Hemophage

Hemophage

by

Stephen M. DeBock

Gypsy Shadow Publishing

Hemophage
by
Stephen M. DeBock

Gypsy Shadow Publishing, LLC.
Lockhart, TX
www.gypsyshadow.com

Library of Congress Control Number: 2015938147

eBook ISBN: 978-1-61950-212-3
Print ISBN: 978-1-61950-254-3

Published in the United States of America

First eBook Edition: April 1, 2015
First Print Edition: April 15, 2015

Dedication

For Andrew and Karyn
Proud to be your dad

Prologue
Hilton Harrisburg Hotel
Harrisburg, Pennsylvania
Saturday, March 19, 1994

"So you're in town for what, a convention? A conference?" The young woman sitting at the bar waited for an answer as she sipped a gin and tonic. Her smile was open and inviting, which indicated to the man that she could be either a high-priced escort or a young woman alone looking for companionship. Whichever, it made no difference to him, and she surely did look fine.

"Neither, lovely lady," he said. "My colleague and I were at a business conference in New York, and we decided to take a detour on our way back home to Charleston."

"I could tell when you said hello that you were from the South," she teased. "You do know that *damn* and *Yankee* are two words, right?"

He shook his head and grinned. "Someday you Yankees will learn how to talk right. I'm Bobby Justis, by the way." He held out his hand and she took it. Her hand was warm, which he wouldn't have expected, as it had just been wrapped around the icy glass. "And?" he said, waiting. "You are—?"

"Naomi. Just Naomi, no last name, if you please. I know, mysterious and melodramatic, but bear with me for now." Her chestnut-brown eyes, a perfect match color-wise for her loose, below-the-shoulder-length hair, stared into his watery blue ones over the lip of her glass. "Now answer me this, Bobby Justis. Unless my geography's way off, Charleston's a straight run down the coast from New York. What made you take a dogleg to Central Pennsylvania?"

"Well, Miss Naomi, Jason and I are Civil War re-enactors back home, and we've decided to come by to pay our respects to the Southern dead."

"In Harrisburg? The War didn't actually get this far north, did it?"

"Matter of fact, no. Biggest recruit depot for you Yankees was here, though. Camp Curtin, it was called." The woman raised her eyebrows, as if to say she hadn't known that. Bobby continued: "The Confederate forces came close, though, but they were waylaid a bit south of here, a little town called Gettysburg. Maybe you've heard of it?"

She picked up on his banter. "Gettysburg. Wasn't that where President Lincoln kept a summer home?"

He tilted his head and knitted his brow. "What are you talking about?"

"Oh, come on, Bobby, your being a Civil War buff and all, you must be aware that the President had an address in Gettysburg?" She winked.

He laughed, perhaps a little too loudly and long, but the woman seemed to appreciate it. She lowered her eyes and lifted them again as she leaned forward and spoke in a confidential tone. "I'm just passing through myself. Traveling with my son. He's upstairs, sound asleep I assume; the hotel has a sitter keeping him company. And—all right, I don't want to tell you my last name because I'm running away—not from the police, an abusive husband. I won't tell you where I'm running from, and I won't tell you where I'm running to. I hope you can understand, and I'm sorry if you can't."

"Don't be sorry," said Bobby. "It's all right." He thought a moment. "You know, most abused women are afraid to leave their husbands, leastways that's what I'm told."

"You're not wrong. But after the third beating I wised up. Rather than going to the police, which is the same as doing nothing, I contacted . . . someone . . . to make some false ID cards for me. Then one day while my husband was at work I emptied our joint bank accounts, bought a used car, and hit the road."

"Wow. That's ballsy. So how old's your boy?"

She hesitated before answering. "He's four."

He ordered another drink for each of them, and after more conversation, during which he took pains to make himself sound empathetic, Bobby placed his hand over Naomi's as she rested it on the bar. She didn't draw it away; instead, she looked into his eyes and gave him a slight nod.

"I have to check up on my little man," she said. "But I'd like to continue our . . . discussion. My suite's on the top floor. Two bedrooms," she added. "Why don't you bring something bubbly for us to drink? Just give me a half hour alone to make sure my boy's asleep and get freshened up, okay, Bobby?"

When the woman opened her door exactly thirty minutes later, Bobby saw she was wearing a hotel bathrobe, open just enough to reveal something filmy and white beneath. Her feet were bare, and her makeup had been skillfully reapplied. Her breath—she stood that close—smelled of peppermint. Bobby's face was flushed as he walked inside, carrying a bottle and two flutes.

"Champagne, as the lady requested," he said.

Naomi placed the bottle in a freshly filled ice bucket and whispered, "Be very quiet, my son's asleep in the other room."

She took his hand and led him into her bedroom, where she had turned down the covers to expose crisp cotton sheets. "Why don't you strip down and climb into bed, and while you're doing that I'll take care of the bubbly."

Bobby was fumbling with his tie as she glided out of the room.

Lying between the sheets and grinning at the tent he'd formed halfway down, Bobby Justis heard the pop of the cork, and moments later the woman entered carrying two filled flutes. She offered him one and they toasted, draining their glasses. A few moments later, he was unconscious, his tent pole collapsed.

Naomi wiped her flute clean of prints and any DNA traces at the lip. She pulled back the top sheet and considered Bobby's pudgy body as he lay spread-eagled in the center of the bed. She knelt next to him and lowered her face toward the inside of his thigh.

She opened her mouth. Her lower jaw extended downward, and downward, farther than a normal human jawbone would allow. From the roof of her mouth, a pair of curved fangs swung down, like those of a pit viper, and she pressed them against his flesh. Blood flowed freely into her mouth, and she sucked it in, barely missing a drop. It was

3

blissful, this blood, better than any poor animal's, better than the drug-addled derelicts she'd sometimes drunk from during her relocation from New Jersey to central Pennsylvania. Naomi drank and drank, growing nearly tipsy on the blood.

She grew aware of company when a tiny hand tapped her on the shoulder.

"Don't be a pig, Mom," said a child's voice. "You're not the only one dying of thirst here."

"Sorry," she said with resignation as she lifted the boy onto the bed. "Don't take too much, now," she admonished. "We don't want to kill him."

"Duh. Look who's talking," he said, looking down at the punctures in Bobby's thigh. He shook his head at the man's limp phallus. "When are you going to learn to go for the throat like they do in the movies, or at least the wrist?" he demanded. "It makes me skeeve, sucking so close to a guy's willie, I told you that how many times."

"And as I've told you before, how many times, over how many years—"

"I know, I know. Too many times, over too many years. Just let me be for awhile."

The little boy closed his eyes as he lowered his lips to the man's thigh. He kept them closed as he drank.

Next morning, Bobby awoke in the bed, fully dressed except for his shoes, and suffering from a splitting headache. He sat up slowly and swung his legs over the edge of the bed. He noted a few spots of blood on the sheets and wondered if the woman had been having her period. *Wait a minute,* he thought. *What the hell's going on here? What exactly happened last night?*

Looking about, he saw that all trace of the woman's presence in the room was gone. He stood . . . and nearly fell over. "Whoa, vertigo," he said. "What's up with that?" He stumbled shakily into the sitting room and from there to the second bedroom, where the baby would have been. Nothing. "Well, good morning and goodbye," he muttered, feeling every bit the fool. He shuffled back to the bedroom and put on his shoes, visited the bathroom and splashed water on his face. Then he left, noting the Do Not Disturb sign on the doorknob in the hall.

4

In the first floor restaurant known as Raspberries, Bobby saw his colleague alone at a table, working on a stack of pancakes. He walked unsteadily toward him and braced himself on the table as he fell into a seat opposite. He shook his head as if to clear it. "Morning, Jason," he mumbled.

"What happened to you?" Jason asked. "You're white as a sheet."

Bobby scratched an itch on the inside of his thigh. "See, I met this woman at the bar last night."

"Uh huh."

"Beautiful she was. And long story short, she invited me up to her room."

"Well, good for you. But you might want to keep your voice down. Some folks at the other tables are looking."

Others, in fact, were looking, in particular at one slim, very attractive brunette dressed in a long-sleeved light gray blouse and black slacks, who stared with coal-colored eyes over the rim of a coffee cup. When she lowered the mug, a hint of a smile played about her lips. Her companion, a burly Mediterranean type sporting a day's growth of stubble and greased, slicked back hair, studied Bobby from the corners of his hooded eyes. Appearance-wise, they made an unlikely-looking couple. Beauty and the beast, for sure.

"Oops, sorry." Bobby leaned forward, bracing himself on his elbows. He shook his head again and blinked his eyes before continuing. "I'm tellin' you, she was hotter'n my granddaddy's pit barbecue."

Jason grinned. "And that's hot."

"Thing is, though, nothin' happened. Leastways I don't think it did." He scratched the itch on his thigh and sat back in his chair as the waitress took his order for juice, coffee, three eggs over easy, ham, grits, and a buttered biscuit. Plus a couple aspirin and a tall glass of water. "Thing is," he said when they were alone again, "last thing I remember we were drinking champagne, and—oh, shit. She drugged me, didn't she?"

"Checked your wallet lately, young stud?"

"Oh no." Bobby reached into his pocket, pulled out his wallet, and sighed in relief. "Well, my credit cards are all there," he said with a grin. "Uh. Wait a minute. Wait. A. Minute."

"What's up?"

Bobby was staring into the bill compartment. "Son of a bitch."

"Don't tell me."

"I had six hundred-dollar bills in my wallet when we checked in. There's only one there now."

Jason chuckled. "Hey, at least she left you something. Damn white of her, you ask me, Bobby boy."

The water and aspirin arrived, and Bobby gulped the pills down. "My stomach's empty, my head's empty, and now my wallet's empty, too," he moaned. "I am so screwed." He paused. "Jason, after breakfast I'm going back to our room, pack my suitcase, and we're going to blow this place. I never want to see this damn Yankee town again."

The dark-haired woman sitting with her swarthy companion nearby paid their bill. They walked out of the room, she sparing a sideways glance at the two men as they left.

Declan Mulligan, principal of Hershey High School in nearby Derry Township, arrived in his office early every morning to devote an hour or so of uninterrupted time to reading the *Harrisburg Patriot-News*. Mulligan was fifty-two, happily married, with two children in college. Refusing to become jaded after two decades in administration, he still genuinely cared for the students in his charge and deeply respected the teachers who guided their learning.

Mulligan sat at his desk, Monday's newspaper spread before him, and shook his head sadly at the story under the banner headline. Harrisburg, like most cities, had its share of crime, but this one was particularly heinous.

Movement in the hall caught his eye. He looked up to see the new guidance counselor walk down the hall on the way to her office. She glanced in, smiled, and said good morning, as she passed. Mulligan thought highly of the woman. She was not only well credentialed; she was also doubtless the object of many a schoolboy's adolescent fantasies. He surmised she was one reason so many boys joined the drama club, where she would assist the director—Dr. Mulligan himself—with rehearsals. A single mother, if she couldn't find a sitter she would often bring her preschool-age son to rehearsals with her. The little boy had an uncanny manner about him that charmed the girls, many of whom said they wished they could take him home with them.

6

The lady's attractiveness brought her no preferential treatment from the principal. Their professional relationship was strictly that. As after-school drama club advisors, however, they were more like siblings. There was never a breath of scandal about their friendship, nor was there any reason for one.

Declan Mulligan stood, newspaper in hand, and walked to the counselor's office. Final rehearsals for *The King and I* were to commence today after school, and he wanted to confirm that she would be available. She said of course she would.

Then she noticed the headline on the folded newspaper in his hand. "What's that about?" she asked. He passed her the paper and she spread it out on her desk.

It could have been a scene from a horror film, the article began. *But this was worse, because it was real. Jason McElroy and Bobby Justis, both 35, of Charleston, South Carolina, were found murdered yesterday in their room at the Hilton Hotel here. Their throats had been slashed and their bodies drained of blood...*

The young woman stopped reading. She placed her palms over the article and looked straight ahead, her expression blank. The color began draining from her face.

Mulligan leaned forward and stared into her suddenly vacant eyes. "Good God, Naomi, what is it? You look like you've seen a ghost."

Chapter One: Naomi
Newark, New Jersey

April Naomi Paris became a vampire in 1972, at the age of twenty-seven. For all appearances, she would never age. She was turned by her son Joseph, who was only four at the time and recently made himself. He would remain four years old, in physical appearance at least, for as long as he continued to exist.

Naomi was barely three months old in 1945 when her mother returned to Newark from California. She had never met her father, a Marine killed fighting the Japanese on Iwo Jima. Before he shipped out, the couple had driven west from New Jersey and bought a house trailer in Highgrove Trailer Park in Riverside, where none of the other residents were native Californians either. All had come from elsewhere, including the park's owner, a retired dentist from Albany, New York. They all shared a pioneering spirit and camaraderie, and the then-pregnant Aimee Christian Paris found a sense of community, especially among other young wives waiting for their husbands' return from the War in the Pacific. Their wedding portrait, the bride in white organza and the groom in his dress blues, was all she had to remember him by. That, plus a stack of his letters, and the lump in her belly, which turned out to be a beautiful baby girl with her father's chestnut brown eyes.

Aimee wasn't the only military wife (and new mother) to receive the dreaded telegram, and as time passed the mood in the park seemed to darken with each passing week, with each visit of the olive green military sedan. Burdened by grief, Aimee sold the trailer, packed up her husband's 1941 Packard with Naomi and all her personal belongings, and on a furiously bright Southern California morning she began the eight-day trek back to her mother's home on Fifth Street, in the Roseville section of Newark.

Fifth Street was a narrow, one-way road shaded by ancient maple trees whose shallow roots had pushed up the slate sidewalk tiles willy-nilly. Parking was on either side of the road. The homes were three-story, two-family affairs, separated by three-foot-wide alleys that led to postage-stamp back yards. Aimee's widowed mother lived on the second and third floors; her elderly landlord and landlady occupied the first.

Dorothy Christian's home, like the others on the block, was old, dating to around the turn of the century. Its peeling exterior paint was lead based, its windows were single paned, and when the wind blew, drafts intruded from any number of sources. The house was hot in the summer and cold in the winter. The basement had two coal-fired furnaces, one for each flat, which needed to be banked for the night before retiring. To get hot water for dishes or bathing, it was necessary to lift a chain anchored to the furnace that went up through the floors to a hook on the kitchen wall. This diverted the flames through a cast iron port to the hot water tank.

Coal was delivered from a truck; down a metal chute that went through a basement window to each of the two bins below. The produce man and rag collector used horse-drawn carts, each man announcing his presence with a voice that needed no amplification. Their horses also made their presence known, leaving behind what the neighborhood kids called road apples.

Dorothy's home stood five doors down from the corner grocery store. Across the street was a butcher shop, and next to it, around the corner on Sixth Avenue, was a dry cleaning and tailor shop, from which Dorothy Christian picked up work as a seamstress. Her reputation was solid, and what she earned combined with her late husband's insurance policy—a policemen, he'd died in a shootout ten years before at the age of thirty-five—was enough to pay the rent, the telephone bill, electricity, and groceries from the A&P on Orange Street, a five-block walk away. Her one luxury was a massive wooden console radio, which allowed her to enjoy operatic music via *The Voice of Firestone* on Monday nights and popular tunes on *Make-believe Ballroom* Saturday mornings. Plus the always-entertaining *Don McNeil's Breakfast Club* Monday through Friday.

9

Soon after returning to her mother's home, Aimee Paris noted that the neighborhood seemed to have gone downhill since she had moved out. Her mother confirmed it. "Lots of lower-class Italians here now," she said in a confidential tone, as if she didn't want the baby to hear. "Puglios next door, for one, always fighting. Cops have to come to the house every couple weeks or so to calm them down." She added, "They have a little boy, Alphonse, about a year older than Naomi. All he hears from his parents is fighting and screaming. And the language—disgusting. Why people like that are even allowed to have children is beyond me."

Aimee put her education degree to work teaching fifth grade at Garfield School, a four-story brick structure three blocks away. Not needing the car anymore—buses to downtown ran along Roseville Avenue, and the trolley line ran through nearby Branch Brook Park—Aimee sold the Packard and gave the proceeds to her mother as rent.

Her mother in turn secretly set up a trust account for baby Naomi's college with the money from the sale.

Dorothy, who worked on customers' tailoring from home, watched over her granddaughter during the day, knowing a joy she'd never experienced before. "When you get married," she told her friend Elsie VanBuskirk, "you think you know what love is. Then you have children, and you have to revise your opinion. But grandchildren? Elsie, let me tell you, they just completely rewrite the book of love."

"I'll take your word for it," said Mrs. VanBuskirk as she dunked a cruller into her tea. "My daughter's what they call a career woman. She and her husband are both too *busy* to have children."

"Well, any time you want, you can come over and play with Naomi. Look at her there in her playpen. What a happy little girl she is."

Chapter Two

Five years later marked the end of Naomi's being a happy little girl, for it was then that she entered kindergarten—and for the first time encountered her neighbor, six-year-old Alphonse Puglio.

From the start, the husky little boy with the black hair and eyes to match became her tormenter on the asphalt-covered playground. By fifth grade, he'd earned the nickname *Alley Oop,* as in the comic strip caveman, from like-minded boys Gerald *Moon* and Nicky *Beans.* Mrs. Paris's daughter proved a convenient target for their jibes. For starters, her last name didn't end in a vowel, which automatically made her an outsider. Second, her mother was a teacher at Garfield, which made Naomi a potential snitch; third, she had made friends with another outcast: Martha, one of only six Negroes in the whole school.

When a playground monitor wasn't looking, the boys would hem the frightened Martha between them and taunt her: "Man, you black . . . *all* black!" Naomi, incensed, once tried defending her, and they yanked her inside their little circle and called her a nigger lover. Which, although she couldn't fully appreciate the connotation, incensed her even more, but she was wise enough to know there was nothing she could do to force them to stop.

Whenever the monitor looked, the boys suddenly became the picture of innocence.

Once, Naomi asked her mother if she could invite Martha to the house to play. Aimee flushed and said she'd love to have her over, but it wasn't a good idea. Then she gave her daughter her first formal lesson in the unfairness of racial discrimination. "Remember who lives next door," she concluded.

By the time she turned eleven and entered sixth grade, Martha had moved away and Naomi felt truly alone in her class of twenty-five—which included Alphonse, who had been retained. As a teacher's child, she was treated as a pariah, a goody-two-shoes who couldn't be trusted not to rat on them for their foul language, petty thefts, or their precocious sexual innuendoes.

"Hey, Annette, nice mouseketits!" Alphonse shouted more than once, and Naomi, although mortified, didn't get the reference until her grandma surprised the family with their first-ever television set and she watched her first episode of *The Mickey Mouse Club.*

The Dumont television came in a huge, heavy, wooden console, very much like the radio. Its twelve-inch screen had curved sides, and tuning was done with a knob that moved a needle on an illuminated face. It picked up Channels 2, 4, 5, 7, 9, 11, and—when the rabbit ears were adjusted just right and reception was good—13.

One of Naomi's favorite programs was *The Adventures of Danny Dee,* which featured cartoonist Roy Doty sitting before an easel. Mr. Doty would narrate a story and illustrate Danny's adventures with his sister Debbie Dee, Pancake the Magician, and Filbert the nearsighted dinosaur. What particularly intrigued her was that the tablet on which Mr. Doty drew had hidden cutouts. When the artist drew a door, he could then open it to show what he had already drawn behind it. Or, if Danny were to throw Debbie a ball, he would draw it on a cutout slide and then pull a tab off screen to move the ball from brother's hand to sister's. After the show, Naomi would often retire to her third-floor room, pull out her artist's tablet, and make her own stories, complete with cutouts.

Saturday mornings were devoted to *Learn to Draw with Jon Nagy.* Naomi would sit before the tiny screen, pad and pencil in hand, and follow Mr. Nagy's step-by-step demonstrations to create drawings that eventually became almost as good as his. Better, according to her grandmother.

When her mother took her to New York one Saturday to shop at Arthur Brown Art Supplies, the sponsor of *Learn to Draw,* Naomi proclaimed it the best day of her life.

There were not many of those days, thanks to Alphonse and his cronies, both of whom lived the next block over on Fourth Street, and who congregated on the corner with him after school. Naomi proved a prime target when she walked home alone.

12

"Hey, Naomi," called Gerald Moon one day as he cupped his hands before his chest. "You've got a beautiful pair of . . ." He paused long enough to see the red creep into her face. "Hands!" The boys thought it was hilarious.

Having no friends in the neighborhood, and fearful by now even of stepping outside the house, Naomi spent her after-school hours in her room. She would draw and paint, but she would also devote time to her schoolwork. Evenings, she would be lulled to sleep by Alan Freed's rock 'n' roll on station WINS. The portable radio her grandmother had given her for her twelfth birthday was a godsend.

Her grade-A homework and test scores made her the joy of her teachers—and the target of her less-academically-inclined peers, which was most of them. The bumpings while standing in line, the Oops, sorrys when someone tripped her, the whispered imprecations when the teachers' attentions were elsewhere, all combined to make her a recluse even in the classroom. She felt she could get lost in a crowd of two. Many times, she wished she could.

Halfway through her eighth grade year, Naomi became especially fearful of what would happen to her in high school. Garfield was a feeder school for Barringer High, a long walk across Branch Brook Park. Its nickname was The Grinder, as the upperclassmen reportedly made mincemeat of the new freshmen. She never shared her fears with her mother or grandmother, but neither was so naïve as not to notice. And it was her mother who saved her from Barringer and restored her faith in other children.

"Have you heard of Arts High?" Aimee asked Naomi one night over dinner. When her daughter answered no, she continued, "Arts High is a city school where the students all take college prep courses, but they major in either art or music. Two periods a day are devoted to their major. You have to take a test to get in, and the art test is scheduled for this Saturday. You can take the bus downtown, get off at High Street, and walk from there, it's not far. Would you like to go?"

During her first year in Arts High, Naomi's personality went through a renaissance. The teachers were great, the art instructors were all professional artists in their own right, and best of all, the kids, drawn from all areas of Newark, became fast friends through their common interest in their respective majors. The icing on the proverbial cake was that fully a third of the students came from predominantly Negro neighborhoods, and there was never a trace of racial tension. *Martha would've been right at home here,* she thought.

The principal made the school's policy clear in the auditorium on freshman orientation day. "We welcome you all to Arts High, but we also remind you that we didn't invite you here; you're the ones who asked to come to our school. Bear that in mind when we tell you that we respect each other, our teachers, and our school each and every day. Any bad behavior will result in your being sent back to your neighborhood high schools."

As far as Naomi was concerned, his speech was unnecessary; she knew she'd love the sanctuary of Arts High.

The only potential problem would be when she came home. The 34 Market bus would drop her off on Roseville Avenue, and then she'd have to walk three blocks through enemy territory to get to her house. Fortunately, the gang usually stayed at the Barringer campus for a while and were rarely in evidence.

But one day, Alphonse was waiting for her, sitting on the steps of his front porch.

All the fears from Garfield swept from her gut into her throat. She almost dropped her books. But Alphonse only nodded to her, and his expression didn't appear hostile. He had a textbook on his lap along with an opened notebook.

"Naomi."

"Alphonse."

"You're good in math, right?"

The newly self-confident part of her wanted to scream, *I'm good in everything, you dumb jerk,* but the resurgence of fear prompted her simply to nod her head. "Yeah, I guess."

"Can you help me with this problem?"

Chapter Three: Alphonse

Now under Alphonse's protection, Naomi's life was nearly perfect. She could almost let her guard down with Nicky Beans and Gerald Moon, and they were always respectful around her. The girls who hung out with them were silent when she greeted them on the street, polite but privately resentful of her favored status. At times Naomi held group-tutoring sessions, and her successes made her realize where her career path lay. *Like mother, like daughter,* she thought as she applied for admission to Trenton State Teachers College. She was a shoo-in.

During Easter break in 1963, the neighborhood gang was looking forward to their high school graduation. The guys would have to register for the draft, but at least the Cuban Missile Crisis from the past fall was over, the missiles were back in Russia, and it didn't look like World War III would be a reality anytime soon. Kennedy was cool, his wife was a looker, and except for the spooks down South demonstrating with that King character, all was right with the world.

Saturday afternoon, Naomi's grandmother asked her to take a dress back to the dry cleaner's for her. Its alteration had been a rush job for a woman going to an Easter party the next day. No longer fearful of the gang, Naomi delivered the dress and was walking back when she saw Alphonse standing in front of his house.

"Hey, Naomi, c'mon inside," he said. "I've got a present for you."

She was taken aback. "A present? What for?"

He fidgeted. "Listen, you done good tutoring me. I'm graduatin' with all C's, which I never woulda done without you."

"Well, that's nice to hear, Alphonse, but there's no need—"

"How many times I gotta tell you, it's Alley, like in Alley Oop?" He pretended to swing a caveman's club. "You know only the gang can call me that, and you're an honorary member." He grinned. "Anyways, come on inside."

She'd been in his house before, working problems at the dining room table as his mother prepared some semblance of dinner. Today, she discovered, his mother wasn't home.

As they stood in the dining room, Alphonse took an oversized comb from the back pocket of his jeans and readjusted his Brylcreemed DA. He cast an appraising eye at Naomi, in her penny loafers, white socks, pleated skirt, and long-sleeved white blouse. Her hair was pulled back in a ponytail, and she wore almost no makeup. But she was still wholesomely attractive, sexy even, without it.

Alphonse broke out a Lucky Strike from the pack tucked in his white T-shirt sleeve and lit it. "LSMFT," he said, parroting the television and radio commercial. "Lucky Strike Means Fine Tobacco."

Naomi wrinkled her nose. "Where's your mother today?" she asked.

"Gone to the A&P. She won't be back, an hour at least." He held out the Lucky. "Want a drag?"

Naomi shook her head and glanced around. For the first time in her life, she was alone in the house with Alphonse.

He reached into the sideboard and produced an unopened pack. "My old lady's," he said. "Parliaments. They've got filters, recessed even. Want one?"

"I don't smoke, Alph—Alley."

He took a serious drag on the Lucky and blew smoke rings before stubbing the cigarette out. "Okay, so your gift. Come with me." He reached for her hand, but Naomi pretended not to notice and kept her hands by her side.

"Where are we going?"

"You'll see."

Alphonse walked through his bedroom doorway. "Come in," he said, trying to keep his tone casual.

Naomi stood in the doorway. "No, that's all right—"

"Look, I'm not goin' to hurt you. I just want to, you know, tell you somethin'. We're close, right, you and me? And let me tell you, you're a real looker, Naomi. Nice tits,

nice ass, great legs, the whole package, you know? We could
be good together, know what I mean?"

She was suddenly trembling. "I really have to go, Alphonse. My grandmother's expecting me."

His mouth drew into a straight line. "I told you, it's Alley Oop, and you ain't goin' nowhere!"

He seized her wrist and spun her onto his bed, flat on
her back. He lay on top of her and held his hand against her
mouth. "Not a fuckin' word, you hear?" he said, all pretense
of friendship replaced by fury at the unthinkable: he'd never been refused pussy in his life. He shoved his free hand
up her skirt and slid the crotch of her white cotton panties
aside. "Dry as a fuckin' bone," he growled. "Well, you don't
get wet soon, you're gonna be hurtin' real bad later."

Naomi whimpered wordless objections and tried to
struggle free.

"Hey," Alphonse said, "Old Chink saying: If you're gonna get fucked anyway, you might's well lay back and enjoy
it."

She stopped struggling, lay limp, and silently wept.
When he penetrated her she bit her lower lip to keep from
screaming, and she forced herself to lie inert, as if she were
already dead.

When Alphonse was done, he noticed blood on the bed-
spread. "Shit, no wonder you was so dry," he said. "Hey,
Naomi, listen." He sounded almost contrite. "I was just tryin' to show you my appreciation for tutorin' me all these
years. You know it was me protected you, right? You were
like my girl; not like the skanks around here, you know,
you're a class act." She turned her head to the side, and
tears spilled as focus returned. She refused to look up at
him. "I thought we was tight, you know what I'm sayin'?" He
thought for a second. "Well, you was definitely tight."

Still looking to the side, Naomi whispered, her voice
tremulous, all confidence lost, "Please don't come near me
anymore."

"Okay, okay, I promise." He stood and zipped up,
watching her sit on the edge of the bed and pull up her
panties. "But one thing, Naomi. Look, I didn't know you
was, you know, a virgin. I mean, you know Maria from
down the street? Hangs out with us? Hell, if that girl had as

many dicks stickin' out of her as she had stickin' into her, she'd look like a fuckin' porcupine." He laughed. She didn't.

Naomi shook her head and stood, her back to Alphonse as she lowered her skirt. She fastened her brassiere, buttoned her blouse, straightened her skirt, and hobbled away. Her face burned almost as much as her vagina.

When Naomi walked into her own flat, Dorothy knew immediately that something was wrong; and when she fell into her grandmother's arms, sobbing uncontrollably, she felt grateful that her mother was spending the afternoon with friends from the faculty. There is nothing like a grandmother's love to soothe a sorrowful child.

When Naomi had cried herself out, the two sat at the kitchen table, facing each other, cups of hot tea between them.

"I was starting to get worried," Dorothy began. "You were taking a long time coming home."

"I'm sorry, Grandma," Naomi said, her falsehoods coming between sobs. "After I left the tailor shop, I figured it was such a nice day that I'd take a walk in the park, go down by the lake for awhile." She looked into Dorothy's sympathetic eyes. "I know I should've come home first to tell you, but I guess I wasn't thinking."

"What happened in the park to upset you like this?"

"I never made it to the park. I was standing on the pedestrian bridge across the tracks when I saw the trolley coming. I looked at it and saw something tiny moving on one of the rails. I thought it was a squirrel and that it would run away when the trolley got close, but it didn't."

She took a sip of tea and looked down at the nearly empty cup. "I looked again and saw that it was a kitten. And that someone had tied it to the track."

Dorothy gasped and put her hand to her mouth. "Sweetie . . ."

"I don't even know if the trainman saw it; he was slowing down anyway so he could make his stop at the platform. But he ran right over the kitten—" The tears came again. "I need to take a bath, Grandma."

"Go," said Dorothy. "I'll turn the water heater on. You take all the time you need."

Naomi sat in the steaming water and furiously scrubbed down her pubic area, over and over again. The story of the kitten had been true, although thankfully she hadn't witnessed it in person. Nicky Beans had done that on a dare when they were all in eighth grade, and she'd overheard him brag about it to Gerald Moon and Alphonse—she refused to acknowledge that ridiculous Alley Oop handle. Like other hurts, she had internalized it and never shared it with her family. She couldn't confess to the rape, she just couldn't. The shame . . .

Her mother and grandmother had been painfully aware of Naomi's difficulties growing up, although neither imagined the full extent of them. On the one hand, they wanted her to have a social life, but on the other they didn't want her socializing with anyone in the neighborhood. And complaining to the parents would've been unproductive. There was old Mrs. O'Grady, a widow who lived halfway down the block. She had tried shooing the kids from in front of her house one day, and that night vandals tossed flaming toilet paper rolls onto her porch. Frantic, she called the fire department and immediately swore out a complaint. But the parents all alibied their kids, and no further action could be taken.

When Naomi began to garner a new respect among the dead end kids who came to her for tutoring, including Alphonse, her grandmother acknowledged it, but told her not to be so sure that the wolves weren't wearing sheep's clothing.

Naomi scrubbed until the soap stung. She let the bar go, and it floated to the side of the tub. She lowered her head beneath the surface. Her long brown hair grew weightless and floated around her head like a gossamer halo. The thought of keeping her head down, of drowning herself, occurred briefly, but she understood intellectually that the shame and the guilt weren't hers. They belonged to Alphonse alone. But for now, emotion chose to override intellect, and the hurt . . .

His words to her when she had left were imprinted on her brain. "You don't tell no one about this, understand? It was a one-time thing. I'll leave you alone from now on, long's you do what I just said. You tell, then I tell everyone how you waited until you knew my mom was out of the house and threw yourself at me. Had this thing for me all these years, what could I do? So. We got a deal? You're smart. Go with it."

Naomi almost imperceptibly nodded her head. "Deal," she whispered.

It would be four more years before Alphonse reneged.

Chapter Four: Robin
London, Seventeenth Century

When Robert Bradford was born in 1593, his mother nearly died at the hands of the middle-aged midwife who delivered him. Equally unfortunate, the strain of the birth on the baby—the sudden desperate yank to get him out severing nerves already stretched too tight—left him paralyzed from the chest down.

The senior Bradford, Avery by name and lawyer by trade, stood in service to King James I, and—had he so wished—had the power to send the midwife to the hangman. Not on the enclosed Tower grounds, where some semblance of dignity was assured, but in the public square, where she would have been paraded before the rabble and pelted with rotten produce and stones before reaching the scaffold, and she without so much as a farthing to tip the hangman—a tip which would ensure a quick snap of the neck rather than lingering strangulation. Such was the plight of the poor; they even had to pay for a clean death. Indeed, the thought of petitioning the king to execute the midwife had occurred to him, but Avery's wife, physically enfeebled but emotionally persuasive, had begged her husband for leniency on the cowering woman's behalf.

When young Robert was able to hold himself up in a chair, his father had a wainwright construct a wheeled wagon for him. The seat cushion contained a hole that opened to a chamber pot on a shelf below, and he deputized the midwife, now in thrall to him, to wheel his son wherever he wished and to empty the chamber pot and clean him after each evacuation of his bladder and bowels.

The smell of the chamber pot, combined later in life with the stench from Robert's bedsores, made some in the court hold nosegays to their nostrils whenever he was wheeled into a room. The midwife, for whom the odor was omnipresent, received no sympathy from the court, as the boy's condition was the result of her own botched procedure.

To pass the time as he grew older, young Master Bradford asked for charcoal and paper and began developing a talent for art, more specifically portraiture. By his middle twenties, he was painting in oils, and members of the king's court had marveled to His Majesty of the young man's talent.

As Robert continued to hone his skills, a well-regarded artist, Daniel Mytens, painted the king's official portrait. James commissioned another artist, John de Critz, to paint Queen Anne's, and after the commission was satisfied, Anne requested a second, less formal portrait of her, to be painted by young Robert Bradford.

The reason for her request was not so much that she wanted another painting, but that she had taken a liking to the fair-featured young man, empathized with his condition, and frankly thought his talent equal to that of Mytens and de Critz. The Danish-born queen was lonely for male companionship, for her husband was more prone to dally with his male courtiers than with her. That he had sired eight children, all told, by her seemed a bitter irony. But that had been earlier in their marriage, and James's tastes had changed since then.

In addition to his penchant for sodomy—punishable by death when committed by others, but rank has its privileges—Anne's royal husband was obsessed with witchcraft's threat to his kingdom. In 1597 he wrote the scholarly *Daemonologie,* and after the translation of the Bible that bears his name was produced in 1611, he devoted himself fully to pursuing practitioners of the Dark Arts. The queen feared for her husband's stability but wisely kept her own counsel.

Robert—Robin to the queen, a name he rather fancied—painted her portrait in her private chambers. It was so well received she commissioned him to paint her three surviving children as well, and in an act of charity—seeing that her ladies in waiting also longed for portraits of themselves—further commissioned him to paint individual portraits of them, too.

It was necessary for Robin to devote extra hours every day to the work, for he had begun to understand that his life was ebbing like a slow tide. His bedsores, although he could not feel them, by now, had grown so large and so deep that one could bury a fist inside them. The stench of their decay had grown stronger now, too. The midwife had to cleanse and perfume him before wheeling him to his appointments.

There was one more portrait to paint, that of Catherine Drummond, a slim beauty with hair black as the Tower ravens, and eyes similarly dark and piercing. They sat alone, as the other ladies found excuses not to be in the same room with the somewhat sanitized but still odorous painter. Catherine, however, seemed to have no qualms. She even closed the door to the chamber, thus ensuring their privacy, and sat closer to him than the others had dared.

"Your features are comely," she said as he directed her to position herself.

"Thank you, Lady Catherine," he replied. "As are yours."

She did not blush as other ladies so complimented might. "Your parents—they are no longer alive?"

"Sadly, that is so. They fell to the sweating sickness some summers ago. Only my midwife, who waits outside these doors, lingers on to perform her menial duties—duties for which I confess I am duly ashamed."

"It is your midwife who should be ashamed. I would have no truck with that churl."

No sooner had Lady Catherine's portrait been blocked out on canvas and a wash applied to the background, than Robin gasped and his color, already pale, began to fade fully from his face. Catherine leapt from her chair and shook him.

Robin's eyes were mere slits. His hands hung at his side, lifeless as his legs. Spittle drooled from the corners of his mouth.

"You cannot die yet!" Catherine suddenly commanded. "My portrait is barely started. Once it is done, *then* you have my permission to die!"

She gripped Robin's head, tilted it back, and exposed his throat. She could sense that his pulse, normally weak, was now nearly nonexistent. Praying to whatever dark gods had sired her, she opened her mouth wide, her lower jaw distending on an unnatural hinge, and lowered a pair of fangs from their resting place against the roof of her mouth.

She bit into the side of his neck and drew the weak flow of blood into her mouth. She sucked hard and swallowed greedily, although nourishment was not her first priority. Robin's own jaw was slack, his mouth open as if he were snoring. But no sound, rasping or otherwise, issued forth.

Catherine withdrew her lips from the wound. Then she held up her wrist and bit into it, holding the wound over the artist's mouth. As her blood pooled inside, she massaged his throat to make him swallow. Her blood flowed down his esophagus, swept through his stomach and into his gut, and was instantly absorbed to merge with his own blood. It circulated, almost lethargically, until it reached his heart—which began pulsing with newfound strength. His newly revitalized organ sent the blood to his brain, and then an even stranger chemistry began.

Catherine's wrist closed without leaving a mark, and she watched as Robin's neck similarly healed, his breathing grew less labored, and his eyelids began to flutter. She held his mouth open and looked inside to see fangs grow slowly from his upper palate, held in place by a newly-formed, muscular hinge. Her practiced fingers were able to feel the nearly undetectable change in his lower jaw where it met his skull. Her breathing returned to normal; she had acted in time.

Now Robin would be able to finish the portrait. And later, if he no longer pleased her, she could dispatch him as she had dispatched the first of her many husbands, with a decapitating blow from the keen-edged sword she secreted among her belongings.

Robin stirred. His tongue traveled to the roof of his mouth and explored the pair of intruders nested there. Then, he both felt—and actually heard—his heart beating with a vitality it had never known. He felt his blood surging through arteries and coursing through veins, and then—*mirabile dictu*—felt it in his legs! He experienced sensation below his chest for the first time in his life, animation that at first tingled and then cascaded through and through with power. His bedsores, those black, fleshy craters in his back and hips and buttocks, began to burn, and it was a blessed feeling, because to feel anything was a blessing. He felt the dead skin slough away as new flesh grew and filled in the wounds. He wiggled his toes—what a feeling, to wiggle one's toes!

And when he opened his eyes fully to see the smiling and coldly-beautiful face staring at him nearly nose to nose, he became aware of something else that he had despaired of ever feeling. Lady Catherine's hand reached under his gown as she pressed her rouged lips to his, as she thrust her tongue into his mouth.

She mounted him there in the wagon, mindless of the awkwardness, and guided him into her. It was over in seconds, with a cry from his lips whose sound she stifled with her own mouth. She stayed there, poised over him on her knees, as he regained his breath and stared at her, like a babe reborn—in his case, born truly for the first time.

He had so many questions, but before he could speak she placed two fingers across his lips. "I will answer all your questions, Robin Bradford, but only as you paint."

His first question was, "Will I be able to stand now?"

"Of course you will. Although at first I suspect you will wobble. You are whole, but with greater perception and stronger senses—and hungrier thirsts—than any of your human peers." She regarded him. "Do not look at me that way. You are no longer human. You are like me, a *strigoi*. Immortal. Kept alive now by the blood of others."

Robin pushed himself up, but Catherine held him down. "Never, never attempt to stand; never display any qualities other than those you had as a cripple. There are ears in the castle walls, eyes in the tapestries. Think of what would happen to you, to us, should the king's minions learn of this new life I have bestowed upon you."

He frowned, mindful of her purpose. "If only so I could finish your portrait, my lady?"

"Albeit so. But you do please me, Master Robin, and so long as you do, and are discreet, you are safe here in the lion's den."

"As much as anyone is safe in the king's court," he reminded her.

The witch-finder Matthew Hopkins had acolytes scattered throughout the kingdom, and there was apparently no shortage of innocent women upon whom to prey, whose capture, torture, and execution—mostly by hanging—justified King James's paranoia.

Accused sorcerers, the couple knew, were treated even less humanely than witches. As blasphemers, as heretics, as deniers of Christ and devotees of the Dark One, they would typically be burned at the stake; or in extreme cases, burned *above* the flames, turned while lashed to a spit to make their deaths more lingering, more excruciating, thus being both instructing and more entertaining to the rabble. Robin and the Lady Catherine would certainly have been treated as sorcerers. In the extreme.

"Your handicap is now and ever will be, so long as you remain at court, a charade," charged Catherine. "A charade you must maintain at all costs. Do you understand?" He nodded as he added flesh tones to the portrait. She continued, "I will provide nourishment for you, and in return you will provide carnal nourishment for me, in my private chambers." Regarding a more practical matter, she said, "You can turn the wheels of your wagon by yourself, as you have for years now. The midwife is irrelevant but for the care and emptying of your chamber pot. At day's end, you will dismiss her to her own pursuits until next morning. She will appreciate the reprieve. And I will appreciate the presence of a man in my bed for the first time in an age."

Chapter Five

Careers in the royal court of England were mercurial to say the least. The rise and fall of Sir Thomas More and Thomas Cromwell during the reign of Henry VIII were historically documented, and those of Sir Walter Raleigh—once a favorite of Queen Elizabeth, now considered a traitor by King James and beheaded—fell into the category of more current events.

Robin Bradford began to fear for his own fall from grace. Not from the king, but from his lover, Catherine Drummond, the *strigoi* who had given animation to his entire body—only because it was expedient to her demand that he finish painting her portrait. Their sexual life was born in passion, with Robin understandably insatiable, but over the few months since it had grown into routine, and the woman's eyes, never truly warm, he now saw as cold and at times bereft of passion.

Queen Anne died that same year, 1619, leaving her maids of honor suddenly superfluous. Many of them suspected by now that Catherine, behind the back of their late queen and thus without her consent, had for some unfathomable and unspeakable reason taken the crippled artist to her bed. Some even suspected that he was no longer a cripple at all, that Catherine was a sorceress with designs of her own. Now that Anne was dead, might she seduce His Majesty, assume the title of queen, and then eliminate her royal husband and find a way to install Robin in his place? Given the king's current penchant for young men, *could* she seduce him? What could the pair be plotting behind her closed bedchamber doors?

To ensure their continued service to the throne, the maids pondered the prudence of compromising the couple by spreading rumors—which to a gossip-hungry court always carried the taint of truth—as opposed to saying nothing, instead currying favor with Catherine, should she indeed one day become their queen.

Robin's aged midwife disappeared one day, and he became discomfited when that very night Catherine brought them fresh blood to share. Her victims, she swore, had all been anonymous, beggars and urchins she had culled from the back alleyways. But this batch did not carry the hint of disease, as so many others did. He drank it anyway; regardless of its source, others' blood was his life. And whereas he hated being a slave to the blood, he reveled in what Catherine's selfish act had otherwise given him.

In the bedchamber one night, Catherine off-handedly admitted that the real Catherine Drummond was dead, and that her own name was Daciana, a Romanian by birth who was already more than a century old.

The real Catherine, she explained, had left her home to become a maid of honor to Queen Anne, thanks to the influence of her parents through a social-climbing friend of a current courtier, one who had never seen the maid for himself. Daciana discovered and befriended her in London, as the girl tarried in the capital before reporting for her royal duties. It was no major matter to kill her as she slept, drain her of blood, toss her dead husk into the alley, and assume her identity.

Daciana's calculating nature allowed her to rise in the queen's service, enjoying more and more influence and gaining favored status.

But now the queen was dead and fortunes were turning. The king's paranoia about practitioners of witchcraft had grown, and Robin felt less and less safe within the castle walls. Mere wounds, no matter how grievous, could not kill either of them, but decapitation or being roasted while alive would surely and completely blot out their existence.

As if that were not enough, Robin began to fear for his own life at the hand of Daciana. She had shown him her sword; told him casually how she had dispatched her first husband, the one who had turned her, and kept his head for years as a souvenir; told him that she always favored giving her human victims, when possible, a lingering death rather than a merciful one.

Robin himself did none of their killing. He stayed in his wagon on the nights Daciana went out to hunt. When she explained to him how he could sneak to the streets unobserved and make kills for himself, he refused, citing the risk if they were caught. But she called his excuses the weakness of the prey rather than the strength of the predator. If her disappointment in him suddenly turned to disgust, he knew his life could be forfeit. Compassion, he'd learned early, had no place in his consort's character.

And so, in the early morning hours following a moonless September night in 1620, as blood-sated Daciana slept, Robin Bradford sneaked out of the castle, leaving his wheeled wagon behind, but taking with him a purse filled with coin, and walked to the London docks. There he added his name to the passenger manifest on a ten-year-old ship scheduled to set sail for the New World. She was of the Dutch cargo *fluyt* class, a hundred feet long with four decks, and boasted a crew of fifty. Her passenger manifest when she sailed that day would carry the names of a hundred two passengers.

One of those passengers was listed as Robert Bradford, no relation to future colonial governor William Bradford.

The ship's name was *Mayflower*.

Chapter Six: Alphonse
Newark, New Jersey, 1966

Alphonse Puglio was frantic. The Vietnam War was escalating furiously, and his best buds Nicky Beans and Gerald Moon had already been drafted a year before. No effin' way was Alley Oop goin' into the Army, no sir. He actually started reading the *Newark Evening News* and visiting the Newark Public Library to find out ways to avoid the service.

The clearest path to deferment was the *husbands with families* provision in the Selective Service Code. Their names were on the bottom of the draft list. But he didn't fit into that category—at least not yet.

He thought about Maria, the bleached-blonde who hung out with the guys back in the day. Good-lookin' skank—if you could ignore the acne scars on her face—with a waist you could still wrap your hands around and have your fingers touch, and a set of sweater puppies that would make Jayne Mansfield look like a boy. Her girlfriends had gotten married and left the neighborhood, but Maria was still around, and still looking at Alphonse as marriage material.

As in, beggars can't be choosers.

Naomi Paris, who, according to Alphonse, always thought of herself as above him—in spite of his having brought her down to his level, so to speak, three years before—was in her junior year at Trenton State. She was the one he'd have preferred to snag above any other girl he knew, but in his case as in Maria's, beggars can't be, whatever. These were desperate times.

So one afternoon, before Maria's single mother had come home from work, Alphonse left off his rubber. Maria noticed, and with eyes moist with happy tears, knew that he wanted to have a baby with her. It didn't take many more tries before she carried his unborn child.

In earlier days, she would've expected Alphonse to insist on a back-alley abortion, but in this case he said he was excited. "Let's get married," he said, "right away. I don't want my kid to grow up a bastard."

They had a small wedding—after hours on a weekday at St. Rose of Lima Church—attended only by his parents and her divorced mother. Her former girlfriends had dropped out of touch, and his own cronies were somewhere in Asia fighting gooks.

The bride wore her mother's wedding gown—it was a little tight around the middle—and the groom wore a charcoal suit he'd bought from Robert Hall, Newark's discount men's clothier.

Alphonse and Maria moved into the first floor flat of his parents' house, after the current tenants agreed with his suggestion that they might be happier, and even healthier, living elsewhere. The newlyweds lived rent-free, as his custodial job didn't pay well, and besides, they'd need whatever money they had for the baby. As for the thought of their giving up cigarettes and sweet *Bali Hai* wine—seventy-four cents a fifth, courtesy of Italian Swiss Colony's fine vintners—it had never occurred to them.

Maria was halfway to term when she and Alphonse learned that both Nicky Beans and Gerald Moon wouldn't be coming home from Vietnam. Heroes, she called them, and even though she implied nothing more than that, her draft-dodging husband—cynics continued to call his kind Kennedy Husbands—thought she might secretly be comparing them favorably over himself.

Had he known that his boyhood friends were anything but heroes, Alphonse wouldn't have felt the need to be jealous of their neighborhood status.

Gerald Moon had gone AWOL during basic training. The MPs had made short work of his capture, his resultant scrapes and bruises the product of his having resisted arrest. At least, so they'd claimed. After some brig time, he was returned to another recruit platoon and given some extra harassment by his drill sergeants. They called it motivation.

Arriving at Tan Son Nhut Airport near Saigon, feeling heat so savage and humidity so intense it was like breathing warm water, hearing the pops of distant gunfire as he stumbled from the plane down the mobile stairs, Moon was overwhelmed. As he and his fellow new grunts marched away from the plane, field transport packs carried high on their backs, they passed a line of unshaven, filthy, haggard-looking, but nevertheless grinning soldiers heading toward it.

"Look at the pussy-faces."

"Welcome to paradise, fucknuts."

"Give my regards to Charlie."

"You'll be so-oooo-rry."

"I'll be good to your mothers, know what I mean?"

The last remark struck a nerve in one of the new arrivals. "My mother's with the angels!" the trembling boy shouted, looking for the offender.

"Right," came a response from somewhere else in the line. "She's fuckin' for 'em."

Before the young soldier could break ranks and leap at the man who had besmirched his mother's reputation, the boy's sergeant stepped in front of him and told him to keep marching. "Those men have the right to say anything they want," the veteran NCO, now about to serve his third tour, said. "And you will too, if you live to go home."

Gerald Moon—rather, Private Monetti—took in everything he heard and trembled in his oversized boots. *First chance I get,* he thought, *I'm outta this hole.*

He didn't last a month. On guard post one night deep in the jungle, he saw his chance to desert. Where he would go, what he would do next, did not concern him. He had seen men get shot and die on either side of him. He'd been peeing in a latrine when a Viet Cong mortar round dropped into the trench he'd been sharing, turning his fire team into bloody confetti. His number, he was positive, was about to come up.

And so Private Gerald Monetti left his post and crept off into the forest.

He managed to find a narrow trail in the blackness and decided to follow it. Somewhere in the back of his mind he remembered learning that taking a trail was dangerous, that it could be booby-trapped, that it was always safer to hack through the undisturbed brush. But he was in a hurry to get as far away as possible as quickly as possible. The mean streets of Newark looked mighty good to him now.

Suddenly a piece of the jungle floor pivoted and gave way, and Gerald Moon fell face first into a tiger trap. The wooden spikes embedded in the packed dirt floor received his body before he even had time to scream.

Private First Class Nicholas Beninato—the former Nicky Beans—was stationed elsewhere in the Nam. He had done his boot training a month before Gerald Moon, and they never saw each other after he left for the train station in Newark. They never said goodbye, never wrote, never kept in touch in any way. He never learned of his former gang buddy's going AWOL from basic, nor of his death, nor of the shame that attached itself to both. He had other things on his mind now, anyway.

He was point man on a recon patrol. A Charlie unit was up ahead somewhere, and the patrol's job was to find out where they were, determine their troop strength, and report how best they could be engaged.

War, it has been said, is ninety-nine percent boredom broken by one percent sheer terror. The numbers didn't hold precisely true in the bush—there was a hell of a lot more terror—but Nicky usually found things to keep him busy during down time. Most of them involved lifting rocks and fallen limbs to seek out small reptiles and amphibians to torture. Salamanders were his favorite. He'd wrap them in an empty cigarette pack and suspend them over his lighter. Hearing the crackle of their bodies inside as they roasted amused him.

But no thrill could match the sight of what had happened to the kitten he'd tied to the trolley tracks back in Newark. There was no shortage of stray cats, and they'd provided endless sport to him and his boyhood buddies.

With a hand signal, Nicky halted his patrol and dropped into a crouch. They spread out around him and listened. They heard sounds coming from just beyond the lush green growth in front of them—human sounds. Voices, in that gibberish tongue. Laughter. *Obviously,* he thought, *Charlie felt pretty secure there. Well, surprise, they wouldn't feel secure for long.*

But a pop from behind the patrol brought him and his men up short. One of them fell forward, a red flower blooming from a hole in the back of his neck.

The men spun around to see a dozen gooks staring at them, grins exposing yellow teeth, rifles at the ready. The enemy soldiers shouted and made gestures that left no doubt as to their meaning. The Americans dropped their weapons and stood, lowering their eyes to avoid the insult of contact.

"Geneva Convention, boys," muttered Nicky as the men were herded into the clearing. "We get to sit out the rest of this fuckin' war in a prison camp. Just be cool, do what you're told, and we'll be fine."

The Viet Cong officer in charge jabbered to the leader of the group who'd captured the Americans. Then he forced them into a hooch with a guard posted at the doorway. The guard faced inside, his expression stern.

"Phase one," whispered PFC Beninato. "Next step, what, Hanoi? Be grateful we're alive, boys. Lewis back there wasn't so lucky."

They were allowed to leave the hooch individually to visit the latrine trench, but they were not fed. Tepid water was given in a soiled bowl they all shared. When he was allowed to use the trench later in the day, Nicky saw soldiers digging holes into which they placed stout tree branches. *What're they, gonna burn us at the stake?* he thought as he passed. *Nah, it's no mind to us. Makin' booby traps, maybe, or snares.*

The next morning, the men were herded out of the hooch and made to stand near the makeshift posts. There were twice as many men as posts, and half the American patrol were roughly but securely lashed to them as their comrades watched apprehensively from the side, enemy rifles pointed at them.

The officer in charge gathered his men—there must have been about fifteen or sixteen all told—and lectured them. Nicky had never tried to learn the language of the slopes, but he could pick up on tone and facial expression, and suddenly he was not as confident of his future as he had been yesterday.

Half of the VC soldiers fixed long-bladed bayonets to the muzzles of their rifles. They lined up ten paces in front of the bound Americans, anticipation writ large upon their faces.

The commander lifted his hand and brought it down smartly, and the men charged, howling. They ripped into the screaming Americans, stabbing at their bodies furiously as they ran past. Then they came back and made another pass, and another. By the end of the third pass, the Americans had been slashed into crimson ribbons. Their bloodied bodies hung limp against their bonds.

Nicky watched his dead comrades being untied by soldiers, most of whom could not have been older than teenagers. They grinned and chattered like little monkeys. Suddenly, he and the others were seized from behind and dragged, struggling, to the posts.

"No!" Nicky screamed. "Geneva Convention! You can't kill prisoners of war, you bloodthirsty fucks!"

His cries went unanswered as he and his men were fastened firmly to the posts. Then the officer in charge approached him. He regarded the American soldier solemnly . . . and spat in his face.

"*That* to Geneva Convention!" he said. "Long 'go, Japan use Chinese brothers for bay'net practice. Now 'Merica Japan friend. Make it your turn." He laughed as a dark stain grew inside Nicky's trousers. Then he stepped back and ordered the rest of his men to fix bayonets, as the first group stood to the side to observe.

Before giving the command to charge, he pointed to Nicky and made some remark. Three of his men jabbered something back and nodded their heads. They looked like kids at Christmas, eager to open their presents. The officer again gave the signal for his men to charge.

Nicky closed his eyes as he heard the footfalls of the soldiers rushing toward him; heard their war cries and the desperate screams of his men as bayonets pierced and tore at their flesh; even heard sucking sounds as the bayonets were yanked free. He tasted dust from the ground as the VC ran by.

Ran by.

They ran by him. They didn't kill him.

Nicky dared to open his eyes. He saw the three Viet Cong soldiers singled out by the camp commander regarding him from a foot or so away, waving their bayonets in front of his face and grinning like Cheetah in a Tarzan movie.

Meanwhile, the others returned for a second run at the stricken Americans. Another charge. Another round of war cries. Another round of screams. The third charge left none to utter even the weakest of wails.

The three men standing before Nicky moved aside so their commander could approach him. He stood inches away from Nicky's face, his eyes nothing short of reptilian.

"My name Captain Vo," he said. "You call me blood-thirsty, yes? Now you see how right you are."

He tilted his head to one side, as a predator might consider its prey before striking. He opened his mouth . . . and kept opening it. A pair of needle-sharp fangs swiveled down into place from the roof of his mouth. They reminded Nicky of a picture he'd seen once of a rattlesnake, where its lower jaw swiveled nearly perpendicular to its upper one.

The captain leaned forward, encompassed Nicky's throat with his mouth, and drove his fangs into the side of his neck. There was no finesse here; he simply bit down— and yanked his head to one side, ripping Nicky's throat out, leaving behind a ragged red tear.

Air whistled through his trachea as Nicky fought to breathe. Captain Vo placed a hand against his forehead and tilted it back against the post, then pressed his mouth hard against Nicky's neck. He began lapping up the blood.

Nicky heard the obscene slurping sounds, felt the warm blood that the monster didn't catch dribble beneath his collar and down his chest, where it cooled. He heard the cheers of the Viet Cong soldiers as they gathered to watch the spectacle. He felt the blood drain from his head, as if he were going to faint. His legs lost their power to hold him up, but the ropes secured him firmly upright against the post. His mind swam in a murky whirlpool, and his last thought before sinking into the darkness was of a kitten tied to a trolley track years before, back home in Newark.

Chapter Seven

Angelo Puglio was born in early 1967, and instead of heading to the cigar store, his father Alphonse made a beeline to his Selective Service office with the baby's birth certificate in hand. Now he was guaranteed placement at the very bottom of the draft-eligibility list, beneath married but childless, and that category below single but in college.

His own college attendance amounted to employment as a custodian at Essex County College, a two-year community college downtown.

From his local draft board, Alphonse hightailed it back to Presbyterian Hospital. Maria, looking haggard but happy, held their son in her arms and with a mother's devotion offered him to his father—who shook his head and said, "That's all right. You hold him." When she frowned, he added, "Hey, I'm so big and clumsy I might break the kid." She acquiesced and drew the baby back to her swollen breast. Alphonse couldn't watch her nurse; there was something gross about watching a baby suck on her tit. Why couldn't she use a baby bottle like a normal mother?

Already, Alphonse was considering the wisdom of insurance—a kind of life insurance for himself— namely, fathering another child to ensure his place at the bottom of the draft rolls in case the first baby died. But Maria, as it turned out, wasn't all that anxious to get it on with him anymore.

So while married life and fatherhood proved expedient, they did nothing for Alphonse's sex life or his self-esteem. Now Maria doted on the baby, while appearing oblivious to her husband's needs. Yes, there was an occasional hump, but she was usually too tired to do much else but lie there. Alphonse got to see sex as something she just endured, and nothing more than hands-free jerkoff sessions for himself.

Often as not, she went to bed with her hair rolled up around empty soup cans. "I hafta look nice for when I take the baby out for a walk," she protested in response to his complaints. The implication that she didn't have to look nice for her husband any longer did not go unnoticed.

It took more than a year before Maria got pregnant again.

As he left for work one morning, Alphonse saw her sitting at the kitchen table in her ratty robe, feeding Angelo from her tit, her hair still in those god-awful soup cans, her belly like a bowling ball, and a lit Pall Mall dangling from one side of her mouth. Only thing to make this picture complete, he thought, would be to see her sitting on the shitter at the same time.

Then he walked outside to catch the bus and saw Naomi Paris pull her old Nash Rambler up to the curb. Her mother and grandmother got out first, all smiles, and he offered a cursory smile back at them. And then at Naomi as her own expression turned sour. He saw the mortarboard in her hand and said, "Well, looks like we have a college graduate on our hands."

Dorothy's smile was cautious, but Aimee's was that of a proud parent. "Yes, and not only that, but Garfield's art teacher just retired, and they offered her job to Naomi." Her grin widened. "Which means we'll be the first and only mother-daughter faculty members in the school's history."

"That's very cool," Alphonse said. "Congratulations, kid." Man, no way she was a kid anymore. She was an absolute stunner.

Her smile was cold. "Thank you, Alphonse."

"Hey, Alley, remember? Like in Alley Oop?"

"Yes, I remember. I assume you're on your way to work?"

"Yep." He waved to the trio. "Heigh ho, heigh ho, as they say."

They watched him walk away.

"He's matured since you left," Aimee said to her daughter. "Married now with a son and another baby on the way. I see his wife occasionally walking their son in his carriage. Always looks very pretty, and dressed fit to kill."

Naomi wasted no time signing up for evening graduate studies at Jersey City State College, a much easier drive from Newark than Trenton. Her major was counseling; even though the elementary school had no guidance counselor on staff, and even though there were no plans to add one, she wanted to gain behavioral insights on the children in her charge. She especially wanted to serve as a resource person for those children who, like her, had been social isolates. She wanted them to know they had a shoulder to cry on.

On a Sunday in late June, Naomi was walking home alone from church when Alphonse, looking frantic, intercepted her outside his house.

"Naomi!" he cried. "I need help!"

"What's wrong?" she asked, wary.

"It's the baby. He's crying and coughing up gobs and gobs of snot."

"Where's your wife?"

"Maria just left for mass, left me alone with him. Please, can you do something? I don't know what I'm doin' here."

"I'm no authority, but I'll take a look."

They walked into his flat, which was silent.

"Where's the baby, Alphonse?"

"In the bedroom, come on."

"He's not crying."

"That scares me even more. Please."

He ushered her into the bedroom. Alphonse Jr. was sound asleep. There was no evidence of sputum anywhere on his bedclothes or the sheet.

Naomi turned to see Alphonse standing inches away and getting closer.

"Not a sound," he whispered. "Not one fuckin' sound. *Capis'?* Don't want to wake the baby."

"Oh, no," Naomi moaned. "Alphonse, you promised."

"Yeah, tough shit. You see that skank I'm married to? Men have needs, and I need a real woman. Now lift your skirt and drop your drawers, and you won't get hurt. I promise."

"You *promise*," she whispered. "Right."

"Yeah, yeah. Just get 'em down."

When it was over, and she had tidied up—"Hurry, before Maria gets home"—Alphonse told her to go out the side door into the alley. She could use her own house's alleyway door, three feet away, to get inside without being seen.

She left by the side door. Defiantly walked up the alley to the sidewalk. Turned left toward her own house. Saw Maria walking toward her a half block away, clothed in the dress she always wore to mass and trailing smoke. Naomi gave her a weak wave before going inside. It was not returned.

Before undressing and immersing herself in the bathtub, Naomi pressed her ear to the bathroom wall and listened. No repercussions, no angry imprecations, no sound of broken china floated from the house next door.

Naomi lowered herself into the hot water and wept.

Essex County College fed its graduates to Rutgers and the Newark College of Engineering. Its baseball team was called the Wolverines, but, as Alphonse noted to himself every time he saw the logo, the only animals native to Newark were cockroaches and sewer rats.

The job paid okay, and as custodian he got to check out some tuff-looking young babes walking the halls between classes. Even some of the darkies looked good, which to Alphonse indicated they had some white blood in them, too.

A couple of the female teachers looked pretty good as well, and one of them was definitely whack-off grade. She was a professor with a foreign-sounding last name that he couldn't pronounce, but it wasn't her name that caught his attention.

She was built for speed, not comfort; slim, long legs, tight ass, small, perky breasts. Alphonse's obsession with large breasts had cooled after Maria had begun using them as nature intended. Add to that her never wearing makeup except on Sundays when she went alone to mass, her hair night-times and mornings perpetually rolled up—with the dark roots showing more and more—and the acne scars that he could no longer ignore. If she were black, he thought, with those sagging tits, she'd be a perfect candidate for a jungle jigaboo photo in *National Geographic.*

This prof was the exact opposite of Maria. Long black hair, dark eyes, red lips, and makeup always perfect. She favored black or dark gray suits and dresses, and her voice when she answered his daily, "How's it going?" when he passed her in the hall was sweet as honey.

Sometimes he imagined she looked at him with a little more than just a casual glance.

Alphonse's position was year-round, despite the fact that daytime classes were not in session during the summer months. Quite often he would see the professor in her room alone, and one day he decided it was time to make his first tentative move.

She looked up as he opened the door, a watering can in his hand.

"Sorry, professor, I don't mean to disturb you, but—"

"Yes?" Even that one word, in that voice, was enough to arouse him.

"I thought I'd water your plants. The leaves are drooping, see."

She looked to the ledge by the window. The administration had placed potted plants in each classroom in an attempt to avoid the sterility of the environment. "I see what you mean," she said. "Please proceed, Alphonse."

He stopped in his tracks. "You know my name?"

"It's stitched over your work shirt's breast pocket," she noted, her lips turned up at the corners.

"Oh, right. Not too obvious." His swarthy face began to redden. *Nothing like making an asshole of yourself in front of the lady.* Still, she did make the effort to call him by name, and that was a start. "I wish I could pronounce your name," he said. "What is it, French?"

"No, Romanian," she said as she stood and walked to where he stood near the plant.

"Romanian. No sh—no kidding."

"But at times like this, when there are no students about, please feel free to call me by my first name."

"And that would be?"

"Daciana."

Chapter Eight

In July of 1967, Newark erupted in riots. Racial tensions had escalated from simmering to boiling since Martin Luther King's speech in Washington four years before, and even Alphonse could see the irony of how the blacks' violent actions conflicted with King's message of peace.

It was early evening when Alphonse and Daciana found themselves virtually trapped inside the college. She suggested he phone his wife to tell her he was safe inside, but he replied, "It'll do her some good to worry about me." Daciana smiled at that, then she asked him if he wouldn't mind doing her a favor.

"Can I trust you, Alphonse?"

"Hey. It's me."

"I mean, can I really trust you? To do something that others might find, oh, unnatural at first and criminal at best?"

"I'm interested."

She lowered her voice, even though they were alone, school having been shuttered earlier in the day. "Can you go outside and find someone near the school, someone who's been hurt enough in the riots that he can't put up a fight, and bring him to me?"

Alphonse eyed her suspiciously. "What is this, some kind of experiment or something?"

"Something." She took a breath. "Will you do it for me?"

"You got it, kid," he said and turned to walk out of her room.

"Meet me in the lab when you get back." She grinned to his retreating back. "Kid?" he heard her say softly to herself. "Who's kidding whom?"

In less than an hour Alphonse returned, dragging with him a badly banged-up young black man. Both had blood on their clothes. "He didn't volunteer to come quietly," he said, by way of explanation.

Daciana helped him place the man's feebly protesting form onto the cold lead bench top, with his head tilted back over the built-in sink at the end, fully exposing his neck. She turned to Alphonse.

"Would you give us a moment alone, please?"

"Sure. Whatever you say."

But after he left the room and closed the door, he stood to the side and peeked through its safety glass window to see just what the professor was doing. He couldn't believe what his eyes were showing him.

Daciana bent over the man's throat. With one hand pressing on his chest to hold him down and the other pushing his forehead back and down, she opened her mouth—opened it wider than Alphonse had thought possible—and exposed a pair of fangs. She closed her mouth over the man's neck, and blood poured forth as she ripped out a piece, then chewed and actually swallowed it.

Next, she planted her face in his open throat, slurping blood as the excess bubbled out and down into the sink.

Daciana fed for what seemed forever, and when she came up for air her face was smeared in blood. She glanced at the door, and Alphonse wasn't quick enough to escape her stare.

He summoned up his bravado and strode into the lab. "I'd'a never believed it," he said. "You're a fuckin' vampire. There's supposed to be no such things as vampires."

"I prefer the word *strigoi,*" she said, forcing her voice calm. "It's more accurate, as its origin is found in my native country. And if you do not mind, I abhor cursing. It shows disrespect for the person being spoken to and a lack of dignity in the speaker himself."

"Yeah, right," he said. "Whatever. That's not important right now, is it? I mean—"

"You mean you have stumbled upon my little secret."

"Well, what were you gonna tell me once you were, um, done?"

"That I had dissected him, reinforcing my knowledge of anatomy, and then have you dispose of the body in the furnace."

Alphonse shook his head as Daciana ran water into the sink, washed the blood from her face, and rinsed her mouth. She looked normal again, and it was hard for him to believe what he had seen just moments ago. She stood erect and regarded him.

"So. We have a conundrum, Alphonse. I suppose I could kill you, make it look like our friend here had broken through the doors and attacked you."

He gulped. "You could do that? Kill me?" In the comic books he read, vampires possessed superhuman strength.

She continued, "Or I could let you live, provided you agree to be my off-hours assistant."

"Uh huh. I can guess what that would mean."

"Providing derelicts to serve my hunger, of course."

"Oh, boy. I'm in deep shit now, ain't I?" The *strigoi* shook her head and lifted an upper lip. He responded, "Well, I'm not gonna say deep *doo-doo,* sorry."

She considered him. He was strong, well built, and crudely good-looking. His practice of wearing his shirt collar up in the back, his belt buckle fastened on the side of his trousers, and his hair in that greasy duck-tail comb, might have been ludicrous, in fact his mannerisms *were* ludicrous, but he did have a certain brutish appeal.

Daciana had long been without a man.

Alphonse stared back at her, not knowing if he should be simply cautious around her or seriously afraid for his life.

Daciana half-lowered her eyelids, and her lips curled up in a sly smile. "Come with me," she said, leaving the body on the bench top for the moment. She led Alphonse into her office and sat him in her chair. Then she unfastened her skirt and let it fall. Her blouse joined it on the floor, and she knelt on the chair facing him, her knees to either side of his thighs. She leaned forward, her face inches from his own. Her breath smelled of copper.

She smiled at his surprised expression. "I believe," she murmured, "that I have found yet another function for you to fill."

Chapter Nine: Robin

Two passengers died during the *Mayflower's* passage, and Robin Bradford was among those who mourned their loss. Indeed, he felt as if he might be partially responsible, as they were among those wretchedly seasick pilgrims from whom he had drawn small amounts of blood as they slept. He joined their families in weeping as the bodies slipped into the sea.

Robin himself never suffered through the *mal de mer.* In fact, he knew he would never feel any taint of illness ever again. Or so Daciana had said, and she had given him no reason to disbelieve her.

One evening back in London, following a bout of vigorous lovemaking, he asked her about the legends of the *strigoi,* or vampire. "Obviously," he said, "we do not sleep by day in our native soil, we are not repelled by the sun, garlic, or the cross of Christ, and I assume we can also cross running water and enter a person's home without invitation. Whence came these tales?"

Daciana chuckled and murmured against his neck as she tossed an arm across his chest. Her lips felt soft as a butterfly's wings, but he knew that death lurked behind them.

"Why, from the *strigoi* themselves," she said. Daciana propped herself up on one elbow and smiled at his puzzled expression. "The first of my former husbands was the one who made me, and at the time I asked him the same questions. Why do we not go to ground before dawn? Why does the sun not burn us to cinders? Why do we still cast reflections in the looking glass? Why can we not change form into that of a wolf or a bat? Why, why, why? And he laughed at me, as I laugh at you now."

"Cease your laughing and answer me the same questions then," Robin said. "Why, why, why?"

She kissed the tip of his nose. "To provide tales with which to frighten children. More importantly, to assure reasonable adults that our kind could not possibly exist; that we are the stuff of fairy tales. The result of which is we can pass among normal humans unnoticed. We do commerce with them, we drink and sup with them, and we enjoy carnal relations with them."

"But we also drink their blood."

"To drink is to live."

"How often must we do that?"

"I do not know for certain. I have gone without feedings for as long as a fortnight with no pains of hunger or thirst. When the longing which is ever present becomes an irresistible urge, I know it is time."

"And why do I not feel pain as your fangs pierce my flesh?" There had been times when they fed from each other before sexually uniting, a particularly heady and vitalizing experience.

"My saliva—our saliva—contains a numbing agent which drips down those fangs and falls first upon the intended wound site. Our donor does not feel the puncture's pain."

"And if we drain the person unto death?"

"He will not become one of us, another fanciful invention of our kind. The transformation is done through a sharing of blood. What the alchemy might be, no one has ever explained. Probably, no one yet knows. It just is."

And so, in the hold of the *Mayflower,* the passenger Robert Bradford would occasionally visit one of the more soundly sleeping passengers and sup from their wrists. He discovered on his own that his saliva, in addition to being a topical anesthetic, also presented the property of rapid healing, leaving a slight rash at the wound site that went away, along with the itching, usually after no more than a few hours.

For Robin, who for his first twenty-six years was a veritable slab of meat; meat with a brain; meat that thought—his newfound physicality, to say nothing of his immortality, was nothing short of a miracle. That others should contribute to his longevity, so long as they did not suffer or die in the process, was more than acceptable.

He believed it a moral imperative that they not die. The Commandment said, "Thou shalt not kill," and Robin, like the religious palmers being transported to a place where they could practice their faith unmolested, believed in the sanctity of both physical body and immortal soul.

Palmers, he mused. Pilgrims. A smile came to him as he recalled the performances in the king's court by Master Shakespeare's acting troupe. When Romeo met Juliet at the masque dressed as a pilgrim, he saw her as a saint and attempted to kiss her. But she teased him and offered her hand instead, saying, "Palm to palm is holy palmer's kiss."

Their dialogue, he recalled, took the form of a sonnet, and Robin went so far as to believe that the author of those plays and sonnets might even enjoy a certain measure of notoriety one day.

As it happened, the pilgrims in Massachusetts Colony eventually grew to be just as intolerant as those religionists in Europe from whose persecutions they had fled. When Roger Williams was banished in 1635, he went on to found the colony of Rhode Island and establish it upon complete religious toleration. Robin Bradford followed Williams and settled in the capital of aptly named Providence.

It took only one bitter Rhode Island winter to convince Robin that yet another move was in order, and he joined a small group of like-minded individuals on a trek south seeking warmer climes. His unchanging appearance would always present a problem, for he never looked older than twenty-six. Every decade or so, he knew he would have to move on.

With a pack holding all his worldly possessions on his back, Robin found his way early one summer in the year 1700 to a small village in the New Jersey Colony on the northern shore of Goose Creek—not a creek at all, but a wide waterway that emptied into a shallow bay the local Indians called Barnegat. The day had newly turned dark when he walked into an inn on Water Street. The interior was hardly lighter, being barely illuminated by a scattering of lanterns hanging from wooden ceiling beams. Dark it may have been, but quiet it was not. Occupying half the room were clusters of men hoisting tankards and loudly toasting a man they called Indian Tom.

Robin placed his pack next to a small wooden table and took a seat. In moments he was approached by a stout, middle-aged woman with cherry cheeks and a pleasant, gap-toothed, smile.

"Evening, m'lord," said the woman. "I be Mistress Applegate, the proprietor. With me husband, o' course, over there servin' the men."

Robin stood. "Pleasant evening, Goodwife Applegate. My name is Robin Bradford, and I seek food and lodging, at the least for one night."

"Manners, he's got. Well, Goodman Bradford, ye've come to the right place. In fact, it's the only place!" Her laugh was as hearty as her figure was stocky. "Now ye've proved yerself a gentleman, so sit yerself back down. Ye look tired as well as hungry." Robin agreed with her assessment and resumed his seat. She said, "Now, tonight's special is venison stew, courtesy of Johnny Irons over there. Shot it early hours this mornin'."

"That sounds splendid. Tell me, Goody Applegate, what's the commotion over there, and who is this Indian Tom the men seem so intent on filling with ale?"

"Aye, that's Tommy Luker, he's gettin' married tomorrow, you know."

"Is that right?"

Mistress Applegate leaned forward. "To an Indian princess, no less."

"Really? So there's no hostility here between the English and the Indians?"

"Hardly, sir. These are Unami, from the Lenape Nation. Peaceful relations, we've got."

Robin nodded and changed the subject. "Might I start my meal with a tankard of ale?"

"I'll draw one for you now, Master Bradford, and dish you up some stew and bread. After ye're done, I'll show ye to yer room upstairs."

"That would be lovely, thank you."

Once he had finished dinner and dropped his pack in the small but tidy room Goodwife Applegate provided for a reasonable sum, Robin returned downstairs and ordered another ale. Soon he was noticed by the revelers—those who were still sober—and welcomed into the group.

Tom Luker was the least affected of the men alcohol-wise, and he took an immediate liking to the stranger who joined the others in toasting his upcoming marriage. "Princess Ann Suncloud," he said. "Imagine that, a commoner like me marrying a princess. Couldn't happen back in England, now, could it?"

Robin laughed. "Hardly."

"And she comes with a dowry."

"No."

"Land along the river, where I hope to run a ferry service across. Oh, and would you know what my last name, Luker, might mean in the Indian dialect?"

"I most certainly would not, sir."

"By goodly coincidence, it means *river*. And you know what else? The river, that is, Goose Creek, belongs to the tribe, and Ann's father is giving the river to me as part of her dowry. Already, folks here are calling it Tom's River."

Robin held out his hand. "And congratulations again, Tom River of Tom's River."

They laughed, and Tom asked what was Robin's trade.

"Before I left England," he said, "I was a passing fair artist. Portraits, mostly. But there's not much call for those around here, I suppose."

Tom thought for a minute. "No, but I'm thinking that maybe I could pay you—not a king's ransom, mind you—to paint a portrait of my bride?"

"I didn't bring my paints and brushes with me when I left England . . ."

"One would think . . . but no, I won't ask your reasons for leaving, sir, none of my business."

"No, it was just that I always intended to travel light and explore the New World unencumbered. But if you have some charcoal I could sharpen, I might be able to present you with a passable likeness. In truth, I'd be delighted to sketch a portrait for you, and charge you not a farthing. Call it a wedding gift."

"Oh, no, sir."

"Oh, yes, sir. I count it a privilege and an honor to render a portrait of a genuine princess. And along with that, I thrill to be able to practice my craft again."

That night, as he lay in his bed under an itchy woolen blanket, Robin recalled how, some seventy-plus years

49

ago, he had painted his last portrait, of the Lady Catherine Drummond—actually, the *strigoi* Daciana—who had transformed him into what he was now.

All of his contemporaries would be long dead and moldering in their graves. Yet he lived on, the blood of the animals he hunted rejuvenating his body nearly as well as that of the humans upon whom Daciana preyed.

Where would she be now? he wondered. Robin had no idea, but he hoped that wherever she was, they would still be separated by an ocean's expanse. He knew she had been growing bored with him, and he likened her at the end to a mantis, which takes the head of her lover as part of the mating ritual. A male mantis he had no intention of becoming.

As Thomas Luker and Princess Ann Suncloud exchanged vows in the tiny chapel perched on a small bluff overlooking the river, Robin Bradford strolled the shore of the wide, cedar-colored river whose name, Goose Creek, would officially become known as Tom's River. He strode along a natural sand beach and noticed a crab scuttling near the edge. Its dark green shell was the size of his hand, broad in the middle and pointed at both ends, and its great claws were white with iridescent blue coloring the tops. Blue-claws, Goodwife Applegate had told him they were, and said that the inn's latest haul would be served to the wedding party in celebration of the happy couple and the merging of the two peoples. "But we'll have more the next day," she promised, "and I'll teach ye how to pick the sweet-tasting meat from the claws and the carcass. 'Tis a slow job, one best accompanied by a tankard or two of ale."

Robin told her it sounded wonderful.

Turning from the river, he visited the general store in the village and purchased the implements he would need to execute the princess's portrait. He spent the rest of the day sketching his new environs, sharpening his eye and re-honing his skills.

It was a week hence when Tom told Ann that his wedding present to her would be a portrait rendered by "the famous English artist, Robin Bradford." Then he contacted Robin to set up a time and place.

They chose an outdoor setting, where Ann would sit in the foreground, with their cabin in midground, and the river and far shore as background. Robin roughed in the cabin and river beforehand, leaving a space for Ann to dominate the foreground. He had yet to meet her.

"She'll be in traditional Unami dress," Tom said. "Just to make it look formal." The local Indians often as not wore much the same clothing as the colonials, commerce among them being the custom now.

"I can't wait to meet her," said Robin.

But their meeting would not go as well as he expected.

On the appointed day, Tom sat his bride outside in a chair he'd brought from inside their cabin. She sat in the morning light, the thin overcast of the day softening the shadows of her sharply contoured face.

Then Robin arrived with his supplies and a makeshift easel.

And Princess Ann Suncloud Luker suddenly had second thoughts.

Tom performed the introductions, and as Robin made to kiss her hand, Ann refused to give it to him. She pressed her back against the chair, her breath coming in short bursts.

"*Ntalemi,*" she whispered as she looked away.

"What are you afraid of?" Tom asked. "And why speak Lenape all of a sudden?"

Robin frowned. "Have I offended you, Princess? If so, it is unintentional, I assure you."

Ann shook her head and directed her gaze at her husband.

"What's the matter, dear?" Tom asked.

Her voice came out a whisper. "*Punihi, punihi, ntalemi,*" she said. "*Ikalia, halapsi!*" she added before she retreated into the cabin, slamming the heavy door behind her and leaving the two men to stare at each other dumbly.

"She said she's afraid and that we should leave her alone. Rather, you should leave her alone. Then she said to hurry and go away." He shook his head. "I'm sorry about that, mate. I don't know what's gotten into her."

Robin could think of nothing to say. But his gaze fastened on the closed cabin door, and he wondered.

"Master Bradford? Robin?"

"Sorry, Tom, nothing. I've heard that some indigenous people shy away from having their portraits done. A few tribes to the north believe that putting their images on parchment steals their souls. Perhaps—I don't know."

"But she never said a word about her soul. She was thrilled with the idea of getting her portrait made."

"I can't explain it then. But please tell your wife that I send my regrets for having disturbed her." He picked up his easel and gathered his gear. "And perhaps it would be better that I leave town and continue on my travels as soon as possible."

The Applegates told Robin they were sorry to see him go, said that the Indians were still a superstitious lot, suspicious of some strangers, whether they deserved it or not. Then they suggested that he head to Philadelphia, a small but growing city on the Pennsylvania side of the river some fifty miles to the west.

"There's a coach that kin take ye right across the colony," said Goody Applegate. "On a road straight as a log."

"Right through a pine forest," added her husband. "Most boring road ye'll ever travel."

"And have a care ye don't meet any highwaymen on the way."

Robin raised his eyebrows. "Highwaymen?"

"Don't listen to her," said Goodman Applegate as he extended his hand to Robin. "By the way, news is there's a paper mill went up near Germantown, not far from the city. Might come in handy for an artist such as yourself."

"Excellent," Robin said. "And where there's paper, there most certainly will be printers."

"And a school, should ye want to teach," said the proprietor's wife.

"Thank you, Goody Applegate, I'll keep that in mind. Now, about that coach."

Boring was an apt description for the road cut through the pines. The day was hot and the air still, and the coach, drawn by two horses, and carrying a man and his wife inside—and Robin, who sat up top next to the driver—went slowly along, raising little dust.

"'Twould be a hell of a thing," observed the driver, "to get a wheel in a gully and snap an axle. Go too fast, you might miss seein' one, and there's hell to pay. Yes, sir."

"I'm in no hurry, Master Phelps," said Robin. "I don't know about the Davises in the coach, though. They seemed anxious to see their children in Philadelphia."

"They'll get there quicker if we don't break an axle."

They chuckled. The road was indeed rutted in spots, with shallow gullies formed by rain runoff or carriage wheels rolled through what had once been mud.

"Something up ahead," said Robin to the driver. "See, there is a wagon on the side of the road."

"Be that a woman on it?" asked the driver.

"Looks to be. Pretty far away still."

The figure climbed down from the wagon—it was definitely a woman—and waved to the coach. Her motions were hurried, and Master Phelps flicked the reins to make a slight but careful adjustment to the coach's speed. When they drew closer, they saw the figure of a man slumped over the driver's bench.

The coach stopped, and the young woman ran toward it. "My husband!" she cried. "He just turned pale and collapsed. Be any of you a doctor?"

Robin hopped down from the coach before Phelps could caution him. The Davises remained inside, but drew the curtain aside to observe.

"I'm no doctor, but perhaps there's something . . .." He climbed onto the wagon and leaned over the man—who suddenly snapped upright and knocked him to the ground. When Robin looked up, he saw a wheel lock pistol pointed at him. The woman held a companion piece directed at the driver.

"We'll have your valuables," said the man, "and then you can be on your way." He jumped down from his wagon and motioned to Robin, who was in the process of rubbing his chin as he stood. "That looks like a fat purse ye've got there, my friend. Why don't we start with you? Jessie, you keep an eye on the driver and passengers."

Robin stood his ground and placed a hand on the leather pouch tied to his belt.

"Maybe you didn't hear me," the highwayman said. "We're starting with you. Are you going to untie your purse, or would you prefer I do it for you?"

"I don't think that would be a good idea," said Robin.

The man's unshaven face darkened. He squinted and aimed the pistol at Robin. "One way or t'other, friend, your purse is mine. And now I'm right curious as to what's in it."

"Hiram, you be careful," said the woman. "You promised no bloodshed."

"No bloodshed if everyone behaves," he amended.

"Master Phelps," called Robin. "Go! Like the wind!"

With that, the highwayman shot Robin dead center of his chest. The blow from the ball knocked him off his feet and onto his back as Phelps cracked his whip and the startled horses took off, ruts in the road be damned. The woman fired a futile shot at the retreating coach.

Then she looked down at Robin, lying still, the hole in his chest seeping blood. Her voice grew shrill. "Damn you to hell, Hiram, you promised this wouldn't happen! Now look what ye've done. Ye've gone and killed a man!"

Chapter Ten

Hiram and Jessie stood a brief time in silence, contemplating the consequences of their actions, while the horse in front of their wagon returned to munching the grass alongside the road. Jessie was right, this should not have happened, no one was supposed to get killed. But Hiram had had it planned so well. After all, who wouldn't stop on the road to come to the aid of a pretty girl in distress?

Once the coach had stopped, the sight of two pistols leveled at the driver and passengers—in addition to a second pair, plus a musket stolen from her father before sneaking off on their path to elopement—should have made it easy for the couple to relieve the passengers of their coin and treasure. "A wedding gift in advance, if you please," said Hiram when he advised her of his plan.

Jessie objected at first, but in the end she saw no other course. With their parents at war over some property they both claimed was theirs, the couple knew they would never get their blessing. Neither had known the story of the families Montague and Capulet and their star-crossed progeny, but even if they had they would have ignored the portents and plowed on anyway. Hiram's strongest trait was his impetuosity; his weakest was a relative lack of intellectual prowess.

If nothing else, Hiram was a man of purpose, and Jessie admired that in him. She accepted his judgment as final and swore she would prove a devoted wife and mother. Many a girl she knew had gotten married when they'd reached her age, and it was unfair of their parents not to put their differences aside long enough to at least bless their children's union.

Hiram was nineteen years old; Jessie was three years his junior.

The young man now found his bluster gone. But he vowed to keep it up, for Jessie's sake, and he strode over to where the dead man lay. He drew a knife from its sheath on his belt and leaned over him. He said, "I'll just cut his purse strings and see what's inside that pouch he was guarding so dearly."

That was when the fallen man's hand gripped his wrist.

Hiram screamed, and Jessie echoed him as the man's other hand snapped up and pulled the boy's face to his. Hiram tried to push away, and in so doing he pulled his head back, exposing his neck. And, compelled by another fierce downward yank, his neck was suddenly encompassed by the jaws of the man he'd thought dead.

The jaws closed, and Hiram was silenced as his windpipe was severed and blood fountained from his neck into the other's greedy mouth. He tried to pull away, but his strength ebbed almost instantly and he collapsed onto the blood-splashed body beneath him.

When Robin Bradford rose, he saw a young woman with a wheel lock pistol leveled at him. She was a wisp of a girl, he noted, long curly black hair, brown eyes, muslin blouse and skirt, and scuffed boots. She was trembling, the muzzle of the pistol doing a little dance as she tried to direct it toward his general vicinity.

"Do you really think that would work?" he asked calmly, through blood that bubbled from his lips and dripped down his chin. "Because it didn't the first time."

"You . . . you killed him. Bit clear through his neck."

"He had a knife; I had no weapon but my teeth. If it be any consolation to you, I would not have killed him had he not tried to kill me. Also, if it be further consolation you desire, please know that until this moment I have never killed another human being. I took no pleasure from the deed." He stared at her, his expression one of friendly sympathy. "Now, why don't you put that piece down before you hurt yourself? You've nothing to fear from me. I was first off the coach to help you, Jessica, remember?"

Her jaw fell slack. "You know my name? How—"

"I heard your companion call you Jessie. I assumed . . ."

She lowered the gun slowly but kept it at her side. "Correctly, Master . . ."

"Palmer," Robin said, thinking quickly. "Avery Palmer. I'm on my way to Philadelphia to seek my fortune there."

"Well, Master Palmer, it looks like you've at least got a future ahead of you. I've nothing now." She began crying as she looked down at the ruined body of her former fiancé.

"I'd suggest, Jessica, that we carry young Hiram's body into the woods for whatever scavengers might enjoy it—sorry, I don't mean to be unfeeling, but once again, he did try to kill me—and then find a source of water with which to clean ourselves. I'm assuming he has a change of clothes I could wear until we get to the nearer shore. Your horse looks content. We can hitch him to a tree as we, um, freshen ourselves."

Later, wearing clean clothes and with freshly scrubbed faces, Robin and Jessica continued on their way to Philadelphia, both of them silent for much of the way. She had not taken notice of the lead ball his body had pushed out and left in the dirt.

Despite his revulsion at having made his first human kill, Robin felt elated for the first time in ages. Young, vital blood was so very hot, and delicious, and rejuvenating. He was over a hundred years old, but he felt as young and powerful as he did when he regained the use of his once-crippled legs, courtesy of the healing blood from the *strigoi* who had made him whole.

"What's to become of me?" the girl asked as she wiped her eyes, finally breaking the silence as Robin took care to let the horse travel at its own pace.

"What do you think?" he replied. "I assume our mutual path ends at the river, where a ferry will be waiting to take me across. I'll board the ferry and you'll turn the wagon around and return to your parents."

She pouted. "I don't want to go home. I can't go home."

"What?"

"I said, I don't—"

"I know what you said. But I don't know why. Might you have family in Pennsylvania, then? People with whom you can stay?"

"None. Don't know a soul."

"Then you're going home. To sleep in your own cradle."

She huffed. "I'm sixteen years old! I'm no baby!"

"Apologies, my lady. To be frank, when first I saw you on the side of the road back there, I thought you to be older. But still . . . the problem is, were you to cross the river into Philadelphia with me, I would see you as my responsibility."

She thought a moment. "I am that, you know. Your responsibility."

Robin turned his face to stare at her. "And what reasoning allows you to offer such logic?"

She looked to the sky first, then back at him, ticking off points on her fingers. "Well, you killed my fiancé, didn't you?" She affected a French accent, overly stressing the last syllable. "My fiancé was responsible for my care and safety. I am a woman alone now. Therefore, the responsibility for my care and safety lies with you."

"You're driving yourself back home, alone."

"But there are highwaymen on the road!"

Robin laughed. "You don't say. And by the way, I share your grief at the loss of your intended groom. You are grieving, I assume?"

Jessie thought for another moment, brows knit, eyes looking at something Robin couldn't see. "I'll tell Hiram's parents that you killed him," she said. "And they'll storm into Philadelphia to find you, Master Avery Palmer."

"My, my. Look, I tremble."

"Stop treating me as a child!" When he returned his attention to the road, grinning, Jessie sneaked a finger into her nose to pick out a crusty booger. She looked at it before flicking it away. "There's something odd about you, you know."

"Oh?"

"Hiram shot you in the heart. I heard the thunk when the ball hit, I saw the hole it made, and I saw you knocked on your back. That was a mortal wound."

"It was a flesh wound," Robin said quickly. "The charge must've been too light, because the ball barely broke the surface. Here, what are you doing?"

"I'm lifting your shirt to see the wound." She was too quick for him to stop her. "Cor! There's not even a hole!"

"What did I tell you? Must've not even broken the surface. It did pack a punch, though."

Jessie shook her head as she felt his chest for some indentation; nothing. "No. It went in. I saw the blood."

"People often mistake one thing for another in a moment of panic."

She stared at his profile as he kept his eyes on the road. "I think you're a hant."

"A what?"

"A hant. You know, someone who's dead and come back."

He laughed. "That's a haunt, child. And as you can tell, I'm very much alive."

"Now he makes fun of my dialect as well as calling me a child, second time today. How old are you, Avery Palmer? You don't look all that much older and wiser than me."

He faced her again and smiled. "I'm twenty-six," he said. "But I've been told I have a boyish face."

She nodded, triumph etched on her features. "Twenty-six's good. You can be my older brother. Or my benefactor, and I could be your ward. Maybe your indentured servant? No, no, put that aside right now, I couldn't be a slave to you. And to have me living with you unchaperoned would cause scandal. No, you'll definitely have to be my brother. We'll be orphans, and you'll be seeking fortune in the city."

"You've thought it all out," Robin said. "Except for the fact that you're going home after I board the ferry."

She lowered her head and stared at him obliquely. "You know, you'll have need of a horse and wagon in the city."

Decades and decades later, Susannah announced to her mistress that a "rather handsome young man" had come to visit, saying he was an old friend. When she produced the visitor's card, Jessica Palmer Stover glanced at it and produced a smile wider than Susannah had seen in quite some time.

Mistress Stover, ninety-one years old, lay in the bed she would never again leave in life. Flowers adorned every horizontal surface, the gifts of admirers and her late husband's associates. The curtains were opened wide, allowing the autumn light to flood the room through its oriel windows. "By all means, show the gentleman in," she said. "And then afford us some privacy, if you please."

"Yes, ma'am."

Robert Bradford stood in the doorway and looked at his aged *sister* with a resigned sadness mingled with love.

His appearance had not changed one whit from when they first entered the city from the New Jersey side of the river named for the Baron De La Warr. He strode to her bedside and leaned over to accept her withered embrace. "Jessie," he whispered. "I got your note."

"No one's called me Jessie in years," she said, "not since Lemuel died." She kissed his cheek with withered lips before releasing him. "You look wonderful, Avery. Or Robert now, I see from your calling card. Will you be going back to Robin next? I dearly like that name, you know; it fits you. Cheery as a bird." She coughed and held a delicate handkerchief with crocheted trim to her mouth. "But then, why wouldn't you look wonderful? You never change." She laughed. "Remember, I was right when I called you a hant."

"Thank you again for keeping the secret, Jessie."

She winked. "You know I love knowing something no one else does." He held her tiny hand to his mouth and he planted a kiss there. She said, "Don't you swing those teeth down, now. If you wanted to make me immortal, the time to do it was when I was a young woman, not a desiccated old husk."

"You're still beautiful," Robert said. "You always will be."

"In your mind, maybe," Jessica returned. "But thank you, love."

"I offered, you remember. When you had grown mature enough to make an informed choice."

"I know. And I have no regrets. A body can grow tired of life."

"Your housekeeper is new."

"Susannah, yes. She's a free black woman. I'm lucky to have her. You know how Lemuel and I hated slavery."

"As do I."

She tilted her head on her pillow. It was so fluffy it looked as if she could lose her head inside. "You were another kind of slave once, if I recall what you told me. To a body dead from the chest down."

"A long time ago."

"I'm curious. Are you still a slave to your body, Robert?"

He thought about it and nodded. "But remember, the only person I ever killed to satisfy that slavery was your Hiram. And that's because he killed me first. So to speak."

Jessica nodded. "My ticket out of my parents' home. Foolish boy. Foolish girl, I thought I loved him."

He decided to change the subject. "You still have the portrait."

"Place of honor, above the mantelpiece. Tell me, was I really that attractive back then, or were you embellishing?"

"No."

"No, what?"

"You were more attractive. I was never satisfied that I'd caught the full extent of your beauty."

"Stop, you're making me blush. At my age, yet." She took a breath. "So, Robert, or Robin, or Avery, did you come back to Philadelphia just to say goodbye to your counterfeit sister?"

"To visit, you mean, not to say goodbye."

"It's goodbye, love, and that's fine with me. I'll be reunited with Lemuel soon. My only regret is that I'll never be reunited with you." She saw the tears in his eyes. "You are the most sentimental man I've ever known. It's a strength to be able to cry, you know, not a weakness."

"Thank you for that," he said as he brushed a fingertip below one eye. "There is another reason I've come back, though, a happy coincidence."

"Which is?"

"As you know, we colonists are boycotting imports from the homeland."

"Because of the taxes that never stop coming, I know."

"Exactly. Before long, Britain will be taxing the very air we breathe. There has been talk, perhaps you've heard, of the colonies uniting to declare our independence from the Crown. As we speak, a corps of volunteers is being formed, soldiers trained to fight from aboard ships rather than across open fields. I'm thinking of joining them."

"The artist prepares for war."

"I fear we will be fighting sooner rather than later, Jessie. And to a land that has given me so much, I've a responsibility to return my service in kind."

"What day is it today?"

"It's tenth November," he said, "1775."

She glanced around the room. "I know the year, fool. Every day, though, every day seems the same. I only know it's Sunday when Father comes by to give Susannah and

61

me communion. Now kiss me goodbye and go sign up for your cause. For our cause. I'll be watching you, you know." She lifted a bony finger. "From up there."

Robert sat on the edge of the bed and leaned into her embrace. "You have ever been more than a sister to me," he whispered, his voice faltering.

"As have you a brother," she said.

They exchanged a chaste kiss, hugged once more, and parted for the last time. As Susannah escorted Robert past the portrait in the parlor, he stopped to stare at it one more time.

"A famous artist painted that for her, sir," said Susannah. "It's her most prized possession on this earth."

"She has another, even more prized, waiting for her in heaven."

"God bless you, sir."

Robert walked down the street to Tun Tavern, where he joined the line of other would-be freedom fighters—Marines, they called themselves—eager to teach the limeys a lesson about what happens when you push a man too far— for far too long.

Robert distinguished himself in the war for independence, and when the British returned in warships in 1812, he joined the military again, under a different name. Indeed, throughout the generations, he served under various pseudonyms in one branch of military service or another in nearly every war undertaken by the United States of America.

During the Civil War, he was attached to General McClellan's Union troops. He admired the men with whom he served, but despised their pompous general—not only for his holding them back from attacking when they should've gone in full bore, but also for the commander's overt contempt for President Lincoln, whom Robert idolized.

He was with Theodore Roosevelt on San Juan Hill; with the cavalry in France during The Great War; in the Pacific following Pearl Harbor; at the frozen Chosin Reservoir in Korea. He sweltered in the steaming jungles of Vietnam, from which he returned home to the scorn of a country he still loved but no longer recognized.

Chapter Eleven: Alphonse

At the same time Robin Bradford was fighting in Vietnam, Joseph Christian Paris—conceived in rape and born a bastard—arrived on the scene in Newark. The year was 1968, the same year that Robert Francis Kennedy and Martin Luther King, Jr., were murdered, and the same year Alphonse Puglio's parents died in a head-on collision while driving drunk, leaving their only son the family home and little else of value. Baby Joseph's unwed mother, April Naomi Paris, had become *persona non grata* among the Garfield School Board of Education members, who didn't want her indelicate situation to set a poor example for the students, especially the adolescent girls. Miss Paris had not passed her three-year probationary period and therefore was not entitled to tenure; she was directed not to return to school the following fall.

Nine months earlier, Naomi admitted to her mother and grandmother that she had been raped late one night while walking from classes at Jersey City State. She said she never knew the identity of her rapist, had not even gotten a good look at his face. It would have killed them to learn that the monster who had really done this lived right next door.

She did report his identity, however, in addition to the actual circumstances, to the Newark Police. She sat across from a male officer at a wooden desk in the middle of a roomful of desks, with other officers circulating or pecking at typewriters. She had to speak up to be heard over the clacking of keys and the questions of the policemen taking statements from other citizens.

"Were you dressed provocatively at the time, Miss Paris?"

"I was walking home from church. How provocatively does a woman dress for church? Listen, check with my minister at Fifth Avenue Presbyterian, Dr. Van Dyke. He can vouch for my modesty, and for my decorum."

"That won't be necessary. Now, did your language in any way encourage Mr. Puglio's alleged behavior?"

"I pleaded with him not to. I begged him not to. And it's not alleged behavior, either, it's actual. As in, he actually raped me."

Furtive glances from the other officers coupled with their cocked ears as the sound of typing stilled.

"Uh huh. And were you in a public place when this alleged rape occurred? Where there might be witnesses?"

"No, I was inside his—oh, God. Are you even listening?"

A day later, Alphonse, alone, was asked to give his side of the story. He shyly admitted to having had *relations* with Naomi Paris.

"Was Miss Paris provocatively dressed at the time, Mr. Puglio? She says not."

"Officer, have you seen those cans? I mean, a tight sweater like the kind Dagmar used to wear on TV, know what I'm sayin'? Like two sizes too small? Aah, she prob'ly wore somethin' loose yesterday so's you wouldn't notice. Am I right?"

"Hm. Did her language in any way encourage your behavior toward her?"

"Listen. We were close in high school, you know? I mean, really close. But nothin' happened between us until she graduated. Then, before she went off to college, she managed to invite herself into my house when my folks were out, and—well, ba-da-bing, it just happened."

"And?"

"And so now she graduates from college, she sees my wife head off to mass, and rings my doorbell. I'm inside tending to my son, who's asleep, and she asks if she can see him. Well, soon's she gets inside, she's all over me like stink on shit, you know? I remind her I've got a wife, and she says she knows my wife's at mass and won't be back for an hour. Now officer, I try to be a faithful husband, but, again, were you able to scope out those cans? I mean, I'm only human."

"So you didn't lure her inside, as she states."

"Hell, no. And don't let my wife know anything about this, okay? Between you and me, you know?"

Naomi was called back to the station.

"Miss Paris, Mr. Puglio states that when you graduated from high school, you both shared an intimate encounter. Is that correct?"

"Intimate, hardly. He raped me then, too!"

"If it was in fact rape, why didn't you report it to the police back then?"

"He threatened me. I was . . . young. Afraid."

"Afraid?"

"Of what he might do to me. To my mother and grand-mother. We live next door. He's a dangerous man."

"I think we're done here, Miss Paris."

Dorothy Christian, now a great-grandmother at only sixty-eight years old, was thrilled to be able to take care of Joseph during the day. She called him the best thing to come along since the invention of the steam iron. Meanwhile, her daughter Aimee, with Naomi's blessing, continued to teach—Aimee hated Garfield now for its treatment of her daughter, but wasn't so foolish as to give up her tenure, sick days, and pension, not to mention a modest salary, by resigning on principle. Naomi herself decided to seek work elsewhere.

Her secondary school alma mater, Arts High, was happy to hire Miss Paris as an art teacher while she worked toward her counseling degree. And when she graduated with her master's the school ushered her into the guidance office, knowing she could be plucked from there to serve as a substitute art teacher if and when necessary—a financial advantage to the school and a professional advantage to Naomi, as she would, on those occasions, be able to observe her charges in a classroom setting.

Ironically, she and Alphonse both took the Number 34 Market Street bus to work, and both got off and on at the same stop, High and Market Streets—but at different times of day. He had applied to work the night shift at Essex County College on a permanent basis, so their paths outside work seldom crossed. It was a blessing for Naomi, for she vowed never to be seen by Alphonse when she was out walking her baby. Never once did she think of her son as his baby, too.

Unbeknownst to Naomi, their schedules were a blessing for Alphonse as well. For more reasons than one.

The professor, Daciana, always taught both afternoon and evening classes, none in the mornings. Which gave Alphonse time alone with her after the last of the students had left the building; which gave him the opportunity to snag some spades from the street to provide her with fresh blood; and which always led to the finest, fiercest sex he could imagine afterwards.

In 1972, four-year-old Joseph's illegitimate father became a vampire.

Alphonse had lured a scrawny beggar, his first woman, into the college with the promise of a free cigarette and a drink. Once he got her inside and the door locked, he throttled her to the point of near death before carrying her over one shoulder to the lab.

Daciana looked at him with a tiny smirk. "Do you want to do the honors this time, Mr. Oop?" she asked, enjoying his grin when on rare occasions she called him that.

"I don't have the teeth for it," he said. "But I guess I could use my pocket knife."

She nodded. "Or . . ."

"Or what?"

"Never mind."

"Wait, are you thinkin' what I'm thinkin'?"

"It might be fun to . . . hunt together."

"Oh, man, I've been dyin' to hear you say that."

"Tell me why, Alphonse. Why would you want to become a *strigoi* like me?"

"Well, in case you haven't noticed, I'm kind of in love with you."

"Men have claimed to love me before, but they have never asked me to turn them." A lie, but it was of no import. "Prove your devotion to me, Alphonse." She looked down at the street woman, who was just now returning to consciousness and wondering why her head hung so low backwards, her neck stretched. Was that a faucet above her head?

"How?"

"Dispatch her."

Alphonse looked from Daciana to the woman. He had never killed anyone before, but that was not about to stop him now. As Daciana pinned her to the bench top, he flipped open the blade on his razor sharp switchblade and placed the tip just under the woman's left ear. She struggled weakly, and as she tried to push away, the blade pricked her skin. Alphonse, seeing the blood begin to trickle back into her ratty gray hair, began a slow circular slice that ended at her right ear. The woman gurgled as he made another, deeper slice along the same path, and blood spurted over her face as her head tilted all the way back as if it were on a hinge.

Alphonse looked at Daciana, waiting for a reaction the way a puppy might wait for a biscuit. She in turn smiled at him and lowered her mouth to the wound.

The vagrant woman twitched once, twice, and then lay still. Her fingers, which had been curled, her opaque nails digging into and drawing blood from her palms, relaxed. Her chest stopped heaving, then stilled altogether.

Daciana lifted her head and smiled, her teeth smeared with crimson, a deeper red marking the lines between them. "This woman's blood was diseased," she noted. "But blood is blood, and disease has no effect upon me. As," she said, regarding Alphonse, "it will have no effect upon you either. After tonight."

His knees went weak. "What do you want me to do?" he said.

"Take this trash to the furnace first. Then come back and take its place here upon the lab bench."

A half hour later, Alphonse reclined on the lab bench, his head tipping over the edge of the sink. He watched as Daciana leaned forward, her ebon eyes mesmerizing, lips parted, tongue slightly extended. Her nostrils flared as her mouth opened, and Alphonse became suddenly aware that instead of turning him, she could be about to kill him.

He tensed. Well, so what if she was? What did he have to look forward to anyway? A peroxide blond skank for a wife, two brats who couldn't shut up to save their asses, a dead end job with no end in sight? *Dead end,* he thought. *Literally?*

He'd miss the sex, though. Not with Maria, there was no sex there anymore, not that she could turn him on if she even tried. With Daciana. White-hot heat under a mane of coal black hair. *Bite me, baby, and let come what may.*

67

As if knowing what was passing through his mind, Daciana whispered an endearment in a language he didn't understand and encased his throat with her distended mouth. He felt two tiny drops against his neck and then the slightest pressure as her fangs pierced his anesthetized skin. They sank deeper, and he could feel a release of blood from whatever vessel there was inside, vein or artery, he didn't know which, and furthermore, didn't give a damn.

She didn't tear his throat out, as she had with all the others; instead, she surrendered her jaws' feral embrace and lowered her lips to the wounds. Then she began to suck.

My God, he thought, *I'm getting wood.* This gave new meaning to the term *sucked off.* He could feel an erection building, without any stimulation at all. He couldn't open his eyes, for fear of seeing the room spin around him. Daciana's lips were soft as a baby's butt, yet demanding as a baby's mouth at her mother's tit. *Don't think about that last part,* he admonished himself as an image of Maria suckling baby Angelo and Alphonse, Junior, materialized unbidden.

"Open your eyes," Daciana whispered, and he was powerless to disobey. He looked deep into twin dark pools over a wash of red, his blood on her lips and tongue. Her fangs were still down.

As he watched, Daciana sank those fangs into her wrist and then tilted it over his mouth. She squeezed the blood out and down, quickly, before the holes she had made could heal. His mouth filled, and he swallowed. It tasted finer than the finest of red wines—although, truth to tell, the wines he was accustomed to would have marked their vintages in weeks rather than years.

When her wrist closed, Daciana bent forward and kissed him. Her tongue darted inside his mouth, and its tip felt the fangs growing along the roof of his mouth. Finally, she sat him up on the lab bench and slid his legs over the side. He looked down and saw the dark spot next to his fly.

"Oh, shit," he said, blood flushing his face. "How did that happen?"

Daciana's smile reflected an air of amused patience. "It's normal," she said. "And it's good, because it will take the edge off. Tonight's lovemaking will last even longer and be more intense than you've ever known." She kissed him. "Welcome to the world of the immortal."

They bid each other good day just as the sun began brightening the sides of the downtown buildings. Alphonse wearily climbed onto the Market Street bus and nearly stumbled off at the Roseville and Sixth Avenue stop. He glanced across the street as another bus pulled up heading for downtown. One of the passengers climbing aboard he recognized immediately: Naomi Paris, heading for her day at Arts High.

Stuck-up bitch never acknowledged him, never in four years, never brought the kid around—not that he especially wanted to see him, but it would've been the right thing to do, show him the kid. Maybe when Maria was out at confession or mass. Well, maybe not then.

A courtesy, though, that's what it would be, a courtesy.

She had no right to brush him off. Maybe it was time to teach her another lesson in doing the right thing.

Alphonse barged through his front door and made a direct path for the bedroom. He passed Maria, who was holding Junior in her arms trying to keep him still, without even offering his perfunctory peck on the cheek. From Angelo's bedroom came angry cries demanding breakfast. "You look like shit," Alphonse said to his wife. "You keep those little bastards quiet, hear? They keep me up with that bawlin', I'll give 'em something to bawl about! And you too!" Then he stormed into the bedroom and slammed the door. He was asleep almost before his head hit the pillow.

Joseph Christian Paris, had he been able to draw a comparison at the age of four, would have considered himself the happiest of children. After all, with three women happily attending to his every need, what little boy wouldn't be happy? Great Grandma (Gammy) watched him during the day, Regular Grandma (Mimi) took over in the afternoon, and Mommy made three when she got home from work. He was a big boy now, and soon he would be going to school with Mimi for kindergarten, where he could play with other boys and girls. Joseph couldn't wait.

He was strapped in his booster chair late one morning enjoying a cup of cut-up fruit when the door buzzer sounded. It was an angry sound, like bees, and Joseph never liked it. Gammy told him to wait a minute, she'd be right back, and gave him a kiss on the top of his head before walking out of the kitchen.

Joseph heard the clump of her footfalls on the stairs leading down to the vestibule, heard her turn the deadbolt, heard the door hinge squeak, heard his Gammy say, "Yes?"

Then he heard the scream.

Cut short.

Thumping sounds.

The door closing, the lock clicking.

Then nothing.

He began to cry.

More sounds. Footfalls coming up the stairs. Heavier than Gammy's.

He saw a man walk into the kitchen. A big man, with shiny black hair and red all around his mouth, looking like a clown he'd seen in a picture book. He had never seen this man before, and he pushed himself back in his chair as hard as he could. The man stopped and looked down at him. He smiled, but it wasn't a happy smile. It was a bad smile. A bad man's smile.

"Hey, kid," the man said. His voice was deep. As he spoke, some red bubbled out of his mouth and dribbled down his chin. He leaned forward until their noses almost touched. Joseph pressed his head against the seat back. He turned it to the side, trying not to smell the man's breath. He struggled against the vinyl strap around his waist that bound him to the chair.

The man grabbed Joseph's chin and turned it to make him look into his close-set, squinty brown eyes.

"I'm your father," the bad man said.

Then he opened his mouth.

When he told Daciana after hours that night in the privacy of her lab, she turned nearly purple and slapped him hard enough to make his ears ring. His face got so hot he thought it might blister. Her nails raked his cheeks, opening them wide and then scratching them open again even as they began to heal. Regaining his wits, Alphonse grabbed her wrists and held her away as she sputtered obscenities at him in a foreign tongue.

"Hey, bitch," he nearly shouted, "you near knocked the fillings out of my teeth. What the hell's the matter here? I thought you'd enjoy it. It's funny, right?"

Silence met his question as the *strigoi* fought to catch both her breath and her temper. Finally, "That you did it at all is bad enough. But to do it *without my knowledge, without my permission!*"

"I didn't know I needed your *permission* to do anything, lady." He relaxed his grip on her wrists, and when she made no move he released them. She lowered her hands to her sides and glowered at him.

Her first thought was, *I must kill the child.*

It was not from compassion that the thought originated. Daciana did not discriminate when it came to a victim's age or any other consideration. Beggar children in any number of countries over any number of ages had succumbed to her thirst. They, after all, comprised the easiest prey. No, it was not compassion; it was expedience that demanded his death.

Had she made a mistake in turning Alphonse? Had she herself succumbed to an appetite long denied? He was a lover such as she had not had in years. Brutal, strong, impetuous—yet it was his impetuosity that brought about his turning of another: a child who would not understand what had happened; a child who could neither explain nor control its urges; a child whose very existence, when discovered, would awaken others to the fact that her kind were in fact real and not the stuff of comic books. Such knowledge could threaten her own survival. Child or not, he must die. And Alphonse, for acting so rashly without her permission? She had felt no real loyalty toward him before. Now . . .

Virtue was a manacle that had never bound her.

"What're you thinking?" asked Alphonse, frowning at her far-away expression.

"I am considering how to deal with this situation," she answered. "Why did you do it?"

"Hey, he's my kid, I can do whatever I want with him, right?" Daciana cocked her head, waiting. "Okay, I did it to get back at his mother."

"The woman you raped five years ago."

He nodded. "She lives next door to me with her mother and grandmother." He paused. "Well, not with her grandmother anymore. Anyway, at no time, never, did Naomi let me see the kid. I'd see her in the neighborhood, like on weekends, and she'd walk right by me, her snooty nose up in the air like I had a load in my pants and she didn't want to have to smell me. Once I put my hand on her arm, just wantin' to say hello, and she spun around like some kind of maniac and almost smacked me. But she wouldn't dare. Did tell me—well, more like begged me—never to touch her again, I'd already touched her enough."

"And? Do you blame her?"

"Well, no. But I asked her if she was sorry about havin' her kid, and those eyes of hers just lit up. Told me that she loved the kid more than anything, but she hated me for being his father. Something like that, but she used more uppity language. Tryin' to make me feel inferior, I guess."

"Inferior. Yes, I would imagine that to be the case."

"So now I decided to teach her a lesson not to fu—excuse me, screw with me."

She studied his face, the defiance there, considered the self-serving justification in his tone. And the—admit it, amusing—irony that attached itself to the situation.

Like father, like son.

But if the son were to live, the mother would need to live, too, if only to care for him throughout his childhood—which, ironically, would endure forever, or until Daciana decided to end it. Which also implied that the mother must be turned as well.

Alphonse, so eager to use his cobra's fangs; the ignorant exemplar of the rule of unintended consequences. Daciana glanced at the floor and chewed her lower lip, then looked up as she recognized another irony, one that could be called delicious: to witness the tension between the child's mother and Alphonse escalate, and escalate, and escalate, over countless numbers of years. How much of him could she endure before the little mouse he described turned into a mongoose?

She began to formulate a plan.

Chapter Twelve

Their ten days' bereavement leave took Naomi and her mother through to the end of the school year. Aimee reported in before the official closing in order to complete the mountain of paperwork that attached itself to the closing of the year. It took three days, during which Naomi stayed home with Joseph. As a guidance counselor, she didn't have the entire summer to herself, just one month from mid-July to mid-August. During that time, her mother would be in charge of the baby.

Aimee herself was fifty-two now, three years shy of retirement eligibility. She had planned to teach until sixty-five, in order to collect social security at the same time as her pension, but since Naomi's forced resignation she had felt a coldness from the administration and a subtle distancing from her fellow staff. As if her presence were more tolerated than welcomed. Perhaps early retirement, then, at fifty-five, to allow her to care for Joseph while Naomi worked full time?

But he'll be attending kindergarten in September, won't he? Yes, she said to herself, *and I can bring him to school with me and bring him home at the end of the day. He would graduate from Garfield around the time I turn sixty-two. With a reduced social security plus my pension, I could retire then.*

And what of Naomi, she thought. *Would she find a man willing to marry her and be a father to Joseph?* This was 1972, after all. The culture had changed as a result of the tumultuous sixties, and there wasn't so much stigma attached to a man's willingness to marry an unwed mother— used goods, as the saying went when she was her daughter's age.

President Nixon had campaigned on ending the military draft, and according to the newspapers the legislation was on the fast track toward approval. Which meant Joseph would have more choices when he graduated high school.

Aimee approved of at least two years' national service between high school and college, the opportunity to give back to the country that had given the young people so much. Plus, it would give the youngsters—both boys and girls—the chance to mature some before heading off to college or a trade. But the venue, she stressed to herself, *shouldn't have to be military only.*

Bitter still after all these years, and remembering the sterile notification of her husband's death at the hands of the Japanese, she didn't want her grandson to enter the service at all.

She still woke up weeping from the frequently recurring dream of how she had found her mother's bloodied body at the foot of the stairs that afternoon. How she had rushed upstairs to see if Joseph were all right. How she had found spots of blood on his bib, but no wounds at all on his person. How he had looked so serene, sitting there in his booster chair, looking at her, blissful and unaware.

Naomi, too, would never forget walking home from the Roseville Avenue bus stop, rounding the corner of Sixth Avenue and Fifth Street, and seeing the emergency vehicles blocking the street outside Number 239; of seeing her elderly landlord and landlady standing on the porch wringing their hands as they spoke in hushed tones to the police; of seeing Alphonse and Maria watching curiously from their porch.

Of dropping her briefcase onto the gray slate sidewalk as she saw her mother step across the bloody threshold into the vestibule, weeping and carrying Joseph in her arms; of the pitying look from her landlady; of the sudden realization that she knew whose body it was in that black bag being loaded into the ambulance.

Naomi sank to her knees, held her hands to her face, and wept like a child. When she looked up, she saw Maria looking at her with an expression of curiosity that might have included a measure of solicitude; but Alphonse's own face was blank. When he saw her looking, he turned and walked into his house.

But what else would she have expected from Alphonse?

Later, an inventory showed nothing missing from the household. The only curiosity was the few spots of blood on Joseph's bib. They were tested for type, and the results baffled investigators; they were a mix of two different blood types, O being Joseph's, the other AB—which matched no one in Joseph's family.

No clues surfaced as the investigation wore on. Near summer's end, the case grew cold. There were no fingerprints other than the family's, no witnesses to Dorothy Christian's murder. The only possible lead could have come from the baby, and the police brought in a child counselor to try to elicit whatever information she could from the boy. He just shook his head when she asked him if he had seen anyone in the house that day other than his Gammy.

Her narrative to the investigative team ended with this aside, "The boy is adorable in both physical and behavioral aspects, with one exception. When I said goodbye to him today, I placed my hand to his cheek as a gesture of affection, and suddenly his little hands grabbed mine and pulled it to his mouth—whereupon he bit it with his full strength, actually drawing blood. I shouted *No!* and drew my hand away, and he reached for it, his eyes focused with a certain fascination upon the trickle of blood on the back of it. He wept as I left, reaching for me; or, perhaps more accurately, for my hand. I assume he is simply going through the biting phase common to all children at one time or another; but I hope he can be trained away from it before he enters kindergarten in September."

"I've noticed the biting," said Aimee during dinner one typically sweltering summer evening as the family, diminished by one, sat down to a cold supper. The floor fan was placed by the open kitchen window, the blades vainly trying to replace the stifling air inside with some of the barely cooler air outdoors. In the city, Daylight Saving Time simply added an hour to the day's heat and humidity. The leaves on the maple trees out front were still as if painted on their branches, and those on the rose of Sharon bush bordering the back of the tiny yard outside the kitchen window were drooping and wilted. It hadn't rained in weeks.

In August Naomi returned to school, her month's so-called vacation over, and Aimee began devoting two days a week to preparing her classroom for the new influx of children next month. Joseph accompanied her in his stroller, the distance being too far for him to walk the entire way.

On one of those days, when Aimee was busy stapling posters to her bulletin board, she turned around to see that Joseph had opened her desk drawer and had stabbed his own wrist with her scissors. Worse, he had pressed his mouth to the wound and was sucking in his own blood.

She rushed to him with a paper towel and pressed it to his wrist as she carried him downstairs to the nurse's office. Joseph tried to tear away the towel, but Aimee held his wrist away from his other hand as tears of anger, frustration, and fear formed behind her glasses.

"Mildred," Aimee nearly shouted to the nurse. "Thank goodness you're here. My grandson cut his wrist with my scissors."

The nurse, some five years older than Aimee, grumbled inwardly; here she had come in early to set up her office and go through some paperwork, and now she had to take care of a kid whose grandmother couldn't be bothered to keep tabs on him. For any other teacher, she might've felt more accommodating; but this was the bastard son of Naomi Paris, the teacher who had brought the public's disdain upon the entire faculty through her promiscuity. One rotten apple, and the reputation of the whole bunch was shot.

"Let's see it," Mildred said, and when she unwrapped the paper towel, she looked coldly at Aimee. "Is this some kind of bad joke?" she asked.

"What are you talking about?"

"Do you see any cut here?" She held Joseph's wrist up for inspection.

"That's impossible," said Aimee. "He was bleeding; he was sucking on the wound." She pointed to the trashcan. "You can see the blood on the paper towel."

"Well, there's no blood now, is there? Not even a trace of a cut." She looked at Joseph's smiling face as he sat on her desk. "Are you all right, boy? Did you hurt yourself? Do you feel sick?"

Joseph tilted his head to one side. "I fine."

Mildred lowered him to the floor and looked at his grandmother. "He says he's fine, Mrs. Paris. And I don't see any reason to doubt him."

"Thank you . . . Mrs. Flynn," said Aimee and left hurriedly, holding Joseph's hand.

Shortly after noon a week later, Aimee answered the doorbell to find a slim, attractive brunette dressed in business attire and carrying a briefcase, standing before her. The woman could've been in her mid to late thirties. Her black hair was pulled back severely in a bun and her makeup was minimal. The heavy eye lining and shadow that had been so popular in the sixties was now passé, but this woman's eyes and lashes were so dark that even without mascara they were somehow compelling. The woman smiled, revealing perfect teeth.

"Miss Paris?" she asked. "Naomi Paris?"

"No, I'm her mother, Aimee Paris. And you are?"

The woman extended her hand. "Dr. Moceanu, Division of Youth and Family Services. May I come in?"

Aimee frowned. "DYFS?" She pronounced it, as did everyone in the profession, *Dye-fuss.* "Is something the matter?"

Dr. Moceanu shook her head. "No, not at all. The city apparently thinks we don't have enough to do, so they're sending agents around to interview the parents or guardians of incoming kindergarteners and to visit with the children."

"Really." Aimee gestured to the stairs. "Then come in. Joseph just went in for his nap."

They sat at the kitchen table and chatted over tall glasses of iced tea, starting their conversation with complaints about the weather and moving gradually into the family dynamic.

"I'm so sorry to hear about your mother," Dr. Moceanu said. "I read about it in the paper and couldn't get it out of my mind. Poor child, to be subjected to that."

Aimee nodded. "Yes. And to tell the truth, from that day to this Joseph has been, I don't know, different somehow. As if he knew that he'd never see his Gammy again and it doesn't bother him at all. But they had been inseparable."

"Does he ask about her?"

"That's what's the most different, I guess. I mean, not once has he said he misses her. It's as if she never existed in his mind." She took a sip of tea. Condensation flowed down the sides of the glass and dripped onto the oilcloth. "Other than that—and the occasional biting—he's the little angel he's always been."

"Did you say biting?"

"Yes, but that's normal with children. They all go through the biting phase, don't they?"

The doctor nodded. "They do indeed."

"Do you have children, Doctor?"

"No, I'm afraid not. I'd have to be married first, and I just never found the right man."

"That's odd. You're very attractive, and obviously smart too. Maybe that combination would intimidate some men?"

"Hmm. Men like that wouldn't be worth considering, would they?"

They shared a soft laugh. Then they heard tiny footfalls as Joseph toddled into the kitchen.

"And this is Joseph," said Aimee.

Dr. Moceanu turned in her chair and leaned over to face him. "Hello, Joseph."

The boy's eyes locked onto hers and he smiled broadly as he walked toward her and held out his arms. She picked him up and sat him on her lap, facing her.

Aimee was startled. "He's never done that before. Normally, he's very shy when he meets strangers."

"Children seem to have a sixth sense about people, much the way, say, dogs can sense whether a new person is friend or foe." She looked into Joseph's eyes. "And you know I'm your friend, don't you, Joseph?"

"You my friend," said the boy.

The doctor turned to Aimee. "I'd like to talk with Joseph about his—you know—and it's usually better if it's one on one. Do you mind?"

"Oh. No, I guess not. Joseph, why don't you show Dr. Moceanu your room?"

Fifteen minutes later, the pair returned to the kitchen, holding hands. Joseph's face was beaming, his cheeks all pink and his little tongue licking around his lips. The doctor's expression was itself almost beatific. "We had a lovely talk," she announced. "And I don't think we'll need to concern ourselves with Joseph's, um, problem anymore."

"You come back?" Joseph asked, looking up.

"If your grandmother says it's all right," said the doctor, looking at Aimee.

"Why—of course it's all right," she said. "I guess. I mean, aren't you busy with your other visits?"

"I am. But Joseph and I have hit it off splendidly, and I think I can justify some return visits. Again, if you don't mind. I don't often connect with children so quickly and completely, and in my professional opinion I believe that Joseph—no, I'd have to say both of us—can benefit from some more time together." She lowered her voice confidentially. "I'm doing my post-doctoral work on empathy in young children, and Joseph would make a fascinating case study. Again, with his mother's and your permission. And," she added, "as you've no doubt already guessed, I do regret not having children of my own." She checked her watch. "Time for my next appointment. Joseph, you be a good boy, and I'll see you soon." To Aimee she said, "I'll be sure to call first; my job dictates that my first visit be unexpected, so I can see the home environment, um, unvarnished, shall we say. My report will read that you keep an exemplary home. Oh, and I think Joseph's biting problem will soon be a thing of the past. Won't it, Joseph?" As the boy nodded, she released his hand and extended hers to Aimee. "Thank you, Mrs. Paris. It's been a pleasure meeting you."

"You're welcome any time, Doctor. Oh, and please, my name is Aimee."

"Then please, Aimee, call me Daciana."

"You did what?" asked Alphonse at work that night. "I thought you were going to kill the kid, and his grandmother too."

"I changed my mind," Daciana said. "A woman's privilege, or so I've been told."

"Yeah, they say women have cleaner minds than men because they change 'em more often."

"A poor joke, Alphonse, nearly as old as I."

"But tell me, why didn't you do it?"

"Because once I met the child, I detected a certain . . . possibility. I have lived hundreds of years, Alphonse, and a long existence can become tedious without new experiences, new challenges to face. I thought it might be entertaining to see what happens with this child as he grows older intellectually and emotionally . . . but never grows a day older physically."

"Huh?"

"You never thought about that, did you?"

"Uh, no."

"Can you imagine what will happen when he reaches emotional puberty? And his body remains that of a child?" Her chuckle contained no mirth. "Frustration, leading perhaps to fury, endless are the possibilities."

Alphonse thought. "Not grow older? That could be bad shit. What'll the kid do about it, do you think?"

"Perhaps that is what we shall find out, you and I."

"Uh . . . huh. So, how was the kid, anyway?"

Daciana pursed her lips. "In a word . . . sweet."

Alphonse stared at her. "Meaning?"

"I mean, I gave him a little taste of me, and I took a little taste of him. To establish a bond between us, and a bit of a snack to tide me over until tonight. I made him promise not to try biting anyone else, because he can take what he wants from me on my next visit. And the next. And so on."

"But how about killing the old lady?"

"In time. The most effective plans often move slowly. I intend to let the victim—in the final case, the child's mother—recover from the first shock, namely, at her grandmother's murder, before hitting her with the murder of her own mother. It's delicious, is it not?"

No, it's sadistic, Alphonse thought, but he knew better than to voice it. Besides, it was only Naomi getting hurt in the end, and she deserved it. "What're we talkin' about, time-wise?" he said.

Daciana raised her eyebrows. "Time? What is time to us? There's no need to rush, is there? We can drag this out as long as we like." She touched her painted fingernails to his stubbled cheek. "Now, what have you procured for me in the lab?"

The whore, gagged and bound and strapped to the lab bench, was still unconscious when they entered the laboratory. A large angry bump on her head testified to the subtlety of Alphonse's persuasive skills.

The victim was probably in her twenties, but street life had aged her to look double that. She was black, as were

all their victims—this was a predominantly black neighborhood, after all—and for Alphonse their race was a bonus; he
made no excuses for his prejudice. As far as Daciana was
concerned, a person's race and ethnicity were moot.

The woman had probably never been pretty, even to
start with. Her brow ridge was prominent and low, her eyes
set close; her nose was broad and flat, with flared nostrils;
and her lips were fleshy and pale against her dark brown
skin. A real two-bagger, as Alphonse would say. And you'd
need to sew the bags together to make one big one, just to
get 'em over and around that dopey Afro.

Her body was rail thin. She wore an elastic tube top over
scrawny breasts, short enough to leave her middle bare to
below her navel. Her skimpy shorts hung so low that a few
strands of curly black hair peeked out above the thick black
plastic belt, and when Alphonse happened to glance up a
leg he saw another tangle of hair; she wasn't even wearing
panties. No stockings either, but she did have on a pair of
clunky platform shoes of the kind that were just coming
into style and made walking a skill to learn all over again.
Women's designers must think women are stupid, Alphonse
thought in one of his rare reflective moments. *What smart
broad would ever want to shove her feet into those things?*

"Wake her up," Daciana said. "It's so much better when
they know what's going to happen. And they realize they're
helpless to do anything about it."

Alphonse slapped the girl's face, and when she came to
he leaned over her head and let down his fangs. Her eyes
grew huge, dilated black dots punctuating jaundiced yellow globes that reminded him of dirty old Ping-Pong balls.
She tried to move her needle-tracked arms, but he had
bound them behind her and tied them against the small of
her back with rope wound tightly around her waist. A rope
around her neck and ankles, plus one more just above her
knees immobilized her on the lead-topped lab bench. She
tried to scream, but the gag not only covered her mouth, it
filled it. *Probably still cleaner than the last thing that was in
her mouth,* he thought.

Daciana stood next to Alphonse, opposite the girl's torso. The victim tried to twist her body from side to side, but
her bonds would not yield. Daciana yanked the tube top to
the girl's waist, revealing breasts so scrawny they reminded

her of a chimpanzee's dugs. None of this mattered to her; mortals were merely cattle to be slaughtered.

But the slaughter of a human need never be humane.

"What the hell's that?" said Alphonse, his attention diverted by the apparatus now in Daciana's hands. It looked like a chrome-plated barber's clipper with a fine-toothed wheel at the business end.

"It's a saw to cut through the sternum." When he frowned, she traced a fingernail down the center of the victim's chest. "Sternum," she said. "Breastbone." She placed her thumb against the trigger, and the blade began whirring, a sound like a dentist's drill. She released the trigger and put down the saw, after casting a long and satisfied look at the whore's sweating face.

"And this," she said, picking up a new instrument and making sure her victim saw it as clearly as did Alphonse, "is what some call a torso splitter." It reminded him of a polished steel carpenter's vise, but one that pushed open instead of closed. There was a wheel geared to a set of jaws that when together, as they were now, came to a point, like a sharp wedge.

The girl's throat strained against a series of screams trapped behind the gag.

"What are you gonna do with that?" he asked.

She placed it against the girl's sternum and picked up a surgical mallet. "I'm going to get to the heart of the matter," she quipped. "But first things first."

Daciana picked up a scalpel and drew the blade slowly down the middle of the woman's chest. Blood bubbled out and ran down her sides, forming glistening red puddles on the flat gray bench top.

Alphonse heard a sound that reminded him of the faraway scream of a cat in agony and realized it came through the thin walls of the woman's throat.

Daciana picked up the saw and bent over the woman. Her face reflected something akin to nostalgia. "Dr. Mengele would be so proud," she muttered to herself. "*Ilsa, She-wolf of the SS,* indeed." The motor whined as the blade began to whir.

Even Alphonse couldn't watch what happened next.

Meanwhile, half a city away, four-year-old Joseph Christian Paris was enjoying the nicest dream. It was of the man who'd said he was Joseph's father, the man he used to think of as bad, and of the nice lady he'd met today, the one who had shared blood with him. In his dream, they were all in his bedroom, drinking blood from some woman. He himself was drinking from her wrist, his father from her neck, and the lady, Miss Daci, from inside her leg. His father's large hairy head blocked his view of the woman's face, but the clothes she was wearing looked familiar.

Chapter Thirteen: Naomi

Naomi Paris sat on the Arts High School stage on Freshman Orientation Day along with the school administrators as the principal, Dr. Fragomeni, gave the same welcoming speech he'd been giving for the past twenty years. It was in fact the same speech he'd delivered when Naomi herself was a freshman. *There was obviously no reason to change it,* she reflected, *as the audience is new each year.* When he was done with his speech, the assistant principal, Mrs. Rascona, followed with hers. She then introduced Naomi as the guidance counselor.

A few of the freshmen, noting her good looks, were already making plans to seek guidance, even though Miss Paris's duties involved mostly juniors and seniors and their college and career plans.

Naomi gave the newbies her best professional smile, but her mind was elsewhere. This was Joseph's first year in school, having just turned five, and she was anxious that he fit in with the other children. Her mother would be there in case of emergency, so that was good, and thanks to that DYFS agent's weekly visits, his tendency to bite had tapered off completely.

Although there was the time she came home one day to find her son biting into a package of raw chopped beef. He pulled his head up when he saw her, and his mouth was covered in cow's blood. Her mother had been in the bathroom at the time; Naomi couldn't fault her for not being there at the moment Joseph had chosen to raid the refrigerator.

Because the DYFS lady had come during Naomi's summertime working hours, Naomi hadn't had the opportunity to meet her, and she regretted that. But her mother had vouched for the woman, especially for her rapport with young Joseph. Aimee had told her that the agent with the foreign-sounding name was actually visiting on her own time now, mostly during her lunch hour. She had offered to serve lunch on numerous occasions, but the offer had always been politely declined. "I'll feed on my little pork chop," she said once, smiling as she began her private visit with Joseph. Their little tête-à-têtes had become so commonplace by now that Aimee never thought to question the reason for them. *Goodness knows,* she thought, *these visits have worked wonders for the little boy.*

"Good news," said Aimee on a Friday afternoon. "Daciana called and said if it's okay she'd like to visit with Joseph tomorrow, get the chance to finally meet you, too. I invited her to lunch, and told her she couldn't say no."

When Naomi opened the door to the vestibule at noon the next day, she saw a thin, attractive brunette dressed in a short-sleeved gray blouse, black skirt, and casual flats. She looked to be in her mid-thirties, with long, loose black hair parted in the middle, the Gloria Steinem look so fashionable these days, gracefully arched eyebrows, and eyes nearly as dark as her hair. Her lips were rouged pink, slightly darker than her cheeks. She held a white box tied with string.

"You must be Naomi," the woman said. "I'm Daciana." She proffered the box. "Some French-glazed doughnuts, for dessert."

Naomi took the box with thanks and added, "Mom says you never eat lunch."

"Not during weekdays, usually too busy. But on weekends I turn into a glutton."

"Well, don't just stand there, Daciana. Come on upstairs. Joseph's excited to see you again."

They all chatted amiably over lunch, and Daciana suggested they delay dessert. "It's a lovely fall day," she said. "What do you say we take Joseph for a walk in the park first?"

"You girls go ahead," Aimee insisted. "I'll clean the dishes and set out plates for the doughnuts. And make a fresh batch of iced tea."

"Mom, don't you want to—?"

"Go. Scoot. Get to know each other. Joseph needs some outside time. Beat it."

Branch Brook Park was two short blocks away. Naomi wheeled Joseph to the pedestrian bridge over the trolley tracks and carried him up the stairs while Daciana lifted the stroller, Joseph's stuffed toy monkey secured in the back pocket. Once inside the park, they wheeled him to the empty bandstand near the lake. Across the lake stood the Cathedral of the Sacred Heart.

"Do you go to church?" Daciana asked as they sat on a bench and watched Joseph play with his stuffed monkey nearby.

"Not that one," Naomi said as she nodded toward the cathedral. "I go to Fifth Avenue Presbyterian, over on Park Avenue. Which used to be called Fifth Avenue at one time, I guess." She faced Daciana. "Do you? Go to church?"

"I prefer not to," she replied. "I've had some . . . unpleasant experiences that I'd rather not go into just now. But I admire people of faith. Faith is important, and I wish I hadn't abandoned mine."

Naomi placed her hand over Daciana's. "If ever you do want to talk about it . . ."

Daciana smiled and closed her fingers around Naomi's. "Someday," she said. "I already know I can trust you, Naomi. Thank you." Her eyes flickered to the front. "Oh, now would you look at Joseph."

The boy was holding the monkey's neck to his mouth and biting it.

"How cute," Daciana said.

"If you don't mind, I'd like to accompany you to church one day," Daciana suggested on one of her later visits.

With that, the by now regular weekend visits transitioned from Saturdays to Sundays, and as Aimee babysat Joseph at home, Naomi and Daciana attended eleven o'clock services at Fifth Avenue Pres. For Naomi, Dr. Van Dyke's sermons had taken on the aspect of routine, of normalcy, of I-know-what-he's-going-to-say-next regularity. They were nothing new, but they still provided a base of strength and comfort for her.

Daciana, on the other hand, seemed to find great interest in what the minister had to say each week. The two friends would walk back to Fifth Street chatting about the message, so close emotionally that one might expect them to comport themselves arm in arm.

When they arrived at Naomi's home, they would find a mid-day dinner prepared by Aimee—at which Daciana, to her hostess's delight, ate heartily, although she never seemed to gain weight—and later, Daciana would insist that she be the one to put Joseph down for his afternoon nap while the other two ladies cleared the table and loaded the new portable dishwashing machine.

Joseph seemed always eager for Daciana's attention, and she herself mentioned how much she enjoyed their alone time.

No one, as Daciana had once said to Alphonse, could resist her charm offensive.

And Alphonse, by mutual consent, had agreed to make himself invisible during Daciana's visits.

"I'm going to ask Daciana to spend Christmas with us," Naomi declared. "She has no family of her own—her parents are political prisoners in Romania, remember—and I think she'd like to share the day with us. Especially with Joseph."

"Funny you should say that," her mother replied, "because I was about to suggest that myself."

Aimee had access to a myriad of Christmas decorations at school, and after she'd decorated her classroom she brought home a dozen or so paper Santas she had cut from an old Clement C. Moore book which featured pictures of the jolly, rotund fellow introduced in the Coca-Cola ads of her own youth. She taped them to the walls of the living room, dining room, and alcove off the porch, where the television resided and where the Christmas tree soon would stand. She brought home cardboard-backed holly wreaths and even hung a mobile of cardboard ornaments from the living room ceiling.

On Saturday, the day before Christmas Eve—when prices would be almost at their lowest—she, Naomi, and Joseph planned to visit the lot on Seventh Avenue and Seventh Street, where Christmas trees were sold, and pick out a tree light enough for the two women to carry home. Already, the ornaments stood in their boxes in the alcove next to the tree stand, the angel with her arms extended before her, as if welcoming all to receive glad tidings of great joy.

Daciana would arrive on Sunday, as usual, but stay overnight for the first time, to welcome Christmas with the family on Monday.

Dr. Van Dyke's holiday sermon, Naomi acknowledged to herself, *was actually inspired.* The junior choir sang like little soprano angels, and the senior choir caroled "The Hallelujah Chorus" so powerfully that many of the standees in the congregation found themselves unselfconsciously wiping their eyes, Naomi among them.

Daciana's eyes were dry but alert, darting from choir to congregants and then returning to Naomi herself.

Back home, the women found the air filled with the scent of Italian herbs and spices, signaling that Aimee had prepared a meal befitting her late husband's Italian heritage. First came antipasto; cheeses, salamis, scallions, olives both green and black, cherry tomatoes, pimientos, and sardines resting on a bed of romaine, bathed in olive oil and red wine vinegar, and sprinkled with oregano. Next came a huge baked lasagna casserole, flat noodles layered with ground beef, Italian sausage, ricotta, and mozzarella, all married to a rich red sauce and accompanied by a tart chianti. Dessert was a mascarpone cheesecake with a slivered almond crust, accompanied by demitasses of espresso, the coffee itself served with hard peppermint candies that none but Joseph seemed to have room for.

The women pushed their chairs back and rubbed their bellies. Daciana declared that she hadn't eaten so well in ages and filled the conversation with effusive praise for Aimee's culinary skills. Aimee blushed, and Naomi cautioned Daciana against giving her mother a swelled head.

Joseph sucked on a peppermint and observed.

Between the dining room and kitchen, a small square hallway gave access to the two bedrooms, the bathroom, and side stairs. Next to the doorway to those stairs stood a small table, and on that table rested the telephone. It rang.

"I'll get it," said Naomi, standing with pretended oh-dear-I-ate-too-much effort. Picking up the phone, she chirped a Hello.

"Hi, Naomi?" came a woman's voice.

"Yes?"

"This is Nina, from DYFS. Hope you don't mind my calling you on Christmas Eve, but when I phoned on Friday school had already let out. Do you have a second?" Naomi said she did. "You phoned originally about one of your younger students, a boy who showed signs of parental abuse, remember? We've intervened and are going to recommend foster care. But that's not the reason I called. If you remember when we spoke you also mentioned that you wanted to put in a good word for one of our staff members . . . a Daciana Moceanu?" She struggled a bit with the pronunciation.

Naomi nodded and said, "Yes, uh-huh." She glanced into the dining room, where Daciana and her mother seemed to be sharing a joke.

"Well, I was kind of focused on your student at the moment, but after I hung up I got curious, because I didn't think we had anyone on our staff by that name. I checked, and we didn't. So I called the home office in Trenton, figuring maybe she worked for another branch, and they might be able to tell me which one. Now, the administrative secretary was busy getting the office ready for the holiday recess, so I didn't expect an answer right away. But she did call back, just before closing time, and told me DYFS had no one who matched that name in their files. Not the first name nor the last."

Naomi remained silent.

"Hello, Naomi, are you there?"

"Um, yes I am. You're sure, Nina? I mean, absolutely sure?"

"Abso-tively, posi-lutely," came the reply. "So anyway, I thought you'd want to know, and I hope you and your family have a Merry Christmas."

"Yes . . . thank you. Um, you have the same. Goodbye, Nina."

Naomi stared at Daciana, who was now making goo-goo eyes at Joseph. She walked slowly into the room and stood by her, looking down at the top of her black tresses. Daciana looked up and their eyes met.

The instinct of a mother to protect her young overrode all the questions Naomi would otherwise have demanded answers to. Suppressing her need to interrogate, she simply said, in a voice so flat it made her mother gasp, "Leave. Now."

Aimee said, "Naomi?"

Her daughter didn't answer. She just stared into Daciana's flat black eyes.

Daciana moved her chair back and stood, expressionless. Without a word, she walked to the coat tree, put on her overcoat, and walked down the stairs.

They heard her turn the lock, open the front door to the vestibule, and close it again.

"What's going on?" asked Aimee, her voice nearly a whisper.

"She's not from DYFS," Naomi said. When her mother began to protest, she told her about the phone call as Joseph looked from mother to grandmother and back again.

"I don't understand it. Why would she say she was? And why would she take such an interest in Joseph?"

"She's my friend," the boy said.

They heard the door open.

"I forgot my overnight bag," called Daciana. "My I come up?"

"Yes," said Aimee. "And while you're here, you might ex—"

She stopped and held a hand to her mouth as they heard two sets of footfalls on the stairs. One was soft and measured, Daciana's; the other was heavy, plodding.

"Oh, God, no," whispered Naomi as her fears became real. Alphonse emerged next to Daciana at the head of the stairs.

They walked into the dining room and faced the others. Aimee's confusion was still manifest in her expression, and Naomi's face grew ashen at seeing her twice-rapist in her home. Joseph frowned in his booster seat and said, "The bad man."

"Not a bad man," corrected Daciana in a soothing voice. "Your daddy, remember?"

"What?" cried Aimee. "It was you?" She swiveled her head toward her daughter. "But you said—"

Naomi bolted for the phone, but Alphonse was quicker and blocked her. She pelted him with her fists, but he only smiled. Finally, as if swatting at a pesty fly, he slapped her across the face hard enough to make her knees buckle and her mouth fill with blood. She spat it in his face.

He licked his lips.

Joseph bolted from his booster chair, stumbled as his tiny feet hit the floor, and began hitting Alphonse on his legs, as high as the boy could reach. "No hit my mommy!" he cried.

"Now, let's be civilized, shall we?" said Daciana as Alphonse pushed the boy away.

With blood dripping down her chin, Naomi said, "How can you say *civilized* when you're holding that knife?" It was the nine-inch chef's knife that Aimee had used to cut the cake.

"It's because I'm the one holding the knife, dear," said Daciana. "And I'd advise you to stay still and say nothing." She looked at Alphonse. "By the way, you must try some of that cheesecake. It's—dare I say it—heavenly."

"Now?"

"Well, maybe you can wait a little bit."

"After we take care of business, you mean."

"Speaking of business, what about your wife and boys? What did you do with them?"

"I sent 'em to five o'clock mass and told Maria to go from Saint Rose's to her mother's. Said I'll meet her there later."

"Ah. Well done." She turned to Naomi. "You'll remember when you told me last week that you had a student you were going to refer to DYFS? And that you'd put in a good word for me while you were at it?" Naomi nodded weakly. "You remember I urged you not to do it? Well, now you know I wasn't being modest. But I figured you just might do it anyway, little do-gooder that you are. So I arranged for Alphonse to be available today after you and I returned from church. That phone call you received? Interesting that your caller beat me to the punch, so to speak."

Aimee spoke, "What is going on here? What are you talking about? Just who the hell are you, anyway, and why are you terrorizing us like this?"

Daciana smiled and turned to Alphonse. "And now might I suggest that you take Mrs. Paris into her bedroom to preserve her privacy?"

"Oh no," Naomi cried. "You can't rape my mother, you can't! Take me instead!"

He grinned at her. "Been there, done that," he said. "Twice, in fact. And tell the truth, both times you weren't worth gettin' my dick wet."

Daciana laughed. "How touching, Naomi. But we have other plans for you, dear. Alphonse?"

"You're gonna wish it was only a rape." He leered at Aimee.

Daciana stepped behind Naomi and held the blade to her throat. She looked at Joseph and said, "Don't worry, my little angel, I'm not going to hurt your mommy." Under her breath, she said, "Yet."

"Let's go," Alphonse said to Aimee and shoved her, protesting, into her bedroom.

"Mom," Naomi uttered, her voice pleading, fearful that she might be saying goodbye.

The door closed behind the two as Daciana stood with the knife's edge dancing across Naomi's throat. "Go back to your chair, Joseph," she said, and the boy obeyed. "Everything is going to be fine, trust me. You know you can trust me, right?"

Joseph nodded, but his face told her he wasn't so sure anymore.

"We have our secrets, you and I, don't we? And we're going to share them with your mommy and your grandma; excuse me, your Mimi."

A sharp cry, a wail suddenly silenced, came from behind the closed door. They heard a soft thump as something fell to the floor. Then nothing.

When the door opened, Alphonse emerged with blood covering the lower half of his face. It was smeared over his neck and blotted on his shirt.

The bedroom was subject to winter's early darkness, and Naomi could see nothing inside. But she didn't have to see to know that her mother was dead.

As dead as her grandmother.

"It was you who killed my grandmother," she accused. "That's right, isn't it? And now my mother? Who's next? Me? And my innocent baby boy? What kind of monsters are you?" She could feel the spittle at the corners of her mouth.

"Funny you should mention that," he said.

"Leave my boy alone. You leave my boy alone." Naomi could feel her Adam's apple bobbing across the blade at her neck.

"Oh, Naomi," cooed Daciana. "Does your little boy have a surprise for you. Joseph, open your mouth, the way you do when we're alone together."

In wary obedience, Joseph opened his mouth. Wide. Wider. Then he lowered his tiny fangs from the roof of his mouth. As Naomi gagged, Daciana lowered the knife and Alphonse stood close, facing them. The two intruders revealed their own fangs mere inches from Naomi's face.

"What are you?" cried Naomi. *"And what have you done to my son?"*

"I believe you know what we are," said Daciana as she retracted her fangs. "And you know what we can do. But, dear Naomi, we offer you a choice."

"What are you talking about?"

"The choice is a simple one. Choose life or death. If you choose to live, it will be as one of us. If you choose to die rather than live as we do, the salient question becomes, what's a little boy to do, alone, without his mother?"

"And I'm sure as hell not going to raise him," Alphonse butted in. He nodded toward Daciana. "She's not either."

"Says the very father who made him—in more ways than one." Daciana cast a glance at Alphonse. He took a small step backward and almost imperceptibly lowered his head. "So if we kill you, for the sake of expedience we must also kill little Joseph. If you choose the former option, we make you into one of us. Which means you get to keep your son, alive, with you. This is your decision, my gullible young friend. Just remember the consequences to your son as a result of your choice."

Naomi sobbed, blood bubbling from her mouth. Her teeth on the struck side of her face were loose. Her life, it seemed, was measured in losses. She had lost the father she'd never known; lost her virginity to a rapist; lost her grandmother, slaughtered in the doorway of her own home by the very creature who had raped her. And now her mother lay dead in her bedroom. Not even given the hideous choice being offered to her.

"Tell me again. What will happen if I choose . . . to let Joseph live?"

"You will continue as before, but with one difference, the need for blood. Not every night like in the movies, but you'll know when you need it. How will you explain your mother's disappearance? That will be up to you. And as for little Joseph, well, I'm sure you'll think of something to keep him happy."

Naomi's breathing grew harsher. She could not let her baby die. Even if he was one of them—a—she couldn't bring herself to even think the word. And couldn't even admit that she could soon be one too.

"Oh, one more thing, my dear. We shall monitor you, Alphonse and I, Alphonse mostly. Should you do anything to betray us, you and your son will not live to see another sunrise. With Joseph I would probably dispatch him swiftly; I rather fancy him, in my way, at least for now. But you, Naomi? You? I love to see people suffer who break confidence with me."

"I didn't break any confidence! It was you—" Tears mingled with the blood on her face. Naomi found herself blubbering.

"Look at the bright side," interrupted Alphonse. "Be good, and you never have to die. Like her and me, we're not gonna die either. You stay lookin' hot like you do, forever. Things could be a hell of a lot worse."

Naomi looked at her son's trusting and adoring face. "I'm going to do this. For you, my little prince," she said as she wept.

"Good, that's settled," said Daciana. "Now, Joseph, listen carefully. We are going to take some blood from Mommy, and then you are going to give her some of yours, just as your daddy did that first day, remember? Then she will live forever, just like you and just like us. Won't that be nice?"

"Where's my Mimi?"

"Oh, she's in the other room, sweetie. Resting."

"Let's get going," said Alphonse. "I've got a family dinner to go to."

Naomi walked with a fatalistic resolve into her bedroom and pulled back the covers before lying on the sheet. She shuddered as Daciana lifted her dress to expose her thighs. At her direction, she extended a hand to the side, palm up, exposing her wrist. Joseph climbed onto the bed and slipped his small hands beneath her arm. Tears were in Naomi's eyes as she told Joseph she loved him.

"I love you too, Mommy," he said and lowered his mouth to her wrist.

At the same time, Daciana leaned forward and sank her fangs into the inside of Naomi's thigh while Alphonse bit into the side of her neck, blocking Joseph's view of her face as he sucked.

Joseph seemed to remember something peculiar about this, but he couldn't place it. Maybe it had to do with Mommy's dress. He'd never really noticed it before, but somehow it looked familiar.

Chapter Fourteen

Naomi awoke suddenly, nerves on fire, head throbbing. She sat up, staring about, and saw Joseph lying next to her, sleeping like an angel.

But he was no angel anymore, was he? He would never be an angel.

She ran her tongue over the roof of her mouth and discovered the fangs. *And neither will I,* she thought. *But Mom, my blessed, murdered mother, will. She's with God, an angel already. Mom, Mom, if you can hear me, forgive me; please forgive me.*

Naomi was suddenly overcome with grief. Joseph stirred, but continued sleeping.

The room was dim. She could hear the alarm clock ticking and turned to look at its white face, blurred through her tears. Six-thirty. Christmas morning.

Through the thin wall, she could hear water running in the bathroom. Seconds later, Daciana walked in carrying a towel and tossed it on the bed before turning on the light. Joseph turned over on his side and kept sleeping.

The *strigoi* smiled and regarded Naomi from behind half-lidded eyes. "Merry Christmas," she said in a tone that reeked of mockery.

Naomi looked at the towel. It had been pure white; now it was blotched with red.

"It's been a long night," Daciana said matter-of-factly. "It's fortunate that your landlords are visiting their children in Florida for the holiday; otherwise, they might have heard me drag your mother's body down the back stairs to the furnace."

Naomi took a halting breath. "You didn't. You couldn't."

"I could and I did, dear."

"Don't call me dear."

"I'll call you whatever I like whenever I like, child. That's the nature of things now."

Naomi stared at her.

"You'll be happy to learn that your mother enjoyed a dignified cremation." She hesitated a second. "Well, it would've been more dignified had the door to the furnace been larger. I had to do it in stages."

"Oh, my God."

"There are some stains you'll have to clean up down there. I'd suggest you use muriatic acid; it works wonders on concrete. As for as the bed linens, I burned them too. No, there's no need to thank me. Dear."

She sat on the edge of the bed and stared into Naomi's eyes as she reached her fingers out to stroke her hair. Naomi jerked her head back and bared her teeth. "Oh, no, dear, like this," Daciana said as she extended her jaw and lowered her fangs. "Here, you try it."

"Go to hell."

"No heaven, no hell for me, I'm afraid. Not for you either, or little Joseph."

"What happens to him now? To us?"

"Why, nothing at all, except for the fact that we'll be watching you for any signs of a betrayal of confidence. You've never seen my sword, dear. But if you do, you will only see it once." She smiled. "You'll probably find you have a taste for raw meat now, organ meat especially, just to quench your thirst for blood. That's how it will start. But eventually, you will crave human blood; in fact, you might even find yourself and Joseph doing a little sharing after a while."

"What happens to Joseph?"

"Well, now, this is the amusing part, the part I'm looking forward to most. You see, Joseph will not only never die, he will never be more than four years old." Naomi took a breath. "That's right, his body will be four years old forever . . . but his mind? Oh, no. As the years pass, he will find himself a grown man trapped inside a little boy's body. And he'll have to pass in public as a four-year-old. Always. Which means he'll always need his mommy nearby. Oh, and can you imagine what a little terror he'll be when he reaches emotional puberty and finds he can't do anything about it? It's delightful!"

"You really are a monster. And to think I—"

"Fell under my spell, yes. But you may take comfort that you're not the first. That was a certain witch finder I met back in 1600s England. He amused me, and our tastes were similar. He and I were practicing sadists more than a century before the birth of the marquis after whom the predilection was named. And the next person I made came shortly after that, a crippled artist who was on the verge of dying before he could finish painting my portrait. Now, I couldn't let that happen, could I? I still have the portrait, by the way. It's exquisite. But where the artist himself absconded to, I couldn't say. What I can say is that they're both still alive, somewhere, I can sense them sometimes. As today I sense Alphonse."

"Alphonse."

"You say that with such venom in your voice, dear. I like that. Yes, he is rather crude, isn't he? But he does have his uses." Daciana stood. "Well, on to more practical matters. You'll have to explain to your mother's school why she won't be back after the holidays—make up something believable, say she married a secret lover and moved away. Whatever. And you'll be the one to see Joseph off to school in the mornings and pick him up afterwards."

Naomi shook her head weakly, still trying to absorb the events of the past day and what the next days, the next years—the next centuries—would bring. What would she do, for example, when Joseph went into first grade but remained the size of a kindergartener? She was aware of arrested physical development in children, something to do with the pituitary gland's delayed production of growth hormone. But how long could she get away with that?

She imagined her son in eighth grade, in high school, still with the body of a four-year-old. Impossible!

Daciana seemed to read her mind. "Yes, your little boy will always be your *little* boy, despite his cognitive and affective growth. I'd advise you to get him home schooled so you can keep your job. After all, you will need money to survive as much as you'll need blood." She nodded, as if seeking a solution to Naomi's problem. "Of course, you'll need to home school him yourself as he grows older, which means you'll probably have to quit your job. Which further means you might have to get daring and use your physical charms to lure men into bed. Then, while they sleep, you can take your fill from them and relieve them of their cash. I'd suggest visiting certain hotels where traveling businessmen stay. The Robert Treat downtown might be a good place to start. And you could bring a container of blood home for Joseph as well. Or even take him with you. There. See how solicitous I am of your needs? Why, I'm practically doing your thinking for you."

"Get out of my house."

"Oh, I was about to take my leave. But be aware that Alphonse will be checking in on you regularly, and I will too, as the mood strikes. One last thing. I would advise you not to not to try to hide from us by relocating somewhere else. After all, you and Joseph are my latest experiment."

"What do you mean, *experiment?*"

"You will learn, my pet, that when one is immortal, one looks for new ways to pass the time. Otherwise, life would be frightfully boring."

With that, Daciana pursed her lips as if throwing an air kiss and walked to the bedroom door. "Tell Joseph when he wakes up that his Aunt Daci wishes him a Merry Christmas."

Chapter Fifteen: Robin
Alexandria, Virginia
1988

Robert Bradford stood erect as the tall black Marine wearing a chief warrant officer's bars on his uniform collar and carrying a courier bag entered his high school classroom. The Marine took a cursory glance at the students' artwork festooning the walls, noticed his daughter's, and extended his hand to the teacher.

"Mister Bradford," he said, his voice deep and mellow. "Marcus Mitchell."

Robert took his hand, the strength of his grip matching the other's. "Good afternoon, Gunner. Good to meet you. Have a seat."

Mitchell gave him a sideways look. "You call me Gunner. Not many civilians know that term."

Robert took a classroom chair and turned it to face the warrant officer. "Staff Sergeant Bradford, actually. Once a Marine," he said.

"Always a Marine. Judging from how old you look, you probably just got out, am I right?"

"A couple of years ago, actually. I hold my age pretty well."

"So why didn't you stay in? As an E-6, you were on your way to a career."

Robert nodded and tented his index fingers to his chin. "I loved the Corps, and I loved serving my country. But sometime during my enlistment I realized I might be of more use to America by serving her children. I'd certainly touch more lives—and," he said with a chuckle, "with slightly less deadly force."

The two men laughed.

"So listen. The reason I asked for this after-school confab isn't to find out how my daughter's doing in your art class."

"That's a relief. You're not here to chew me out. Rowena said you used to be a D.I."

"No reason for an ass-chewing, son. She tells me she's doing great in your class, her report card is great, and . . . keep this to yourself, now . . . I think she might even have a girly crush on you."

"Oh dear. Is that why she picks every opportunity to tease me?"

"That's her way of showing affection. Sorry about that."

"Don't be. She's absolutely charming. And if I were a teenager again—"

"Don't go there."

They laughed again, at ease in each other's presence—unlike some parent-teacher conferences where the parents blamed the teacher for their children's poor grades. His colleagues' mantra, "Failure to learn doesn't imply a failure to teach," wasn't always received in the way it was intended. Fortunately, as an art teacher, he had few if any complaints; in fact, having a conference at all was rare for most of those in the non-3Rs universe.

"Okay, then. So the reason for our conference is?"

Marcus Mitchell opened his courier bag and withdrew an eight-by-ten photograph of himself, his wife, and his daughter. In the photo, he wore his dress blues, his wife a one-piece dress that looked like silk, and his daughter a preppy, button-down navy shirt tucked into cuffed khakis, with a sweater tied loosely around her shoulders. Judging from Rowena's age in the photo, it was probably about two to three years old.

"Beautiful," said Robert. Then he looked at Marcus and paused a beat. "And if I may say so, it's a blessing that your daughter gets her looks from her mother."

"You got that right. Kim-Ly is so beautiful that when we're out together folks think she's my hostage."

"I believe that too."

"So anyway. Rowena tells me you sometimes sketch pencil portraits of the kids and give them to them."

"Yes, when there's a few minutes near the end of the period. I haven't sketched Rowena yet, but the year isn't over."

Marcus shook his head. "No, no, nothing like that. See, it's my wife's birthday coming up in a month, and what I'd love to do is give her a painted portrait of herself."

"Ah. That's absolutely outstanding, Gunner."

"And if you can do it, from this photograph, I'd like to commission you to paint it."

Robert took the portrait and studied it for a long time. Finally, he said he'd be honored to take the commission. It had been a long time since he'd painted a formal portrait in oils.

The men discussed the size of the portrait, the background Marcus wanted painted, and any other touches. Then Robert gave him the price. "That's without a frame, of course. You'll have to have it framed yourself."

"It's still less than I'd expected. Does that mean you're not as good as Rowena says?"

"That'll be up to you to decide. Let's call the cost the Semper Fi discount. But listen, Mr. Mitchell—"

"Marcus."

"Marcus. And I'm Robert. Growing up, I was Robin, but the kids I played with started calling me Christopher Robin and asking where's Winnie the Pooh, so I went back to my baptized name. That aside, let me lay out the deal. First, I'll prepare a sketch on canvas, in graphite. That's a fancy name for a pencil, by the way; makes it sound more impressive. And expensive. Once that's done, you'll come in and approve it. Then I'll block out the background behind your wife, in oils, to make sure the colors are what you want, and you'll come in to approve it again. Or if it doesn't meet with your approval, have me correct it. Next, I'll work on your wife's likeness, and you'll need to approve that, too. I'll need your okay, basically, at every stage, because frankly, I don't want to do all this work only to hear you say you don't like it."

"Only fair."

They worked out a timetable and Marcus offered a deposit, which Robert refused. They also agreed that the project would be kept secret, and that Rowena would learn about it at the same time her mother did. Handshakes were exchanged and Marcus left, his smile white against his dark brown skin.

Robert looked again at the photograph. *Handsome family,* he thought, and that night in his modest condominium he stretched a canvas over a wooden frame and began to sketch.

He awoke next morning thinking of Daciana. It was a stream-of-consciousness thing, stemming from his meeting the day before with Marcus Mitchell. Normally, when veterans meet they discuss, among other things, their various duty stations and when they served there. If Marcus had asked that of Robert, the teacher would have been in a bind. He hadn't put on a uniform since he'd returned from Vietnam, and judging by his youthful appearance, he would've been too young to serve in that conflict. He would have had to make something up on the spot, and dissembling wasn't his area of expertise.

But serve in Vietnam he had, in a Recon unit, leading a team of fellow grunts through the steaming jungles searching out the enemy's position and reporting back its location, manpower, and armament. Most of the time, his team was able to return to base camp without being detected.

Most of the time.

Except for that terrific firefight in which he and his men were ambushed by Viet Cong regulars; when those not killed outright were tortured to death solely for amusement.

And there was that commander, Vo he said his name was, crowing like a rooster, who took an interest in Sergeant Bradford when the Marine refused to scream in pain and refused even to die no matter how egregious his wounds.

When Bradford's company, alerted to danger by the recon team's prolonged absence, eventually arrived in force to engage the enemy, Bradford—suddenly forgotten in the surprise attack—leaped upon Vo and went hand-to-hand with him.

The Viet Cong commander was shocked at his prisoner's vitality, in light of the fact that he'd supposedly been so weakened by torture he needn't even be bound anymore. And awe worked to Vo's disadvantage as the two grappled upon the dusty ground, neither able to use a weapon other than his hands.

And in the Marine's case, his teeth.

Bradford swung down his fangs and tore first at the side of Vo's neck—a gout of blood burst into his mouth—and then at his face, tearing a piece from his cheek as he pinned him to the ground.

Held firmly to the earth and stunned at the sight of Bradford's fangs, Vo desperately lunged upward and bit into the closest thing available—the Marine's throat. Blood spilled onto his face and coursed through the hole in his cheek. He swallowed involuntarily just before the Marine snapped his neck, twisting it well beyond ninety degrees. Vo lay still, his eyes open and bulging. Robert Bradford would never forget that face.

The frenzy of the firefight demanded Sergeant Bradford's immediate attention, and as the wound in his own throat healed he rejoined his comrades. Later, when the VC had been destroyed to a man, Bradford took another look at the motionless body of Captain Vo. He left the scene knowing he should've decapitated him, just in case, but to do so in front of his men, battle-hardened though they were, would have raised questions he wasn't prepared to answer.

And this morning that thought led to his turning at the hands of Daciana, the *strigoi* who called herself the Lady Catherine Drummond, in the court of King James I.

Where is she now, he wondered. His maker could be anywhere in the world; their last contact had been just before he'd fled from her and from England in 1620. It wasn't that he wanted to see her again, ever, but there were times recently when he almost *felt* her presence somewhere nearby.

The snooze alarm went off again, and Robert arose, attended to his normal bathroom routine, and, dressed only in his undershorts, walked into the kitchen and took the last of the blood from the refrigerator. He heated it to slightly above room temperature on the electric range and sipped it slowly as he prepared the rest of his breakfast.

He would need more blood soon. Today was Friday; tonight he would cruise Northwest Washington, around 14th and U Streets, where prostitutes often strolled as their johns trolled. It was where he had met Delilah, a thirty-something, overweight hooker who had thought he was joking when he whispered to her that he was a vampire and only wanted her for a small volume of her blood. They negotiated a price and conducted their business at the bottom of a flight of concrete steps that led to an abandoned basement flat.

Delilah was surprised at the lack of pain when he bit gently into her wrist, but she nearly passed out as she watched her blood fill the plastic container he produced. "It's only a pint," he assured her, "the same as if you were giving to the Red Cross. You won't die, I promise. In fact," he continued, "if you're willing, I can come back and visit you on a regular schedule." She looked at him, her eyes the size of saucers.

"Now, let me tend to your wound." He licked the two dainty holes, leaving a layer of saliva, and almost immediately the blood stopped and they began to close. "You're going to feel an itching, like a rash, for a day or so, but after that everything will be back to normal. Now, Delilah, the Red Cross recommends eight weeks before donating again, and I'll honor that with you. But I will want more blood before eight weeks are up, and maybe you can help me there by recruiting one or two friends to help. I'm not a killer, Delilah, you can tell that, right?" She nodded, still a little woozy but mentally alert. "That said, I can't have my secret revealed to anyone but you and your, um, professional colleagues. You must all swear to absolute secrecy, for any number of reasons you can think of. That said, if any knowledge of what I am does get out, I will, regrettably, have to kill you, on principle alone, and your friends too, do you understand what I'm saying?"

"I do, Mister—"

"Call me Lestat," he said with a wink.

"All right."

He paused to see if she'd caught on. Obviously not. "You've earned twice your usual fee with this transaction, Delilah, so you have a good reason to be faithful to me."

"I do, Mr. . . . Lestat. That's a funny name, by the way."

"It's French."

"Oh. Okay. So, when do you want to meet my friend?"

"Say, two weeks, same time, at the top of these stairs? You'll be with her of course."

She nodded and looked at her wrist. It had completely healed and was already starting to itch.

Chapter Sixteen

By the time of Marcus Mitchell's first visit to Robert Bradford's condo, the artist had concocted a plausible narrative of his time in the Corps. After the warrant officer voiced his approval of the first stage of the painting, the two men sat down over the kitchen table, broke open a couple bottles of beer, and exchanged anecdotes from their years as Marines.

Robert told him that he'd enlisted in 1972, did his boot training in Parris Island, South Carolina, and advanced infantry training at Camp Lejeune, North Carolina, as did every recruit, and then reported to Marine Barracks Washington to serve with a ceremonial unit. After that two-year tour of duty, he transferred to the Second Division back at Camp Lejeune and served as an office pinky for the rest of his enlistment.

"I was a pinky in Nam," said Mitchell. "Had the good fortune to meet Kim-Ly in Saigon. And yes," he said as he emptied his second bottle and opened a third, "we got married before she got pregnant. Did it the old fashioned way."

"I'll drink to that, Gunner."

"Good Marine'll drink to anything."

Robert went on to say he'd shipped over for six years for drill instructor school, where he'd learned he enjoyed teaching. After two years on the grinder, he returned to Lejeune, where he was assigned keeper of the Security and Classified files in Division HQ. His Top Secret clearance from his time in Washington was reinstated, and following that tour he finished his enlistment at the President's retreat in Camp David, Maryland.

"So what's David like?" asked Mitchell.

"If I told you . . ." Robert began.

"Yeah, yeah, I got it. While you're resting . . ." He held up his empty bottle. "Next time, I bring the six-pack."

Robert took two more bottles from the refrigerator, careful not to reveal the nearly empty flask of blood behind them.

"So, after I got my walking papers in 1982, I enrolled in Monmouth College in New Jersey—I'd taken a couple years' worth of correspondence courses from there while I was in David—and got my teaching degree in '84. Taught high school art in Toms River for a couple of years before relocating here. Always loved the D.C. area."

He did get his degree from Monmouth College, and he did later teach in Toms River, but both happened much earlier than 1984. Everything else he told the gunner was fiction. But the contrivance worked.

"I grew up in the area," Mitchell said. "Not far from the Barracks at Eighth and I Southeast. Where you and the other pretty boys marched. Used to go to the parades on Friday nights in the summer when I was a kid. Fact, that's what inspired me to enlist."

After Mitchell left, Robert chased the last of his beer with the last of his blood. Time to renew his supply soon. Meanwhile, he reflected on how the Gunner had bought his story. Actually, they had probably served in Vietnam at about the same time.

Following his discharge in 1972—the same year that four-year-old Joseph Christian Paris, in Newark, was made a vampire and who, on Christmas Eve, turned his own mother—Robert decided to head to New Jersey himself, specifically to Toms River, for no other reason than nostalgia. He had left more than two hundred years before and never returned. He was curious to learn how the town had fared since the days when he'd befriended Thomas Luker—and so frightened Tom's Indian bride.

Toms River, the former Shrewsbury in colonial days—the name had since been bestowed upon another town one county north—was in the throes of decline, the newly-constructed Ocean County Mall already beginning to draw consumers from the town proper to the ever-expanding outlying area. Strolling the town, Robert found an art gallery on Main Street and was surprised to learn that all the beautiful oils on display were the work of one man, H. Hargrove, and that the artist himself had his studio in an area behind the gallery's rear display wall.

The two formed an immediate bond as they discovered that neither had had an art lesson in his life and yet were both accomplished artists—a coincidence Hargrove discovered upon his first visit to Robert's Jamestown Village apartment and saw the portraits adorning his walls.

"I'd love to display your work in my gallery," Hargrove said, "but it's a signature gallery, which means all the work has to be mine."

Robert found employment in Toms River High School South, teaching art. This was the town's original high school; now it was one of three, the others eponymously designated North and East. He was delighted that the sports teams were called the Indians in honor of Tom Luker, and he loved the school song commemorating his one-time friend's legacy:

> Oh, old Indian Tom was the man who gave his name
> To the high school upon the hill.
> And the glory of his vic'tries and the honor of his fame
> A-a-abide here among us still . . .

Victories? thought Robert. *Tom ran a ferry service. His only victory, so to speak, was the wooing and winning of Princess Ann Suncloud for his bride.* But no one seemed to know much about her these days. Robert still wondered what she had seen in him that made her so fearful.

Sitting in his kitchen, staring at the empty blood flask, he abandoned his reveries and remembered that he had an appointment with Delilah tonight.

Waiting near the intersection of U Street and Fourteenth, NW, as arranged, a clearly upset Delilah had an unexpected companion tonight. The man had a wiry build, with eyes that reflected the light from the distant street lamp. He wore black from head to toe, his skin barely lighter than his clothes. Were it not for his eyes and the glitter of gold chains around his neck and wrists, he could have been invisible.

"Oh, shit," Robert muttered to himself.

"I'm sorry," whimpered Delilah. "I didn't want to tell him nothing, he made me tell, I promise, tha's the truth." She was trembling, and even in the dim light Robert could see perspiration beading her forehead.

"You Lestat?" growled the man. "The vamp man?"

"And you are?"

"Never the fuck mind who I am."

"Delilah."

"He beat it out of me, Mr. Lestat, I swear."

Robert looked squarely into the pimp's eyes. "You beat your women, do you?"

"Hafta keep 'em in line. You got a problem with that?"

"Actually, I do."

"I don' believe that shit she tell me, that you a vampire. You just some pervert think's he's a vamp."

Robert gave his most disarming smile. "Why don't we just go down these steps? That's where Delilah and I normally conduct our business."

"Don' you try bullshittin' me, mothafucka." he pulled a snub-nosed revolver from behind his back. "You tellin' me you ackshally drink her blood?"

Delilah took a step backward.

"That's all right, Delilah," Robert said, his voice calm. "I know it's not your fault. I have no intention of killing you."

The pimp scowled and leaned into Robert. "Whut's that s'posed to mean? Killin' her? That be my job, she don' produce."

Mr. Lestat kept his voice steady. "But she does produce, doesn't she? Why don't we just walk down these stairs? You wouldn't be afraid, would you?"

Robert led the way, followed by Delilah and her pimp.

Only Robert and Delilah walked back up. Once on the sidewalk again, she took a last look down at the body, at the shredded neck, at the head haloed by a spreading circle of blood.

"Obviously, I won't need your services this evening, Delilah—I've drunk my fill and filled my flask—but I want to pay you anyway."

"Th-th-thank you, Mr. Lestat."

He handed her the pistol and the pimp's jewelry.

"Police will chalk it up to robbery/murder. Or a turf war. Whatever, it doesn't matter to me. I'd advise you to keep the pistol, but pawn the gold."

"Yes, sir."

"We'll have to find another location for next time."

She told him of another deserted flat on another block nearby.

"Excellent. And Delilah, stay away from pimps from now on. I don't like them."

Robin had killed many a man, in wartime, in the line of duty. He always regretted each death. Most of his enemies were men like him, sworn to and fighting for their nation's cause. But there were others, whom he considered vermin, whose deaths, like that of Delilah's pimp, he didn't regret at all. In fact, dispatching them quite often made him feel he had done the world a service. This night, for example, he slept the sleep of the just.

Robert met Kim-Ly Mitchell for the first time when Marcus brought her to his condo, where the finished portrait stood in one corner of the living room, on an easel covered by a red velvet drape. Their daughter Rowena was with them, hesitant at first to step inside, feeling awkward at seeing her teacher outside his classroom for the first time.

The story Marcus—wearing civilian clothes tonight—had given his wife was that he was taking the family to dinner, and that they'd be joined by one of Rowena's teachers, Marcus's treat, as a thank you for taking an interest in Rowena's artwork and his encouraging her academically. Rowena was quietly suspicious, but her mother bought the tale.

Robert greeted the family warmly and offered drinks. Marcus pointed out that the paintings on the walls were all done by their host, and during conversation Kim-Ly asked if Robert were working on something now.

"As a matter of fact, I am," he said. "Would you care to see it?"

"I would," said Marcus, on cue, and Rowena chimed in her agreement, eager to see what her teacher's work looked like in progress.

When Kim-Ly was in position directly before the easel, Robert lifted the drape. She stared for a brief moment before babbling incoherently. As her knees began to buckle, Marcus stood behind her to offer physical support—and judging from her reaction, she needed it.

"Happy birthday, babe, a little early," he whispered in her ear, and as his wife turned to embrace him, his daughter, struck dumb for perhaps the first time in her life, stared at her teacher, who stood apart from the three and wore a modest smile.

"What the heck," Rowena said, and threw her arms around Robert. Marcus's grin indicated that Robert was welcome to hug her back, and he was delighted to oblige. Kim-Ly was next to embrace him, and Marcus shook his hand in a grip that could crush walnuts.

Marcus checked his watch. "Time to go," he said. "Hope you like Vietnamese food."

"Never tried it," Robert lied, "but I'm game for anything."

"It's called Vo's Vietnam," said Kim-Ly.

"Did you say Vo?" asked Robert, experiencing a sudden flashback.

"My maiden name, but no relation. Vo in Vietnam is like Smith in America."

"Well then," he said, his smile betraying a sense of caution, "let's get going."

Vo's Vietnam occupied a small but deep storefront on an Alexandria side street. The smells of ginger, cinnamon, and mint spiced the atmosphere, and the party of four all inhaled deeply as they entered. A hostess guided them to their table, where they were greeted by a smiling server, who identified himself as Hiep.

"Everything here's good," Marcus said to Robert, "but seeing as this is your first time, you might want Kim-Ly to order for you."

"I defer to your wife's indigenous expertise," he replied grandly. It had been more than fifteen years, but the tonal inflections as Kim-Ly and Hiep conversed brought back vivid memories of his time in the Nam—none of them pleasant.

Kim-Ly ordered *nem cuon* all around to start and then added *bun bo Hué*. To follow the salad rolls and soup, and with a nod to her husband, she added a main course of *chá lụa*, a sausage dish made from lean pork and potato starch.

As they waited for the salad rolls to arrive, she translated her conversation with Hiep.

"I remarked that I hadn't seen him here before, and he told me that he was indeed new to America. Then I noticed that a lot of the wait staff were new to me, and he said that was true too."

"Why the turnover?" asked Robert.

"He could not say. Only that Colonel Vo regularly adds staff to the restaurant from Vietnam. He has an agent in Ho Chi Minh City who recruits people who can speak some English and are willing to come to America to work. Perhaps, once the people are acclimatized to their new surroundings, they seek work elsewhere. Restaurant work, you know, is very stressful. That is why Marcus always leaves a big tip," she said with a wink at her husband.

"So," Robert said, "this Colonel Vo was in the army?"

She said, "I assume so. We never met him to ask. He always seems to be somewhere else when we're here."

Marcus growled, "He'd better have been on our side." Then he laughed. "But who gives a rat's, um, rear end anymore," he said, glancing at his daughter. "We're all supposed to be friends now. Right, Rowena?"

"Right, Daddy. And you can say rat's ass if you want. I've heard worse at school, believe me. Right, Mr. Bradford? You must hear it all the time."

Robert agreed. "Our usage of language has deteriorated badly. These days, your contemporaries use the F word as commonly as your dad's generation used to say Darn it."

Marcus nodded toward his daughter. "And how about my little dependent there? She cuss like a drill instructor?"

Robert glanced at Rowena. "Tell the truth, I never heard her utter an obscenity. At least not while I'm around. But now that you mention it, I'll keep an ear out. And report back promptly."

"Thanks, Benedict Arnold," the teenager remarked through a grin.

"Well, at least we know you stay awake during American History class."

They all chatted like old friends throughout the meal, but in the back of Robert's mind drifted the uncertainty of who this Colonel Vo was. He remembered the Viet Cong officer named Captain Vo, whose neck he'd snapped, and realized that in the unlikely event he had survived, he might have added rank before the war's end. Then again, this Colonel Vo, the one who owned and operated the restaurant here in Alexandria, might be someone else entirely—and probably was, considering the ubiquity of the surname. Further, he might even have been a civilian who added the rank to his name to effect respect and authority.

Still, something intangible bothered him. It was almost as if he felt the presence of a being like himself, lurking behind the distant door marked Private.

Robert and the Mitchell family became fast friends, and at Rowena's graduation two years later, he sat in the audience with Marcus and Kim-Ly as their guest, instead of on stage with the rest of the faculty. At home afterward, Rowena insisted that he visit her room to see her graduation present.

"It's a Macintosh," she said. "My parents figured that since I'm heading off to college in the fall, I'd need a computer to write my papers. It's got a word processing program and a printer that makes typewriters obsolete. Isn't that great?"

"Welcome to the brave new world," said Robert with a grin.

"I've decided to major in English," she informed him. "I mean, I love art, no offense—"

"None taken."

"But I really love English. Creative writing, expository writing, even grammar. Maybe I could be a reporter, and then work my way up to an editor. Or I could write magazine articles, or books."

"Or teach."

"Please. No offense, but I don't know how my teachers deal with some of these kids. No problem for you, of course, everyone loves art. Everyone loves you."

Was a blush stealing into her coffee-colored cheeks?

Robert paused for a moment before asking her what college she was going to attend. He knew she'd been accepted to many.

"Criterion, in New Hampshire. Far enough to be away from the Gunner's microscope, close enough to come home on holidays and summers."

"Come on, Gunner's retired now. Don't tell me he still watches you like a DI on a recruit."

"Hey, Mr. Bradford, what do you think? I wouldn't be surprised if he were standing outside my door right now listening in."

"I heard that!" boomed through the door, and as it opened they all laughed. "I wasn't snooping, by the way, I just came up to tell you that your mom's got dessert ready."

"Sure, Daddy, like I believe that." And they shared another laugh as they made their way downstairs to the dining room.

But Robert took another look at Rowena's computer as he left the room. He had read that research was being done regarding an international computer network that could connect personal computers like Rowena's to a giant database, making a vast array of information available to the public. If that were ever to come to pass, it might be helpful in fulfilling an obligation he'd never put far from his mind; one he'd assumed forty-five years earlier, as a Marine once again, this time fighting in the Pacific Theater of World War II. And he hoped that if it allowed him finally to discharge that obligation, the opportunity wouldn't come too late.

Chapter Seventeen: The Obligation
19 February 1945
Aboard USS *Missoula*
Off the coast of Iwo Jima

Corporal Joseph Paris, USMC, age twenty-six, stubbed his cigarette out in an empty section of his steel mess tray. Morning chow was steak and eggs, which meant today was the day. Forty days ago, his troop ship steamed from Pearl Harbor in a seventy-mile-long convoy nearly nine hundred ships strong, bound for what the enlisted men were only told was *Island X*. Loose lips, and all that.

Sulfur Island, *Iwo Jima* in Japanese, was actually part of Japan, just as the Territory of Hawaii was part of the United States. Iwo had been formed by Mount Suribachi, an extinct volcano that squatted at the southern end of the island. From this distance, it reminded Paris, as it did so many others, of a woman's breast. Women—wives, sweethearts, the girls they'd left behind—occupied every man's mind, almost every waking hour of every day; and the fact that many of the seventy thousand assault Marines would never live to see another woman again made their longing all the more poignant.

The Army Air Force had been bombing the island for seventy-two days, and the Navy's battlewagons had been bombarding it from offshore since the convoy re-formed two days ago.

Paris turned to the man sitting next to him and said, "You think there'll be any Japs left for us, Doc?"

Pharmacist's Mate John Bradley, at only twenty-one the senior Navy medical corpsman assigned to Easy Company, said he didn't know.

What neither of them could anticipate was that in four days Doc Bradley would make history as one of the six flag raisers on Suribachi, captured in that immortal Joe Rosenthal photograph . . . and one of only three to survive.

After the war, Bradley would be racked by night terrors for years, his wife bearing compassionate but impotent witness to his nightmares. He would live the longest of the three survivors, dying of a stroke at age seventy; Rene Gagnon would find his own fame fleeting, and accept employment at a succession of menial jobs until his death at fifty-four; Ira Hayes, suffering from survivor's guilt, would descend into alcoholism and die at age thirty-two.

No battlefield veteran ever came home intact.

But for now, Bradley and Paris tried to control their tension with mundane conversation in the crowded chow hall, where today the chatter was eerily subdued. "Your squad members call you Frenchy," Bradley said. "Are you? French, that is?"

Paris shook his head. "Eye-talian through and through, Doc."

"Huh. So how does an Italian boy end up with fair skin and blond hair—and without a vowel at the end of his name?" asked the corpsman, taking a final drag of his own cigarette.

"My grandfather was from the Lake Como region, way up north. Lots of blonde, fair-skinned Dagos there. Close to Switzerland and France, lots of intermingling."

"Yeah, I can imagine."

"I was named after my *nonno,* Giuseppe Antonio Parisi. When he came to the U.S. as a young man he Americanized it to Joseph Anthony Paris."

"J-A-P," observed Bradley. "Pretty unwelcome initials these days."

The two met again on deck, where they watched the continued naval bombardment of the island. The roar of the big guns was almost enough to make a man's ears bleed. Nobody could survive a pounding like that for long. Taking this target would be a cakewalk.

So why were they all so nervous?

Paris was thinking about his wife, and about the infant daughter he'd never seen, except for a photograph in the last batch of mail from home. Thinking, too, about the trip to Paris he'd promised to take them on after the war, after the Krauts were driven out of France. For at least the hundredth time this week, he called to mind their wedding reception, their first dance as man and wife, and what they considered their song, "April in Paris."

Their daughter was conceived during his last leave, and when Aimee wrote him with the news of her pregnancy, he wrote back that whether it was a boy or a girl, the choice of a name would be hers alone. When the baby was born, on New Year's Day 1945, Aimee had her baptized April Naomi.

"April N. Paris," he said aloud, and Bradley looked at him.

"What about it?" the corpsman asked.

"Oh. That's what my wife named our baby daughter. Surprised you could hear me over this racket."

Bradley smiled. "I was afraid you were about to break into song. Now, that would be a racket."

"Someday we'll get there," the corporal said. "To Paris. Farthest we've ever traveled from our home in Jersey was Maine, on our honeymoon."

"Maine," said Bradley. "Ever get to Bangor?"

"Every day, doc, at least once." Paris's eyes crinkled at the corners as Bradley groaned. "Yeah. She tells people what she saw the most of in Maine was the hotel ceiling. But she wasn't complaining."

"This a private party, or can anyone jump in?" asked another Marine as he sidled up to Paris.

"Hey, Rembrandt," said Paris. "Meet Doc Bradley." They nodded amiably.

Bradley said, "Name stenciled over your pocket says Bradford, not Rembrandt." He nodded. "Don't tell me. You're an artist."

"At your service, Doc."

"Rembrandt's my first fire team leader," Paris explained under the roar of the big guns. "He drew caricatures of the guys in the squad on the way over."

"Some guys play cards to pass the time," Bradford said. "I brought my sketchbook."

Paris added, "He did a really beautiful pencil portrait of me, too. Suckin' up to the squad leader. I told him to keep it in case I don't make it back and be sure to give it to my wife and baby daughter. Who I would call Naomi, by the way, and I told Aimee as much in my last letter. I mean, April's a nice name and all, but hey, she was born in January."

Doc Bradley shook his head. "Now why would you think Bradford here would make it and you wouldn't?"

Paris said, "Because in every bad war movie, the one with the most to live for always dies, and the one with no family to come home to gets to live. It's a formula."

Bradford twirled an index finger around his temple. "Welcome to my world."

"Yeah, yeah, Rembrandt. You still got the address of the trailer park in Riverside, right?"

"Still taped to the inside cover of my sketchbook, right where you saw me put it."

"Thought you lived in Jersey," Doc said.

"We do. But I moved Aimee to Riverside because when we get back stateside, we'll get our discharge papers in San Diego, and while you guys are humpin' it home across the good old US of A, all horny for the girls you left behind, I'll already be hum—well, never mind."

They shared a nervous laugh. Then came the signal to assemble. "Time to move out, I'm afraid," Bradley said. He checked his watch. The time was 0700. The big guns went suddenly silent. "Catch you on the beach."

The landing craft reached the shore, lowered their gates, and the Marines charged out, their legs calf deep in water, rifles held high, helmets strapped securely beneath their chins. They reached the sand and plopped down on black granules that felt fine as talcum powder. Their ears were alert for gunfire; their eyes searched for enemy movement.

There was none. The men moved farther inland, in a crouch, more troops filling the spaces where they'd been.

Time passed, and more men, thousands more, waded ashore. They still saw no sign of enemy resistance. The interior appeared lifeless, an indication that the bombings and big guns had done their job. Paris glanced from side to side, checking on the twelve men in his squad. One of them, a cocky Georgian in Fire Team Two, shrugged his shoulders and stood up.

"Keep down, Cracker, you dumb shit," yelled Paris as the private fished a cigarette from his breast pocket.

"Hey, Frenchy, come on," he drawled. "Nobody here but us moe-huckin' Moe-rines. Place is dead." He placed the cigarette between his lips. But before he could strike a light, his face burst in a welter of bone, blood, and brains. Paris heard the distant pop a split second later; bullets, after all, traveled faster than sound.

Suddenly the island exploded with gunfire, coming from hidey-holes and caves, and from the heights of Suribachi, pinning down the troops in a withering defilade. The Japs had dug a network of protective tunnels into the hills, and now they were firing down from them at the Marines. They'd waited, waited until most of the invading force had come ashore, providing ever more targets for their rifles, mortars, and artillery. The aerial and Naval bombardment had had no effect upon their subterranean city.

Paris shouted for a corpsman, and in seconds John Bradley was there, attending to the fallen private. He took one look at the man's ruined face, glanced back at Paris, and shook his head. Another call came, and Bradley was gone, scrambling over the sand to the next stricken soul. When they fired their bullets, the men's rifles also spewed out the stinging smell of cordite, and the air was heavy with the rotten-egg stench of the sulfur that gave Iwo its name.

The remaining squad members stripped the dead man's ammo clips from his cartridge belt. Each clip held eight .30-caliber rounds, a supply that was quickly exhausted in the fight. Every few seconds, a ping would signal an empty clip's being ejected from an M-1 rifle; soon the beach was littered with clips—along with the bodies and body parts of Marines mowed down by Japanese forces. The black sand was blotched with blood; Paris likened it to red pus, even though he knew pus was yellow, like the motley remains of Cracker's skull that had stuck to the wet legs of his own utility trousers.

The noise, oddly, was even worse; the pop from far-away rifles, the ping of ejecting ammo clips, the shouted commands of officers and NCOs, the screams of the grievously wounded, the explosions of mortar, the whoosh of a flame thrower as its operator incinerated Japs inside a hidey-hole, the rat-a-tat-tat of machine guns and Browning automatic rifles. The din created an ear-splitting soundscape of competing and discordant babel.

Their world became defined by three words: fire, duck, and cover. Battle plans always worked, Paris had been ad-

119

vised by a combat vet, right up until the first shot was fired; from that point on, everything was FUBAR—fucked up beyond all recognition. Stay alive, keep your buddy alive, and be first to kill the sonofabitch who's trying to kill you.

"Move out! Move out!" came the platoon sergeant's call from behind him, and Paris urged his remaining squad forward.

One of them caught a burst of machine gun fire that blew through his wrist. His rifle fell to the sand, his hand still gripping the stock, and he stared dumbly at the stump that poked out of his sleeve.

"Corpsman!" shouted Paris as the man dropped to the ground, and Doc Bradley appeared as if from nowhere. He was applying pressure to the wound as Paris and the others snaked forward on their elbows. Behind and alongside them, thousands of fellow Marines were doing the same.

Ahead was a small rise, more like a wrinkle, which he thought might provide at least some small cover. Paris belly-crawled toward it. Suddenly, a burst of nearby gunfire.

"I'm hit!" screamed one of his riflemen. "Shit! Shot me in the fuckin' ass! Aw, Frenchy, it fuckin' burns, man!"

Paris glanced behind him and saw the man writhing, arms flailing, rifle abandoned. A furrow had been plowed into his body, from his belt line across his right buttock, where it terminated at a hole blasted in his left inner thigh.

Another sound caught his ear, a creak like a gritty hinge. Paris spun his head forward and saw at the base of the rise, not twenty feet before him, a camouflaged trap door spring up, scattering dirt to either side. From the darkness within the hidey-hole, a series of yellow flashes sent bullets over his head; one ricocheted off his helmet, snapping his head to the side, temporarily deafening him. He shook his head, seeing stars.

A hand gripped his ankle—the wounded rifleman, reaching for help. Paris tried to yank his foot away. Still disoriented, desperate to free himself, he rose to one knee and attempted to push himself forward; and at that moment the enemy machine gunner stitched a tight pattern across his midsection. Then he swung the piece back, creating another stitch directly across the first. The fusillade completely severed Paris's upper body. He felt his trunk slide forward, leaving his legs behind, felt the thud as his torso hit the ground. Strangely, he felt no pain.

Paris could actually see the grinning face of his killer. But his final vision was that of a photograph of his wife, holding the baby girl he would never get the chance to meet.

His last thought was, *Yes, I'd definitely call her Naomi.*

Chapter Eighteen

Upon receiving his discharge papers in San Diego, Marine Sergeant Robert Bradford made his first civilian stop at a stationery store downtown. There he bought an artist's portfolio in which to store his sketchbook, including his most important portrait to date: that of Corporal Paris, Joseph A., KIA on Iwo Jima two years earlier. He'd been charged with delivering the portrait to Paris's widow Aimee, and—remembering the value to Jessica Stover of his portrait of her nearly two centuries ago—he vowed to keep that commitment. He also vowed not to tell her the gruesome details of her husband's death; nor how he had avenged it by diving into the hidey-hole from alongside and tearing out the throats of the machine-gunner and ammo handler using only his fangs.

Robin's second stop was the Greyhound Bus Depot, where he bought a ticket to Riverside. Once there, he took a cab to the Highgrove Trailer Park and asked the manager where he might find Mrs. Aimee Paris. The owner/manager, who called himself Doc, told him that soon after she received word of her husband's death she sold her trailer, packed up her baby girl, and went back to New Jersey—Newark, he believed—to live with her mother.

It was a sad farewell, Doc recalled, lots of hugs and kisses. She left no forwarding address with him, he added, though she might've with some of her friends in the park. He directed the Marine to the appropriate trailer sites, but when Robin asked Aimee's women friends, their response was only that she had told them she'd be moving back to Jersey and promised to write with her address. But she never had.

With his travel allowance from the Marines, Robin bought a bus ticket to Newark. As he rode, unbidden thoughts recurred about the battlefields of the Pacific, where he had surreptitiously harvested a cornucopia of blood from enemy soldiers; since then, pickings had been slim. Robin had vowed never to kill for sport, quite the opposite of his feral maker, Daciana.

Late one night, at a layover in Saint Louis, he found a drunken vagrant passed out in the men's room of the bus terminal and was able to soothe his thirst. The vagrant would wake up next morning with a headache, an itch on the inside of his his elbow, and a ten-dollar bill in his shirt pocket.

Finally, Robin arrived in Newark. In the Essex County telephone book he found a sizeable amount of numbers under Parisi, but none under Paris. Undaunted, he spent scores of nickels pay-phoning each family, asking the parties if Joseph Paris, a Marine, was any relation. His search came up empty.

Corporal Paris had never thought to mention his wife's maiden name, and Robin didn't have enough nickels to call everyone in the Essex County phone book with a Newark address. Not that he would have: Newark was the largest city in the state, and even with a vampire's longevity he acknowledged that by the time he'd found Aimee Paris, she'd probably be dead from old age. And good luck with finding the daughter, who by then would probably be married and carrying her husband's last name.

Robin's release placed him in the Marine Corps Reserves, and when the so-called *limited police action* in Korea broke out, he was recalled to duty. So much for continuing his search for Joe Paris's wife and daughter.

In 1955, a civilian once more, Robin used his GI Bill benefit to secure a place in Monmouth College in West Long Branch, New Jersey. He graduated four years later with a degree in art education and found a welcome at Newark's Arts High School. He lived in an apartment in nearby East Orange, and every year he would peruse the new phone directory for a residential listing under Paris, always without success.

As usual, it was necessary for Robin to vacate his position as his lack of aging threatened to become noticeable among the staff. So it was that in 1967—one year before a young unwed mother named April Naomi Paris joined the faculty as a guidance counselor—Robin Bradford left Arts High and reenlisted in the Marines to fight for his country yet again, this time in a land halfway around the world called Vietnam.

In 1972, Robin was issued his latest set of discharge papers, this time in Philadelphia. Rather than hide in his civilian clothes as so many of his combat brothers had been advised to do, he wore his Marine Corps greens out of both pride and defiance. Whether the war was justified or not, whether it served no purpose other than to feed the military-industrial complex that his idol President Dwight David Eisenhower had warned the nation against, Sergeant Robert Bradford knew that ultimately his service was still dedicated to the freedoms he had fought so valiantly for during the Colonies' War for Independence.

True, a cynic might downplay his patriotism, citing the fact that knowing one could not die made it easier for one to engage in battle. But from Robin's perspective, it presented the opportunity for acts of heroism that resulted in the saving of numerous comrades' lives. The small leather satchel containing his Bronze and Silver Stars and a host of Purple Hearts served as proof of that; more valuable, however, were the notes and letters from those he had saved and from their families and friends that filled the bulk of the space.

Most people ignored him as he strolled the streets of one of his adopted cities. Tun Tavern, the site of his original enlistment back in 1775, had long ago burned down. But he still could pay his respects to Independence Hall and the nearby Liberty Bell and visit the home of Elizabeth Ross, today referred to as Betsy. And to pass by the house that was once home to the vivacious and beloved Jessica Palmer Stover.

Jessie, who some two centuries ago had stepped off the ferry at the landing in Philadelphia posing as his young sister; whose beauty attracted many a wealthy bachelor; who married a fiery abolitionist whose tracts were the talk of Philadelphia; who was widowed in middle age and left wealthy; and who would never take another husband, knowing that no other than her Lemuel could provide her the same degree of love and happiness.

Today, although Robin was largely ignored, some he passed slid him glances of scorn; not one of the faces thanked him for his service. As day turned to dusk, he found himself in South Philadelphia, an area quickly going to ruin. Strolling toward him, shoulders bobbing and weaving, heads rocking from side to side, came a pair of men a few years younger than his own apparent age. They wore caps with the visors to the rear and matching lightweight black satin jackets. One looked at the other and nodded as his buddy smirked. They parted as if to let him pass between, but when he came abreast one of them held out an arm.

"Wuzzup, baby killer?" one asked, his smile showing a gold-capped front tooth.

"Yeah," said the other. "You think you some shit, comin' in our hood wearin' a piece o' shit uniform like that?"

Robin looked stoically from one to the other. "A little early for you gentlemen to be out, isn't it? Don't you work best after dark?"

"Hey, you some kinda psychic, man?" Gold Tooth turned slightly so Robert could see the white stitching on the back of his jacket. It read *Urban Vampires,* with the legs of the *M* elongated, pointed, and tipped with red.

"Jacket gangs?" said Robin. "That is so 1950s."

"Oh yeah?" said Gold Tooth as his buddy nodded. He withdrew from beneath the jacket a twin pair of needle-sharp knives. "Here's our fangs."

The sidewalk suddenly grew deserted. The few pedestrians nearby instantly found some interesting shops in which to browse. Doors opened, bells tinkled, doors closed.

"I like them," Robin said. "You looking to chip some ice with those picks?"

"Ol' Sarge here thinks he's funny," said the other, whom Robin likened to a fireplug—short, stocky, solid.

"Maybe ol' Sarge wants to laugh out the other side of his mouth," suggested Gold Tooth. "Maybe I'll just give him a ear to ear grin."

His buddy reached up as if to flip off the Marine's barracks cap. Robin's hand grasped his wrist and held it firm.

"I wouldn't do that," he said. His voice remained calm, nearly impassive, and that gave Fireplug pause.

"This neighborhood, the visor goes to the back, man. That's cool."

Robin cracked the ghost of a smile and lowered Fireplug's wrist before releasing it.

Gold Tooth held a knife to Robin's side and nudged him toward the alley. "I bet you got some cash on you, Sarge. All servicemen has cash on 'em. Cash we give 'em with our taxes. And that's just bullshit, man. Why we pay you to kill little babies? Now I want my money back."

"What taxes?" asked Fireplug.

"You don't want to do this, Goldie."

"Ooh, he call me Goldie. Well, listen, Sarge, I got a coupla knives here says I do."

"I can't let you kill me."

Fireplug pushed him into the alley, and the pair held him against a brick wall. "What you gon' tell us now, mister Marine? That you know kah-rah-tay? That your hands is deadly weapons? Cause we know that's bullshit too."

"Do you have weapons too, little man?"

Fireplug's eyes widened and his nostrils flared. "We see who's the little man, Sarge." He pulled out a gravity knife and flipped the blade open.

Robin cast his eyes left and right. They were definitely alone and unobserved. He shrugged his shoulders and sighed. "I guess there's no way to avoid this," he said. "But before I kill you, would you at least tell me how many innocent people you've killed? Just to ease my conscience, you understand?"

"Son of a bitch," said Gold Tooth and grunted as he shoved both blades through Robin's uniform blouse and up under his ribcage. He let go the knives and took a step back, grinning. "Countin' you, that's more kills than I got fingers. How's that?"

Robin didn't move and didn't raise his voice. "Look, now you've cut my uniform," he said. "But thank you for your honest answer. I never killed a baby, by the way. Although I'd guess you might have the intellect of one."

With that, he pulled the knives out and drove one into each of his attackers. One punctured Gold Tooth's chest, and the other went through the smaller man's eye and into his brain. Robin yanked the knives free. Fireplug crumpled, lifeless, as Gold Tooth staggered back against a wall.

"You know," Robin said, "it's people like you who give people like me a bad name." He opened his mouth and released his fangs.

Gold Tooth's eyes showed more white than dark as he whimpered and sank to his knees. "Oh, God, please," he whimpered. "I beg you, I wasn't gonna—" He never got to finish the sentence, as Robin placed the point of one of the knives beneath Gold Tooth's chin and drove the point up all the way to its hilt. He left the knife imbedded there and with a handkerchief wiped his prints off the handle. Then he dragged Fireplug over and wrapped his fingers around it. He wiped the other knife down and placed it in Gold Tooth's hand.

He imagined how the scene would present itself to investigators as he surveyed it for a brief moment.

"I'd normally stick around for a drink, fellas, but in the interests of time I think I'll have to pass."

He returned to the sidewalk, looked both ways, and crossed the street. Some shop doors opened and people looked cautiously out. He hailed a cab and took it to his hotel. Next day, he would have a tailor stitch shut the holes in his uniform blouse and shirt. And then he would hand his papers over to the reserve unit to which he'd been assigned. His reserve classification was Inactive, meaning he didn't need to make monthly meetings or attend two-week training sessions in the summer. It suited him well. He had done his duty to America many times over. Maybe it was time to let others carry the torch.

Like all true patriots, Robert Bradford held a deep and abiding love for his country.

Like all true warriors, he also hated combat.

But he hated capitulation even more.

Chapter Nineteen: Naomi
1989

Naomi Paris hated capitulation too, but since 1972 her life had become one capitulation after another. Seventeen years had passed now since Joseph and she had been made vampires. She'd already had to make two job transfers from her beloved Arts High School, first to Central High and then to West Side High. Not showing one's age, for a mortal, was a blessing; to an immortal, it could easily be a curse.

Her elderly landlords had passed away, and Daciana Moceanu bought the old house at 239 Fifth Street, subsequently deeding it to none other than Alphonse Puglio—who kept the transaction secret from his wife and collected Naomi's rent for himself. Daciana had given her instructions she was never to leave the city without their permission. Not only was the house their property, Naomi was as well.

And then there was Joseph.

That was the ultimate capitulation, the ultimate outrage. He was twenty-one years old now—twenty-one, legally already three years into adulthood—but he was still trapped in the body of a four-year-old. What pain her son suffered! None of the teenage hormones had kicked in—they never would—but mentally, emotionally, his libido was raging. And he vented his frustrations on his mother. Who else did he have?

Naomi, meanwhile, needed to figure a way to nourish them both, and she ended up taking Daciana's direction. Periodically, she would spend a weekend in one of Newark's hotels, telling anyone who asked that she was traveling with her young son. She would prowl the lounges, seek a lone traveler, take him to her suite, drug him—Daciana supplied the proper quick-dissolving powders—and drink from him. When she was sated, Joseph would gulp down his fill. She made sure that they never drained their victim to excess, and when they were finished, Naomi would take enough of his money to pay for her room and meal expenses. Then she would take some more, leaving him with what she surmised would be enough to pay his own tab should his credit cards be maxed out. Her goal, thus far proved correct, was to assure that when he woke up he would be too embarrassed to actively seek her out or report the incident to the authorities.

The process, though repugnant to Naomi—she might have had the face and figure of a seductress, but clearly not the inclination—was no less off-putting to Joseph. All of his mother's victims were men, and he was desperate for a woman. Finally, after much argument and shedding of tears, Naomi agreed to try to find a woman for him.

She sat at the bar of the Robert Treat Hotel, alone, sipping a pink lady. After a few moments, a middle-aged man sat on the empty stool next to her and tried to strike up a conversation. She ignored him. And that was enough to entice a woman to take his place after he left.

The woman introduced herself as Joan. She was rail thin, had honey-blond hair cut boyishly if not brutishly short, and wore minimal makeup. Her suit was severely cut, almost mannish. Drawing a cigarette from her purse, she asked Naomi if she had a light.

"Sorry, I don't smoke."

She rummaged through her purse. "Oh, never mind, I found one. Do you mind?"

Naomi shrugged and gave her a weak smile.

"I take it that's a yes." She put the cigarette back in the pack. "It's okay, I'm going to quit anyway. So, are you in town for business or pleasure?"

Later, after Naomi had drunk her fill, Joseph walked into his mother's room. He climbed onto the bed, looked at Joan, lying naked and spread-eagled, and cast a scornful look at his mother. "You call this thing a woman?" he said. "It's a man with a cunt!"

"Joseph!" Naomi cried. "You will *not* use that language in my presence! Do you have any idea how *hard* this was for me?"

He tilted his head to one side. "Point of fact, Mom, not that you should need reminding: I look like I'm four, and I

sound like I'm four, but I'm not four, and as far as not using that language in your presence, when am I *not* in your
presence? Shit, woman, when can someone who looks like
me *not* be in his mother's presence? And please, don't talk
to me about being hard. Hard's something I'll never be."

Naomi found herself shamed.

"All right, I understand. But save the scatology for
when I'm at work and you're at home alone. And, as a favor
to your mother, please keep the *Playboys* in your room. As
a mark of respect."

"I subscribe for the articles," Joseph said, his mouth
twisted.

Naomi rolled her eyes. "Are you going to drink, or not?
And do you want me to leave the room?"

He shrugged. "Yeah, okay, thanks, I guess, and close
the door after you."

The next female pickup, a month later, was a volup-
tuous looker slightly past her prime named Patty. Dark red
fingernails, lipstick to match, deep violet eye shadow, long
blond hair. "And tits!" exclaimed Joseph. "You did good,
Mom."

As she sat in the next room, imagining Joseph's exploring of a woman's body, imagining his delight followed by his
inevitable impotent frustration, Naomi glanced toward the
ceiling.

"It's for my son, I'm doing this for my son," she said,
as if explaining herself to her now long-dead minister, the
Reverend Dr. Theo Van Dyke. "Wouldn't you do the same
for your son? Judge not, lest ye be judged," she quoted.
She gave a half-hearted chuckle. "Listen to me," she said
to herself. "Oh well, I suppose the good news is I'm not
Catholic. The priest would have a field day with me at confession. Then again, he might even call in an exorcist; or a
guy named Van Helsing, with a crucifix and a wooden stake
and reeking of garlic."

In January of 1990, Naomi told Alphonse that Joseph
wanted to go to Disney World during Easter break.

"Why? He's too old. I mean, he looks like a kid, but
still . . ."

She cast him a look. "No thanks to you."

"Still bitter, after all these years."

"Especially after all these years."

She had stopped at Essex County College on her way home from school. It was the only way she could meet with Alphonse, aside from being inside his house or hers—something she was loath to do.

"Where's your boss?"

"Teaching a class."

"So, do I need permission from both of you before we go?"

"I'll tell her. I'm sure it's okay, long as your plane tickets say round trip."

Once they arrived at the Magic Kingdom, it became obvious why Joseph had wanted to come. The warm weather meant young ladies in shorts and halters, ladies who were too eager to ooh and ahh at a cute little four-year-old who wanted to hug them, girls who'd giggle and say How cute! when he pressed his face to their bosoms.

While waiting for a table at one of the park's restaurants, they met a young family from Ohio. "This place is so amazing," the mother said. "Normally, we take our vacations at Hershey Park . . . oh, it's in Pennsylvania," she said in response to Naomi's frown. "It's not as expensive, and it's a lot closer to home. We had to save up to get here, but just look at little Daphne's face. It's worth it."

"Thanks, Vera," Naomi said. "I'll have to check it out. Back home in Jersey, we used to take day trips in the summer to Great Adventure. It's a safari ride as well as an amusement park, but it's getting awfully expensive, and the lines for the rides go on forever."

The husband said, "And these lines don't?"

Daphne, four years old, looked at Joseph and shyly attempted to get his attention. But his eyes were fixed instead on her rather attractive mother.

"Maybe we'll check out Hershey Park next time," Naomi said. "Thanks."

It was then that Joseph cocked his head and took a serious look at Daphne.

Tables for larger parties were more readily available than those for three or two, so they decided to eat lunch together. Daphne and Joseph were given crayons and paper placemats festooned with Disney characters for them to color while their parents looked at their menus and ordered. Naomi and Vera got on well, for all intents and purposes leaving Tom out of the conversation. He cast bored glances at the children as they colored. Daphne's coloring was more like scribbles, with her hand jerking back and forth, whereas Joseph's was contained well within the lines. But then Joseph glanced up, saw he was being watched, and scratched the crayon across the lines in mimicry of Daphne's efforts.

The two families discovered they were staying in the same hotel, and Vera, inspired, suggested that she and Naomi drive to downtown Orlando after dinner to do some shopping; Tom could watch the children. "Mommies' night out," she announced.

They left them in Tom and Vera's two-room suite, the mothers admonishing the children to behave and Vera instructing Tom to keep an eye on them.

Soon as Vera closed the door, Tom turned the television to a sports channel and told the kids to amuse themselves. Maybe they could play in the bedroom; Daphne had some stuffed Mickey and Minnie dolls Mommy and Daddy had bought her yesterday.

Daphne and her new friend—Joseph called her Daffy, using his little-boy charm—repaired to the bedroom. Tom smiled, grabbed himself a beer from the mini-fridge, and returned his attention to the TV.

When Tom's back was turned, Joseph quietly closed the bedroom door.

Just before the women returned, Tom heard the toilet flush. "Wash your hands," he called through the door. It opened just as he was getting ready to turn his attention back to the tube. Joseph stood there, his face a mask of concern.

"Daffy sick," he said.

"She looks anemic," the doctor announced when Vera and Tom—with Naomi and Joseph in tow—rushed her, unconscious, to the dispensary.

"Could it be something she ate?" asked her mother.

"Is she allergic to anything?"

"Healthy as a horse," said her father.

Unnoticed by the others, Naomi gave Joseph an accusatory look. He returned his most charming smile. And licked his lips.

The doctor again: "There seems to be a rash inside her thigh. It looks recent."

"Maybe from one of the rides?" Tom suggested. "Something in the seat rubbed against her?"

Vera said, "You were supposed to be watching them, honey."

"They were okay. They were playing with dolls in the bedroom."

"Behind a closed door, you said."

"All right, so what, behind a closed door? They're kids; what're you implying?"

"Never mind. We can talk later." She cast a self-conscious look in Naomi's direction.

"She's coming around," said the doctor.

"You all right, sweetie?"

Daphne nodded to her mother. "Mm-hmm."

"Sweetie, what were you and Joseph doing in the bedroom? Were you playing with your stuffed dolls?"

"Uh uh. Play doctor."

"Oh, God."

All eyes fell to Joseph, the picture of studied innocence. He looked from his mother to Daphne's parents, and he began to sob. He'd learned long ago to affect tears on command, and he employed that skill to the fullest now.

"Joseph," said Naomi as Tom and Vera stood silent, "what did you do?"

"Nothing, Mommy."

"Not nothing," said Tom. "Something."

Naomi glared at him, then back at her son. "Joseph?"

"Nothing!" The water works were putting in overtime now.

The doctor continued his examination. "Doesn't seem to be anything else to see here, folks. Aside from the rash and being pale—and that could be from any number of things—Daphne here appears to be fine. What do you think, Daphne?"

"Fine. Tired. Head hurts. Got a itch."

"Give her some children's Tylenol and have her drink lots of water. This is Florida, it's hot, and kids get dehydrated very easily."

"Vera, I'm so sorry."

"You're not the one who should be sorry, Naomi." Vera glanced at her husband, whose expression ranged from sheepish to defensive and back again. "Kids will be kids. She probably got dehydrated, like the doctor says. Maybe a bug could've bitten her on the thigh, or something she ate might've gotten to her. Look, she's going to be fine, so let's just forget it, okay?"

Naomi thanked her and forced a smile. Joseph, his sobbing suspended, smiled too. Daphne herself smiled as her father lifted her from the exam table. Tom, however, wasn't smiling at all. And chances were he wouldn't be for quite a while.

"You will never—*never*—pull a stunt like that again," hissed Naomi when they had repaired to their room.

"No harm done, Mom. I'm just the one who took the initiative this time. Hey, I learned from the master, as they say. Or would that be mistress?"

"Joseph, her father was *in the next room.* And she's a *child.*"

"A real sweet child, at that."

Naomi sensed something in his tone.

"Real sweet," he added, licking his cherubic little lips. "Her blood. Must've been like mine tasted when Alphonse turned me."

She glared at him, a look forged in fire. "Don't ever mention his name to me, I've told you that."

"All right, all right, truce. But you've got to know, Mom, that I have needs too. I'm so frustrated there are times I want to bang my head against the wall, just so I can feel better when I stop. I want a woman." He looked her in the eyes, his expression pleading.

"I don't know what to tell you, Joseph. You want a woman . . . and I want a man."

"What?"

"Hello? I'm not a nun."

Joseph almost managed to look contrite. "Never thought of that."

Naomi shook her head. "Want a glass of milk?"

"Coffee would be better."

"Sorry. I forget sometimes."

"Okay. I still like milk."

She found the coffee envelope and emptied it into the room's coffeemaker. Moments later, they were sitting at the desk sipping from Styrofoam cups. Neither worried about not being able to sleep; caffeine had no effect on them.

"Want to talk?"

"About what? Men? There are some things a mother doesn't share with her son. I shouldn't have said what I said before."

"Yeah, but you did. You're a looker, Mom. If you weren't my mother I'd be hot for you myself."

She shook her head. "Thanks, Oedipus. One more cross for me to bear."

"Relax. I don't even peek when you're in the shower. I'm not a perv. Tell the truth, though, I'd really love to get a look at Daciana naked."

"*Name.*"

"Sorry." He made a zipper motion across his lips.

Naomi took another sip. "I do need someone to talk to, and because of our . . . unique . . . situation, you're the only one I really can."

"So talk. Remember, I'm really an adult. Growing up, you home-schooled me for years, all those nights after you came home from work. Even though, no matter how much I learned, no matter how much you taught me, there's no way I could ever get a job. Without a job, what value do I have, never mind to the world at large, to myself? It's like I'm a professional welfare sponge, refusing to work so's I can collect benefits from Uncle Sam. Do you even know how degrading that is?"

She admitted, apologizing, she hadn't considered it.

"I never told you this before, but even though I might've fought the home schooling at the time, I appreciate it now, even if it just opened my eyes about how much I'm missing. Which leads me back to the sex. Look. During weekdays when I was alone, I watched TV, but the soap operas just frustrated me, everybody shacking up with everybody else, and nothing I could ever do about it for myself."

Naomi shook her head. "I'm so sorry."

"Not your fault, though, is it? Around you, at least, I can act my age. So tell me, why haven't I ever seen you with a boyfriend?"

"Joseph, I have only experienced sex twice in my life, and both times were with . . . him. Both times it was violent, and it hurt—more emotionally than physically. Frankly, I'd love to be intimate with a man I love, but I just can't afford to love a man. Look at me. I'm a vampire. I'm immortal. Neither of which exactly makes me marriage material."

"So why not go for a quickie sometime? Like, with the guys you seduce for their blood? I'd stay out of the room until you told me you were done."

Naomi shook her head. "Those men were all married. I could always see the pale stripe on their ring fingers where their wedding bands were."

"So?"

"So, number one, and call me old fashioned, I'd need to love the man before I was intimate with him; and number two, I can't be intimate with someone I know is an adulterer. I have a conscience."

"They don't."

"It's not them I'm thinking of, it's their wives."

"Yeah, and their wives could be banging the pool boy or something when their husbands are gone. Cat's away, and all that."

"I don't play tit for tat, Joseph."

"Ooh, I love it when you talk dirty."

Naomi crumpled her empty cup. "Enough. Bedtime. Promise me you'll never try to seduce a child again; it's just . . . I don't know, immoral."

"Hah. That's rich. Case in point, right here. But okay, Mom, I promise. So, it's two more days in Florida, and then back home to Newark. Shit. Some home. But I heard Vera say something about that place, Hershey Park. Like the candy bar. Want to try it this summer? For your darling four-year-old's sake?" He batted his eyelids. "I can't promise not to look, but I will promise not to touch. At least, not with my teeth."

Chapter Twenty: Joseph

He let his mother kiss him goodbye and watched her from the second floor porch as she walked toward Sixth Avenue, turned left, and disappeared behind the corner butcher shop on her way to the bus stop on Roseville Avenue.

He waited until he saw Alphonse Junior, next door, slink off to whatever crime boss he was working for these days. He wondered how many knees he'd cap today, how many teeth he'd knock out. He'd heard Junior one day across the alley, through an open window, yelling at his mother when she demanded to know what he did for a living. He left nothing out, then threatened her if she ever told anyone. "I wouldn't do it myself, Ma, but trust me, it would get done. And it'd be your fault, not mine. *Capisc'?*"

He waited until Junior's mother left the house, heading for mass, as Mom told him she'd done every day since her older son, Angelo, had OD'ed eight years ago at the age of fifteen. Mrs. Puglio had stayed skinny as the years passed, not fat like so many Italian mamas. But fat or not, she was still about as attractive as a Bronx Zoo orangutan. *Face it,* he thought, *Italian she may be, but Sophia Loren she's not. That's the problem with women. They lose their looks.* He thought about his stack of magazines, as frustrating to him as they were pleasurable. *Even those models, they can't look as good as they do in the pictures. Mom told me their photos are airbrushed to make them look better. Well, my sex life is a fantasy anyway, doesn't hurt to add to it, I guess. And,* he thought, *even if the models do get ugly as they get older, there are always new ones to take their place. I mean, who remembers Marilyn Monroe anymore? She was the first Playmate of the Month, and where is she now? Answer: dead. But at least she didn't have to get old and ugly.*

He stood on the porch chair until he saw Alphonse Senior, his maker, walk around the corner of Sixth Avenue and Fifth Street and approach his house. Then he leaned over the railing and called to him.

It was the first day of school, fall semester.

"What do you want?" asked Alphonse after Joseph let him inside. "I've got some sleep to catch up on."

"I want a favor," he said. "I want to see Daciana."

Alphonse looked at him from beneath beetled brows. "How come?"

"It's private."

"Private, huh? How private?"

"If I told you, it wouldn't be private then, would it? Listen, I just want to talk to her, is all. Would you tell her that? She can come over during the day, when Mom's at work."

"She works too, ya know." He scratched dirty fingernails through his greasy black hair. "But she doesn't have any morning classes, now I think of it. So yeah, I guess I can tell her you want to see her. Anything else?"

"No. You should get some sleep; you look tired."

The next morning, he answered the bell to admit Daciana. She wore black low-heeled shoes, black stockings, a black skirt, and a silky white blouse. Her long hair fell below her shoulders, and her fingernails and lips were painted and glossed a matching shade of red. Blood red, he observed.

She could have carried him up the stairs to make the climb quicker, but she afforded him the dignity to lead her, taking one step at a time, reaching for the next step when both feet were planted on the first.

He topped the stairs and walked into the living room. He sat on the sofa and patted the cushion next to him. Daciana nodded, the corners of her mouth turned up, and sat beside him, so close he could smell her subtle perfume.

"So, I assume you enjoyed your trips to Disney World and Hershey Park." She hadn't seen him since before Easter break; monitoring the comings and goings of Joseph and his mother was Alphonse's job.

Joseph nodded. And confessed what he'd done to Daphne at Disney World.

"Well done, but be careful," she cooed, her voice like butter. "You must take care not to compromise yourself.

138

Because compromising yourself could in the end compromise me. And we wouldn't want that, would we?"

He acknowledged her unspoken warning. "But there's more," he said.

"I'm listening."

"Mom read me the riot act afterwards, but I figured what the hell, if she can do it so can I."

"Tell me you were careful. Where did you puncture the little girl?"

"Inside her thigh. But I felt like some kind of pervert, I mean, sucking from a four-year-old girl."

"I understand."

"But here's the thing." He fidgeted next to her, looking up at her face, forcing himself to look directly into her nearly black eyes. "Look, I'm . . . horny." He took a breath. "There, I said it. I need a woman. And the bitch of it is, there's no way that can happen. You know what I mean?"

Daciana's stare met his. Was there a spark of sympathy there? Or was it amusement?

"I do. You cannot even please yourself, much less a woman."

He looked down so she couldn't see the frustration manifest in his eyes. When he looked back up, he said in a voice that betrayed a slight tremble, "But maybe there is a way I can please a woman, someone who understands my situation. Maybe I can please you."

"Oh?"

He slid his tiny tongue in and out. "I've read the magazines. I know there are certain things that women like."

"Do you now?"

"So . . . what do you say? Can we try it, you and I? You should know how I feel about you."

"I say, little Joseph, I may be many things, but being a pedophile is not one of them."

He smashed his fists against his thighs. "Don't call me little! Damn it, I'm an adult, and thanks to your boyfriend I'm trapped in this goddamn baby's body. I hate it!"

"That's something you should discuss with your father, not me."

"And don't call him my father! I hate him!"

"But he is your father. And your maker. It was his decision to turn you, not mine. And he did it without my blessing, behind my back, without any thought to the consequences. To him it was a joke. But it's not funny at all, as well you know. It was terribly unfair, both to you and your mother, but life doesn't come with a guarantee of fairness, does it? I reprimanded Alphonse, but in the words of Lady Macbeth, what's done is done."

"Maybe you should've killed me. Killed Mom and me both."

Daciana thought. "Maybe we should have. It would've made my life less complicated, to be sure." She tilted her head. "Wait. What was it you just said, that you have feelings for me?"

Joseph blushed, but he refused to release her from his gaze. "You're not Aunt Daci to me anymore. Haven't been for years. You're beautiful, and I love you."

Daciana's expression didn't change. It was as if she had been carved from marble.

"There. I said it. Now it's your turn."

"My turn. To do what?"

"Damn it, I'm not going to cry, I promised myself that. Don't you have any feelings for me at all? Daciana? Talk to me."

"You are crying. And wipe the snot from your nose."

"Talk to me!"

"What is it you want me to say?"

"Isn't it obvious? I want to make love to you."

"You can't."

"I can! At least . . . at least, let me see you . . . without your clothes. Please? Please, Daciana?"

She sighed, stood, and faced him. "All right. I will remove my clothing, on condition that you remain on the couch and do not attempt to touch me. You may look only."

"Like a centerfold?"

"Like a living centerfold. Consider it a step up."

He had no choice but to comply.

Daciana nonchalantly removed her clothes, draping them over the arm of the sofa. This was no strip tease, there was nothing sexy about it at all. It was a clinical thing, as if she were disrobing in a clothing store's dressing room. There was no passion in her face; nonchalance might have described it better. She turned around, giving him a full circle view of her body.

Joseph stared at her breasts. Her figure was slim, and her breasts were proportional—smaller than he'd like, but more than a mouthful was wasted anyway. Least, that's what he'd overheard from talk on the street, teenage boys smoking on the downstairs porch. Her pubic area was downy and dark, and he longed to explore her.

"Get your hand away from your crotch," Daciana admonished.

"Sorry, I couldn't help—"

"You could help it. The show is over." She dressed quickly, either oblivious to or ignoring the perspiration on Joseph's forehead. "Now, is there anything else, or may I return to work? I've a class in an hour."

"Daciana, I love you," he said. She didn't respond. "When can I see you again?"

"Again? Joseph, if the police were to have walked in a few moments ago, they would have arrested me for contributing to the delinquency of a minor."

"Come on, that wouldn't happen, and you know it. If the police come at all, they go next door when Alphonse and Maria start their scream fests. Look, I get the pedophile bit. It's not fair, but I get it. But at least, I'm begging you, come over once in a while to talk to me, keep me company. I'm lonely, Daciana, you don't know, you can't know, and my mother? She doesn't count."

She reached into her purse and scribbled something on a note pad. "This is my phone number," she said. "You may call me at home once a week, and if I'm not busy we can talk. Perhaps, when your mother is at work and I have the time, I might even drop by." She tore off the page and handed it to him. It contained only the number, not her name. But it was enough. She turned without another word and walked toward the stairs.

"I love you, Daciana," he whispered to her back. He slipped his hand once again into his baby denim coveralls, and after many desperate and futile minutes, he gave up in frustration and let the tears spill forth.

Chapter Twenty-One: Robin

Young Robin Bradford had been impotent too, until Daciana had made him whole. But his initiation into sexual discovery could hardly have been called lovemaking. As a member of the queen's court, Daciana—that is, the Lady Catherine Drummond—told him she had to be careful with her nocturnal assignations. She would usually slip out unseen, pass herself off in London's back streets as a whore, and when the deed was done, she invariably killed her partner, tearing out his throat and leaving him to bleed out—after first satisfying her other, unnatural thirst.

When she took Robin to her bed, his ardor was physical, purely passion. They rutted like rabbits, and even after Daciana's portrait was completed she welcomed him to her chambers at night because, as she admitted, he provided her with the best, the most exciting . . . recreation . . . she had had in ages. Which became a tacit acknowledgment that Robin served at her pleasure. And so long as he continued to serve her pleasure, his life would not be forfeit.

Today, nearly four hundred years later, he often wondered what had become of his first—no, not first love, certainly not his mistress. If anything, he had been the kept one. There were random times over the years when he almost felt she was aware of him somehow, that she knew he still existed, and that if she called out to him he would be tempted to join her again.

But, in keeping with the verbiage of nearby Washington, he swore to himself that even if called, he would not serve.

By the spring of 1992, Robin knew it was time to move on. He received a commitment from the Fine Arts Department of the University of Maryland in College Park and submitted his resignation to Alexandria's T.C. Williams High School.

Before the term ended, he told Marcus and Kim-Ly Mitchell of his plans and accepted a dinner invitation to Vo's Vietnam as a going-away present. A new server greeted them, a lovely young Vietnamese woman who glanced surreptitiously at Robin as she took their orders. And again throughout the meal, when she wasn't busy with other tables.

"She seems to like you," said Marcus. "Maybe Kim-Ly could arrange for—"

"Don't even think about it, Gunner. I'm leaving town, remember?"

Marcus ignored him and motioned for the girl. "Say, young lady," he said when she came to the table, playfully gauging Robin's discomfort. "There was a server here named Hiep a while ago. Would you know what happened to him?"

Robin let out his breath.

"No," she replied. "Lots of turnover here. Colonel Vo helps people find jobs with better pay, replaces them with others from Vietnam. He gives them a new life. Very good boss."

"I see," said Marcus, with a sly glance at Robin. "You know, we've been eating here for a long time, and we've never met the colonel. We'd like to tell him how much we enjoy the food. And the service."

The young lady shook her head. "The colonel is not in tonight. I am sorry."

"Another time, perhaps. Thanks."

"Way to make me squirm," said Robin after the server had left. "I'll get you for that." He took a drink of water. "So, what do you hear from Rowena?"

"Doing well. She's a junior now. Having issues with some of the libs who don't understand her Corps values, if you get my drift, but overall she's okay. She doesn't write you?"

"We exchanged a few letters early on, but you know how that goes. Busy. I understand. Everyone moves on."

One thing positive about his move, Robin acknowledged, was that College Park wasn't that far from Delilah's territory in Northwest D.C. And when he drank from her that summer, he noticed her blood had a subtly different taste.

"Delilah, I hate to say it, but I believe you have VD."

143

"What's that, Mr. Lestat?"

"Oh, I guess you call it STD these days. Used to be called venereal disease, and in the very olden days, we—I mean, they—called it the French disease."

"Musta been really old days. Everybody's got something these days, not just the French." She tilted her head. "You can tell that, huh? From drinkin' it?" He nodded. "Does that mean it's bad for you?"

"It doesn't affect me. But listen, you've got to see a doctor." He gave her more than her usual stipend. "Take this and get yourself some penicillin. Please."

"You're a good man, Mr. Lestat. You're right, I been feelin' kinda low, figured some honky—'scuse me—some customer give me the clap or somethin'."

"Take care of yourself, Delilah. When I see you again, I expect to get a good report." He glanced at her wrist, which was already beginning to heal. "And I'll know, won't I?"

"Charity Bledsoe?" Robin called as he took roll the first day of class. An attractive coed raised her hand and offered a pleasant smile. "Wouldn't have sisters named Faith and Hope, would you?"

"Right on," she said, her smile open and wide. "I'm the baby. Parents are religious nuts."

"Lucky for you, you weren't born a boy. Should I take it you're not as religiously inclined as your parents?"

"Please, Professor Avery. Too much of a good thing, you know."

"So I hear." He continued calling out the students' names, mentally associating them with their faces and cordially promising to get them straight sometime around the end of the semester, which elicited their chuckles.

Miss Bledsoe was easily the best-looking young woman in the class, something he noted first with an artist's eye. She was of medium height, but that was the only part of her that could be called average. She had curly blond hair that she wore like a crown. Her eyes were big and blue, her nose the classic button, her lips and nails painted pink. She usually wore a loose-fitting top that billowed forward when she stood and leaned over her sketches, and what he saw beneath stirred him in a way that shamed him.

144

But she was also a college junior, around Rowena Mitchell's age, and he, despite youthful appearances, was— inappropriately older. And presumably wiser. Which was the problem with his love life, he reminded himself. He was easily attracted to physical beauty, but he'd found no one who possessed the degree of maturity and perspective that extreme longevity brings—an unfortunate impossibility for him. There had been women who had opened themselves to his attentions over the years, and some—those who had assured him their fancy was passing—who had shared his bed. But he always left those interludes frustrated. He knew he was seeking love, but knew he was doomed never to find it. The sex was a release, and he rationalized that it was so for his partners as well, albeit not exactly for the same reason. And they never deduced *what* he was, even though they would sometimes wake up with a headache and a slight rash on their necks, something they invariably attributed, with fondness, to a hickey.

Between classes one day, Robin drifted to the library— nowadays called a media center—and happened to see Charity Bledsoe sitting at a study carrel staring into a computer screen as she typed on a keyboard. He remembered Rowena's glee at getting her own personal computer for her high school graduation present, but he'd never bought one for himself.

Charity turned around and saw him. "Hi, Professor Avery."

"Hello, Miss Bledsoe. You look engrossed. Is that research you're doing?"

She gave a short laugh. "Not really. I'm emailing a friend back home."

"Where's home?"

"Lancaster, Pennsylvania." She pronounced it LANK- ister, which reminded him of Lancashire in England. He told her as much. "Yeah, it's pronounced like the English version. Maybe the town was named after it, I wouldn't know. Wouldn't care, really." She pulled a chair from the empty carrel next to her and scooted over. "Sit down, take a load off."

He sat beside her as she logged out. She gave off the scent of citrus. It brought back memories of Daciana, who at times used to perfume herself by rubbing her skin with oranges imported from Spain.

"I'm rather a novice at computers," he said.

"Really. Well, let me educate you." Due to the confines of the carrel, they sat so close he could feel the warmth of her body and wondered if she could feel his.

Down, boy, he cautioned his crotch.

"So, what's Lancaster like?" he asked, determined to keep his eyes from her neckline.

"Oh, it's okay, if you like farmland. Rolling hills, lots of green, lots of cows . . . and tons of manure. Nature's fertilizer. In the spring, when the wind's right, you don't want to be anywhere near Lancaster, believe me." She wrinkled her nose.

"Sounds like parts of the English countryside. The hills, the greenery, more sheep than cows, though."

"You've been to England?"

"Um, yes, but it's been a while."

"I'll take the beach any time. Give me the sun, the surf, and the sand. Give me gobs of suntan oil, a blanket, and my bikini, and I'm set for life."

Charity's body in a bikini? *Down, boy, and I'm not telling you again.*

They met weekly at the carrels, where Charity gave Robin what turned out to be expert tutelage. As she liked to tell him, she was a natural blonde, but that didn't mean she was a dumb blonde. He quickly realized the latter and cautioned himself constantly that he wanted no evidence of the former.

Which was not entirely true, though, especially when they shared study space in the carrel.

She taught him how to work on a word processor, how to create a spreadsheet for attendance, assignment, and grading purposes, how to import artwork of the Masters from other sources into a PowerPoint presentation. Robin was an apt and eager pupil, but the day finally came when he asked Charity if there were a way to locate persons using the Internet feature.

She cast him a coy glance. "Who would you be looking for?"

"A woman I've never met, actually."

146

"All right, my interest is piqued."

"She's the wife of an old friend, who's passed on. I have a message he asked me to give her, but he never gave me her address."

"Well, that's not too swift."

"It's complicated. He died before he could tell me. Just that she lived in New Jersey."

"And how old would this widow be?"

Robin thought. "I'd assume that she'd be somewhere in her seventies."

"Oh." Charity brightened. "Well, give me her name and let's see what we come up with."

He told her the name was Aimee Paris and spelled the first name for her. Her fingers flew over the keys, and a list came up. Hundreds of names or variations of the name.

"Wait," she said, "I'll narrow it down. New Jersey, right?" More keystrokes, another long list. But no Aimee Paris among the names. "Seventies, you said? Maybe she's dead by now."

"I'd thought of that. They had a daughter, that much I know. I could pass on the message to her."

"What's her name?"

"April. She was born in 1945."

"Let me guess. In April."

"No, January. First, I think."

"New Year's Day baby. Well, all righty then. That would make her about fifty, right?"

"Forty-eight, actually. I see you're a math major."

"Ha . . . ha. Okay, here we go again." Another list popped up. Nothing in New Jersey. "Maybe we should expand the search." She added the neighboring states and came up with a listing for A.N. Paris in Hershey, Pennsylvania. "That's the best I can do for you, Robert. Hershey's not all that far from Lancaster, by the way."

She had slipped effortlessly into calling him by his first name. He knew that a wall should exist between teacher and student, but their roles had reversed for the computer tutelage, and he felt uncomfortable correcting her.

Spring break was coming up in a few weeks, and Charity informed him that she would be going to Daytona with a group of friends. He refused her invitation to join them, telling her that he was thinking about heading for Hershey instead, to see if he could find the mysterious A.N. Paris.

"Could be a man, you know. Albert, or Anthony, Andrew maybe."

"Yes, it could be a wild goose chase."

"Where do you live, Robert?"

The question caught him off guard. "I've . . . an apartment nearby."

"Do you have a computer there?"

"No. I use the ones at school here."

"You need one at home. Before the break, let's go downtown and buy you one. When it comes to picking computers, I'm a walking *Consumer Reports.*"

Early on a Saturday, Charity picked him up in her compact sedan and drove him to a store she frequented in downtown Washington, where she said he could get the best deal. In his apartment that afternoon, she set his hardware up, established an Internet connection and email account for him, and guided him through his introduction to the operating system. After a soup and sandwich lunch, she installed his Office program and talked him through a few operations. When they were done, it was dinnertime.

"Let me take you to dinner," Robin said. "It's been a long day, and you've been a huge help."

"Let's eat in," she said, and with that she walked into his bedroom. When he didn't follow her, she called back, "Coming? Your dinner's warming up."

Robin followed her and saw Charity standing beside his bed. She was unbuttoning her blouse. Her smile was anything but demure, and her movements were calculated and slow.

"Charity, are you sure you want to do this?"

"Listen to me, Robert. I told you before, I'm not a dumb blonde. The media center has all kinds of manuals that could teach you how to operate a computer system. But you didn't go to them, you went to me. I know the way you stare at me when you think I'm not looking. So tonight, we're going to stop screwing around . . . and start screwing around."

She tossed her blouse onto a bedside chair, sat down on the bed, and took off her loafers and jeans. The bra was next to go. Still the seductress, she lowered the straps and peeled the lacy cups slowly down until her pale pink nipples popped out. "Peek-a-boo," she said.

Robin stood rock still; his need, however, was evident.

Charity noticed. "You wear boxers, don't you? Nice. I think we're going to have some fun tonight, Robert."

"Charity?"

"That's right, it's Charity. Not Chastity. Now Robert, I understand you're not sure about this, so let me explain something, and pardon me if I sound a little Machiavellian. People have seen us together on campus, and I happened to tell a couple girlfriends that I was spending the day here with you. They're jealous, by the way. So here's my proposal: we have sex; I'm talking raw, serious sex. And if you walk away from this"—she rolled her panties down across her hips, past her buttocks, and leaned forward to let them drop to the floor—"I go crying to the dean that you seduced me, and your career is over. I hate to put it in those terms, but I have to tell you, I've wanted you from the first day in class, and I always get what I want. Oh, and by the way, do you think it was by accident that I just happened to be in the media center the day you found me there?"

"I give up, Charity, you're right about my attraction to you." He could almost taste her blood.

She ran the tip of her tongue over her glossed lips. "I told you before, I'm not a dumb blonde." She glanced down. "But as you can see, I am a natural blonde." He took a small step forward. "Excellent. Now come to mama; dinner is served."

Charity woke up next morning with a slight headache and an irritating itch on her neck. The bed was empty; from the kitchen came the smell of bacon frying. "Yum," she said. "My kind of man."

Naked, she left the bed and headed for the mirror that hung over the dresser. As she leaned forward, her head started to spin. "Whoa," she said, bracing herself on the dresser top. "Holy shit," she murmured. "That's some kind of hickey he put there. I don't remember him doing that at all. It's so—so *high school.*" She found a robe in his closet and put it on, and then—still a little dizzy—made her way to the kitchen.

"Good morning, lazybones. How do you like your eggs?"

"I hate eggs."

"Pancakes then?"

"Perfect. I smell coffee." She poured herself a cup and added sugar and cream. After taking a sip and pronouncing it good for what ails you, she stood alongside Robin and slipped her hand inside the back of his boxers for a squeeze.

"Nice. But you might want to stand back; the bacon spits."

"Speaking of, that first *spit* last night almost blew the top of my head off. How long since you got laid, Robert?"

"A lady shouldn't ask those questions."

"Who said I'm a lady?"

"Good point."

"And the second and third time last night—I mean, where do you get the stamina? You wore me out! Not that I mind, of course."

"You passed out, if I remember. You were very sweet, by the way." He ran his tongue across the roof of his mouth, playing its tip against his fangs. "Now, if you'll excuse me, I have pancakes to make."

They ate in silence, staring at each other as they fed pancakes and bacon into their mouths.

"You didn't use a condom last night," she said as they cleaned the dishes. "It's okay, I'm on the pill."

"I guess I should've told you. I'm sterile. I'll never be a father."

"Well, you may be sterile, but you're sure not impotent! So as far as we're concerned, the pill's redundant. Kind of like a back up. Which means we don't have to worry about my getting knocked up."

"And we're not looking to start a family together either, are we?"

"Definitely not. But I still wish you'd come to Daytona with the gang." She winked. "Especially now."

"Not a chance, Bledsoe. Especially now. I don't want to publicize our relationship. Keep it private."

"So you're telling me this isn't a one night stand? You do want me back, even after I manipulated you into this affair?"

Robin chucked her gently under her chin. "And what makes you think you're the only one who was doing the manipulating?"

They enjoyed sex for sex's sake intermittently during the week and always on weekends. Always, too, on Sunday mornings Charity would awaken a little lightheaded, with what she thought was a hickey—sometimes on her neck, others on a wrist or elbow, still others on the inside of her thigh. She never remembered Robin's putting them there. But she never complained either. She reached a point where she'd wake up, head throbbing, and immediately seek out the telltale rash.

She flew down to Daytona with her friends, promising to save up her libido for her return, and Robin, now that he was alone, turned his attention to his computer. He called up A.N. Paris, but the information simply said Hershey, Pennsylvania. The town was about two hours away, and Charity had left him the keys to her car. He intended to leave the university at the end of the school year—Charity would be a senior next fall, and the way things were evolving, he thought there might be a danger—not so remote anymore—of her lust's turning to love. It was something he couldn't allow, as his feelings for her were driven solely by hunger, on two fronts.

"Let's see," he said to himself as he gazed at the screen. "If this really is Joe's daughter, she'd be in her late forties now. What profession might she have taken up back in, say, the 1960s? Nursing? Teaching?" He keyed in a request for Hershey information and saw that Penn State had a teaching hospital there. He found a list of doctors on staff but no information on nurses or technicians.

Under schools, he read that the founder of the town, Milton S. Hershey, had bequeathed a school that today provided both school and home environments, from kindergarten through high school, to children living in poverty. *I like this guy Hershey,* he thought. *Capitalism with a conscience.* He searched the faculty list; no A.N. Paris.

Next he went to the Web site of the public schools. Again, he seemed to strike out—until he saw a tab labeled Welcome Aboard. He clicked and found the page listed new faculty coming in the fall, and one of those names was A.N.

Paris, who would be added to the high school's guidance staff. No photo, no indication of gender. Worth a shot, he thought.

"Looks like I'll be heading to Hershey for a few days," he said to himself.

The three Hershey schools—elementary, intermediate, and high—stood side by side, with athletic fields behind them, and across the street an immense greensward sporting soccer nets. The town itself reflected its identity as a company town, with the main street—Chocolate Avenue—being lit by streetlamps in the shape of Kisses. In his wanderings, Robin drove by an amusement park, a huge hotel upon a nearby hill, a sports/entertainment arena, and a massive hospital complex. Neighborhoods were clean and tree-lined, and the township boasted a large library, community swimming pool, and ball fields—on Cocoa Avenue, which met Chocolate at a T intersection. Robin decided he liked the town. He also thought he might enjoy living there for a while.

Before he'd left Maryland, Robin had had the foresight to inquire if any of the three schools needed an art teacher. His timing was perfect: the superintendent was interviewing for the position, and yes, he could fit Mr. Bradford into his schedule.

By the time he returned to the university, Robin carried the superintendent's recommendation for the post of middle school art teacher for the 1993-94 school year. At the next board of education meeting, his appointment was confirmed.

When Charity returned from Florida, more sunburned than tanned, they resumed their relationship with vigor. When she asked about his visit to Hershey, he said it was nice but a bit too bucolic for his taste. He preferred the Washington area, for its museums, its history, its big-city ambiance. As for the mysterious A. N. Paris, he told Charity her suspicions had been confirmed: the A stood for Alfred.

The day after classes adjourned for the summer, Charity kept Robin in bed, getting up only for bathroom and meal breaks. The next morning, promising that their last twenty-four hours of lovemaking should hold him until she returned in the fall, she drove home to her prim and proper parents' house in Lancaster, where for three months she would live a life of enforced chastity. "Pure as the driven snow," she said. "Sadly."

The first thing Robin did after she left was change his email address. He cleaned out his apartment, bought a used station wagon, and checked out with the administration. He told his department head he'd accepted a position in the Chattanooga, Tennessee, public schools. He thought he might drive downtown and say goodbye to Delilah, but he wanted to be in Hershey before dark, and Delilah only came out after dark. So he drove north to Pennsylvania and left no trace of himself behind.

"You're a prick," he told himself as he crossed the state line. "You used that girl—for sex and for blood. But then," he countered, "she used you too, for what she needed. So it was reciprocal, no harm done." He passed a tractor-trailer with the Giant Foods logo on its side. "But you didn't tell her you were bugging out, did you? Afraid of a scene, a break-up? Huh. You have no trouble when it comes to fighting for your country, oh no, you've stared death in the face lots of times, but when it comes to breaking off a relationship, Robin Bradford, you're a coward. Figure that one out." He took a swig from a bottle of soda—it wouldn't be good to be stopped by a policeman if he had blood on his breath.

He hoped once her fury at his desertion had worn off, Charity would be discreet and, further, wouldn't try to find him, if only to vent her spleen. But if she did try, and if she checked with the university office for a forwarding address, she'd end up scanning the Internet for a Robert Avery, somewhere in Tennessee. When in fact, he would be living just thirty miles from her home.

Meanwhile, Robin would be looking forward to his new teaching assignment and to meeting Miss—Mrs.—Ms.—Mr.?—A.N. Paris, the guidance counselor in the high school next door. Corporal Joe Paris's portrait still lay pressed in his sketchbook, tucked into a pocket in his artist's portfolio. Perhaps, he hoped, he could discharge his nearly fifty-year obligation at last.

Chapter Twenty-Two: Naomi
Early August, 1993

"What the hell, Mom?"

"Never mind. Just pack all your clothes and personal belongings—you might want to leave those magazines behind—and put your things by the stairs."

"But where are we going? This looks permanent."

"I'll explain when we're done. I'm busy now. Just trust me, Joseph."

The intolerable humidity of their last summer day in Newark produced streams of sweat that ran from their faces into their lightweight tee shirts. Dark stains saturated their underarms. But Naomi was the happiest of dervishes as she gathered her clothes and kitchen utensils, their toiletries, their few mementos. By late afternoon, a pile of suitcases and supermarket bags stood like silent sentinels at the head of the stairs.

Naomi checked her watch. Alphonse would be leaving for work any moment. Time for a break, time to wait. She sat Joseph at the kitchen table, and as he sat, sullen, she struggled to put everything into words, in the proper order. She nodded her head and began:

"Joseph, do you remember last February, when I told you—and you know who next door—that I wanted to spend the four-day Presidents Weekend with some of my friends on the faculty learning to ski in the Catskills? I'm sorry to say, it was a lie. Instead, I went to Hershey for my final interview with the school superintendent. When we visited the amusement park a few years ago, you remember I left you alone for a few hours one afternoon. I told you I was going to do some shopping in the outlets, if you remember."

"You never lied to me before. Why start now?"

"Just listen, please. I went to the board offices and submitted my résumé. I couldn't tell you then. I wanted to, but

I was afraid to. Afraid that word would somehow filter . . . next door, and from next door to that woman."

"In other words, you don't trust me."

"I do. Trust you. I trust your intentions, honey, I really do. But you know what the road to hell is paved with. Besides, I really didn't have much hope for a position. The board secretary showed me a four-drawer file tower and told me it was filled with applications to teach in Hershey. She was very pleasant, but she said the best she could do was file it with the others. She advised me against holding out too much hope."

"But they did hire you." His face couldn't mask his uncertainty, his anxiety. She had to calm him.

"Honey, it's going to be fine. You told me during our last visit to the Park that you liked it there. You liked being in Hershey. Well, now we'll be living there full time."

"You're running away."

"We have a lovely, two-story, furnished town house waiting for us. Two bedrooms, two full baths—you'll have your own suite, honey—plus a half bath on the first floor. And the rent is less than we have to pay *him* next door to live here. It'll be perfect for the two of us."

She looked at her son's face, at eyes that blinked furiously. If he weren't chronologically twenty-five by now, she'd think a four-year-old was about to cry.

Naomi checked her watch. She patted Joseph on the shoulder and walked to the porch. Right on time, there was Alphonse leaving for work. She waited five minutes more, in the event that he might've forgotten something inside his house. Then she turned around to see Joseph standing behind her. His face, once a mask of indecision, was now cast in stone. It wasn't a look she liked.

She brought him to the porch rail. "See that little Honda Civic down there? That's ours. I bought it yesterday. I'm going to start loading it up. I want to be on the road before dark."

After school had been in session for a month, the Derry Township Board of Directors sponsored its annual evening social hour to welcome new faculty members. It was held in the Hershey High School gym, where tables and chairs were set up and the staff were encouraged to mingle not

155

only with their own peers, but also more importantly with the faculty of the other schools. "We're a family here," the superintendent said in his opening remarks, "and like family we want to know everyone, enjoy everyone's company, and even help each other out whenever we can."

Deborah LeVan, a math teacher at the high school, whispered across their table to Naomi. "Same speech every year. Dr. Sponagle's a nice guy, but he likes to think this is Mr. Rogers's neighborhood." Naomi matched her grin for grin and sipped her punch. "Oh, by the way, have you seen Robin Bradford yet? Hubba hubba."

"Robin? That's a girl's name. Deb, may I remind you you're a married woman? To a man, no less?"

Deb smirked. "Robin's a man, you jerk. And he's hot."

"Robin . . . oh, you mean like Robin MacNeil on PBS news?"

"Well, he sure ain't like Batman's boy wonder. I always had my suspicions about those two, by the way. Come on, I think I see him over there."

"Must I?"

"He teaches art, kiddo. In the middle school. You told me you used to teach art. So you have something in common."

A sigh. "All right, lay on, MacDuff."

"That's more like it."

Deb dragged Naomi to a youngish-looking teacher talking to the middle school's media specialist—a position once known as librarian. The older woman was gushing about how much his students seemed to love him, especially the seventh- and eighth-grade girls.

Deb butted in. "Hate to interrupt, kiddies—well, not really—but I want my friend Naomi here to meet Robin. They're both artists."

"Naomi?" said the new art teacher. "One of my favorite names." He looked at her skeptical expression. "No, really, I'm not trying to . . . oh, never mind."

Naomi and Deb exchanged quick glances.

"Naomi Paris," said Deb. "And this is Robin Bradford."

"Naomi . . . Paris," he said. "You would be the new guidance counselor, right?"

"Hi." She stuck out her hand and they shook. "Where are you joining us from?"

"Alexandria, Virginia. You?"

"Newark, New Jersey."

"Newark." He cocked his head, as if uncertain about something.

"Yes. I was a guidance counselor there, as well as a substitute art teacher."

"Multi-talented. I'm afraid I'm just a one-trick pony."

Naomi glanced around. Both the media specialist and Deb had melted into the crowd.

"Can I get you a refill? Your glass is empty, and there's no danger of getting drunk on this."

"Thanks."

She watched him as he walked toward the refreshment table. *Good-looking guy,* she thought. *Deb was right. But he's got to be only in his mid-twenties, thirty at most. Probably thinks I am too. Which could make things mighty uncomfortable for this old gal—especially one with a kid who's been four for twenty-one years and counting—if he asked for a date.*

When Robin returned, Naomi mentioned she'd been thinking of helping the high school principal, Dr. Mulligan, stage the spring musical. "It's *The King and I.* We'll be tapping some of your middle-school kids for the children's roles, he tells me."

"That's great." He nodded. "I've always loved theater. Um . . . do you think you might need some help with set design, supervision, anything like that?"

"You're volunteering. People never volunteer. Long hours, no pay . . ."

"You're volunteering. Besides, I think it might be fun."

"I do too. I'll tell Dr. Mulligan on Monday."

When they parted company, Naomi shook her head and for the nth time cursed her condition. Then she heard something odd. Robin's back was to her, so she couldn't be quite sure, but it sounded as if he'd mumbled something to himself like, "Too damned young."

Chapter Twenty-Three: Alphonse

"Alphonse, come here and see: angel's wings."

Alphonse still had no stomach for Daciana's sadism with the chest spreader. Whenever she used it, he would turn his head until she was done. The victim, of course, was still alive when she made the cut, slammed the spreader through the sternum, and cranked the torso open. Even though the victim was always a useless piece of shit, it didn't deserve to die that way.

She had been away most of August, and when she returned in September she made no mention of her absence—of where she had gone, what she had done—and Alphonse had learned by now not to delve too deeply into Daciana's affairs. Besides, he had some unpleasant news to share with her and wasn't sure how to go about it. He knew she'd be royally pissed.

So for now, he turned around to see what she was talking about.

The victim, a white male vagrant this time, lay as usual on the lead-topped lab bench, his head hanging down over the sink. Daciana had reached inside his chest cavity and pulled his lungs up, spreading them to either side of his chest: angel's wings.

"The Vikings used to do this," she said. "They considered it high humor. That was before my time, but I just read about it and thought I might try it."

The lungs were weakly inflating and collapsing. The vagrant was still alive, but barely. Alphonse glanced inside the cavity and saw the man's heart, struggling to keep the body alive. He nearly puked.

Daciana bent her head forward, bared her fangs, and sank them directly into the vagrant's heart. His body twitched—once, twice—and then slipped into merciful release. Alphonse heard her suck from the heart, and when she brought her head back up her face was stained crimson.

"Your turn," she said, as she tore the man's heart free and handed it to him.

He was repulsed at first, but after he drank, he had to admit it was delicious. And he never gave a thought as to who this man was, what he had been, what had caused his downfall and decay. Which is to say, business as usual.

Once they were finished—Daciana cleaning the tools, sink, and bench top, Alphonse dismembering and burning the body in the antiquated furnace—they repaired to the empty faculty lounge and enjoyed their culminating activity: feral and ferocious sex, their heat contrasting with the cold tile floor on which they lay.

They didn't want to leave telltale stains on the ratty garage sale sofa, and they didn't think the old springs could absorb the punishment anyway.

Later, in what one might call pillow talk without benefit of pillows, Daciana asked him why he never performed oral sex on her. Why was he so urgent, so fierce?

Alphonse made a face. "Real men don't do that. Come on. You pee from that thing."

She sighed, remembering Joseph's plea. "Real men don't believe in foreplay? They don't believe in pleasing their partner? Alphonse, I swear, you are getting so predictable." She arched an eyebrow. "And predictable becomes boring."

Alphonse swallowed.

"Apropos of nothing, I've not seen your son since school began. He's probably pining away, poor thing. Yes," she said, considering. "My first class starts at two. I might just surprise him with a visit tomorrow."

He thought, *If you do, you're the one who's gonna be surprised.*

"Uh . . . there's no way to say this that it won't piss you off, so I'll just say it."

"There's a problem?" Her expression turned dark.

"Thing is, when I went to collect the rent this month, the place was empty."

"Empty? What do you mean, empty?" She bolted upright and stared at him.

He sat up and eased back a few inches. "All their personal stuff was gone. They flew the coop, probably when I was at work."

Daciana sat silent, still as petrified wood, but her eyes bored into his, and they frightened him. Finally, she spoke: "Why haven't you told me?"

"I, uh, was waiting for the right time. You were busy, and—"

"Don't." Her tone carried condemnation. It frightened him. "Where have they gone?"

"I have no idea. No clue. Naomi never said anything to me."

"What about the boy?"

"He didn't either; probably she never told him."

"A secret is a secret until two people know it," she acknowledged, her voice less threatening now. "Do you see what your foolish act all those years ago has done? Now we have two *strigoi* loose and unconstrained."

Alphonse said, "But don't you have some kind of mind control or something? Some way to find out where they are?"

"I can sense my creations sometimes, and sometimes I can even influence them. But Joseph and Naomi are your creations, not mine. And you're not adept enough yet to influence them." She shook her head. "I need you to find them."

He had a thought. "Hey, what you said before, does the kid go down on you or something?"

She slapped him so hard his cheek blazed. "Don't you *dare* make light of this! Now listen to me. I have just accepted a position to teach at Criterion University in New Hampshire for the 1994-95 year. I have to leave Newark at the end of this school year. You have until then to locate them for me."

"Where do I start? And, what do you mean, you're leaving?" He rubbed his cheek; it still smarted.

"You must realize I can't stay too long in any one position. I don't age. Neither of us ages, but no one notices you." If she realized she had hurt him, she didn't show it. "As for where to start, that is up to you. Hire a detective if you must."

"With what, my good looks?"

"I won't dignify that with a response. I can supply whatever money he demands." After a moment, she added, "I can't tell you how disappointed I am in you, Alphonse. I don't like to be disappointed. You have this one chance to redeem yourself, and I would advise you to start working on it as soon as your shift is over."

He looked at the floor. Cold as the tiles were, her voice was colder.

"One more thing, Alphonse. No sex for you until the situation is resolved."

He looked up. "Does that mean I don't get victims for us anymore either?"

"Oh, no. You will get nourishment as you always have. And I will share, as I always have. But I don't need sex from you. As a matter of fact, there is an associate of mine on staff who has taken a liking to me. I've put him off, politely, for a while. Maybe it's time to entertain his ardor. At least for a while."

Alphonse left the building as the sun rose, a broken man. On the bus ride back to the Roseville Avenue and Sixth Avenue stop, he managed, reasoning through a maze of illogic, to assign blame firmly to Naomi for having put him in this situation. Never once did he think that had he not raped her all those years ago, none of this—none of it— would have happened. The cause-effect relationship never entered his mind.

Ripples in a pond, to him, were no more than ripples in a pond.

Chapter Twenty-four: Joseph

He missed her.

He had been so good for so many months. Thanksgiving, Christmas, New Years, the bitter Central Pennsylvania winter. Now it was March, spring in a week or so, and he hadn't seen Daciana since last June, and that was nine long months ago.

He missed those hypnotic eyes, those red lips, that long black hair; and that one mesmerizing view of her in all her nakedness. He so longed for the opportunity to do what she had denied him. Damn it, despite outward appearances, he wasn't four years old anymore, he hadn't been for decades! It wouldn't be pedophilia!

He knew why he and his mother were hiding; she had explained it again and again, but she had no idea of the grief it was causing him. Just because she couldn't allow herself to fall in love didn't mean he had to forsake it as well. The fact that she could have sex but wouldn't, whereas he couldn't have sex but would—if he only could—just intensified his frustration.

He wondered if Mom wasn't relaxing her prohibition against romance with that artist guy, Mr. Bradford. At rehearsals, he noticed that the three of them—including the principal—seemed pretty tight. Lots of times, though, Bradford—Mr. Bradford to her when kids were around, Robin when they weren't—was working with backstage crews while his mother was coaching the players with Dr. Mulligan. There were no subtle looks between them, no secret smiles. Totally professional. Still . . . there were times he thought he saw the teacher look at his mother with a funny expression on his face, as if he wanted to ask her something but decided against it.

The high school and middle school girls at the evening rehearsals loved him. What girls in their right mind could resist a Gerber-baby-cute four-year-old? Answer: none. It was a fact of life. And when they picked him up and hugged him, their physical contact gave him temporary respite from the loss of Daciana. But they were only pleasant diversions, not distractions.

He wondered what she was doing now, whether she missed him as much as he missed her. He'd thought time might ease the pain of separation, but Daciana was his first love, and first loves have a fascination all their own. Plus, they linger. He loved her so much that he couldn't remember exactly what she looked like, which vexed him all the more. It was wrong, it shouldn't be that way. Each element of her face he could picture, but he couldn't put them together in his mind to form a coherent whole. What was wrong with this picture? What was wrong with him?

And then there was the issue with his mother.

She couldn't have known when she uprooted him that he'd been seeing Daciana privately. She couldn't have known his fascination, his infatuation with—no, his love—for her. But in the end it wouldn't have made any difference to his mother, that much he knew. She hated Daciana. Mom was number one, it was all about her. He hadn't been positive of that at first, but as time dragged on and his longing intensified, so too did his disaffection for his mother. It was like one of those laboratory balances: as his love for Daciana weighed down one stage, it lightened his love for his mother on the other. He hated it when she picked him up at home, as if he were still a baby. He hated it when she talked to him as if he weren't an adult. He hated it when she took offense at his sometimes obscenity-laced language—as if she had the right to correct him. In fact, there were times he had to admit he hated his mother more than anything.

And that too he had to hide. Because considering their enforced symbiosis, what else could he do?

It was early March, spring of '94. Tech rehearsals would begin soon, when the sets, lighting, sound system, and costumes and makeup all came together; when the actors finally got a feeling for the final production; when the director could adjust the size of a spotlight; critique the makeup under stage lighting; tweak the choreography; evaluate the sound system; and give final notes to the players. It would be an intense time for everyone. Everyone, that is, but Joseph Christian Paris.

He still had Daciana's private phone number. It was tucked into a pocket of the denim coveralls he'd worn on the day she'd disrobed for him. He'd placed them on the bottom of his drawer and never worn them since. One of his jobs at home was to put his clean clothes away, so there was no danger of his mother's finding it. He unfolded the paper and gazed at the number as if staring at a treasure map.

He wanted to call her. He'd wanted to call her the very day they moved to Hershey.

But he faced a conundrum. They—no, Mom—had run away to be free from Daciana and Alphonse. His mother had sworn him to secrecy, and he had to admit her reasons were good. Alphonse had raped her, and for that he hated him; further, he had made Joseph immortal—but at a price Joseph was loath to pay; why couldn't the creep have waited until he reached puberty at least?—and for that, he hated him even more. But he did love Daciana, and he believed she loved him too.

If he did phone her, told her where they were living, would she come to Hershey to see him, alone? Would she perhaps take him away with her, back to New Jersey? He could even put up with living in Newark, next door to Alphonse. He had to admit that hearing him yell at his wife from across the alley could be entertaining at times. Better, would Daciana consider taking him to her place instead? Come to think of it, where *did* she live?

What kind of house did she have? Apartment? Condo? Did she live in the city, or perhaps in a single-family home in the suburbs? He had no idea, had never thought to ask. But anywhere she was would be infinitely better than anyplace Alphonse was.

His mother wouldn't miss him. No, that wasn't fair. She would at first, he was sure, the way you worry about a pet that's run away, but as time passed what a relief it would be for her not to have to worry about him anymore! She could concentrate on Mr. Bradford if she wanted. She could even sleep with him without worrying if her *little boy* would hear them. With Joseph gone back to Jersey with Daciana, they'd both benefit. There was no down side.

He knew his mother had made reservations for the two of them at the Harrisburg Hilton for Saturday night, in order to score some fresh blood. Suppose he were to call Daciana and tell her their plans—just like the old days at the hotels in Newark and Manhattan—and suppose he told her that if she were to drive down, say, Monday morning while his mother was at work, she could come to their town house and take him back home with her?

He'd have to convince Daciana that his mother proved no threat to her or Alphonse, that she was still as discreet as ever. He'd have to convince her to let Mom live her life as she pleased; and have her promise not to tell Alphonse any of this, promise to keep him out of their life together, altogether.

It'll be fine, Mom, he said to himself. *You'll see. Bradford seems to be a nice guy, he seems to like you. Hey, if it works out you can turn him and you can both live forever.* Yes. It would work for everyone, all around. Except for Alphonse, who was a piece of shit anyway.

He walked into the kitchen, stood on a chair, and removed the wall phone from its cradle.

At the college later that night, Daciana, peering through half-lidded eyes, asked Alphonse if the detective he'd hired had had any luck finding Naomi. He said the guy was in New York, checking leads. Daciana told him to pay him for his time and fire him. She knew where Naomi was, and she and Alphonse were going to pay her a visit—of sorts. To let her know they knew where she lived and convince her that she would never be free of them.

"Your job later," she said, "will be to keep her under your thumb—or any other part of your body that you might wish, it makes no difference to me—after I leave New Jersey this summer. Your job now, however, is to pack an overnight bag. You and I are going to spend this coming weekend in Harrisburg, Pennsylvania."

Chapter Twenty-Five: Naomi
Monday, March 21, 1994

It could have been a scene from a horror film, the article began. *But this was worse, because it was real. Jason McElroy and Bobby Justis, both 35, of Charleston, South Carolina, were found murdered yesterday in their room at the Hilton Hotel here. Their throats had been slashed and their bodies drained of blood . . .*

Naomi assured Dr. Mulligan—in a voice she tried to keep from quavering—that she was all right, and when he left for his office she picked up her office phone and called home. It seemed to take forever before Joseph picked up.

"Joseph, are you all right?"

"Sure, Mom. Why wouldn't I be?"

"Because they know we're here."

"Who?"

"Can't you guess? I don't know how they found out, but they actually killed the guy we drank from Saturday night. Both him and the friend he was traveling with. It's in this morning's paper."

"No shit."

She winced. What's with kids today and their casual swearing? It was an old song, and this wasn't the time to sing it to him again. "Listen, I want you to make sure the doors and windows are locked, and don't answer the door unless you know it's me. Do you understand?"

"Yup."

"What's that noise?"

"Huh? Oh, I leaned against the wall and the chair moved."

"I thought—never mind. Just be safe. I'll come home right after school and take you with me to rehearsal tonight." She paused. "I wish I could come home and pick you up now, but . . ."

"Calm down, Mom, everything's fine, I'll be okay. We'll figure this out later."

Naomi's second shock of the day came when she unlocked the front door and found the note on the kitchen table. She read it over, several times, then collapsed into the chair and cried. She cried through what would ordinarily be dinnertime, their dinnertime together. And now it was nearing the hour when she had to be back at school. There was no calling out sick during tech week; her presence was mandatory. Dozens of people from cast to crew to Declan Mulligan and Robin Bradford were depending upon her.

What to tell them as to why Joseph wasn't with her? She thought hard and decided simply to tell Declan and Robin that her son had gone back to Newark to live with his father. That he liked it better there—which, for all the wrong reasons, was absolutely true. The staff and students knew she was a single mother, but she'd kept the personal details private—thus relieving herself of the need to lie—and while her colleagues might have been curious, they were also too polite to pry.

So much for the first aid, Naomi thought. *But what about the wound itself?* When would that begin to heal, and how? What treatment could ever cure the hurt? Guilt coursed through her like a deluge from a breached dam. *My fault, my fault, my fault. I failed him. He's my son, and I failed him.*

But to be fair, what mother had ever had such a challenge?

She grabbed an apple from the basket on the kitchen counter. *I have to eat something,* she said, before heading back for rehearsal. She bit into it, and her teeth sank into mush. "Perfect," she muttered before spitting her mouthful into the trash and following it with the rest of the apple.

Naomi read the note again. "Don't come for me," it concluded. And he signed it *Joe,* not *Love, Joseph.* It was all she could do not to scream.

Robin saw immediately that something was wrong. As the players sat for makeup and the band began tuning their instruments, he drew Naomi aside and asked if she were okay. She said yes, just sad that Joseph had gone back to Newark today, to live with his father.

"I'm sorry."

She smiled weakly. "Because of Newark, or because Joseph's gone?"

"Mostly because you're sad, no matter the reason."

She shrugged her shoulders. "Thanks. I'll survive. Time heals, and all that."

"Indeed it does . . . most of the time."

"All right, that's being cryptic."

"Story for another time. Meanwhile, if you need an ear, or a shoulder . . ."

She gripped his hand; and when she saw some students watching and exchanging looks, she released it immediately. "Thanks, Robin. And judging from the giggles over there, I think I might've just started some speculation. Tomorrow it'll be all over the school."

"Ah, grist for the rumor mill."

"Sorry."

"Don't be. Keep them guessing." Dr. Mulligan had just assembled the cast and crew and was giving notes. "Come on, we should be part of this."

They sat apart during notes, Robin with the tech crew, she with the players. After Dr. Mulligan finished and called places, he drew Naomi aside.

"I'm fine," she said without waiting to be asked.

"Good," he said. "I was afraid the article in today's paper still had you upset."

"No. Horrible as that was, I'm upset now because Joseph went back to New Jersey today to live with his father."

"Oh. I didn't know he was still in the picture. His father, I mean. It wasn't any of my business, so I didn't ask."

"For which I'm grateful. Thanks."

"Anything I can do . . ."

"No, but thanks again."

"Actually, I called you over—excuse me. Orchestra, ready for the overture—I wanted you to see Robin's artwork for the program cover." He reached into his briefcase and drew out a twelve-by-sixteen-inch oil painting depicting the students playing Anna and the King of Siam, in makeup and costume.

Naomi caught her breath. "It's . . . it's beautiful. Like I'm looking at a photograph."

"With your art background, I knew you'd like it."

"The kids are going to love it."

He reached into his briefcase again and pulled out a print of the same painting, on heavy, acid-free paper, ready for framing. Handing it to her, he said, "Robin's going to give each cast and crew member reproductions like this at the cast party when the show wraps. I told him he might want to sell prints as a fund-raiser for next year's play."

"Or as souvenirs of this one. Or both."

He told her to keep the print. "I know what you're thinking: what's a man with that kind of talent doing teaching school? And I guess the answer would be, some people follow their calling instead of following the money."

"And thank God for them. Actually, though, I'm thinking the style reminds me of one of the paintings in a coffee-table book I have at home. *Portraits from Colonial America.*"

Declan Mulligan shook his head. "Wow. That's some eye you have. You look at an artist's style the same way an English major looks at an author's. Me, I couldn't tell Faulkner from Hemingway, but then again I majored in math."

He signaled for the overture to begin, and they took their places.

Naomi returned that night to an empty home, for the first time ever. It reminded her of a crypt, not that she'd ever seen one, but what she imagined one would look like. There wasn't a sound except her breathing, which was more a series of sighs. Even with the lights on, it seemed somehow dark. She put her tote bag on the dinette table. It was full, and as it tipped over, a corner of the reproduction Declan Mulligan had given her peeked out.

She needed a diversion. Joseph was gone, a part of herself gone with him. That she loved him despite his origins, despite what had been done to him as a four-year-old, despite his desertion of her, despite all of that, her mother's love for him was undeniable. But he was in fact an adult now, and he had made his decision to leave as an adult, not as a child. She herself was forty-nine, although she still didn't look a day older than when she was turned at twenty-seven. In a sense, she too was trapped, in a body nearly half the age of her mind.

Naomi pulled the print from her purse and opened *Portraits from Colonial America*. She turned the pages until she found "Portrait of Mrs. Lemuel Stover," credited to an Avery Palmer. Its style was so similar to Robin's it stunned her. If anything, she noted, Robin's was even more nuanced, with shading and highlights that made the subjects on the print even more photorealistic than the Palmer painting. It appeared a stylistic evolution of sorts, from Palmer to Bradford.

She looked at the artist's signature: A. PALMER in tiny, neat block letters in the lower right corner. Then she looked at the lower right corner of the playbill cover: R. BRADFORD, in identically small, identically neat block letters. Both were so faint they would be easy for the casual viewer to miss entirely. She harkened back to her days as a student in Arts High. Miss Hopper had said, "A true artist makes his signature inconspicuous. The painting is what he wants you to see. And that's what people should see. If you want them to see your name splashed across the canvas, paint a sign instead."

Naomi slept very poorly that night.

Final dress rehearsal Thursday night was a disaster. Notes were forgotten; the sound board malfunctioned; actors flubbed lines or missed their cues; the middle-school students who played the king's children forgot their stage business and looked more like displaced audience members. Naomi looked like she was on the verge of a breakdown.

Standing before the students, Dr. Mulligan grimaced, his face the picture of disappointment, and his notes to them following the performance reflected that look. But privately, after the cast and crew had left, he was the picture of calm. "Bad dress, boffo opening," he assured her. Or tried to. "All part of the game," he said to Naomi. "You'll see. Robin, am I right, or am I right?"

Chapter Twenty-Six: Robin

Experience proved the principal right. The opening night crowd—hardly unprejudiced—gave the cast a standing ovation, and in Naomi's opinion as well as that of the more objective adult staff, it was well deserved. The standing Os continued throughout the show's two-weekend run, and at the wrap party Dr. Mulligan presented every member of the cast and crew with the print of the program cover. Mr. Bradford himself presented framed copies to Anna and the King and autographed the heavy paper backing. Dr. Mulligan then gave special recognition to Ms. Paris, calling her indispensible to the success of the play. She stood, blushing, as the students cheered them all.

The following Saturday afternoon, Robin hosted an adults-only party in his modest town home to celebrate the play's success. The refreshments were wine and finger food, but the highlight of the afternoon for the guests, all of whom had worked in some capacity on the play, was the display of art on his walls. Portraits, landscapes, and still lifes by various artists graced every room, and he was happy to give the people a tour.

"This is one of my favorites," he said as he pointed out a still life consisting of fruit and vegetables displayed in an arched alcove set in a stucco wall. "It's called *Abbondanza*, which is Italian for Bonanza. The artist is a gentleman I met a while ago, H. Hargrove." He pointed to an orange in the painting. "See that little fly perched on the orange? First time I saw it, I thought it was real. I even tried to shoo it away." They laughed. "It's what made me decide, after some hemming and hawing, to buy the painting."

Naomi, however, seemed unable to take her eyes off another painting. "Robin, is this an original?"

"That one? Yes, as a matter of fact. It's a portrait by a man named Palmer. I bought it at an estate sale."

"Really. The style. It's very much like your own, isn't it?"

The other guests gathered close.

"He's better than I am, but yes, his style did influence mine."

Naomi looked as if she were about to say something.

Declan Mulligan asked, "Is that the painting you told me about, the one in your book?"

She nodded.

"This painting's in a book?" asked Robin. "You have it?" Another nod. "I'd love to see it. I just might have something valuable here."

Sunset approached, and as the others prepared to leave, Naomi offered to stay and help Robin clean up. A few others also volunteered, but he shooed them out. "Place isn't that big," he told them. "We'd be in each other's way. Naomi and I can whip through this in no time. Thanks anyway. See you all Monday."

Some of the volunteers cast playful glances at him and Naomi as they left.

With the kitchen sparkling and the dishwasher running, Robin made a fresh pot of coffee. "Thank you for staying," he said, the steam from his mug rising before his face.

"You're welcome." She stirred her cup and stared into his eyes.

"I have a question for you, and I hope you don't think I'm prying."

"Should I be nervous?"

"I don't know about you, Naomi, but frankly, I am. I'm very nervous."

"You? You're the picture of calm."

Robin released his breath. "On the faculty register, you're listed as A.N. Paris. So Naomi is your middle name." She nodded once. "Might your first name be April? As in April N. Paris?"

She sat up straight, then gave a nervous laugh. "Good guess. It's a bad pun, I know. Mom's idea. She told me Dad went along. See, 'April in Paris' was the song they danced to at their wedding, and he promised after he came home from the war that he'd take her to Paris for a second honeymoon.

But he never came home. I never knew him. Robin. What's behind that look on your face?"

"Naomi, I don't know if I dare continue. If what I suspect is true, a commitment I'm sworn to keep is about to be satisfied. If it's not true, I'm going to make a damned fool of myself."

"Robin, give. What's going on?"

"All right. Here goes. Was your mother's name . . . Aimee?" He spelled it, to be sure. "Was your father named Joseph, like your son? And was he killed on Iwo Jima?"

She sat up straight and pressed herself against the back of the chair. Her expression reflected something akin to fear. "How would you know that?"

"And were you born on New Year's Day?"

"That's it. What are you, Robin, some kind of perverted stalker?" She braced her hands on the table and pushed her chair back from the table, preparing to leap to her feet and bolt for the door. "Believe me, I don't need—"

"In 1945?"

She froze, then slumped back into her seat; her jaw dropped; and her answer came out a whimper. "Yes."

He exhaled audibly. "Thank God. I have been looking for you, April Naomi Paris, for nearly sixty years."

"But you're not . . . you can't be—"

"Listen, please, just listen, and accept what I tell you. I was a friend of your father's. He was my squad leader on Iwo Jima. He told me about you, about your mom, about how much he loved her, about that second honeymoon in Paris he'd planned. And how much he loved the little girl he never got the chance to see. He said April was a nice name, but he liked Naomi better, and he wrote your mother that in one of his last letters. Meanwhile, I've been carrying something with me all these years. It's a gift. I was supposed to give it to your mother, but I was never able to find her. It's something he wanted you both to have." He saw her tears forming, saw her hands tremble. "Please wait here; I'll be right down. When I'm done, I'll answer any and all of your questions."

He returned from upstairs with an artist's portfolio, opened it, and slid a drawing encased in a clear plastic envelope across the table toward her. It was a beautifully rendered pencil portrait, a bust of a young Marine in his utility uniform. He wore a helmet canted slightly to the side, its straps unfastened, and he held a freshly lit cigarette in the corner of his grinning mouth. "Your father," he said. "Corporal Joseph Paris, United States Marine Corps. As I said, he was a friend, a very dear friend. This is what he looked like, as we were getting ready to ship out. It's yours now."

She stared at the portrait, stared at Robin, her mouth open.

Then he said, "How long have you been a vampire?"

All color drained from her face, and she fainted.

Naomi came to lying on Robin's sofa, a pillow under her head and a thicker one under her feet. Her host sat on a kitchen chair he'd pulled up alongside. He had a mug in his hand, but no steam came from this one.

With his free hand, he helped her to a seated position. "I thought you might need this," he said as he offered the mug.

She recognized the coppery smell. With a hand she fought to keep from shaking, she accepted it and looked inside. "It's . . . blood."

He nodded. "Voluntarily given, I'd add. For a fee, naturally."

"You're . . . really like me."

He said yes.

Naomi sipped from the mug, then tilted it to her lips and took deep gulps. When she'd emptied the mug, she handed it back. "Thank you."

He handed her a napkin. "I saw you looking at Jessie's portrait earlier. You're very perceptive, you know. And to answer the question you're about to ask, yes. But how did you know I was the artist?"

"Oh, wow. When I was a student in Arts High—"

"You went to Arts High?"

"Yes. Don't tell me—no, let me answer your question first. My teachers told me that one way to analyze the quality of a painting is that if there's a drape, or a full pleated skirt, it should appear almost three-dimensional when you look at it. But if you cover everything but the drape or skirt, it should look two-dimensional. It's a *trompe l'oeil*. Kind of like the fly on your Hargrove painting. The Stover painting has that quality, and so does the painting of Anna in her ball gown on the play program."

"You are very perceptive."

"Who was Mrs. Lemuel Stover?"

"A dear friend, for many years. In fact, Jessie was the first person in my life up to that time whom I could truly call a friend. Also the first friend who knew me for what I was, for what I am, and it didn't matter to her. When she first realized it, she called me a hant."

"A hant?"

"In today's terms, a haunt; a ghost; a creature of the night. But she had no fear of me. We remained friends from her adolescence until her death of old age."

"She didn't ask you to turn her."

He shook his head. "No, even as she came to terms with her mortality, she never asked to be turned."

"On the subject of mortality. You asked me before I, um, left you for a bit, how long since I was turned. I was twenty-seven. And I've been twenty-seven for some twenty-two years."

"And I've been twenty-six, give or take a year, since . . . get ready . . . 1619."

She gasped. "You can't be. You're, what, four hundred years old?"

"And then some. But people tell me I don't look a day over three fifty."

"Huh. So many questions, Robin, so much I have to know."

"I'll answer what I can. And offer a few questions of my own."

She nodded toward the mug. "I hate to be a pig."

"There's more in the fridge. I keep it hidden in the back." He walked into the kitchen, conscious of her eyes following him, and returned with a stainless steel flask and a second mug. "To secrets shed," he said and clinked their mugs. "And secrets shared." They drank in silence.

Naomi placed her empty mug on the coffee table. "Do your . . . fangs . . . hinge on the roof of your mouth like mine?"

"Indeed. But don't say I'll show you mine if you show me yours." He chuckled, and Naomi surprised herself by smiling.

"Where do you get your supply from? Unless you don't think I should know."

"Soon after settling in, I found what you might call a volunteer in Harrisburg, a section known as the Allison Hill district. It's a pretty tough neighborhood, but she's a pretty tough cookie herself, and no one bothers me when they see me coming. I guess I'm under her protection. I visit Jasmine once every week or two. We make an appointment—aren't cell phones wonderful? The woman thinks I'm a weirdo, that I'm really play-acting, because she doesn't actually feel my fangs, and by the time she comes around the wounds have healed." He held up the flask, empty now. "I take this and a small funnel with me. By the time I've drunk my fill, she's already woozy and either doesn't notice or doesn't care. Plus, she's always a little high on something anyway and passes out before I start to fill the flask."

Naomi looked pensive. "I don't believe I'm saying this, but . . . does this Jasmine person have a friend?"

She shared her story into the night, and when Naomi mentioned the name of Daciana, Robin—who had abandoned the kitchen chair for the sofa's matching loveseat—bolted upright.

"What is it?" she asked.

"Daciana: slim, long dark hair, dark eyes, a voice so smooth it's almost hypnotic?"

"Yes."

"Naomi, we have a common sire. Or sire-ess, whatever. Daciana made me too."

She looked at her lap and then back at Robin. "Even more ancient than you are, then, no offense intended. It's true, she and Alphonse were both involved, but it was my little Joseph who actually made me. After that monster Alphonse made him first. Which was after Daciana made Alphonse, of course. Joseph I could forgive, he was only four. The other two? Never." She added, "You remember that double murder in the Hilton a few weeks ago?" He said yes. "That was Daciana's doing. Hers and Alphonse's. It was their way of showing me that I couldn't escape, that they'd always find me."

"I assume it was Joseph who blew the whistle."

"He believes he fell in love with her—remember, he's four years old in body only; he's in his twenties chronologically—and he believes that she loves him too. That she can see beyond the physical, that they're true soul mates. Huh. Whatever that means."

"I would challenge the concept that Daciana ever had a soul. And I'm sorry for your son. Life must be hell for him."

She shook her head and stared at her lap. "It is. And speaking of Daciana, I wouldn't credit Alphonse with a soul either. He's the one who killed my mother and grandmother in cold blood. Sorry, no pun intended. Joseph's note . . . his note said he was going home to Newark to be with Daciana. It didn't mention Alphonse, but he was with her, he had to have been. Daciana couldn't overpower two men by herself, and Alphonse is very strong. I'm worried about Joseph, worried to death, but there's nothing I can do. I was holding him a virtual prisoner in my house, and frankly, that's how he must've seen himself. I can't blame him, but I do fear for him. He's still my baby. I guess he'll always be my baby."

Then she looked up and asked the question that was on both their minds: "What do we do now?"

Chapter Twenty-Seven

"It's past midnight," Robin said. "Do you feel well enough to drive home?"

"I don't think I want to go home." Naomi stood and walked to the kitchen table, where her father's portrait lay.

Robin followed and stood behind her. He didn't touch her; she looked fragile enough to break. "You don't have to if you don't want. I have a spare bedroom upstairs."

"I know."

"You know?"

"I live two blocks away. Same development, same floor plan. I walked here."

"I didn't know we were neighbors."

"I didn't either, until you wrote your address on the invitation. And thanks for not thinking I'm trying to seduce you." She turned to face him. Her eyes were tired.

"Wouldn't dream of it." He smiled gently. "All right, not a hundred percent true. But lovemaking isn't what you need right now, and even if you said you did, I wouldn't attempt to take advantage of you. I've never been a fan of exploitation."

"Robin, let me explain something." She folded her hands to her chest. "Only twice in my life have I had sex. Two times. And both times it was more the sex that had me than the other way around, and let me tell you, it was beyond ugly. You can imagine. Or maybe you can't. But to be frank, I don't even know what real lovemaking is like."

"Allow me to let you in on a little secret. For all intents and purposes, I don't either, although my reason isn't so traumatic as yours. I didn't dare let myself fall in love, ever."

"For the obvious reason. But what a toll it must've taken on you, to deny yourself that."

"You're right. I'll admit, I never denied my physical needs, but while emotion was definitely involved, devotion never really played a huge role."

She looked at him from beneath drooping eyelids and forced a weak smile. "Who would expect a young, virile man to deny himself sex for four hundred years? But Robin, do you know what I need most of all right now? A hug. A warm, comforting hug. Can you do that for me, Mr. Robin Bradford? Or would you prefer Mr. Avery Palmer?"

He opened his arms, and like a letter in an envelope, she folded herself inside.

Robin lay in bed, the night-light in the hall outside his open door casting a wan halo on the wall and carpet. He couldn't sleep. *Finally, Joe,* he thought, *you can rest in peace. I'm so sorry about what happened to your wife and her mother, and I'm sorry for what happened to your daughter, but she's safe now, she's safe with me. And I promise you, I'll keep her safe for as long as she allows. She's a beautiful girl, Joe, inside and out.*

He wondered if Joe could actually hear him, wherever his spirit might be.

He heard movement in the hall, the shuffling of bare feet on carpet.

"I couldn't sleep," said the silhouette in his doorway.

"Come in," he said.

She wore only her bra and panties. As she sat on the bed and drew the covers back, he noted that her undergarments were purely utilitarian, in no way designed to be alluring. A modest two-piece bathing suit would reveal more skin.

"Can we cuddle?" she asked. "I need to be cuddled."

"Get under the covers and back up to me."

They nested like spoons in a drawer. He draped his arm across her waist, and before he drifted off he felt her raise his hand to her lips and kiss it.

Naomi awoke to an empty bed and the smell of coffee and—and Taylor Pork Roll. A salty slice of heaven she hadn't tasted since she left New Jersey. As she propped herself on her elbows, she saw Robin standing in the doorway with breakfast on a tray.

"Enjoy it," he said with a grin. "Because this is a one time only deal."

"So you say." She looked at the tray, atop which sat a toasted hard roll filled with pork roll, cheese, and a fried egg. Coffee on the side.

"What time is it?"

"Almost noon."

"Oh."

He set the tray before her. "I already ate. Want company?"

"Please."

He sat on his side of the bed and leaned against the headboard. "It's good to have you here," he said.

"It's good being here—with someone who knows me for what I am as well as who I am."

"And who really does care for you, regardless."

She took a bite of the sandwich and sighed. "Aren't we the pair?" After a few more bites, she said, "Robin, how did my dad die? Did you see it?"

"I did. He was cut down by machine gun fire while he was trying to save a member of his squad who'd been hit. He died instantly." This was not entirely true—but it was kinder than giving her the gruesome details. The image of Joe's body, being stitched back and forth by a hail of bullets until his torso fell from his hips would haunt him forever. No need to extend that image to his daughter's psyche. "I managed to kill the gunner myself a few seconds later."

"Thank you." She studied his face. "You're my hero."

She put down her sandwich as he took her hand in his. He said, "The heroes are the ones who didn't come home. The rest of us were just lucky." He considered that a moment. "The rest of them, I mean. It's not hard to risk your life when you know you can't be killed."

Naomi stared at him. "I think there's more to it than that. Were you ever seriously injured, though?"

He thought back. "I was shot a few times during the Revolutionary War, the War of 1812, and the Civil War. I survived the Spanish-American war without a scratch. In the Great War—that's World War One to you—I was bayoneted and later exposed to mustard gas. It burned like the fires of hell. People like us might not be able to die, but as you can testify I'm sure, we do feel pain."

"Poor baby." Her look said she wasn't being sarcastic.

"Should I go on?"

"Yes."

"Okay. I was shot a couple of times in World War Two, although not in Iwo. Then came Korea. Freezing cold, and frostbite burns just as much as heat. Vietnam? Stabbed, shot, caught shrapnel from a grenade. Decided to sit out the Gulf War."

"Who would blame you? But Robin, did you live just to fight wars? I mean, is that what you do?"

"Naomi, listen. I know you've heard the cliché that no one hates war more than a warrior. Like most clichés, it's true. I just wish people would understand, I mean, really understand that. We're not a bunch of hired hit men. Thing is, though, we love our country more than we hate fighting. I lived during the reign of kings, remember, and I know how very special this government of the people, by the people, for the people experiment is. And how fragile. It needs to be protected, whether the average citizen knows it or not."

"And that's why you do it."

"That's why I do it. And remember, I never had to leave a girlfriend or family behind."

"Because you never had either." He said that was true. "How lonely you must have been."

They loaded the dishwasher and sat at the dinette table enjoying the rest of the coffee.

"I still can't believe you're four hundred years old," Naomi said.

"Don't spread the word. People will want to know my secret."

"I remember a line from *Hamlet:* 'There are more things in heaven and earth, Horatio, than are dreamt of in your philosophy.'"

"Would you believe I saw *Hamlet* performed by the real Shakespeare troupe? They called themselves The King's Men. And that *your philosophy* was originally *our philosophy,* meaning *what we've been taught?*"

"Ordinarily, no, and the difference wouldn't have meant that much to me anyway. I can't imagine everything you've seen, everything you've experienced."

"One other thing, and I might as well tell you now, despite my middle-class appearances, I'm very wealthy. Over the centuries I've made money, invested it, gathered items

181

in one era and sold them as antiques and artifacts in a much later one. But my real wealth, our currency now, yours and mine, is simply time. We may invest it wisely or squander it foolishly, but either way, we are none the poorer for it, always the richer."

She sipped from her mug and stared into the blueness of his eyes. "That sounds almost rehearsed."

"Actually, it very nearly is. It's something I've thought of, reflected on, many times. As you will now, if you haven't already."

"I think of it sometimes, our immortality that is, as a curse."

"It can be that. But only if you allow it."

"So, speaking of time, I repeat my question of last night: what do we do now?"

Now, the living present, went on until the end of the school year in late May. They worked in separate buildings, far enough apart that rumors seeded during play rehearsals were soon gone fallow. Year's end brought a flurry of activity for both youngsters and adults: the former fretting about taking their finals, the latter fretting about the tedium of grading them; the former looking forward to the final dance, the latter wondering if their students would miss them as much as they would miss their students; and both looking forward to a well-earned summer respite.

Friday evenings, Naomi would walk to Robin's home or he would walk to hers, where one or the other would cook. Nighttime would find them sharing a bed, always platonic, she wearing sexless pajamas and kissing him on the cheek before rolling over with her back to him.

One Saturday morning after an evening at his place, Robin awoke early and decided to take a jog around the neighborhood. As he neared Naomi's townhouse, he saw a gunmetal gray Ford Crown Victoria standing out front, its engine purring. Taking caution to appear disinterested, he glanced briefly at the driver as he jogged by. Naomi's Civic was in the driveway, as usual; the single-car garage was barely wide enough to fit a car inside without banging the door against the wall when getting out or in.

The Crown Vic's license plate showed the car was registered in New Jersey.

When he arrived back at his townhouse, Robin saw Naomi cooking breakfast. The smell of sausage patties permeated the air, and he saw the waffle iron was hot and ready for batter.

"Time for a shower?" he asked.

"Not if you value your life," she replied.

"Your will, my lady."

After they'd eaten, Robin told Naomi about the Ford with the New Jersey plates. Her expression soured.

"Alphonse," she said. "Has to be. He's checking up on me, making sure I haven't tried to run away again. You didn't see anyone else in the car, did you?"

"If you mean someone in a child's seat in the back, sorry, no. But if I'd known it was Alphonse . . ."

"What?"

He looked at her, his expression steel. "I'd have killed him without a second thought—but with extreme prejudice." She stared at him, shocked. He said, "I've come a long way, baby."

The school year ended. The students fled into summer and the staff wasn't far behind. After a few hugs, wishes for a great vacation, and waves, they too dispersed to their summertime pursuits. Most would be back, voluntarily, in late July or early August, already preparing their classrooms for the new school year.

Later that night, Naomi joined Robin for the first time on his excursion to Allison Hill. Jasmine was waiting, and she had brought a friend whom she introduced as Shoniqua. If Jasmine looked formidable to Naomi, Shoniqua looked downright fearsome. Every inch of her face and body, at least what they could see, was decorated either with tattoos or piercings. When she opened her mouth, a gold ball showed in her tongue, and what looked like a diamond stud was affixed to an incisor. She inclined her head at the introductions but said nothing. No one offered a handshake.

Jasmine led them to what she called her crib—a dingy flat with tobacco-browned windows and walls, bare light bulbs, and furniture that had probably been picked up from the side of the road. Money was exchanged, and the women sat on wooden chairs next to a Formica-topped table.

Jasmine handed her friend a pill and a dirty glass half-filled with a clear liquid—not water, but vodka. The two of them swallowed and drank, smiled, and lay their arms on the tabletop. "Pleasure doin' business with you, Mr. Lestat," said Jasmine as she and Shoniqua rested their heads on their arms and slipped into stupor.

Naomi frowned at him. "Lestat?"

"Shh. Tell you later."

"No need. I've read the books, too."

"Now, like this," Robin instructed as he took Jasmine's free arm and delicately sank his fangs into the crook of her elbow. Naomi observed and followed suit with Shoniqua. They drank their fill and then filled a pair of steel flasks, using a plastic funnel to catch the flow. When the flasks were full, they applied a coating of saliva to the wounds and bent the elbows up. Almost immediately, the holes in the women's arms healed, and a rash began to form.

"All's well," said Robin as he placed their arms on the tabletop. "Let's go."

They returned to his town house and placed the flasks in the refrigerator, showered separately, and returned to the living room wearing pajamas and light robes. Then, like roommates thoroughly comfortable in each other's presence, they watched television for an hour, caught the late news, and went to bed.

As usual, Naomi kissed Robin on the cheek before turning her back to him. "Cuddle?" she said, and he rolled onto his side against her back. He draped his arm around her waist, again as usual, but at that moment something changed.

When she took his hand, he expected her to bring it to her lips for her customary goodnight kiss before drifting into sleep. Instead, she placed his hand on her belly—it was bare, her buttons unfastened—and drew it to her breast. He cupped her softness, felt her hardened nipple, and heard her draw in a breath. Then she rolled toward him and kissed him for the first time on the lips; tentatively at first, but then with a passion she could neither deny nor constrain.

Neither of them said a word; there was no need.

They lay in silence afterward, bodies glistening in the nightlight's glow, their breathing nearly normal again. Robin cradled Naomi in one arm, and she snuggled her head into his chest as he stroked her face and hair with his free hand. When his fingertips found her lips, she kissed them.

He knew not to ask her questions; whatever he said would sound insipid. He waited. Naomi's fingers slid slowly down his torso; her fingernails teased him with exquisite tenderness; and she felt him harden again.

She rolled on top this time, and their motions became almost agonizingly slow—exactly what they wanted, to make their lovemaking last. And this time, whispered endearments, breathed into each other's ears, accompanied their passage to mutual climax.

Next morning, Robin asked Naomi to let the lease on her town house expire and move in with him—as in, today. "But promise me you'll buy some sexy nightgowns and underwear," he said, and she kissed him and assured him she would. "I'll head to the mall today. Last night, thanks to you, was probably the best night of my life. And tonight, watch out, because it's going to get even better. Be advised, mister, I'm coming for you."

"My, my, when did you become the predator and I the prey?"

"Do you object, my vampire lover?"

"Who, me? Predate away, predate away."

After breakfast, they walked to Naomi's town house with the intention of filling her trunk with her clothes and transporting them to Robin's. When they walked inside her door, they saw that the answering machine had a message. "School?" she wondered. "Did I forget to do something?" She pressed the Play button. The voice didn't carry Declan Mulligan's gentle lilt. It was husky, low, coarse—a voice she knew too well.

"Hey, Naomi. Alley Oop. HUmboldt 3-3989. Yeah, I kept your old number active. I'll be at your house Monday at nine if you wanna talk. Just callin' to tell you your kid's dead.

"Oh yeah, that's Area Code 201, by the way, in case you forgot."

Chapter Twenty-Eight: Alphonse

Why she had to take the damn kid back with them was beyond him. Listening to him yak yak yak from the kiddie seat in the back of the car was like to drive him nuts. All he, Alphonse, wanted to do was screw with Naomi's mind, put the fear of God into her, but no, Daciana had to stop at her house and pick up the brat. And he was waiting there for her, all his stuff packed by the door.

She hadn't mentioned that part of the arrangement.

The kid hated him, he knew. Not that he was learning it for the first time, mind you. Daciana had told him as much one night at the college, like she was putting him in his place or something. Women could be cruel. Or, he thought, maybe she was getting Alphonse mentally prepared for some kind of empty nest situation, a little tough love. After all, she'd be leaving after finals for some Podunk school in New England, and he'd still be here in Essex County College, mopping floors and dusting desks, returning home to a whining nag.

Joseph was returned to his old house, and Alphonse had to supply him with food and other essentials, because even in a nice neighborhood—and this wasn't a nice neighborhood—you couldn't let a four-year-old walk to the corner store on his own. It was a bullshit situation, but he had his orders.

Orders. Like the time a couple days ago when she ordered him to take the kid to work with him. They were gonna play a game, she said.

Some game.

There was this chick who always stuck around after Daciana's last class of the night, sucking up to the teacher, asking about this and that, scientific bullshit that Alphonse didn't understand and couldn't have cared less about. Was she a suck-up? Was the kid a lez? The only thing about her that interested Alphonse was her figure—like, to die for. As for her face: not a two-bagger, definitely not, but not something you'd stop and stare at if you passed her on the sidewalk either. Her name was Darleen D'Andrea; that much he knew. Good Guinea name at least.

That night after class, the chick stuck around as usual and, as planned, Alphonse strolled in with Joseph in tow. Darleen liked to cream when she saw the kid. "How cute!" she said, her voice up a notch or so. She said to Daciana, "Your little boy?" Daciana smiled and nodded, like a proud mommy. "What's his name?" She told her. "Joseph! What a handsome little boy you are!" She squatted, her short skirt riding up to her thighs. "Come here, let me hold you!"

She was really layin' it on thick, but Joseph played his part perfectly and ran into her arms. In fact, he buried his face in her boobs, and she squealed and actually held his head there like she was getting ready to nurse him. Alphonse half expected Joseph to motorboat her, with his head tucked between those lung warts, blubbering. That's what he'd do, given the chance. But Joseph didn't. Kid could've won an Academy Award for cutest performance by a baby vampire.

"Joseph wanted to see where Mommy works," Daciana said. "Mr. Puglio here was sitting with him while class was in session, but now we're going to give him a tour of the lab." She looked at Darleen, who slowly released Joseph and stood up. "Would you mind, Darleen, joining us, so we can do a kind of demonstration lesson for Joseph? It's not too late for you, I hope."

"I'd love it," Darleen said and glommed onto Joseph's little hand.

"Let's go, then."

The three of them walked to the lab, their footfalls echoing in the now half-darkened and empty corridors. As they walked, Daciana casually asked the girl about her family and social life. "I feel I would like to know you as a person, rather than just another student, Darleen."

The girl's face lit up like the neon sign in front of the old Empire Burlesque house back in the day.

"Well, Dr. Moceanu, I don't know what to say, I'm so . . . I don't know, flattered. I mean, no teacher has ever taken any personal interest in me before." She considered a minute. "Well, except for this lech in high school bio, but I told him to fuck off, know what I mean? Oops, sorry, Joseph, I normally don't use that kind of language."

Joseph looked up at her and blinked his eyes, as if he'd fallen in love with her already.

"But anyway," she said, getting back to Daciana's question, "My folks live in Montclair, but I stay with my boyfriend here in the city."

"Oh? And your parents? Do you see them much?"

"Nah. They're my way or the highway people, you know what I mean, and when I told them I was going to live with my boyfriend they freaked and told me not to come back until I came to my senses. I mean, they only met Luis once, never even gave him a chance. Maybe it was the tats, maybe it was the multiple earrings, I don't know. But hey, that's parents for you, right? I mean, present company excepted and all, you know?"

Daciana nodded, all smiles and saccharine. "And your boyfriend? Luis, you said his name was?"

"Yeah, well, he's all right, I mean the bloom fades after awhile, you know what I mean? Sometimes he doesn't come home for a few days, sometimes it's like I'm not even there. I mean, if I were to just, like, disappear, I don't think he'd even notice."

"That's a shame, dear. Let me assure you, right now, you have great value to me."

"Am I blushing, Professor? Because, I mean, I feel my cheeks getting hot."

Alphonse, walking a few steps behind the trio, was invisible to them. But that was about to change, once they got to the lab.

Which they did, another few yards down the corridor. Acting the gentleman, he opened the door for them and they walked in, Daciana standing at one end of the lab bench, beside the built-in sink, with Darleen facing her, and Joseph releasing the girl's hand to stand beside Daciana. Alphonse stood behind the girl, ready to spring into action when it was time.

"Now, Darleen," Daciana began, "we have some lab equipment that I haven't shown the other students, but I'd like to share it with you. It's rather esoteric. Do you know what that means?"

"Uh-huh," Darleen said with a slight shrug that told them she didn't know at all, but was trying to make a sophisticated impression.

"Good. I appreciate your sense of scientific inquiry. I have from the start, you know. Why don't you just sit on the lab bench here, make yourself comfortable, while Mr. Puglio gets it out for us?"

"Okay." She hopped up and planted her buttocks on the bench. Her legs hung over the side, her feet well clear of the floor.

"Mr. Puglio?"

He reached into a cabinet and withdrew a leather mask consisting of a full-face piece and a series of straps and buckles for cinching it to the back of the head. The front had a T-shaped opening for the eyes and nose. Below it, where an opening for the mouth would be, the mask was solid. It looked like it was made a long time ago.

Darleen frowned. "What's that?" she said.

"It's called a restraining mask," Daciana said. "Used during the Inquisition to keep the cries of victims muted while the torturers did their work."

"But...I mean, what's that got to do with, with...?"

Before she could finish, Alphonse shoved the girl onto her back so hard her head banged against the bench top, rendering her nearly unconscious. Before she could recover, he fastened her to the bench as Daciana strapped the mask around her head and cinched the buckles painfully tight.

Darleen opened her brown eyes then, and they reflected the intensity of her fear. She struggled uselessly against her bonds. Her shouts died inside the mask.

Then Daciana lifted Joseph onto the bench and handed him a scalpel. Darleen saw it and her body went into convulsions.

"It's okay, Darleen," he said in his little boy's voice. "This isn't for you, it's for your clothes."

Joseph unbuttoned and parted Darleen's sleeveless blouse and sliced delicately through her bra straps. The bra fastened in the front, and he unhooked it and peeled it aside.

Her skirt was next to go—a slit up the side, and it parted. "Like the Red Sea," Joseph said. Her panties were bikini style, with lacy fringes around the top and crotch. He sliced through one thin side and pulled the panties free, casting them to the floor. Her shoes were last to go, leaving her naked on top of the bench. "Oh, man," he said. "What I would love to do to you."

Daciana said, "Why don't you, then?"

The man-boy looked shocked. "Really? You don't mind? It's okay with you?"

"Of course, dear. As long as it's not *with* me. Besides, you've been very patient, and all things considered, I believe you deserve a treat."

Inflamed with lust as he was, Joseph never considered the phrase *all things considered.* "Darleen, you just relax. You're going to love this."

As the girl lifted her head to look down in disbelief, she saw what she'd once thought was an adorable little boy drive his face between her splayed legs. She tried to recoil, to twist away, but her bonds would not allow her. Instead, she could only weep, tears dripping onto the edge of the mask's crude cutouts.

Next, Joseph crawled up the girl's body and ravished her breasts with his hands, mouth, and teeth as Daciana looked on and Alphonse looked away. When Joseph was finished, puncture marks surrounded Darleen's small dark nipples. He looked up and showed her his tiny fangs. Darleen thrust her shoulders again against the bench top, arched her back, and twisted her body from side to side. The spasms from her throat gave evidence of her non-stop screams. The three vampires could actually hear some of her nearly muted cries as the part of the mask covering her mouth vibrated.

The other two joined Joseph in the feast, Alphonse sucking from the inside of the girl's elbow and Daciana from one side of her neck while Joseph moved back down to the inside of her thigh, his fingers as busy as his mouth. Darleen's eyes began to roll back into her head, and when Joseph looked up and noticed, he picked up the scalpel he'd left on the bench top.

"Darleen," he said to the dying girl, his voice raspy now, no longer a little boy's at all, "do you remember I said this scalpel wasn't for you, it was just for your clothes? Well, I lied. Sorry, but I need to do this." As Daciana and Alphonse stood back, he slashed the girl's throat and buried his face into the wound, sucking deeply.

When he was sated, he looked up at Daciana with a bloody smile, which she returned. Then he glanced back at Alphonse and offered him a scowl—which was also returned.

The next day, Alphonse wondered if Daciana would actually take the kid to New England with her. Like as her son or something. Sitting at his kitchen table, drinking coffee and smoking a cigarette, with Maria at morning mass as usual, he reflected upon his own sons.

Angelo was the first, his get-out-of-Vietnam baby. Dumb shit hooked up with some punks and then got hooked on drugs when he was in Barringer High. Well, Alley Oop might've been a punk too, but he never took drugs or dealt them. Man had to have some standards.

He'd wanted to name him Alphonse Junior at first, but Maria said no, she wanted to name him after her father, like he was some kind of saint. Hell, her old man was mostly an absentee father and a drunk to boot. And his support payments, when they came at all, were either late or too little. Go figure. So they named him Angelo, like the angel he wasn't, and Alphonse found himself playing second fiddle all of a sudden. Now he was only good for bringing in the bucks while Maria oohed and ahhed over the little prick.

Like she used to over his big prick.

So years later, when the police called and told them to come down and identify Angelo's body, it was his job to stop his wife from going off the rails, all hysterical, embarrassing him in front of all these strangers in white coats and blue uniforms.

It was when the second kid came, just a couple years after Angelo was born, that Alphonse got his way with the name. While the boys were growing up, Angelo made Junior's life miserable, always picking on him, getting him into trouble.

So when Junior was ten, Alphonse—as much to give the kid a break from his brother's taunts as get him out of the house, to give Alphonse Senior some peace and quiet—enrolled him in the Boy Scouts. Every Wednesday night, Junior walked to Garfield School's basement, where Troop

28 met. He earned his Tenderfoot badge, then his Second Class and First Class badges. He went on weekend camporees, even spent a couple weeks in the summer at Camp Mohican in Blairstown, up near the Delaware Water Gap.

But Junior wasn't your All-American boy, no matter his rank and his merit badges. He was a sadist, like Alphonse's buddy Nicky Beans, now long dead. He liked to torment the spooks and the Riccans, and if he came upon a stray animal, the animal was bound to meet a grisly end. Alphonse told him once about how Nicky had tied a kitten to the subway track—why he told him, he didn't know—and sure enough, Junior found a pregnant stray cat, and—well, enough of that.

At least Junior managed to survive through high school. He was smart enough not to get involved with the druggies. He worked for some guys downtown these days, never told him what he did—Alphonse never asked, either—but he brought home cash and never paid income tax. Never paid for room and board, either, and Maria never asked the little dickhead for it. Tough as he was, looking at her the way he often did, maybe Maria knew better than to ask. Maybe he did, too.

Every year, Junior would take a couple weeks' vacation and go hiking, of all things. Said he was still a Boy Scout at heart. He never told his parents where he was going, and they figured it might be better that they not know. But Alphonse, who still read the newspaper—mostly on the job, while perched on the john—did notice that every year, coincidentally during Junior's vacation time, some hiker somewhere would always be found savagely murdered on some backwoods trail. And the cases were never solved.

Maria never read the paper, except for Sunday, when she looked for bargains in the circulars. She began going to morning mass every day after Angelo's death, which was fine by Alphonse, as he got home after she left and was usually asleep (or pretended to be) when she got home. Then she'd hit the Guinea red and her smokes, maybe make some pasta for his dinner before he left for the college. He used to complain about it—macaron' every night, can't she cook something different for a change? But no more. Why bother?

Maria used to be a looker, in a skanky kind of way. Now her looks were gone, her voice sounded like a frog, and her eyes were sunk in. She was skinnier, too, like she could hide behind a broomstick. Maybe she had cancer or something.

He was aware of his own looks now, of the fact that he looked no older than he had when Daciana turned him, twenty-seven years ago. He was sixty and still looked to be around thirty at the most. He'd changed his hairstyle— the days of the DA were long gone—and had begun adding touches of gray around his temples. If Maria were to say anything about how he never seemed to age, he would credit it to his Mediterranean heritage and his clean living. But she never said a thing. Probably didn't even notice. Or if she did, she didn't care.

Clean living? If she only knew. Knew how some nights, usually once a week, sometimes twice, he would lure some spook into the school with promise of a smoke or, in the winter, of warmth, and then truss them up and take them to Daciana for draining. Sometimes she'd do it quick and clean, but other times she'd get . . . imaginative, she called it. Those nights, he might have to excuse himself and come back later for sloppy seconds.

The sex, though, was always first rate. He wondered if she'd find someone like him when she went north to that new job. *Not friggin' likely,* he thought.

The faculty member she'd said had an interest in her never existed. She'd just told him that to keep him in line. She was good at keeping him in line.

Complicating things was the brat, Joseph. He was his responsibility, Daciana told him whenever he complained. Reminded him of the fisherman's wife: You caught it, you clean it. He got it, but he didn't like it. Kid treated him like shit, he did, his own father. Now he's telling Daciana that he expects her to take him with her, that he can't stay in Jersey with Alphonse; that he loves her and knows that she loves him. He proved he was worthy of her love—at least in his own mind—with the way he handled that snatch Darleen.

Well, if Daciana did take him, he could rent out the house next door. In fact, he could even sell it. Neighborhood was going to shit anyway, what with the Puerto Ricans starting to move in down the block. He wouldn't tell Maria. She still didn't know that he'd been collecting rent from Naomi before she skipped town and that he stashed the cash in a separate bank account. She didn't even know that Alphonse owned the house.

After their blood orgy last night with Darleen, Daciana told him that her responsibilities to the college were nearly satisfied. The term was done, the students were gone—last night's class closed out the term—and she just had grades to post and administrative paperwork to fill out before her final checkout in a day or two. Then she would be heading north to New Hampshire. Before she left, however, she and Alphonse would to pay a visit to little Joseph. He wondered what that might be about. He wondered, too, what was to become of himself. She had in the past casually mentioned how she'd *disposed* of men who'd disappointed her, or who had lost their value to her. He would do anything to assure that his head remained firmly attached to his neck.

Including keeping his switchblade knife hidden in his pocket, for whatever good that might do. Still, a guy couldn't be too careful these days.

When they opened the door to the second floor flat of 239 Fifth Street, they saw two suitcases at the foot of the stairs. The same suitcases that Joseph had brought with him from Hershey. Alphonse scowled when he saw them, but Daciana smirked. Slung over her back, and looking totally out of place, was a gem-studded leather sheath sporting a coat of arms that depicted a dragon inside a shield. The hilt protruding from the top was wrapped in oil-stained leather, the hexagonal-shaped end cap inlaid with gold and ivory. Her appearance reminded him of the female warriors he'd seen in samurai movies.

He himself, as directed, carried a supermarket bag with two full-body aprons inside.

Daciana breezed up the stairs, where tiny Joseph stood waiting. Alphonse followed, wondering if the boy had seen the weapon. Without preamble, she shooed Joseph into the bathroom.

"I don't need to go to the bathroom," he protested. "I'm ready to go with you. Didn't you see my bags downstairs?"

"To the bathroom," she said again.

"Why?"

"Because I said so, Joseph. Because I said so."

Alphonse had to hold back a smirk when he saw the boy pout; but then, there was that vicious-looking sword strapped to her back. Joseph in fact did notice that. His face showed something other than confidence. He too had heard about the sword.

Joseph was told to sit on the lid of the toilet, and Daciana and Alphonse stood over him. She reached into the pocket of her black slacks and handed Alphonse a ring. It was heavy gold, with a delicately cut emerald center surrounded by tiny diamonds. The inside of the band was engraved. "Once I'm gone," she said, "you can take it to an auction house that specializes in antiquities. It once belonged to Queen Anne, wife of King James the First of England."

He looked at the ring. "What? You're saying it's old?"

She shook her head, her lips tight. "Yes, Alphonse, it's old. It dates from the early 1600s. I appropriated it after the queen died." He furrowed his brow. "Oh, don't look so surprised. All her ladies in waiting helped themselves to at least some of her baubles; it was our job to inventory her treasures, you see. It was understood among us that we might liberate one or two pieces of her loot, discreetly of course, not so many that their absence would be noted. We considered it a token of appreciation for our service."

Joseph's head swiveled from one to the other. "You were a lady in waiting, to a queen?"

Daciana ignored him, her eyes still on Alphonse. "You will reap a huge sum for this. If you invest your gains wisely, you will be able to live off the interest they accrue without ever needing to work again. Further, I want you to sell both this house and the one you share with your wife and relocate near Naomi. Let her know you are there, watching her."

"Um . . . why? What's going on?"

"Please understand, Alphonse, you remain alive at my pleasure, as I might have need of you again at some future time. I am reasonably confident, having experienced the . . . *inconvenience* that resulted from your early impetuosity"— she glanced at Joseph—"you won't jeopardize yourself. That said, the indelicate situation before us is all of your doing, and you must assume responsibility for undoing it."

Joseph squirmed. "Undoing it?" he said. "What do you mean, undoing it?"

Daciana ignored him. "And understand too, Alphonse, I shall be checking on you myself, mostly unannounced, to see that you are keeping Naomi in line." He waited, his question unspoken. "Yes, my Mediterranean minion, I am being charitable, to both you and Naomi, which is something I am not especially known for. I have my reasons."

He fingered the switchblade knife in his pocket. "Okay. But for the record, once you're not around, how will you know if I'm doing what you told me to? Suppose I don't want to sell the house and move near Naomi?"

"Trust me, I have ways of knowing. A maker always knows. Further, you will keep in regular touch with me. I will buy a separate cell phone dedicated to our correspondence. As will you."

Alphonse took a half step back as he studied the expression on Daciana's face. "Naomi could be a threat, you've got to realize that. If she wanted to, she could expose you as well as me. Why not go down to Pennsylvania and off her yourself, just to be sure there was no threat? She can't be of any use to you anymore."

"Alphonse, she never was of any use to me. Remember, this Joseph-Naomi turning was your doing. I would've been happier if I'd never met or even heard of Joseph and his mother. But you, metaphorically speaking, fouled the nest. So, would I be more secure if she were disposed of? Certainly. And one part of me wants to take you up on your suggestion. But as it stands, even if I were so inclined, I don't have the luxury of time. Criterion University phoned this morning and told me they needed me there day after tomorrow at the latest. School is letting out for the summer, and the administrative offices need to get me processed in before their personnel go on hiatus for a month. Don't ask, Alphonse. One doesn't challenge the bureaucracy."

"Especially if you're a new hire."

"Especially."

"But there's another reason that I choose not to terminate her existence. At least not yet."

"Oh? Like what?" She didn't respond. "And what's the reason for that shit-eatin' grin on your face?"

"Excuse me?"

"Sorry. But you know what I mean. Something's cooking inside that head of yours."

"There is. First, I've thought about it, and another part of me actually prefers keeping Naomi alive, at least for the time being. She is anonymous and discreet, we know that, and because of her discretion she doesn't pose a threat to someone's eventually discovering my existence. She doesn't kill, as we do, and her victims are always people who stand to lose more than gain were they to set the police on the trail of some beautiful woman who seduced and then robbed them. Frankly, you pose the bigger threat."

"No comment. So what's the other reason, then?"

Daciana looked from the boy to Alphonse. "I think, fundamentally, Naomi paints herself psychologically as a victim. Certainly of you, what you did to her, to her family, to the bastard you sired and then, compounding the sin, made a *strigoi*. But I also think she's being wound like a coiled spring, tighter and tighter, whenever you're around her. Someday, she might just come unsprung in front of you and snap."

"Uh-huh. And?"

"And that's why I want you near to her."

"You mean, to keep her from snapping?"

Daciana chuckled. "No, silly. To *make* her snap."

That threw him. "Huh? Why?"

"Trust me. I think you'll enjoy seeing the fire in her eyes as she transforms in the blink of an eye from a mouse to a lion. The meekest animal, when cornered . . ."

"Yeah, yeah, yeah. I get it."

"And then you may destroy her. Cut off her head with that knife you always keep in your pocket. The one you're manipulating now."

Alphonse started. He hadn't realized he'd had his right hand in his pocket, fingering the handle of his switchblade. Looking sheepish, he removed his hand and held it at his side.

"But you will ensure that when she does snap, it is at the right time and the right place. Which is to say, without witnesses and without any means of tracing the deed back to yourself. And then, you must report to me every bloody detail. Make me re-live the kill, vicariously. And after that," she concluded, her voice transitioning from demanding to beguiling, "we might discuss your moving to New Hampshire to be with me. To hunt together."

Alphonse brightened. "That's more like it."

Joseph, his head moving from one speaker to the next as if following a tennis match, finally reasserted his presence. "Hey. You two. You forgetting about me?" he said.

"Ah, yes—Joseph, Joseph, Joseph. I haven't forgotten you at all. In fact, I noticed just now you didn't show any emotion at all when we spoke about your father's killing your dear mother. I find that . . . interesting." Daciana unslung the sheath from behind her back and held it before her. She addressed Alphonse. "This artifact is even older than the ring I gave you. And much more valuable. It is not to be yours, by the way. You see the crest, yes?"

"Yeah, a dragon, so what? Dragons are a dime a dozen on things like that."

"But not the one on this scabbard. In my born tongue, the word for dragon is *Dracul*. The word could also mean devil. And this sword and this scabbard date back to my own youth."

"What are you saying, this comes from, like, some Dracula movie?"

"Dracul. The -*a* added to the word means *son of.*"

"Okay. Son of the dragon, son of the devil. Cool. But that movie guy's just a story, right? I mean, I never read the book, but—"

"So you do know there was a book first. That's reassuring. The real Dracula—that is, Vlad Tepes, son of the warrior prince known as Dracul—is no story. He was real, also a prince, and also a warrior—for Christ, if you can believe it, fighting against the Moslem armies of the Ottoman Turks. But he was not a *strigoi* . . . although he did have a taste for blood. For a time, Alphonse, Prince Vlad and I were lovers. And despite his delightful cruelty when it came to punishing others, he loved me, and he knew how to please me. When he was of a mind."

"What happened to him?"

"Killed in battle, the story goes." She offered a sardonic smile. "His head was never found."

Joseph said, his voice almost pleading, "But he was mortal, and he's dead, and now you're my lover, isn't that right, Daciana? I mean, after that girl in the lab, you know I can do the same for you, and I know you'd love it, I promise. As for your past lovers, I can forgive—"

"*Forgive?* You can *forgive?* Who are *you* to tell *me* you forgive?*" Her voice was a lash, and his head snapped back as if struck.

Joseph's voice grew high, a four-year-old's whine coupled with a young man's urgency. And fear. "You love me. I know you love me."

She laughed. "I love no one but myself."

"But you're taking me with you. You told me so."

"I lied. You're familiar with promises broken, I assume?" She slid a finger across her throat.

Daciana drew the sword and gently lowered the scabbard to the floor. The blade was polished, engraved with lettering in a language Alphonse did not know. "The English," Daciana explained to Alphonse, as if Joseph weren't even there, "used an axe to decapitate those deemed unfit to live. The condemned would have to tip the headsman with coins to ensure that the blade was sharp enough to cut through with a single stroke; otherwise, the procedure could get quite uncomfortable. The French, however, used a sword similar to this one. The condemned could kneel upright to receive the stroke rather than placing his head on a block of wood. Much more dignified, wouldn't you agree? This, of course, was long before the invention of the guillotine."

Alphonse looked from the sword to a suddenly sweating Joseph and back to Daciana. Her eyes were emotionless black orbs.

The man-boy broke out in tremors. He nearly foamed at the mouth as he stuttered through spittle. "You can't. No, Daciana! All right, listen, don't take me with you. Alphonse made me, I'm his son, I'm his responsibility. You said so. His, not yours. Look, you want him near my mother. Okay. He can take me back. I'll go back to living with her again, I can keep an eye on her every day, and everything will be fine, just like before. I won't say anything to anyone, I promise."

"I just made your mother your father's responsibility. I don't remember saying anything about you. Now, I want

199

you to take off your clothes, Joseph. All of them. No, don't get down from the seat."

Quaking, he obeyed. A moment later, he stood at eye level before them, naked, shamed, profoundly fearful for his life. "Daciana. You can't be doing this. After all the time we've spent together!"

Daciana snorted. "Our time together? Compared to what? My five hundred years and more of existence? You are but a snap of the fingers." *Snap.* "Like that. So. On to the business at hand. Your mother, she has studied art, has she not? Of course she has, she told me as much back when she thought we were friends." He nodded and began to blubber. "She told me she loved fine art, especially the art of the old masters. I have a certain connection to fine art as well. So tell me. Did she ever show you a certain painting by Raphael titled 'The Wisdom of Solomon'?"

"No," he said through sobs. "Never heard of it. Why? What's going on?"

"Alphonse? Need I ask you?"

"Who the hell's Solomon? Some Yid?"

Daciana shook her head. "Never mind. Just reach into your bag, take out an apron, and hand me one of the others. Loop yours around your neck and tie the straps around your waist."

Alphonse did as he was told.

Joseph tried to leap off the toilet lid and run, but Alphonse constrained him with a headlock. His fusillade of tiny kicks and panicked punches had no effect upon his maker.

Daciana put on her own apron and said, "Excellent. Now, Alphonse, you grab one ankle and I'll grab the other. Hold him upside down over the tub."

Joseph shrieked like a pig in a slaughterhouse.

Alphonse knew he would never forget what happened next. Even though, once again, he couldn't force himself to look.

Chapter Twenty-Nine

The phone rang Monday morning at nine, right on time. Alphonse let it ring four times before answering. "Yeah."

Naomi's voice would've broken the heart of someone who harbored any modicum of compassion. Which is to say it didn't affect Alphonse at all. "Yeah, he's dead. Daciana killed him. Like Solomon with the baby, but this time, ol' Solomon went through with it."

He pulled the phone from his ear and held the earpiece to his chest. "Holy shit, that broad can scream." When the vibration against his shirt subsided, he said, "Listen, cryin' won't bring him back. I mean, look at it this way, all your problems raisin' him are over, you should be happy. Now stop blubbering. I've got more to tell you."

He heard the sound of gasps mixed with groans, on the other end of the phone. "Okay. Now, Daciana's on her way to some college in New Hampshire, Criterion, I think she said, to teach up there. But before she left she told me she wanted me to move close to you. Keep an eye on you, you know?" He listened to her for just a moment. "Quit your whinin', I'm not gonna do it right away, I've got responsibilities of my own up here. But understand, Daciana's got some mumbo-jumbo way of keeping track of me and knowin' what I'm up to. Says she'll be checking up on me, and that means I'll be checking up on you. But once my responsibilities here are settled, I will be moving close to you, like she told me to, make sure everything's copacetic, got it? So you be cool, don't say nothin' about nothin', and everything'll be all right."

Shit, he thought. *I just realized. Daciana may be a real bitch, but the worst part is now I'm her bitch.*

"Oh, one more thing," he said. "I don't suppose you'd want your kid's clothes and things, so I put them in one of the Dumpsters I used to dump the body." He almost said *body parts* but caught himself. He broke the connection when he heard Naomi wail again.

And after he hung up, he realized that he'd never once referred to Joseph as *our* kid.

Damn, Alphonse realized, he actually was glad to finally be rid of Daciana. One down, one to go. Sure, Daciana was fun at first, but she'd become so naggy, so damn demanding; so demeaning. But now she was gone, the kid was gone, and ... but there was still Maria, wasn't there?

He was supposed to auction off the ring, sell the houses, move to Pennsylvania, and keep track of Naomi; that was what Daciana had said. But she wasn't around now, and as time passed, her phone calls to his burner cell grew farther and farther apart before stopping altogether. He might not have been home free—Alphonse knew he couldn't trust her—but the longer he could stay where he was, the better he liked it. After all, he liked his arrangement at Essex County College. The night shift worked fine for him. He could still wait until after hours and snag a vic from the street. Only difference now was that with the new gas-fired furnace he couldn't burn the bodies there; instead, he had to put them in heavy duty contractor bags and toss them into Dumpsters somewhere on the outskirts of the city.

As for the ring, soon after Daciana's departure he took a day to research auction houses at the Newark Public Library and found one that dealt in antiquities. He made an appointment—and nearly laughed out loud when the representative stared at it with eyes like Barney Google and almost dropped his chin to the floor. Alphonse told him, when asked, that the ring had been passed down through the family for generations, that family tradition had placed it as originating somewhere in England, and that he had no idea how valuable it was. It brought him a fabulous price at auction, even after the auction house's cut, just as Daciana had said it would. Enough to retire on right now if he wanted to.

But then, again, there was Maria.

He'd loved the fact that marrying her and having Angelo kept him out of the army and out of Vietnam. That was true. But he'd never had any affection for Maria herself.

Which meant he had no love for Angelo either. Or Junior. They were just . . . there.

Now Angelo was dead, and Junior was some kind of mob enforcer, and his wife reminded him of a cross between Olive Oyl and Ma Kettle. Skinny as hell, droopy tits, dumpy clothes, the whites of her eyes the color of the Dago red she drank. By now she'd forgotten all about the tattoo incident, which at the beginning had been a real thorn in his side.

The tattoo incident. So many years ago he'd nearly forgotten it. Shortly after they got married, Maria asked—no, make that demanded—that he get a tattoo to show how much he loved her. He wanted no part of that—he'd heard the needles hurt—and offered to carve their initials in a tree instead. The old fashioned way, right? But she insisted on a heart inked on his upper arm, with an arrow through it and her name on a ribbon below it. He told her no, and she told him no sex until he did, so when he couldn't stand his enforced abstinence any longer, he relented. What he'd heard was right: the needles did hurt like hell. He jerked so much that the lettering came out sloppy, and the so-called artist wouldn't take a cut on the price. Said it was Alphonse's fault, not his.

Funny thing, though, years later, after the night Daciana turned him, he woke up next morning with red and blue ink on the sheets, and his arm was bare once again. That was when Maria accused him of getting a temporary tattoo instead of a real one. As if. Nag, nag, nag. She turned into a real harpy. By that time, though, any thoughts of sex with her liked to turn his stomach, so he just let the bitch, well, bitch and enjoyed real sex with Daciana.

Still, he had to be here for Maria. He couldn't bring himself to desert her, what with her mother now dead and all. And while Maria was alive, he couldn't bring himself to move to some hick town in Pennsylvania to keep an eye on Naomi. But he could do the next best thing. He used some of the interest money from what he called his ring account to hire a private investigation company in Harrisburg to check up on her regularly, keep track of her comings and goings, things like that.

The PI told him she'd moved in with her boyfriend. His weekly drive-bys confirmed the fact that they remained together for the 1995 school year, as her car was still either in his driveway or in an overflow parking spot nearby. She bought a new car in 1998, and that was the only new piece of information that he could report. They lived just like any other married couple.

Maria died in early 2003. Cancer, the doctor said, in addition to emphysema and cirrhosis of the liver. Or, in terms that Alphonse could relate to, she totally fucked herself up. It was later the same year that his second son, Junior, was killed by wild dogs, or wolves or something, on the Appalachian Trail somewhere in Massachusetts. Police identified him by dental records, because there wasn't that much left of him otherwise.

There happened to be another couple on the same site, in a tent, a young married couple who Junior had evidently stabbed to death before the animals got to him. The cops and forensic people couldn't understand why the animals that ripped him apart left his victims, which were already bloody as hell, totally alone.

Now, though, Alphonse was free from responsibility, and a door into a world of options opened up. He sold the house that Naomi and the kid had lived in—to a family of Puerto Ricans, but at least they weren't spooks—but kept his own house next door until he figured out just what he wanted to do with the rest of his life.

You know, he thought, *it just might be fun to stalk Naomi for a while, make her life miserable. Wind her spring. Make her snap. Dare her to do something about it.* He didn't concern himself with the thought that by doing so, he'd be following Daciana's directive like a puppet on a string. In fact, he barely thought of his maker at all anymore.

Daciana hadn't been in touch for years now. It was as if she had fallen off the edge of the Earth.

Chapter Thirty: Naomi

They waited until two years after the terror attacks of 2001 before driving to Shanksville to visit the United 93 crash site. Robin turned at the hand-lettered sign onto a quarter-mile-long unpaved road that led to a gravel parking lot bordered by protective steel rails of the type that line the shoulders of sharply curving roads. The sky was gray, and a mist kept the intermittent windshield wipers busy.

He turned off the ignition, looked at Naomi, and got out of the car. She waited until he opened her door for her—even in this so-called liberated age, Robin refused to let his deference to women die. He held an umbrella over their heads, favoring hers, as he wore a ball cap whose visor shielded his eyes. They walked to a temporary shack, where a park ranger stood, her expression conveying a sadness that time had not dulled.

Naomi could identify with that look. The summer after Joseph died—rather, was murdered—she spent in a limbo so bleak and painful that not even Robin's empathy and compassion could enter, nor could they salve. When school reconvened in late August, it was all she could do to keep up appearances as the totally put-together guidance counselor and assistant drama coach. If anyone on staff asked her how her son was doing with his father, she would nod and say he was doing fine, thanks for asking.

She would sometimes wake up at night in a sweat, the image of Raphael's *The Wisdom of Solomon* blazing in front of her, then seeing Joseph, held upside down by one ankle, in the grip of the swordsman whose face became Daciana's. Her groan would immediately awaken Robin, who would wipe her forehead and face with a damp washcloth he kept on the nightstand and soothe her as well as he could with endearments and caresses.

It took two years to break the dreams' regularity. Now they came less frequently, and they were more of a staged tableau than reality. Time heals, but never completely; scars remain, they always remain.

"You all right?"

Robin's question broke her reverie. She said yes, and they walked to the edge of the grass and stared. In the distance across the field stood two tall posts, and between them was strung a huge American flag. Behind the flag was a shrub-covered mound—or was it two, she couldn't be sure—that marked the site of the crash.

At their feet, lining the edge of the grass, had been planted forty metal angels, each about two feet tall, each marked with the name of one of the passengers or crew. One angel had a rosary around its neck; another wore a knit cap; yet another had a tiny knit sweater tied around its neck by the sleeves. "That angel is one of the flight attendants," explained the ranger. "Her sister put it there. She said she was always complaining she was cold."

To the side of the ranger's shack stood a high, chain-link fence. Around the bottom or attached to it were mementos: a rock painted by a child with the number 93; a papier-mâché airplane in United livery made by another child; Saint Christopher medals and more rosaries; personalized tee-shirts from various schools and organizations to mark their visits; plaques bearing the names of the passengers and crew; hand-written notes, the ink faded and the paper puckered by time and weather.

The mist, now a gentle rain, descended upon them, a gray shroud to blanket the scene in cold comfort. They stood and returned their gaze to the giant flag, at the blotched green earth behind, they as immobile as the metal angels at their feet. The water streaking their faces came not only from the rain.

Naomi turned to Robin. "I can't stay. I'll see you back at the car."

He followed her moments later. She handed him the keys as he sat behind the wheel.

"Look," she said. "At the rail."

On the slats of the gray metal guardrail, visitors had scrawled notes in indelible markers: *Proud to be an American; You are not forgotten; Never again.* And the two words that encapsulated and enshrined it all: *Let's roll.*

"You want to rejoin the armed forces," said Naomi. "Join the war on terror."

"Part of me does," he admitted. "But . . . a bigger part of me says no."

"It does?"

"The part of me that's a part of you, and always will be."

She unfastened her seat belt, leaned over, and kissed him. "Thank you."

"I still love my country," he said. "But I think I've done enough for her; and besides, now I've found something—rather, someone—to whom I pledge an even stronger allegiance." He started the engine. "Let's roll."

In February of 2005, Robin announced over dinner, "Much as we love living here in the Sweetest Spot on Earth, it's past time we thought of relocating. We're not getting any older, you know."

Naomi laughed. "I never thought I'd hear it stated quite that way before. But you're right, people are starting to notice. Declan Mulligan thinks I have a portrait at home that ages instead of me. Pretty perceptive, for a math major. But before we move, are you going to make an honest woman of me?"

It was his turn to chuckle. "Do you really want to go for a blood test?"

"Oops, never thought of that. What do you think they'd find?"

"Frankly, I've no idea. Maybe nothing, maybe something. Want to take the chance?"

"I don't think so. Time to move out of my comfort zone, I guess. After all, it's not the mid-twentieth century anymore."

"Common law marriage is no longer on the books, is it?" Robin said. "I wouldn't think so. Single people live together all the time these days. I do feel conflicted sometimes, though, to tell you the truth."

"Your British propriety still with you, after all these years?"

"Centuries," he corrected. "It's called imprinting, and yes, I'm afraid it is. But when I was born—where I was born—a promise of marriage was the same as a contract of marriage. So, Naomi, my love, will you enter into a promise of marriage with me?"

"You're a little late, there, old chap. I committed myself to you years ago. I do hope you don't mind, though, if I keep my maiden name; Mistress Bradford, or even Goody Bradford, both sound a little hokey to me. I'll still be known as your wife, and who checks couples' marriage licenses these days anyway?" She kissed him.

"Well, April Naomi Paris, a.k.a. Mistress Bradford, if only between us," he said, "now that's settled, do you have any place you'd like to relocate to?"

"Anywhere but Newark."

She had not seen nor heard from Alphonse Puglio since that horrid telephone call more than a decade ago. Perhaps he'd forgotten about her and moved on with his own detestable life. As for Daciana, she was hundreds of miles away, teaching college in New Hampshire, or so Alphonse had said in that call. So Naomi didn't want to move anywhere to the north if she could avoid it. Keep as many miles between themselves and those two as possible.

There was another reason, too. More than once Robin had asked her where he might find Alphonse, his Newark address, and every time she had denied him the information. "I respect your position, but I do want very much to find him," he'd said.

"And what would you do if you did find him?"

"I've said it before. Catch him when he wasn't looking and decapitate him. What? Now, stop looking at me like that. I wouldn't roast him over a spit, I'd be quick about it."

"But sneak up on him from behind? Really? Doesn't sound like a fair fight to me."

He took her hands in his. "Naomi, my beautiful naïf, outside of a boxing ring, there is no such thing as a fair fight. The term is an oxymoron. Real fighting isn't a sport, it's not a game, and a sense of honor and fair play has no place there; in fact, if anything it's a handicap. The object is to kill the other person before he gets the chance to kill you. Period."

She pondered his words. "I never thought of it like that. But in matters of life or death, I guess, what else could it be?" Naomi kissed his cheek. "It's over, sweetheart. Alphonse has been out of our lives for ages. Can we just forget it? Concentrate on a place for us to live instead?"

What she did not say was that if push came to shove, Alphonse was her problem, not Robin's. And should the problem ever resurface, she would have to solve it herself.

Robin shrugged his shoulders and returned to the subject at hand. He said, "I've been online. There's an artist in New Jersey I told you about years ago, H. Hargrove. The one who painted *Abbondanza,* there on the dining room wall. He has a Web site now. I emailed him to see first if he remembered me, and second to see if he had any advice about opening a signature gallery of my own."

"Did he remember you?"

"Yes, matter of fact he did. He advised me not to open a gallery in a small town, not enough exposure. Go to a metropolitan area, especially one that's upscale economically. So I'm thinking the Washington, D.C. area. What do you think?"

She tilted her head. "I'm not all that comfortable with living in the inner city, and commuting could be a problem, too, from what I've heard about Washington traffic. Did you consider that?"

After further discussion, they agreed to spend weekends looking in the District's suburbs for both business and housing opportunities. Robin suggested Maryland over Virginia, as he knew a couple, no doubt retired by now, who probably still lived in Alexandria. "Having them chance to see me today, no older than when I taught their daughter back in the 1980s, would lead to a lot of very uncomfortable questions." So Maryland it was.

In the spring, Ms. Paris and Mr. Bradford tendered their resignations to the Hershey/Derry Township school district. Dr. Mulligan sent Naomi on her way with a letter of glowing recommendation; the principal of the middle school did the same for Robin. After school adjourned in late May, they moved to a small, white brick, two-story house in suburban Maryland. Later that summer, the Robert Bradford Signature Gallery and Studio opened in Silver Spring, with a portrait of his beautiful wife gracing the display window. And in the fall, April Naomi Paris, B.S, M.A., began work in Silver Spring as well, in the guidance department of the Montgomery Blair High School.

Meanwhile, in Newark, Alphonse Puglio received a final accounting from his private investigator in Harrisburg. Along with the bill was a note advising him that Ms. Paris and her boyfriend, Mr. Bradford, had left the area and were now residing at 1205 Prospect Street, Takoma Park, Maryland, 20012.

Chapter Thirty-One

Naomi was assigned the incoming freshman class, and one of her first challenges came in the form of a slight blond 14-year-old named Ali Samples. A pretty girl who didn't realize her prettiness, Ali stood in front of Naomi's desk with eyes downcast and lower lip trembling. She didn't sit until Naomi asked her to, and even then she couldn't bring her green eyes to bear on the new counselor.

"How can I help you, Ali?"

The girl's shoulders shook, and she heaved a sigh. Finally, she looked up. "I'm being bullied," she said.

"Uh huh. Tell me about it."

"It's Sophie. Sophie Bienkowski. Do you know who she is?"

Sophie's reputation had preceded her from her middle school days. Naomi answered that she had heard the name but hadn't met Sophie yet.

"She picks on me all the time. Calls me stupid. I'm not stupid. Make her stop."

"When you say she picks on you, is it physical? Does she hurt you?"

"Oh, no, nothing like that. But she's been picking on me since we were in grade school. We've always been in the same classes, and when it comes to group work, the teacher always seems to assign us to the same group. I can't make any suggestions without her laughing at me, telling everyone else not to listen because I'm stupid."

"So this has been going on for a while."

"Years." Ali wrung her hands, brought her fists to her eyes, and repeated her mantra. "Make her stop."

Naomi sat silent and looked at Ali. Finally, she said, "Have you talked this over with your parents?"

"Uh huh. First, they told me to talk to her, to ask her to stop. But she just laughed at me. So then they told me to ignore her. But that doesn't work either."

"Of course not."

She sniffed. "You know that?"

"Certainly. A bully knows that trick and just tries harder to make you crack. Makes it more of a challenge and makes it even worse for you."

Ali seemed about to cry. "That's right. So what do I do?"

Naomi tented her fingers. "Try giving her a neutral reaction."

"Neutral? How do I do that? What does that mean, anyway, neutral reaction?"

"Think about it. When someone calls you stupid, what do you want to do? Fight back, deny it, insist you're not stupid, right? That just gives her more reason to fight, to get the last word. And we already know what happens when you try to ignore her. So the next time, just say this: 'Thank you for sharing.' It acknowledges what she's said without fighting back, and it doesn't give her any new ammunition to use against you. How can she attack a simple thank you? It's neutral."

Ali blinked back tears and tested the words. "Thank you for sharing." She said it a few more times, and each time her face seemed to gain confidence. Not much, but some.

"Just don't tell Sophie where this came from," Naomi cautioned. "Don't say, 'Ms. Paris told me to tell you.' Let her think it comes from you. Because if you do tie me to it, well, she's got you again for crying to the counselor."

She took a breath . . . and actually smiled. "Got it. Thanks, Ms. Paris."

One problem solved, Naomi thought as the door closed.

Not exactly so. A month later, the girl was back, weeping again.

"What's the matter, Ali?"

"I did what you said, and you know, it worked, it really worked. But now Sophie's got Gina going after me too."

"Really? Well, congratulations, young lady. You've won!"

"Huh? What do you mean, I won?"

"Don't you see? Sophie couldn't conquer you by herself anymore, so she had to bring in reinforcements. You've neutralized her. You win!"

Ali thought about it. She smiled. "You're right. I do win."

"So what do you say when they both try to bully you?"

"Thank you for sharing!" Ali took her hall pass and walked to the office door. Before leaving, she turned around and said, "Ms. Paris, thank you for sharing."

I can't wait to meet Sophie, Naomi thought.

But it wasn't Sophie who came in next. A month later it was Gina, the supernumerary tormenter. She wasn't crying; instead, she was highly pissed.

"My friend's telling lies about me behind my back. It's not fair."

Naomi didn't ask who the friend was. "Tell me something, Gina, do the lies hurt you?"

"What do you think? Of course they do."

"Well, my dear, I hate to tell you this, but that's your fault."

"What? What kind of guidance counselor are you?"

Naomi chuckled. "In the first place, you'd better learn the difference between a friend and an enemy."

"Come on, I know that."

"Really? Which one tells the truth about you, a friend or an enemy?"

"A friend." In a tone that said, you nimrod.

"And which one tells lies about you?"

"An enemy."

"But you just said your *friend* is telling lies about you. Does that make sense? By your own definition? Is she really your friend?"

"Um . . . no. No, I guess she's not."

"Then, why does what your enemy says matter to you? Shouldn't you just shrug it off? Why give someone whose opinion clearly doesn't matter the power to push your buttons?"

"I . . . I don't know."

"You don't have to give her that power, Gina. You control that, not she. So take control, girl."

Gina grinned. "High five, girlfriend!"

"Just don't tell Sophie you heard this from me."

"How'd you know it was Sophie?"

"Goodbye, Gina. Have a good day."

Someday I'm going to have to meet this Sophie, thought Naomi.

And then she took a moment to review her own relationship . . . with Alphonse.

That damned phone call notifying her of Joseph's death was the last time they'd spoken. For all she knew, he was still living in Newark, two hundred miles away. Even better, he might be keeping Daciana company, farther away in New England. So why did she still shudder every time she thought of him? Why did she still give her enemy the power to push her buttons? *Physician,* she thought, *heal thyself.*

Sophie Bienkowski managed to avoid guidance appointments for three years: she managed to be absent that day; or, she had a test that period; or, she just cut. Finally, Naomi managed to snag her in the hallway.

"I've got to get to French class," she said.

"You've got study hall next period. I checked your schedule."

"Yeah, well, I have to study."

"Sophie. My office. Now."

Once settled in the chair, Sophie propped her feet against Naomi's desk and pushed herself back. She slouched, trying to make herself both invisible and defiant at the same time.

It would be hard for Sophie to look invisible. Her Goth look was passé these days, but she kept it going. Her clothes were basically black, although sometimes she wore red tops, cut indecently deep. Today she wore a bare midriff that exposed the ring in her navel. Her eyes were lined so deeply she looked like a parody of Alice Cooper, and her long dark hair was typically streaked with spray-on color, sometimes purple; today, red. By now, her reputation for trouble was accompanied by her reputation for being the easiest lay in the school. *Round heels, they called it in my day,* thought Naomi.

"So what do you want to *guide* me on?"

Ah, petulance. "Nice to meet you too, Sophie. Or would you prefer Sophia? That's the name on your permanent record."

She shrugged her shoulders and kept her face defiantly blank.

214

"You're a smoker, yes?"

"So what? You gonna lecture me?"

"No, why would I do that?"

"Smelled it on me, huh?"

"Pretty fresh, too. Like you've just come from your daily smokes break with Mr.—"

Sophie started. "What're you, Sherlock Holmes?"

"No. I just know that you duck into the boiler room with the custodian every afternoon."

"So, you gonna tell my folks?"

"No. Why would I?"

Another shrug. "And no lecture either? What, you don't get paid enough to care about us?"

"Ooh, touché. Good one. No, Sophie. I do care, very much. But I also know, or at least I suspect, you believe that as a grownup I can't possibly relate to the world of teenagers. Further, you might be thinking, *If she's so smart, why ain't she rich?* You're probably aware of the canard that goes, *Those who can, do; those who can't, teach.* Am I right?"

"*Canard* means duck in French."

"Well, la de dah. Something stuck. Good for you, Sophie. There's another definition to the word, though, which you might want to look up sometime." She opened Sophie's permanent record. "I don't really have to look at this today, I've been looking at it for three years, but it looks official if I open it." She cracked a smile; it had no effect. "All right, then. You graduate next year—or at least you're scheduled to."

"Ooh, la de dah to you, too."

"Do you have college plans?"

"Never took the test, whaddya call it, SAT?"

"That's all right. The community college has open enrollment. You can go there for two years, get your associate's degree, and then transfer your credits to a four-year school. It's convenient, and it's cheaper too."

"BFD. That's Big Fu—"

"I know what it means. Are you saying you have no plans for after high school?"

"Yeah. Getting out of this place. And out of your hair. You don't have to *care* about me anymore—not that I believe you or anyone else in this dumb school ever did."

215

Without another word, she stood up and walked out, closing the office door firmly behind her.

That went well, Naomi thought. *Not.*

In January of 2009, Naomi was in the Takoma Park library when she was stunned by an explosion so severe its concussion actually made the walls vibrate. It turned out to be the Pep Boys Auto Service Center nearby. Dozens were killed, and authorities later neither confirmed nor denied that the attack was linked to terror. No known terror group claimed responsibility, at least not any that was revealed to the public.

One anomaly that stuck with her, in addition to the apparent information blackout, was the fact that just before the explosion she saw a Hasidic Jew sign off a computer, walk outside, and step into a van. The date happened to be a Saturday, and she thought that Hasidim weren't allowed to drive on the Sabbath.

Months afterward, during the Memorial Day weekend, four senior girls from Blair were killed when their car careened up the off ramp on the Capital Beltway and ran head-on into a moving van. In tribute, the four seats assigned to them were left vacant at graduation ceremonies. And Sophie's chair, Naomi noted, was also unoccupied. *Why am I not surprised?* she thought.

But she was very much surprised later that summer, when the news reported that Sophie's nude body was found in the San Juan Mountains of southwestern Colorado, at the bottom of a cliff. She'd apparently been kidnapped, possibly at around the time school let out, and taken out West where she was killed. Once again, information about the circumstances surrounding her death was nearly nonexistent.

Sophie was hard to like, but that didn't mean she deserved to die. That night Naomi sobbed in bed, snuggled against Robin's shoulder. Sophie's student record had shown she wasn't stupid; quite the opposite. The girl had had promise, potential. But she hid it, the way a miser might hide a gold ingot in plain sight—by painting it gothic black.

Naomi's vacation was four weeks in July, and upon reporting back to school in August she learned that Ahmed

Mansoor, the custodian with whom Sophie had sneaked smokes, would not be returning to school. The principal hinted to her privately that Mansoor, or *Monsieur* as the students called him, was suspected of some kind of criminal activity, but the police couldn't be forthcoming, as the investigation was ongoing. He hadn't returned to work since school let out. Naomi wondered privately if, their being partners in crime, so to speak, his disappearance had anything to do with Sophie's.

The first day of school that September—teacher preparation time only, two days before the doors officially opened to students—Naomi reported for the traditional welcome back staff breakfast. The cafeteria was filled with teachers looking rested and recharged, querying each other as to how their summers went, what they did, where they vacationed.

The cafeteria served fresh fruit, doughnuts, bagels—*no bagels can match Jersey's,* Naomi thought—cream cheese, butter, and various jams. Plus coffee, tea, and bottled ice water, all courtesy of the PTA.

Following the meal, it was time for the typical new school year rah-rah speeches from the superintendent, head of special services, and building principal. It fell to the principal to introduce new staff members, which he did with gusto, extolling each individual's qualifications and welcoming him or her to the professional staff of Montgomery Blair High School.

Naomi sat back and made note of the new arrivals, intending to meet them sometime during the day to welcome them personally. They would be piled high with administrative paperwork, so her visits would be brief. Finally, the principal acknowledged the last person on the list of newcomers.

"As you might be aware, Mr. Mansoor is no longer on the custodial staff, but I'm pleased to note we've managed to find a most qualified replacement in the person of—he's sitting in the corner back there, please stand up—Mr. Alphonse Puglio, who comes to us from New Jersey."

Chapter Thirty-Two: Alphonse

As the commercial says, the look on Naomi's face when he stood up: priceless. *She thought she was rid of me,* he said to himself as he acknowledged the polite applause from the others. *Now she's scared shitless . . . again.* It was a good feeling, a feeling he hadn't realized he'd missed, to have that much control over another human being.

Well, not quite human, but hey.

She was still hot, all this time later, just as he—with the gray toner removed from his hair—looked less than half his sixty-plus years. In fact, by his own rather biased standards, he looked pretty hot himself.

'Course, fraternizing with the female faculty here would be a no-no. First place, the few women on staff were mostly middle-aged, married, and physically past their prime. Besides, he didn't want to muddy the waters. He took this job for one reason only, and that reason occupied one of the guidance offices.

After Daciana left town and Junior and Maria died, Alphonse decided to take a page from Naomi's playbook and leave his job before people started noticing that, despite his artificially grayed temples, his appearance was still youthful. He put his house on the market, sold it quickly, and followed Naomi to the Washington, D.C., area.

With the proceeds of his two house sales and the windfall from the auctioning of Daciana's ring, he could've bought a substantial home in an upscale neighborhood. But prudence dictated that he rent a modest home for the moment and live modestly as well—while his fortune earned compound interest and made full-time employment unnecessary.

Alphonse satisfied his blood urges with late-night drives to downtown D.C.'s tenderloin; but his donors, none of them volunteers, never lived to see the next day's dawn.

Their deaths rated barely a paragraph in the *Washington Post*.

Early on, he tracked down the address his Harrisburg P.I. had given him, and as he drove slowly by the white brick house at the bottom of a horseshoe-shaped street at the bottom of a hill, he saw two cars in the driveway. Was she still living with the guy from Hershey? Only one way to find out.

Next morning, he got up early and followed the guy's car to Silver Spring, where he saw him open the doors to a shop on Georgia Avenue called the Robert Bradford Signature Gallery and Studio. Alphonse parked in a public garage and walked to the storefront gallery. He stopped dead when he saw the portrait in the window. The likeness was perfect: Naomi, looking better than ever. Ageless, in fact.

A young man, *the* young man, opened the door and joined him on the sidewalk.

Alphonse gave him a twisted grin. "Some broad, huh?" He made a fist with his right hand and swung it up, stopping it suddenly with his left, a gesture that had obvious meaning in the Italian sections of Newark.

The man glowered. "That happens to be my wife," he said.

Alphonse slid his right arm back, holding his left hand in place. "Oh, *scusi.*" It was all he could do to stifle a laugh.

The man just looked at him, silent.

"Well, I've, um, got someplace I've got to be," Alphonse said as he took his leave.

Damn, Alphonse thought as he returned to his car. *His wife? Had to be the guy she was living with in Hershey. And he looks young too. Which means she must've turned him into a vamp like herself. Like us,* he added. That meant there were now two of them; maybe more? No, he didn't think she'd make more. But it was possible.

This required closer monitoring, so he contacted a realtor to inquire about listings in the Takoma Park area, and she found him one on Glenside Avenue—just around the corner from Naomi's house on Prospect Street. He followed her to work one day, too. *Well, now,* he thought, *she's still a schoolteacher. That makes sense.*

He took a series of handyman jobs, just so neighbors wouldn't be suspicious of seeing his car sitting idly outside the house during working hours. Like most other homes built in this post-war neighborhood, his house had no garage. Meanwhile, he kept scanning the want ads until, in the summer of 2009, he found exactly what he was looking for: a custodial position, effective immediately, at the Montgomery Blair High School in Silver Spring.

Now that Naomi had seen him, Alphonse decided to play it cool and let her sweat for a while before paying her a visit. After school two days later, after most of the staff had gone home, he opened her office door without knocking and stood there, watching her typing on her computer's keyboard.

She heard the door open and said, "Just a minute." Then she looked up. Her face turned pale, and she leaned back in her chair and pushed it away from her desk, thumping against the wall. Her voice registered barely above a whisper: "Leave me alone."

Alphonse plopped himself in the chair opposite her desk, then looped a leg over the arm. "So, surprised to see me? Gonna ask how I found you?" She stared. "Not gonna give me the satisfaction, huh? That's okay, I don't mind. Hey, I met your hubby the other day. At his studio, you know? Nice picture in the window, by the way. No one would ever guess you're, whatchacallit, a *strigoi*. I like *vampire* myself, never did get used to Daciana's uppity foreign words. Oh, and I'll bet you turned your hubby too, right? Otherwise, well, you know the drill. He gets old and dies, you don't."

Her voice remained faint, barely in control. "Please . . . leave me alone. You've done enough damage already."

"Hey, babe, here's my deal. You keep my secret, I keep yours. But you don't run, you don't try to hide from me anymore. Because now you know for a fact you can't hide. I'll always find you. You leave for a weekend, you tell me. You take a vacation, you tell me that too." He was winding the woman's spring, as Daciana had put it, and he found he rather enjoyed it. No, he actually found great and glorious glee in it.

"Surely you don't have any contact with . . . her any-more, do you? It's been years, Alphonse, years."

"It's Alley Oop, babe, remember? Nah, those days are over. But now you ask, matter of fact I do check in with her, every coupla weeks or so." It was a lie, but he relished the fact that she didn't know the truth. *She might've lost interest in Naomi,* he'd thought, *but to lose interest in me? Oh well, why try to figure out what a broad thinks? Vamp or not, she's still a broad.*

"Why are you doing this to me, Alphonse? Stalking me? Keeping me under your greasy thumb?"

He chuckled. "Greasy thumb? That's cute. So here's the reason, babe. It's because I can."

He made good his promise of secrecy, however, as did she, barely exchanging glances if they happened to pass in the hallways. During the 2011 summer break, she be-grudgingly notified him that she and her husband were go-ing to Ocean City for a week, gave him the address of the hotel, and told him when they'd be back. She also implored him—for the nth time—not to make himself known to her husband, for although he knew that a vampire named Al-phonse existed, Robin still believed he was living in Newark. Alphonse shrugged. *Makes no difference to me,* he thought. *Guy's an artsy-fartsy pussy. What could he possibly do to me?*

The 2012 school musical would be *Shenandoah,* a Civil War-era play that demanded a strong male cast. The direc-tor was the head of the English department, Mr. Petillo, and he chose senior Brandon Bracconeri to play the lead role of the family patriarch. Brandon was renowned through-out the school as having a voice to die for. He was already picked to go to some New York school, Julie-something, af-ter graduation.

He was also gay, which for some reason he couldn't explain, infuriated Alphonse. Put simply, he attributed it to the fact he just hated fags.

But the other kids in the cast didn't seem to mind. Matter of fact, at after-school rehearsals, they joked good-naturedly about it with him. "Don't turn your back on Brandon," one cautioned; another joked about his putting hamsters up his ass; yet another laughed about their mak-

221

ing Brandon the *butt* of their jokes. And Brandon laughed along with them.

But he laughed *at* Alphonse. And that was unforgivable.

Alphonse had requested the late afternoon/early evening shift for that year, specifically because Naomi would be working with Mr. Petillo as assistant director. It gave him access to continued exposure to her, a continued reminder of his surveillance and dominance. Good-looking snatch that she was, he figured she was one of the reasons so many boys tried out for roles. But none of the boys disrespected Alphonse; mostly, they ignored him. Except for Brandon.

"Pugslie," he called him, as in, "Hey, Pugslie, there's some dirt on the stage, we could slip. How about a clean sweep once in awhile?" Or, "Pugslie, have you ever thought about ironing your coveralls? You look like a slob." Or, "Pugslie, that hair style is *so* over. What're you, a throwback to disco?" On and on, loud enough so nearby cast members could hear, but low enough not to be overheard by Mr. Petillo. And Alphonse could do nothing but hate him from afar.

Naomi—Ms. Paris in public—knew about the brat's harassment, she had to, but she didn't do anything about it. Probably enjoyed it, the smug snatch. *Let her get her licks in,* he thought. *He who laughs last.*

Then one day Alphonse overheard something that set his mind racing. It was in the boys' locker room, when they were getting ready for evening dress rehearsal. None of them knew he was there, standing behind the middle bank of lockers. A couple of the boys were confronting Brandon, their voices anything but jovial.

"You promised me you'd have it. I already gave you the money."

"Me too. I'm gonna need it, bro, these rehearsals are killin' me."

"You'll get it, guys, I swear. I told you, my distributor's out of town making more. When he comes back, you'll get your stuff. And it's gonna be prime, believe me."

Making more? thought Alphonse. *We talking meth here?*

An idea began to form. And when it did, it posed the question: Do it now or after the play closes? It proved easy to answer. As in, immediately.

Later than night, as Brandon unlocked his Porsche, the last car left in the student lot, Alphonse walked over and stopped him. "You need some shit, kid?"

"Pugslie?"

"Mr. Puglio to you . . . if you want my help."

"I don't know what you're talking about."

"Oh, I bet you do. Your distributor's out of town, right? He's making more?"

Even in the dim light of the lot, Alphonse could see the boy's face turn pale.

"How do you know—oh, shit, you were in the locker room tonight."

"Yeah. And, to help you out, I took the liberty of making an emergency telephone call, to a certain friend of mine."

"Pugs—Mr. Puglio, what're you saying?"

"Show me the money." He'd heard that line in a movie and liked it. It cut right to the chase.

Brandon reached into his back pocket and drew out a wallet. It was fat with bills.

"How much you got?" Brandon told him. "All right, here's how it works. We go to the drop-off point, we meet my guy, and I give him two thirds of your cash. He gives you as much as that'll buy. I keep the other third. Finder's fee." Brandon gulped. "You good with that?"

"Do I have a choice?"

"Everyone has a choice."

"Yeah, right. Okay, when do we make the deal?"

"Now. Tonight. I told you it was an emergency call, asshole. Now get in the car. And put your cell phone in the glove box."

"My folks'll be wondering where I am."

"I don't give a flying fuck about your folks. You're a smart boy, you'll make up something to tell them. Phone in the glove box, or no deal. And we never had this conversation, *capisc'?*"

Brandon looked apprehensive, but Alphonse knew he really didn't have a choice. This was big time shit, who knew that the fucking janitor, of all people, would have a drug line? The boy slid into the car. As he did, Alphonse put colorless latex gloves on his hands before touching the handle on the passenger's side. The punk didn't notice in the weak interior lights as he fumbled with the key.

Alphonse directed him to Rock Creek Park, in Northwest Washington, where he pulled off the road near a stone bridge over a walking path. They walked down the hill, stumbling a little in the dark, and ended up under the bridge.

Brandon looked around, eyes blinking in the deep darkness, breath coming in nervous bursts.

"Where is he? Your guy?"

"Relax. I told him to be here at midnight. It's five of. And if he's late, we wait. You got a problem with that?"

Brandon shifted his weight from leg to leg, turning first to face one end of the stone tunnel and then the other.

"So you're a homo," said Alphonse.

"Huh?"

"Queer. A fag. Tinker Bell. Wear green on Thursdays."

"What're you talking about? Yes, I'm gay, everyone knows that, no big deal. Lots of theater people are gay; dancers, actresses, actors."

"Yeah, yeah, I know. Like Rock Hudson."

"Who?"

"Never mind. Oh, here he comes now."

"Where?"

"Over there."

Brandon turned his head to where Alphonse pointed. He saw nothing. But he felt a pair of strong hands grab his head. It was the next to last thing he ever felt, the final being the sudden snap of his neck.

Alphonse dug into the boy's wallet and drew out the cash. "You can never have too much money," he muttered. Then he fell to the boy's neck with his fangs and ripped out his throat.

Brandon's heart wasn't pumping blood anymore, so drinking from his neck was like sucking through a blocked straw. Alphonse took off the boy's windbreaker and bunched it under his butt to elevate it. Then he bent his knees up. Gravity brought the blood more freely to his lips. Another pint or so he drained into a Nalgene bottle that had once held cleaning fluid.

Queer blood tastes the same as straight blood, he noted. *Guess we're all God's children, after all.*

When he had drunk his fill, Alphonse pulled the windbreaker free and placed it over Brandon's face. He grinned as he decided to leave the boy's eyes open. *Something to freak out whatever jogger happens to find him tomorrow.*

He took the boy's keys, returned to the Porsche, and started the engine. Driving carefully, making sure to keep within the posted speed limits, he returned the car to the students' lot, parked it in the same spot it had been, walked to his own car in the staff lot, and drove home. Inside, he chucked the latex gloves and ran his coveralls through the wash. As they were drying, he took a look at his hairstyle. He didn't see anything wrong with it, but now that he studied it he thought he might be due for a new look. And when he took the coveralls from the dryer, he decided then and there, late as it was, to iron them.

Chapter Thirty-Three: Robin

"I'm so sorry about your student's murder," Robin said as Naomi arrived home, red-eyed, the next night. "It's all over the news."

"Drug deal gone bad," they say. She reached into the refrigerator for the flask and poured herself a small glass. "Considering the circumstances, I feel guilty drinking this."

"At least, ours is voluntary, and the donors are still alive. Did you learn any details, beyond that the boy's throat was cut and that he was robbed?"

"No."

"No indication that he'd been drained of blood."

Naomi did a double take. "No. Oh, please, no." *I hadn't thought of that. What if...*

"I've noticed you've been acting a little . . . differently lately. Is everything all right?"

"Beyond what just happened to Brandon, you mean?"

"Yes. You seem a bit edgy these days. It started even before the play rehearsals began. I don't know, it's as if you expected someone to jump out of the shadows and holler boo."

"No, everything's fine. Really."

Robin felt it prudent to change the subject. "Bereavement aside, on a practical note, what happens now with the play?"

"Well, everyone's shocked, of course, but Gary Petillo said he's putting one of the sons in Brandon's role, and one of the bit players will take on the son's role. We'll be rehearsing all night tomorrow, probably. Gary and the two boys have been given off so they can spend the day in the auditorium rehearsing. I'm printing up a dedication page to insert into the program, to the memory of Brandon Bracconeri."

She took a final swallow and rinsed the glass in the sink before putting it into the dishwasher. "They say someone must've picked him up at school after rehearsal and driven him to Rock Creek Park. His car was untouched, and his cell phone was in the glove compartment."

"You look exhausted."

"I am."

"So go to bed."

"I will, but I don't know if I'll be able to sleep."

"I'm sorry for your loss, sweetheart. I know he was one of your guidance cases."

"Thanks. You coming to bed?"

"After I check my emails. Some people have seen my Web site and are making inquiries. That's a good thing, right?"

She kissed him, lingeringly, on the lips. "Good night, my love."

"Good night, my lady."

Robin opened his laptop and clicked on the mail icon. The screen popped open, and as he scanned the inbox he saw a name he recognized. He opened the message immediately.

Mr. Bradford,

Hi, it's Rowena Mitchell, your favorite student—ha, ha— from high school. I'm living in Boston now and on a whim happened to Google your name today. Wow. You're a famous portrait artist, a big step up from a schoolteacher, yes? I guess now that you're obviously retired, you have the time to create your own work rather than critique other kids' stuff. Your Web site is beautiful, by the way; love the portrait of your wife. Did you paint it when she was a young woman, or are you a cradle robber? ;-)

Right, I'm still the smartass kid you knew back when. Anyway, I'd love to hear from you, if you even remember me, that is. My husband and I are thinking about coming to the D.C. area this summer, visit my parents, see the sights. I'd love to catch up with you in person. Since you and my dad were both Marines, maybe all six of us—you and your wife, my dad and mom, and Matthew and I—could take in a Moonlight Parade at the Barracks together.

Can't wait to hear from you.

Love, as always,
Rowena

Robin read and reread the message. Rowena Mitchell. Marcus and Kim-Ly Mitchell. Memories, memories of the warmest kind. His first impulse was to jot off an immediate reply, tell her he'd love to see her again. He'd loved Rowena like a daughter, loved her parents, and many times he'd wished he could contact Marcus and Kim-Ly, perhaps revisit one of their favorite restaurants in Alexandria, Vo's Vietnam. But how could he explain his physical appearance after all these years? He still looked like a twenty-something, whereas they—whereas Rowena—would have aged normally.

He punched up his calculator. Rowena would be almost forty now, which meant her looks probably would have, if anything, grown more lovely as she matured. Her parents? Marcus was in the Vietnam War; how old would he and Kim-Ly be? Somewhere in their sixties?

He punched in more figures. *If I said I was twenty-six when I met them, I'd be, what, now? Somewhere in my fifties? A teacher could retire at fifty-five, so Rowena wasn't off base when she figured I'd retired from the classroom to paint full time. But there's no way she could accept my looks as they stand, and old age makeup only works in movies. Now that she's gotten in touch, I dearly want to see her, see her parents again, but how can I do it?*

Houston, we have a problem.

He would discuss the matter with Naomi.

And that would have to wait until after the play closed.

The play nearly closed after opening night. Individual band members would stop playing to cry; the young actor who took Brandon's place playing Charlie, who was supposed to fake pathos in his graveyard soliloquies to his late wife, sobbed openly; and in the emotional final scene, where the church congregation sings, "I am ready, you can pass the cross to me," every cast member broke down in tears.

From the audience itself came spontaneous bursts of emotion, as one person or another thought about the murdered young actor who had shown such promise, cut down not in his prime, but before it.

At curtain call, the substitute Charlie held before him a portrait of Brandon Bracconeri, an enlargement of the headshot taken for the program, and more tears flowed from the standing crowd.

But in the back of the auditorium, unnoticed by Robin, who sat in the front row, a husky, swarthy man dressed in dark blue pressed overalls and leaning against a broom, muttered to himself, "Come on, people. The kid was a prick. And a fag besides. What's the big deal? It's all bullshit."

On the second night, the players fared better, and by the next weekend, the final performance was—for a high school production—first rate. Naomi dragged Robin to the obligatory, if this time subdued, cast party, but they made their excuses and left before it wrapped. Back home, Robin showed Naomi the email that he'd been sitting on for more than a week.

"You've told me about Rowena," she said. "You were close to her and her family back—when?"

"When I taught high school art in Alexandria, late 1980s. Her dad was a Marine, her mom Vietnamese. He was black, or what the politically correct call African-American these days."

"Uh huh. All right, why the smile?"

"I just remembered what Theodore Roosevelt said once about hyphenated Americans. He hated the term almost as much as he hated being called Teddy. Said there's no such thing as Italian-Americans, or Irish-Americans, or any other ethnic-Americans. You were Americans, first, last, and always."

"And you probably heard it from his own lips, too. But back to Rowena. What are you going to do?"

"What do you think? I'd love to see her again, but ..."

"It wouldn't hurt to write back, maybe have her bring you up to date as to what she's been up to since you last saw each other."

"But what about her suggestion we meet up this summer?"

"Don't mention it. At least not for now." She yawned. "Sorry, honey, it's late, and it's been a long day."

"I'll stay up a bit and think up a reply."

Hi, Mr. Bradford (sorry, hard to get used to calling you Robin, but I'll try),

Thanks so much for getting back to me. You were one of those special teachers, and even though I majored in English, not art, your influence stayed with me. In a nutshell, I went to Criterion University in New Hampshire, as you might remember, and when I graduated got an editor's job at Jones Publishing in Boston. I married a great guy, had a son, and lost them both—to death, not divorce. Too much detail to put into an email; I'll wait 'til we get together.

I've since remarried, a chemist who lived aboard a boat in New Jersey. She's a 42-foot trawler yacht, and you'll like her name: Semper Fidelis. *Matthew's company relocated to China, but he decided he'd rather stay here with me (And who could blame him?).*

The boat is berthed here in Boston, and in a couple of weeks we plan to travel the Loop: down the Intracoastal Waterway, around Florida, up the Mississippi to the Great Lakes, and down the Erie Canal to the Hudson River before swinging north to our home port. She travels at about eight knots, so it'll be a slow cruise, but as Matthew says, when you're where you want to be—i.e., on the boat—what difference does it make how slow you go?

Anyway, our plan is to motor up the Potomac to visit my parents for a week or so before heading back to the Chesapeake and points south. I must see you; we must have a family reunion. I use that word advisedly, Mr.—okay, Robin—because when we knew each other during my high school years, Dad and Mom said you were like family to them. And to me, too . . . but 'nuff said about that.

I'll have my laptop with me on the cruise, so I can keep you up to date on when we're slated to arrive. One does not etch plans in stone when one is traveling on a boat.

Love,
Rowena

"She went to Criterion?" asked Naomi. "Isn't that where Daciana went to teach after she left Newark?"

"That's what you told me. Should I ask if she knew her?"

"I don't know. She might ask how we know her."

"I can say I painted her portrait once. Which is true. I just won't say when."

Dear Robin,

I knew Daciana Moceanu, yes, but not from school. Long story, painful, really, but before I go into detail, be advised she's dead now. (Oops, redundant. My dear friend Claire, another grammar geek, would tell me that she's dead *automatically means* now. *She's a stickler for grammar and usage; drives people crazy sometimes, but you have to love her.)*

You were uncharacteristically non-committal, by the way, when you asked if I knew Daciana. Maybe you thought I could be friends with her and wouldn't want to offend me by offering an opinion of her. So I'll tell you right off, in my typically blunt way, that the woman was evil made flesh, and I hope you can agree with that assessment. If you can't, you don't know her at all.

Matthew and I are packing some gear and taking it to the boat, so I'll have to cut this short. More later. Can't wait to see you again.

Love,
Ro

Chapter Thirty-Four: Naomi

She sought him out, after school, in the custodians' office. And there he sat, feet propped on his metal desk, leaning back on two legs of his chair, cleaning his fingernails with the wicked-looking switchblade he always carried.

"What're you doing here?" he asked as he lay the knife onto the desk. "Not that I mind. Want to sit down?" He leered at her. "On my lap? We can talk about the first thing that comes up."

Some things never change. "I'll stand, Alphonse. I just have a question for you."

"Okay."

"When's the last time you checked in with your maker? You know, to tell her that I'm being a good little girl and minding my P's and Q's?"

He frowned and lowered his chair. "What's it to you?"

"Just wondering."

"Why just wondering?"

"Because I happen to know she's dead."

"You're shitting me."

"Robin got an email from a former student who went to the college she was teaching at. I told him to ask if she knew her, she said yes, and added that your beloved subhuman savage was dead."

"She called her a subhuman savage?"

"No, that's from me. Actually, she said something like she was evil incarnate. That means evil made flesh."

"*That means evil made flesh.* Suddenly you're the stuck-up bitch again. Think you're better than me."

Physician, art thou actually healing thyself? "I know I'm better than you, Alphonse. But that's beside the point. Daciana is dead, so you don't have to pretend you're still monitoring me for her."

He stared at Naomi, his close-set brown eyes narrowed to slits.

"How did she die?"

"She didn't say."

"I wonder how she bought it." He leaned back in his chair again and picked up the knife. "So it's only you, me, and your prissy little hubby left on the vampire circuit."

She flinched. If he only knew what her *prissy* husband wanted to do to him. And was eminently capable of doing. Naomi began to wonder why she even bothered to try preventing it anymore. "It looks that way."

"Well, Naomi, old girl, that doesn't mean I'm going to stop keeping tabs on your comings and goings. Why, you ask? Because I like it, I like stalking you, keeping you on your toes, keeping our little relationship a secret from your sweetie-pie husband."

Naomi stared at his smug grin. "We don't have a *relationship*, Alphonse. So why don't you just . . . just . . . autofornicate?"

He frowned for a second and then grinned. "Aw, listen to the little lady, too prim and proper to even tell me to fuck myself."

"Why lower my standards to your level?"

"Ooh, aren't we the . . . whatever." He grinned. "Oh, by the way, your phone number? It's a 431 exchange, isn't it?"

Phone numbers were printed in the staff directory. "So what?"

"So's mine. Now."

Naomi opened her mouth, but no sound came out.

"That's right, you sanctimonious snatch. Ooh, listen, I used a long word. Lots of syllables. How about that?" He gave her a wide grin, but there was no mirth in it. "Looks like we're neighbors again, you high-falutin' *cunt.*"

Instead of driving home, Naomi stopped at Robin's gallery. He was alone in the studio, touching up a portrait. They kissed hello, and he began cleaning his brushes as they spoke.

"Love, are you still obsessed with finding Alphonse?"

"I wouldn't say obsessed, but yes, if you'd give me his address I'd be happy to take a drive to Newark and pay him a visit."

"You're saying you'd really kill him. Even after all this time."

"Absolutely. There's no statute of limitations involved here. If anyone deserves to die . . ."

"But Robin, you do have to admit there's no such thing as the perfect crime, right? Forensics is so sophisticated today that someone somewhere would be able to track you down, I know it."

"Uh huh. And for someone like me, a life sentence would be . . . now, that would be something to contemplate, wouldn't it?"

"Please don't make a joke of this."

"All right. So why are we beating this dead horse again?"

"Well, with Daciana dead, I thought that Alphonse might be irrelevant."

"Like the body of the snake, now that the head's been severed? I don't know. He could still be dangerous on his own. But as long as he stays in New Jersey, far from us . . ." He paused. "No. Belay that. If anything, the creep is a serial killer. I'll bet if I picked up a New Jersey crime report I'd find a slew of unsolved murders, people with their throats torn out."

"Then let the Newark police track him down."

Robin returned to his brushes. Naomi took a breath and strolled through the gallery, pretending to study the display of portraits. *You wouldn't find all of those unsolved murders in Newark,* she thought. *At least, not anymore.*

Naomi returned to him, her expression tentative. "Remember, if it weren't for Alphonse, you and I would never have met. So, in a way . . ."

"Point taken. I'll thank providence for that, not him." He cleaned the last brush and capped the solvent. "On another note, I just got another email from Rowena. Her husband's out provisioning the boat for their cruise, and she's at home suspending their utilities, mail service, whatever. She said she's tried phoning her parents in Alexandria, but she just gets their machine. They'd been on a cross-country road trip, but they should be home by now."

"Don't they have cell phones?"

"She had to leave messages there too. So Rowena's asking me if I can go down and check up on them; they're at the same address as when I knew them before. She'll send me the key."

"Don't her folks have a neighbor to keep an eye on the place for them?"

"Yes, but she's elderly and kind of scatterbrained, and she lost the key. Which Rowena just found out when she called her today. The neighbor, a Mrs. Cooper, claims she hasn't seen the gunner and his wife since they left on their trip. Frankly, Rowena doesn't trust the old lady's mental competence all that much anymore, says she'd feel better about my checking out the house for her. We're a lot closer than she is."

"So does that mean we have our weekend planned?"

"A trip to Alexandria, Virginia. With sightseeing in the nation's capital on the side."

The key came the next day, along with a hand-written note offering profuse thanks. It also gave them Rowena's cell phone number, Matthew's number, and a tentative departure date for their cruise. *If anything looks suspicious, if there's any evidence of foul play,* she wrote, *call me and Matthew and I will fly down ASAP. Otherwise, we'll keep in touch via email. Or, you can call me. I'd love to hear your voice again.*

They reserved a room at the Marriott Crystal Gateway Hotel in Pentagon City for Friday night, and on Saturday they drove to Marcus and Kim-Ly Mitchell's town house. As they opened the door, an elderly lady hailed them from an address two doors down.

"Hello, are you Rowena's friends?"

"Yes," called back Naomi. "We're Robin and Naomi. Would you be Mrs. Cooper?"

"That would be me," she said. "If you need anything, just let me know. And stop by after you're done for some tea. I don't get many visitors."

"Thank you, Mrs. Cooper, we'll do that."

Inside, aside from a layer of dust, everything appeared normal. A large framed oil portrait dominated the living room, drawing Naomi to it immediately. "Mrs. Mitchell?" she asked.

Robin nodded. "Nice to see her in a place of honor."

"She's beautiful."

"Yes, fortunately Rowena got her looks from her mother. Her father's a bear."

"Look at the answering machine. It says twenty-seven messages." She pressed the button.

Mom, Dad, it's me. Hope you had a great trip. Matthew and I will be coming down to see you this summer, aboard Semper Fi. *Maybe we can do some cruising together. Call me back. Love you both.*

"Twenty-six to go," Naomi said as the machine automatically went down the list. Each message grew increasingly more tentative, troubled, and finally urgent. As Naomi listened, Robin checked all the rooms and reported that except for the dust, everything was "Marine Corps squared away."

After finishing their inspection, they knocked on Mrs. Cooper's door and were happy they hadn't just left without saying goodbye. The woman had prepared tea and laid out scones and marmalade for them. She appeared to be somewhere in her early eighties, a little stout and a little stooped, with a crown of permed white hair over heavy-lidded blue eyes and crows' feet that on her looked more like laugh lines. She wore a flower-print housedress that probably dated back a generation or more, white stockings over thick ankles, and sensible black shoes.

"I'm from England originally," she said as her guests sat down and put linen napkins in their laps. "So I can tell you these scones are genuine, not the stuff you get in the stores."

Naomi pronounced them delicious.

"My dear, have you ever traveled to England? No? Well, let me tell you that what Americans call English muffins are no more English than, than, than French fried potatoes are French."

"I've heard it said, Mrs. Cooper, that Canadians don't have any idea what Canadian bacon is either."

She beamed at them. "Clever girl," she said to Robin. "You keep her."

"Oh, I plan to."

"So, all is well in the Mitchells' house?"

"Yes, fine."

"I'm so sorry I misplaced the key. I'm sure Rowena must be worried sick."

"We'll let her know that everything's okay," said Naomi.

"Well, when you leave, don't you dare leave Rowena's key with me; I'm sure to misplace that too."

They drove back to their hotel and ate dinner at Ted's Montana Grill, the chain owned by media mogul and restaurateur Ted Turner. They ordered bison filet mignons, rare and bloody, which somewhat assuaged their sanguinary needs.

"I wonder if Delilah is still working," Robin mused, and then had to explain to Naomi. "We'll call Rowena from our room, and then I'll take you to a certain neighborhood I know."

Ensconced in their hotel room, Naomi sat cross-legged on the bed while Robin dialed Rowena's number. "I'll put it on speaker, so you can join in," he said.

One ring, two, and the connection was made. There was a pause before Rowena answered. "Hello."

"Rowena, Robin. You're on speaker so Naomi can join in. How are you? It's been forever."

Another pause. Dead silence. Awkward silence. Someone had to fill it.

"Hi, Rowena, I'm Naomi. We checked your parents' home, and everything looked in order. Marine Corps squared away, Robin says. We met Mrs. Cooper too, she's lovely. Served us tea and scones."

Finally, Rowena had something to say. "Um, Naomi, this is going to sound strange, or then again maybe not, but Mrs. Cooper phoned me after you left. She said you and Robin were, her words, now, the *cutest young couple.*"

Robin closed his eyes and groaned. Naomi reached over and held his hand.

Rowena continued: "Again, her words, Robin, not mine. But you're old enough now to be retired. I know Mrs. Cooper isn't the most perceptive person in the world, and her eyesight can't be twenty-twenty, but she *can* tell young from old."

Naomi said, "Rowena, I . . . don't know what to say."

"Well, I think I do. I also think you both know what Daciana Moceanu was. And I want you to understand that I know it too. So my question is, will I be shocked at your appearance when I finally see you again?"

After another awkward pause, Robin said, "Under ordinary circumstances, yes, you would be. But these aren't ordinary circumstances, are they?"

Rowena's voice, metallic through the phone's tiny speaker, came through strong, her meaning unambiguous. "Let's cut through the bullshit, Robin. How old are you, really? And when did Daciana turn you?"

Chapter Thirty-Five: Robin

"I was born in the year of our Lord 1593, or thereabouts, in London. Daciana—then calling herself Lady Catherine Drummond—turned me around 1619, when we served in the court of King James the First. She was one of the queen's ladies in waiting, and I was a portrait artist in the royal court. I was a paraplegic then, confined to a wheeled chair with a hole in the seat to catch my droppings." He heard a grunt from the phone's speaker. "Yes, Rowena, it wasn't pretty. Infection from my bedsores put me near death, but Daciana wouldn't let me die before I finished the portrait of her that I'd already begun. When she turned me, my body became whole for the first time. Afterward, she took me to her bedchamber, and we became lovers—no, not lovers; make that sexual partners, because love never entered the equation. I finished the portrait to her satisfaction. She might even still have it somewhere, come to think of it. But I knew that Daciana was a danger to me should she become disenchanted, so one night I fled the castle and shipped out to America. I haven't seen her since, which is nearly four hundred years. Now, Rowena, it's your turn. Tell me the details of your own experience with Daciana."

"Too much to tell on the phone. But Robin, as a *strigoi*, please assure me you haven't been influenced by Daciana's—her proclivities."

"You're asking if I'm cunning and cruel. You should know better than to ask, Rowena. I'm disappointed."

"You're right, I'm sorry, spoke without thinking. I'm just so—so confused right now, what with my parents off the grid, and now I learn this about you." She paused. "Naomi, are you—"

"Afraid so."

"By Daciana too?"

"Sort of, like third generation, I guess. She turned the man who raped me and fathered my son. When my boy was four, for reasons I'll never understand, his father made him *strigoi*. And it was my son who turned me. Years later, Daciana killed him . . . and please don't ask me for the details."

"I can't imagine. My God, Naomi. She killed my son, too, and I understand about not wanting to relive the details. She killed my then husband, too. We have a ton of grief in common, girl. I can't wait to meet you. Oh, and since you're not the monsters that Daciana was, you might want to think of yourselves as hemophages rather than *strigoi.*"

"Pardon?"

"Daciana added another scalp to her belt, metaphorically speaking, and actually got married, to a science professor at Criterion who knew what she was and euphemized her vampirism by calling her a hemophage—a blood eater, if you will. He had a theory that she had a genetic disorder he felt he could cure. As if she wanted a cure, but she humored him. He's dead too, by the way, and that's another story. After he died, she started seeing my boss at Jones Publishing, which is where our paths crossed. Now my boss is dead too. Are you getting the picture?"

"Rowena," Robin cut in. "I have to ask. Are you and Matthew, what is it, hemophages like us?"

"Again, that's too long a story to tell on the phone, but I'll fill you in when we see you in a few weeks. Meanwhile, can I ask you to do one more favor for me?"

"Ask."

"You remember the restaurant my folks liked, Vo's Vietnam?"

"Of course."

"If it's still there, would you mind asking if anyone on the staff has seen them? That would be one of the first places they'd go to after they got back from their trip."

"We will do that. Tomorrow. I'll call you back afterward."

"You know I had the maddest crush on you when I was in high school, right?"

Naomi laughed. "Rowena, he's blushing."

"Really. Some things never change. I'm blowing you a kiss, teach. Call me tomorrow."

The last time Robin had been to Vo's Vietnam was in 1992, with Marcus and Kim-Ly Mitchell, a farewell dinner before he left to teach at the University of Maryland. The restaurant was still there, still busy, virtually unchanged in the intervening years. Naomi had never eaten Vietnamese food, and Robin cautioned her that she might want to ask the server to tell the chef to tone down the spices. She told him to order for her.

He did notice one change, though, namely the prevailing gender of the wait staff. Whereas before, they had consisted mostly of men, now the balance had shifted. And the women were all young and attractive, some especially so.

"Watch your eyes, buster," said Naomi.

"I don't have to, you're watching them for me."

When the server arrived to take their order, Robin asked if she might recently have seen a couple somewhere in their late sixties or early seventies, a black man and his Vietnamese wife. This was their favorite restaurant. She frowned, as if trying to remember, at the same time staring fixedly at Robin's face, as if he looked somehow familiar. Finally, she said no. He asked if she could check with the other servers, and after she took their order to the kitchen he saw her conversing with them, pointing to his table. When she returned later with their meals, she reported that no one had seen a couple matching that description in the restaurant. He thanked her, and as they ate, Robin couldn't help but notice that some of the other women cast glances at them, quick, furtive looks that after a while proved a bit unsettling.

Naomi noticed his discomfort. "You seem to have a fan base."

When it came time to present the bill, another striking-looking young Vietnamese woman came to the table. "Good evening, lady and gentleman. I am the manager, Tien. If you would like, I can check with the colonel to see if he or some of the servers who are off tonight have seen the couple you asked about. He's not at the restaurant this evening."

"That's very decent of you," Naomi said.

She gave Robin a paper and pen. "If you will write your telephone number, I can call you when I find out if he's seen them."

"You're an angel, Tien," said Robin with a quick wink, which Naomi saw. He wrote his cell number and handed the paper back. "I'll wait for your call."

Outside the restaurant, Naomi asked Robin what the private joke seemed to be between him and the manager.

He laughed. "I remembered from my tour in Vietnam. *Tien* is the Vietnamese word for angel."

"Cute."

"But there is something."

"Yes?"

"This is going to sound like *they all look alike to me,* but I could almost swear that the manager could be the twin of the server who waited on Marcus, Kim-Ly, and me back in 1992."

"But that was what, twenty plus years ago? Maybe she's her daughter."

"Maybe."

Shortly after they entered their hotel room, Robin's cell phone rang.

"Good evening, Mr. Bradford, this is Tien from Vo's Vietnam." He returned the greeting. "I've just spoken on the phone with Colonel Vo, and he says he remembers seeing the customers you mentioned."

"Ah. Recently?"

"Yes, he said a few weeks ago. But the colonel's out of town on business this week. He said if you can come back to the restaurant next Saturday, he might be able to help you."

"That would be great. I appreciate it."

"He says to come at closing time, that's ten o'clock, so you can talk privately, without interruption."

"Tien, you really are an angel. Thank you. We'll see you Saturday."

Next, Robin called Rowena and explained that they'd be meeting with Colonel Vo on Saturday night. After a brief word with her husband, she came back on the line.

"We've decided to postpone our cruise and take a plane down to D.C. I want to meet the colonel myself. Can you pick us up at Dulles next Friday?"

"You look absolutely beautiful," Robin said as Rowena embraced him in a hug that almost took his breath away. "What're you, training for a weight-lifting competition?"

She released him. "Sorry. Don't know my own strength sometimes. And you, you look just the way you did decades ago. Who would believe you're really our senior citizen?"

"That hardly describes it, luv," said Matthew, shaking Robin's hand. "He's beyond that. He's a super-annuated citizen, an antiquarian's delight. Good to meet you at last, Robin. I'm Matthew Collins."

"Good to hear a northern English accent again," Robin said as they walked from the concourse to the baggage claim.

"And where is your lovely bride?"

"Still at school, I'm afraid. It's a staff in-service day, kids are off, and Naomi's responsible for writing a report on one of the workshops. She promises to be home in time for dinner; meanwhile, she prepared lunch for us this morning. It's in the refrigerator."

Matthew's expression turned coy. "Bloody good of her."

Rowena slapped Matthew's shoulder. "Careful what you say, bud. By the way, is *super-annuated* even a word?"

"How should I know? I just made it up. And a word means what I want it to mean, luv, no more, no less. Now, shall we be galumphing on?"

"Beware the Jabberwock, my son," Rowena quoted. "Matthew's been reading Lewis Carroll," she explained. "Again. He found a facsimile in my library of Carroll's original text, in his own printing."

Matthew picked up their suitcase from the carousel. "Fascinates me," he said. "We live in a kind of Wonderland now, don't we?"

Robin agreed and said, "Turning to more mundane matters, I hope you're both okay with cold cuts and salads."

"By *cuts*," said Matthew as he slid a finger across his neck, "you wouldn't mean literal . . ."

Rowena slapped his arm. "Stop it, you fool."

They laughed. The ice was broken, and the three of them strolled from the airport like old friends.

After their lunch—Robin was surprised at how much Rowena and Matthew could put away—his cell phone rang.

"Mr. Bradford," the sweet feminine voice said, "This is Tien, from Vo's Vietnam."

"Yes, Tien. Let me put you on speaker."

"Of course. Colonel Vo says he would like to entertain you and your wife on his yacht tomorrow, if that would be convenient."

"On his yacht? That's quite a surprise."

"The colonel tells me the couple you mention—the Mitchells—have been loyal customers for many years, and to honor them he would like to offer their friends his hospitality."

"Tien, that sounds . . . perfect. We happen to have guests with us right now, and they happen to be the Mitchells' daughter and son-in-law. They just flew in from Boston and I'm sure they would love to meet Colonel Vo as well. If he can accommodate them, that is."

Tien's normally bright voice suddenly seemed to sparkle. "That would be wonderful. I'm sure the colonel would be thrilled to see their daughter again."

Chapter Thirty-Six: Naomi

Long day, glad it's over, thought Naomi as she sat at her desk organizing the notes on the workshop she'd attended. Initially, she'd thought the subject one she couldn't relate to, but as it unfolded she found it fascinating—having primary grade students sit at their desks not on chairs, but instead on large bouncy balls. "Little children tend to fidget," the presenter reminded her audience. "It's what they do, and it's not natural to make them sit still in hard chairs." She said students tend to focus better when they're allowed to move; plus, keeping their balance on the balls helps them to stay alert; and, in addition to training their core muscles to maintain that balance, they also tend to have better posture.

"I understand that sitting on the balls can help get some of that excess energy out," Naomi asked, "but is there an improvement in actual learning?"

The presenter acknowledged what Naomi was thinking. "We all agree that education seems to belong to the fad of the month club, am I right? Whole language, new math, cooperative learning, conflict resolution; not to mention that hideous attempt to eliminate phonics in the primary grades. Remember that?" All the workshop attendees groaned. "I see you do. But although the evidence is largely anecdotal for now, it seems to improve learning to an *almost* statistical level. What it does best is improve the test scores of kids diagnosed with ADD and ADHD. The more hyperactive they are, the better their improvement seems to be; again, not statistically significant yet, but anecdotally very promising."

This will bear watching, Naomi thought as she compiled her notes. Her cell phone rang—Robin. "Yes, the workshop went better than expected, I'll tell you all about it when I get home. I assume all went well at the airport? Rowena and Matthew arrived okay? Good. Just finishing up here, be home in a jiff. Well, maybe a little longer than that, you know the traffic."

As she hung up, Alphonse walked in. He carried two coffee mugs.

"Everybody's gone," he said with a smirk. "Nobody here but us chickens."

The wind left Naomi's sails. "What do you want, Alphonse?"

"Just trying to mend fences," he said as he put one of the mugs on her desk. It was three-quarters full. Of blood. "Here's a little peace offering."

"What's going on? Where did you get this?"

"Never mind where. It's good. Trust me."

"Trust you? *You* want *me* to trust *you?*"

"Look, it's okay." He lifted the other mug to his lips.

"No, stop. Give me that one."

"Jeez. All right, here." He exchanged the mugs. "Happy now? Drink up." He swallowed the blood in three gulps and licked his lips.

Still cautious, Naomi sipped from her own mug. It was chilled, of course, to keep it fresh. She took a swallow and felt the familiar surge of satisfaction as it danced across her taste buds and sent a welcome rush to her brain. *Why is he being so nice all of a sudden?* she wondered. But whatever the reason, the blood was very good. She drank more.

Alphonse, still standing, looked down at her with an inscrutable expression. Funny, she found herself compelled to blink her eyes to keep him in focus.

"It's the fag's blood," he said. "I saved it for this special occasion."

She stammered, her tongue growing thick. "Brandon? It really was you? You killed Bran—?"

Then she passed out.

Naomi awoke with a headache. She was in the nurse's office, lying on one of the patient beds. She shook her head and tried to sit up, but realized her hands and ankles had been tied to the rails. And that she was humiliatingly naked.

Alphonse entered her field of vision and quickly shoved a wadded washcloth into her mouth. She tried to push it out with her tongue, but it was no use. He wrapped duct tape across the gag.

"Daciana's fairy dust," he said. "Just like you used to use back in the day. But now you're the one on the receiving end. What's it like, huh?"

Naomi twisted her head from side to side and yanked on her arms and legs, trying to free them.

"Like my little trick with the mugs? And you think you're so smart." He leered at her. "Bet you think you know what I'm gonna do to you next, right?"

She arched her back and pulled away, but her bonds held.

"Wrong. Don't flatter yourself, bitch. Lookin' at you now, I wonder what I saw in you in the first place. Oh sure, you may look hot as ever, but the fire's gone, leastways it is for me. You're old news, Naomi, old news."

Naomi dropped her hips back onto the bed. Her head pounded.

"See, when I was with Daciana, she told me that sharing blood with another vamp was a pretty good high. And she was right. Like the kids say, it was awesome with her. But she's not around anymore—and according to you, she's not coming back—so you'll have to do."

Alphonse lowered himself to his knees and poised his head above Naomi's thigh. "Just like you used to do it, right? Your kid told me. Used to skeeve him out when you did it to the men, sucking so close to their dongs. As for the women, though, well, he really enjoyed that. Said he got a coupla nips in too, get it?" He laughed. "Okay, baby, your turn now. Relax, I'm not puttin' my mouth anywhere near your pee hole."

When he'd gorged on her blood and pronounced himself properly *awesomed,* Alphonse tore off the duct tape and removed the washcloth from her mouth. "Sorry, you don't get any of mine," he said.

Naomi, weakened from loss of blood, could do nothing but lie still as her heart pumped furiously and her blood cells rushed to reproduce. *Too much, he took too much,* she thought.

Alphonse retrieved the mug containing the drugged blood and tilted it toward her lips. "Open wide, sweetness, we're going to take a little drive, and I need you to be unconscious."

It was dark when Naomi awoke, dressed again and unfettered, headachy and still somewhat weakened, but growing stronger. She lay on a bed of gravel, inside some kind of brickwork tunnel. The air was still. Alphonse stood over her, holding his knife. The blade was still encased inside the handle, but when he saw that she was conscious he made a show of pressing the button that released it. It swept out and snapped into place. She could see the glint from the long narrow blade, reflecting a dim streetlamp somewhere outside the tunnel.

"Rock Creek Park," Alphonse said. "Same place I killed the homo kid. Figured if I off you here, it'll give the cops something to think about. You know, tie things together, make 'em think there's a serial killer on the loose. Course, unlike the fag, they won't find your head with those pretty little fangs in it. No, afraid that's going to have to go to the fishes in the Potomac." He straddled her legs and knelt.

"Daciana told me to wind you tight as a spring, and to be there when you snapped. And then kill you. In private, no witnesses. Like right now. I figure you're about as wound up now as you'll ever get, and frankly, I don't care whether you snap or not. Personally, I don't think you've got the balls." He laughed softly. "In fact, I know you don't."

Naomi looked into his cold eyes as they drew ever closer, saw his smirk as he brought the tip of the knife closer and closer to her throat.

"And Daciana's not around anymore, is she? Say bye-bye, bitch," he said.

Naomi's vision suddenly flamed red. It was as if she were seeing Alphonse through a film of blood. His face filled her entire universe. It seemed to ripple in front of her eyes.

Her lips drew back in a snarl. And something exploded inside her brain, blowing out a lifetime of fear and fury.

Acting purely on instinct, Naomi jammed her knee into his groin with all the force she could muster.

Alphonse screamed as he dropped the knife, rolled over, and clutched his crotch. His face turned feral. He growled. "I'm gonna teach you to fight fair, bitch!"

Naomi struggled to her feet, head still throbbing, but with her full strength returned. Ignoring the knife, she delivered another wicked kick to his crotch, just as he was removing his hands to help himself stand. He gave out another shriek and fell back again.

"Know what my husband taught me, Alphonse?" she nearly shouted. "He said *fair fight* is an oxymoron." Her words, punctuated by sharp breaths, burst forth in staccato volleys. "You know . . . what an oxymoron . . . is, Alphonse?" She kicked him again, bringing tears to his eyes. "You must know . . . what a moron is . . . You see one . . . looking back at you . . . every time you shave!" Another fierce kick, another groan. "Best time . . . to kick a man . . . my husband said . . . is when he's down . . . because you don't want him . . . to get up again."

Naomi delivered a kick to his midsection, for her grandmother; another to his face, for her mother; and a return kick to his groin, for her son. She tired of shouting, using her energy instead to continue raining blows upon his body.

Exhausted, barely able to breathe, Naomi finally backed herself against the tunnel's cold stone wall. She looked at Alphonse, groaning on the gravel. He looked up at her. *Oh no,* she thought.

He had found the knife. His fingers wrapped themselves around the handle, but for the moment at least he seemed too weak to grasp it tightly.

Naomi cursed herself for not picking it up herself. What to do next?

A swift kick would dislodge it, she thought. *But then what? I have no idea.*

Much as Naomi hated Alphonse, she wondered if she could make herself kill him, make herself cut through his throat and sever his spinal column. She approached his doubled-over, barely moving body and took aim at the knife.

But when she drew her leg back for the kick, Alphonse snapped an arm out, grabbed her other ankle, and yanked her off her feet. She fell flat onto her back with a thud. The sudden blow knocked the wind from her; try as she might, she couldn't draw a breath.

Alphonse rolled on top of her, his knees pinning her arms to the gravel. He lifted the knife, and as she watched, helpless and horrified, he drove the blade into her throat. She felt it stop only as the tip ricocheted off her spine.

The hole through Naomi's trachea shocked her system, and a rush of air flowed into her lungs again; not through her mouth, but through the fluttering slit in her neck. She couldn't scream even if she'd wanted to; the wound was beneath her voice box, where air no longer could reach.

"Wanna holler now, scumbag?" he growled. "No? Didn't think so." He was breathing hard, still hurting and gasping for air himself. "So now I'm gonna do you slow, one cut for every kick in the nuts. You ready for the first? I'm thinking of your eyeball. What do you think? Huh?"

He held her head against the gravel with his left hand, and with his right he poised the knife above her left eye. With one last surge of strength, Naomi twisted her head free, dropped her fangs, and sank them into his left wrist. Alphonse screamed and yanked his hand back, trailing blood. His eyes were bloodshot, his face flushed, his features infused with insatiable rage, rage coupled with a lust for blood. Her blood. This time, all of it.

He made a fist and delivered a blow that fractured her cheekbone.

Naomi dropped her head to the stony earth. All her energy was sapped. There was nothing more she could do. She watched her killer again reclaim his position over her, watched him bare his teeth, watched him hold the knife in both hands, blood dripping from his left wrist.

"Get ready, you cunt," he muttered. "I'm gonna drive this blade clean through your fuckin' skull."

Naomi closed her eyes.

As her ears picked up a low growl.

From behind Alphonse, a black form detached itself from the shadows and leaped upon him. A pair of elongated jaws clamped themselves halfway around his head.

His shocked yelp lasted but a second; then it became something else, a keening wail Naomi would never forget.

The thing held his head firmly between those tooth-studded jaws. Slowly, inexorably, as Alphonse's body vainly contorted and thrashed, the jaws began to close. His eyes nearly burst from their sockets; his jaw distended; his fangs pivoted impotently into place. Naomi heard a loud crack, then another, and a short series more, as Alphonse's skull began to splinter.

And then his skull gave way in a welter of gore as the thing shook its snarling black head.

Naomi stood and gaped at the spectacle as her own body continued to repair itself. She watched the beast—a great black wolf—dig its snout into Alphonse's shattered skull . . . and linger there. Nauseous, and barely able to collect her wits, she forced herself to lean, wobble-legged, against the tunnel wall.

And that was when she saw Robin rush in to embrace her; when she saw, over his shoulder, another man, watching the wolf without a trace of alarm, holding what looked like a woman's clothing draped over his arm; when she saw the wolf itself draw its snout from Alphonse's empty skull and begin to change its form, ever so slowly, delicately even, from lupine to human, until finally it—she—stood before her, naked, a beautiful, exotic-looking woman with milk chocolate skin and dark almond eyes.

"You must be Naomi," the woman said, smiling through the blood that smeared her face. "I'm Rowena. At your service."

Chapter Thirty-Seven: Robin

It was Alphonse's head that wound up in the Potomac, with the rest of his naked body left under the bridge for the police to ponder. Robin looked at Alphonse's license and was surprised and disturbed to discover that his house stood just around the corner. He wondered if Naomi had known, and he vowed to discuss it with her later, when their emotions had settled down.

After Matthew tossed Alphonse's head to the fishes—his pitching arm was a powerful thing—he drove Rowena back to Takoma Park, following Robin, who drove Naomi in her car. Naomi herself slumped in the passenger's seat, head down, breathing through her mouth, eyes barely open. Finally, she uttered, "What exactly happened back there? And *what is she?*"

"First things first. When you didn't come home, and you didn't answer your cell, we suspected something might be wrong and decided to drive out to the school to find you. It was nearly dark when we arrived, and we saw your car leaving the lot. I was about to honk the horn, but then I realized it wasn't you driving but someone else—a man."

"It was . . . it was Alphonse."

"Alphonse. So I gathered." He fought to keep his tone level. "The man who according to you was still living in Newark."

"You're angry, honey, I can hear it in your voice. But can we save my explanation for later? Please?"

Robin exhaled through his nose. "All right. So I turned the car around and followed. Tracked him as far as Rock Creek Park but then lost him somehow. That was when Rowena told me to pull over. She knew your scent from the house and decided she could track you faster and better than I could. Like a bloodhound."

"Emphasis on *blood.*"

"She's a hybrid of sorts. Calls herself a metamorph. When we pulled over, Rowena tossed off her clothes and transformed herself into the blackest, sleekest, most beautiful—well, you know. Then she bolted off. Matthew and I followed, but we couldn't keep up with her. When we finally found your car, parked near the bridge over the jogging path, Rowena was already in the tunnel beneath it."

"Saving me."

"Doing what I wished you'd given me the pleasure of doing a long time ago."

"Honey, can we—"

"I know, later."

Naomi unbuckled her seat belt—superfluous, she'd once idly thought, for people who can't die—and leaned against Robin's shoulder. He put his arm around her and drove one-handed to their home in Takoma Park.

After Naomi had showered and dressed in clean clothes, the four sat around the dining room table. It was empty; no one's mind was on food.

"As Robin told you, Matthew and I are metamorphs," said Rowena. "My friend Claire made me, and I made Matthew."

"Involuntarily, I might add," said the former Brit. "But I was mortally wounded at the time, so if she wanted to keep me alive, she had no choice but to, um, bite me."

Rowena said, "You'd better keep that smile plastered on your face, mister."

"Why certainly, luv. After all, a smile would look ridiculous anywhere else."

"Please," interrupted Naomi, still shaken. "I need more."

Rowena continued, "All right. Claire and her soon to be husband saved my own life by killing Daciana just as she was getting ready to rip my throat out. They had taken their wolf forms then, which I'd been totally unprepared for. Up to then, I'd thought vampires, werewolves, and such were myths.

"Daciana was part wolf by that time, too—another long story—and she was able to tear them up pretty well, Dale especially. In fact, he suffered a mortal wound. But Claire forced Daciana's blood into Dale's mouth and gulped some herself. *Voila,* their bodies healed, but in the exchange, they changed from pure lycanthropes into hybrids. Which is what we are now."

Robin said, "Both werewolves and vampires, then."

"Best of both worlds. And a couple of years later, when I came down with terminal cancer, I turned to Claire and begged her to save my life by turning me. Believe me when I tell you it wasn't an easy decision."

"What's it like, being a metamorph?" asked Naomi.

"Different," she said, her expression unreadable.

Matthew added, "It's not easy, at least at first. You're a vampire, so you want blood. And you're a werewolf, so you're strong and feral. You, pardon the pun, tend to wolf down your food and eat a lot, because you're basically feeding two—your human self and your wolf self."

"No full moon fixation, I assume," said Robin.

"None whatsoever," said Rowena. "You can change any time, and to any degree. Matthew was right, it's strange at first, but as a wise man once said, there's nothing so strange as the way the strangeness wears off the strange."

Naomi blinked.

Robin looked at her. "Please tell me why you didn't let me know that Alphonse was here and not in New Jersey. I could've killed him for you—and saved you the trauma you went through tonight."

Naomi looked down but said nothing.

Rowena answered for her. "If I were Naomi, Robin, I'd feel that this was my fight, not yours. I wouldn't want to be the proverbial damsel in distress, to be rescued by her knight in shining armor." She tilted her head toward him. "Especially a guy who came from the era of knights in shining armor."

Naomi looked at her and inclined her head, as if giving permission to continue.

"Plus, she was probably afraid that you'd leave clues, fingerprints, DNA evidence on the scene. You've served in the military, so your prints would have to be on file."

"The last time was a long time ago."

"Do you know how long fingerprints are kept on file?" He admitted he didn't. "The defense rests. Anyway, you get my point. I think, and correct me if I'm wrong, Naomi, but from what Robin told us while you were in the shower, I think you might have suffered from a kind of poor me syndrome. And you were trying to overcome it, one day at a time." She paused. "How'm I doing?"

Naomi reached across the table and gripped her hand. "Perfect."

Robin looked at Rowena and back at Naomi. "Do metamorphs have ESP too?"

"Just a good dose of feminine insight," she said.

"My insight's not feminine at all," said Matthew.

"No, you big hunka love, you're all man, and you're all mine."

He laughed. "Prisoner of love."

Robin stifled a yawn. "Sorry about that," he said. "But I think it might be time for us to turn in."

"Good idea," said Rowena. "We have some work to do before breakfast. What time's reveille?"

Robin set the alarm for three-thirty, and under cover of darkness, the foursome walked to Alphonse's house, let themselves in using his key, and—wearing rubber gloves—sorted through his papers. He kept his password file conveniently next to his computer, and a quick check showed hundreds of thousands of dollars in his checking and savings accounts.

"You said he was a school custodian, Naomi?" asked Matthew.

She took a look at the statement. "Holy cow. How could a janitor save so much money?"

Rowena gave her a look. "I would think our mutual acquaintance might have had something to do with that."

"I know that when we were living in Newark, Daciana bought our house after the landlords died. When I paid Alphonse the monthly rent, I thought it was going to her, through him. Maybe she gave the house to him, and he sold it. Would that account for all that money?"

"Couldn't say. What are property values like in Newark?"

Matthew interrupted. "We can talk about this later; time's wasting. Now, Robin, in the years I was consulting for Uncle Sam, I sequestered my government pay in an offshore account. The work our team did, you see, was of the clandestine variety, so I figured one good turn deserves another, at least as far as taxes are concerned."

Robin said he should have thought of that himself. Ages ago. "We'll discuss that shortly," Matthew said as Rowena stood behind him and massaged his neck and shoulders. "Meanwhile, let me do some finagling here."

He checked passwords and security questions and within minutes had all of Alphonse's assets transferred to his own account. He printed the receipt and handed it to Robin. "Back at the house, we'll set up an account for you and Naomi, and I'll transfer the funds to it. Consider it a belated apology from the late and unlamented Alphonse Puglio. Right now, though, I think it's best we vacate the premises while it's still dark. I suspect the police will be visiting sometime today, depending upon when they identify the body."

"Rowena and I can take Alphonse's clothes to a Goodwill box in Silver Spring, near the high school, and dump them there," Naomi said. "While we're gone, gentlemen, you might consider what you'll be preparing for our breakfast."

Rowena high-fived Naomi. "Good one, girlfriend and victim no more. Keep those boys in line."

After a Saturday morning breakfast that could've served eight but was consumed by four to the last rasher of bacon, link of sausage, and crumb of toast, Robin's phone rang. It was Tien, and Robin put her call on speaker. She bore news that the colonel had experienced airplane delays and didn't arrive at Reagan National until just before dawn today. Would they mind if he postponed their cruise until tomorrow? Robin spoke for them all when he said tomorrow would be fine.

"Excellent," she said. "Can you be at the National Harbor at, say, two o'clock? I can meet you there and take you to the boat."

"We can do that, thank you. One question, though, I'm curious. Was the colonel really an officer in the army?"

On the other end of the line, Tien laughed softly. "Ah, Mr. Bradford, you think he might be a colonel like your Colonel Sanders? Honorary title? I confess, you are right. His father was in fact a colonel in the Vietnamese army back in the day—on the right side, I might add—and when he was a boy his father called him his little colonel. The imaginary title stayed with him, and he decided he liked it. As a busi-

nessman, it gives him a certain prestige, an authority, if
you will, when dealing with associates and subordinates."

"I see. Well, thank you again, Tien, and be sure to thank
the colonel for his offer. We shall see you tomorrow at two."

When he keyed off, Robin turned to Rowena. "What are
you thinking?"

"Frankly, I'm thinking this might not pass the smell
test."

"What do you mean?" asked Naomi. "I thought it
sounded very gracious."

"All the times we went to the restaurant back in the
day, and Robin, you can back me up on this, we never met
the colonel, not once, never even saw the colonel."

Robin said, "And you'll remember when she called before, Tien said that he would be delighted to see the Mitchells' daughter *again.*"

Matthew said, "Maybe something lost in translation?"

"Hardly," said Robin. "Tien speaks like a natural-born
American. Listening to her on the phone, could you tell she
was anything but American?"

"You're right," said Matthew. "So, what do we do? Do
you think there's some subterfuge going on? Because, quite
frankly, it's been a few years since I was exposed to subterfuge, and I'm not at all eager to renew the acquaintance."

Robin and Rowena exchanged looks. "We go," she said.

Naomi stood and began gathering the dirty dishes. Rowena followed suit, sarcastically mentioning that the wom-
en would do their duty in the kitchen so the men could talk
of important matters women need not be privy to. Then she
cast them a glance, and they got the less than subtle hint.

"Woman works from sun to sun," lamented Matthew as
he picked up his plate, "but husband's work is never done."

"You know, Matthew," said Robin, "back in my day—
I mean, *really* back in my day—the man was king of his
castle."

Naomi looked over her shoulder. "Up thine, sire."

Following a somewhat fitful night's sleep and another
substantial breakfast, the four were on the road headed
toward Maryland's National Harbor. They met Tien on the
dock fifteen minutes early. She greeted them warmly, es-

pecially Rowena and Robin, whom she referred to as extra-special guests.

"I hope you're hungry," she said. "The colonel and his staff have prepared a lovely luncheon."

"Aren't they supposed to be at the restaurant?" said Robin.

"Different crew on Sunday from Saturday," she explained as she led them down to the three floating docks that, seen from above, would form the letter *E* jutting from the wider main dock. Tied to the top of the *E*, broadside to the river, was a yacht that seemed to go on forever. Its twin diesels were softly thrumming, gently kicking up spray from the exhaust pipes in the stern.

Matthew's jaw dropped. "What is this?" he asked, his voice barely audible.

Tien spoke with what sounded like an owner's pride as she pointed to the Vietnamese word stenciled on the stern. "Her name is *Giang*," she said and pronounced it *zaahng*. "It is a woman's name and means *river*. The colonel was thinking the river of time when he named her."

"Northern pronunciation," mumbled Robin to himself.

"Pardon me?"

"Oh, just thinking out loud. Rowena's mother tried to teach me some Vietnamese a while back. She said in the South the word for *river* is pronounced *yaahng*."

Rowena stared at him.

"Oh," said Tien. "Well, the boat. She is a one-hundred-foot Hatteras motor yacht. She has twin diesel engines, thrusters at both bow and stern for easy maneuvering at dockside, state of the art electronics, and five staterooms."

"This is beyond being a liveaboard yacht," said Matthew. "She's a floating palace. She must have a crew, yes?"

"Believe it or not," Tien said, "it can be owner operated, but the colonel keeps a crew of three aboard when he cruises." She smiled modestly. "I comprise one third of the crew."

"I assumed as much," said Matthew. When she tilted her head, he added, "You know it's every yachtsman's dream to have a beautiful female crew."

"You are a charmer, Mr. Collins," she said as Rowena nudged him.

"I have a beautiful crew too," he said, gesturing toward Rowena.

"Nice save there, Slick. But a little late."

"Shall we board?" asked Tien.

The aft deck, or cockpit, was covered for shade by the extended boat deck above, and set up with a buffet table spread with all manner of appetizers, some of which only Rowena and Robin could identify.

"The colonel will be with you shortly," Tien said. "He is preparing to get under way. Please sit and begin. My crewmates and I will cast off the lines, and once we're under way the colonel will come aft to greet you."

The foursome filled their plates and sat on deck chairs as the yacht pulled away from the dock and began to build up speed as it left the no wake zone.

"A bit more elegant than our *Semper Fidelis,*" Matthew observed.

"But not nearly so intimate," said Rowena. "Give me *Semper* any day."

"I'd love to get a look at the steering station."

"You'd love to get your hands on the wheel, wouldn't you?"

"That I would, luv."

"I'd like to lie out on the upper deck and get some sun," said Naomi.

"Yeah, you could use a tan, lady," Rowena said with a wink. "I've already got mine."

Robin said, "The colonel will probably give us the fifty-cent tour once he's handed over the piloting duties to one of the crew. In the meantime, I believe these appetizers are still calling my name."

"Careful, honey, leave some room for the main event."

"Yes, the main event." Robin turned toward Rowena, who had joined him for his second trip to the serving table. "You know, you've given us only the sketchiest account of your life since college. I don't mean to bring up the subject of you-know-who, but her story does seem to link us in ways that neither of us could've imagined."

"At least back in the day."

"Back in the day, yes."

"Not to change the subject," Rowena said, "but I'm still on pins and needles here about what Colonel Vo knows about my parents. For starters, where the hell are they? I mean, the cruise is nice, the hospitality and all, but a

259

simple statement over the phone would've been so much simpler."

"Simpler, yes," came a deep voice from behind them. "But I'm told I'm not a simple man. And I did want to see you again, Ms. Mitchell. May I call you Rowena?"

Robin stared. The man looked to be about his own apparent age, perhaps a few years older. He was dressed in a navy polo, tan shorts, and deck shoes, but Robin could imagine him—or his father—in the battle dress of the Viet Cong.

"You must be Mr. Bradford," he said, extending his hand. "Colonel Vo. And this is Mrs. Bradford."

"Naomi. Very nice to meet you."

"And this is Matthew," said Rowena with a gesture. "He's a boater as well."

"Really." They shook hands.

"But my boat is less than half the size of this one. I trust you'll allow us a glimpse of the pilothouse? I'd be fascinated."

"Ah, of course. We can start our tour at the bridge station. Just up this staircase."

Rowena, clearly agitated, placed a hand on the colonel's arm. "Excuse my impatience, sir, but my parents? You said you had news."

He proffered a wide smile. "Ah, my dear, forgive me. Be assured the news is good; your parents are well. But please indulge me a few moments longer. I delight in hopeful anticipation, followed by the joy of fulfillment. Your Christmas, it should come as no surprise, is one of my favorite holidays for that very reason. So, please?"

"You have a family, then," said Matthew.

"Oh, yes. You have already met one member. Tien."

"Your wife?" asked Robin, but for answer Vo simply smiled over his shoulder as he led the group topside, where they saw Tien at the covered steering station, which was mounted three steps down from the boat deck, and just aft of the forward bulkhead.

Vo pointed to the left. "That stone fortification on our port side is Fort Washington. It was built in 1809."

Matthew added, "And nary a shot was fired from it."

"We have a historian on board," said Vo.

"Amateur, believe me. But I do know that it was the city of Washington's only defense against an assault from the river."

"Then you will be able to tell us what we are approaching on the starboard side."

"Of course. George Washington's home, Mount Vernon. You can see the ferry dock at the base of the rise. Above it's the mansion. Man of many talents, he was—surveyor, farmer, soldier, general, two-term President . . ."

Rowena shuffled her feet and looked around. She coughed exaggeratedly. It seemed to have no effect upon their host. She cast a stern look at Matthew, as if urging him to stop speaking so she could get down to the news she most wanted to hear.

"Let me show you to the main deck," Vo said. "We can talk more comfortably there."

The party climbed down the aft stairway to the cockpit, where the table had been cleared while they were above.

"Your family again?" asked Robin, gesturing to the table.

"You might say that."

"You have them well trained." Robin winked at Naomi's cordial sneer.

The saloon—what a company sales brochure would refer to as the salon—was as large as if not larger than many a contemporary living room. A curved settee occupied the port bulkhead, along with a pair of upholstered chairs and a coffee table. The starboard side contained a built-in credenza that extended into the dining area and abutted the galley. Above the credenza was a bank of large windows that matched those on the port side, in effect bringing the outdoors in.

As Vo showed off the area to Robin and Naomi, Matthew pulled Rowena aside. "Do you smell anything cooking?" he whispered.

She wrinkled her sensitive nose and shook her head.

"Nor do I. The spread on the stern deck was supposed to be only appetizers."

"What I smell," she whispered back, "is a rat. Matthew, if something horrible happens, keep yourself in check until I give you the word. Please?"

261

He said he would as they, Robin, and Naomi took places on the settee as Vo selected one of the chairs for himself. Tien joined them seconds later, explaining that Phuong had the helm and Lan was below.

"Your children?" asked Robin.

"Of sorts," answered Vo. "I do not mean to be evasive. Soon all will be clear," he said as the engines throttled back to idle, the boat slowed to a stop, and they heard the twin anchors on either side of the bow being lowered. "Very good. We are here." The boat backed slowly until it stopped short, indicating the hooks were set. The engines went silent. Through the windows, the guests saw they were moored in a small cove near the northern bank of the Potomac.

"Ah, here is Phuong now."

Naomi and Robin stared. Phuong looked to be the same age as Tien. If she wasn't their child . . .

Another woman entered, nearly a clone of the others, if a tad younger, equally beautiful. All three wore clothing identical to Vo's, except for the tighter feminine cut of the shorts.

"And Lan. All is secure, then?"

She smiled and said yes, casting her eyes on the others.

"Good. Then we can begin."

"About time," Rowena whispered to Matthew.

"Please, join me below. Phuong, I assume all is ready."

"Yes, Colonel."

They took the stairway amidships down to a short companionway with a closed stateroom door on either side. Vo smiled at them as they gathered before him, the three Vietnamese women bringing up the rear.

"This is the surprise I alluded to, Rowena. Your parents, I am happy to announce, are already aboard, and they can't wait to greet you." He opened the stateroom door. And then he shoved a hidden hypodermic needle into her neck as the three women did the same, simultaneously, to each of the others.

Chapter Thirty-Eight

When the foursome came to, they found themselves trussed hand and foot with yellow nylon anchor line, and sitting side by side on a single berth facing another berth three feet away, parallel to them. On that berth lay what was left of Kim-Ly Mitchell.

She lay still, covered with a blood-blotched sheet, her pitifully thin body cruelly bound to the bed with ratcheting straps. Hanging from an IV stand was a bag of clear fluid, which drained into her right arm, next to the bulkhead. Another IV needle had been inserted into her left arm, and from it drained a controlled drip of her blood. A catheter led to a urine bag that hung out immodestly from beneath the sheet. Its contents were brown. Kim-Ly's face was pale, her jaw slack. She barely breathed. Her eyelids flickered briefly as she seemed to recognize her daughter.

Vo stood at the head end between the twin berths; the women stood by the feet. Their faces were no longer lovely, no longer sweet; instead, they radiated lust—lust and hunger. Lan actually salivated as she watched Kim-Ly's blood drip into its sac. She wiped the spittle from her chin against the short sleeve of her powder blue shirt.

Rowena sat speechless. Her mother's image grew blurred as she looked through tear-filmed eyes. She tried to say something, but nothing but a stuttered exhalation came forth. Her lips closed and opened, as if she were beginning to mouth the word *mother*. It came out, "Muh—"

Matthew looked from Kim-Ly—or what used to be Kim-Ly—to Rowena, to their hands bound before them. He cast a meaningful look at her, but she returned his glance and, gritting her teeth, shook her head no.

"You are wondering if you might snap the line, yes? But it is too strong, and nylon doesn't stretch the way cotton line does," Vo explained. "This line can secure the boat to the bottom in the roughest seas, and *Giang* weighs nearly three hundred thousand pounds. It would take more than a mere mortal's strength to snap it. And as for the knots, my . . . wives . . . are highly skilled in that department. Isn't that right, my loves?"

Naomi sobbed quietly. Robin suspected her tears were more for Rowena than themselves. She knew what it was like to lose her mother—and her grandmother and son as well—to a vampire. Robin himself sat stone-faced, eyes boring into Vo's.

"So you recognize me, Marine dog? I knew you at once, the first time you entered my restaurant nearly twenty years ago. You had your chance to kill me once before. Now it will be my turn to kill you. And unlike you, I shall not fail."

Rowena looked at Robin and nodded toward Vo. "You . . . are responsible for *this?*"

Robin stared back, his expression contrite. "Vietnam. Yes, like your father, I was there. Vo and I were fighting hand to hand. There was blood, lots of blood, from both of us. I managed to snap his neck, turned it almost a hundred eighty degrees, enough to kill anyone. Meanwhile, everything around us was chaos. I left him lying there, so I could fight alongside the others in my unit. I believed Vo was dead. He should've been dead."

"In fact," the one time Viet Cong captain said, "I was dead. At least I believed so. But then, to my surprise, the strangest thing happened. And later, that strange thing allowed me to enjoy much sport with American prisoners. And it also provided me with another form of pleasure." He dropped his jaw and lowered his fangs. Then he nodded to his women, and they did the same.

"Brides of Dracula," said Robin. "You made them."

The four captors retracted their fangs. Vo said, "A long, long time ago. And they have continued to make me . . . very, very happy. Eternal love in exchange for eternal life."

"Sick," whispered Naomi.

"My mother," said Rowena. "Why her? Where's my father?"

"Why her? Why, to entice you, Rowena, to return to me. Your parents came back from their long vacation, and where did they stop first, even before going home to unpack? Vo's Vietnam, of course, for a welcome home meal. I noticed your mother and father on the closed circuit screen in my office—I am there every night, contrary to what I've directed you be told—and decided it was finally time to introduce myself. They dined with my compliments that night. And later that same night, my lovely wives and I dined on them."

Matthew's lips drew back as he looked again at Rowena; but again, she shook her head. Redness crept into her cocoa-colored cheeks.

"When they came to, on this yacht and tied as you and your friends are, Rowena, I informed your parents that I had grown extremely infatuated with you, even when you were but a schoolgirl. I observed you from my office, of course. Frankly, and I will put it as indelicately to you as I did to them, I wanted to have you for myself. Make of you another of my wives. Look at you, your heritage. Part African, part Vietnamese, your beauty is exotic." He studied Rowena's face. "Alas, your parents stubbornly refused to reveal your whereabouts, refused to call and invite you to Alexandria for a little visit. So I decided to keep your mother here, alive, until she decided to cooperate. Or until you grew curious about your parents' whereabouts and decided to come down in person to investigate." He laughed. "As you did. So it seems I don't need your mother's acquiescence anymore. But if you want her to continue to live, Rowena, I would suggest that you accede to my wishes. Volunteer to join my brides in a life eternal. I will make a good lover for you, as my wives will attest."

The women looked furtively at one another. Lan cast her eyes upward. But Vo didn't notice, his attention focused on his latest, and longest lasting, object of desire.

Rowena looked at her mother, pain writ large on her face, her fingers twitching as if to restore circulation. "That's not living."

Vo sat himself on a small nightstand between the berths and rubbed his palms together. The three wives stood still, eyeing the prisoners, and gazing also—one observer might say devotedly, another somewhat cynically—at their sire, obedient omegas to his all-powerful alpha.

"Your father is here too, Rowena, in case you're wondering. He's in the stateroom across the passageway."

"You fucking ghoul."

He laughed. "For years, Rowena, I enjoyed watching you on my closed-circuit television, fantasizing about you, from the privacy of my office. Alas, you were too young then, even for me. But I recognized your potential."

Lan began to giggle. "Too young? I was only—" Tien cast her a look. She stopped talking and looked at the stateroom sole, as if she'd found something there to interest her.

"Then you left for college," Vo continued, "leaving me bereft. But your parents continued coming to my restaurant, and sometimes with this Marine dog, the one who had tried to kill me. I was outraged when I first saw him, on his first visit with you and your family; I wanted to kill him immediately. But no, I also realized I owed to him my later good fortune. Still, I decided, he must die, and he must die at my hands. I wanted to devise a plan to kill him properly—that is to say, painfully, lingeringly. But sadly, the day-to-day business of running a restaurant interfered, and I waited too long. The Marine dropped out of sight and, after a time, your parents did as well. I feared my opportunity to add you to my . . . collection . . . had passed. But your parents at last returned, albeit without him"—he gestured toward Robin—"and the rest, as they say, is history."

The women cast their eyes on Rowena. Phuong actually smiled at her, as if giving her greeting. Were they welcoming her to the fold, or were they instead just happy to have their sexual obligations pared back by the addition of one more slave?

"Your father, I must say, was oh so happy to meet me at last—former enemies, now comrades, that's the American way. What a surprise lay in store for him. For both of them."

"I've got a surprise for you, too," Rowena mumbled, then caught herself when Matthew jerked his head toward her again, eyebrows arched, waiting. She shut her mouth, lips tight together.

"What would that surprise be, Rowena?"

She paused a moment. "You're not getting me."

"Oh, but I am. And your lovely Caucasian friend, too."

Naomi looked at Rowena, saw no reaction from her.

And your little dog, too, thought Robin. *As if.*

"Everything has come together," Vo continued, beaming a smile that in other circumstances might be construed as beatific. "You call that serendipity, I believe. Please me, and your mother lives. Or I give her a mercifully quick death, whichever you decide. That said, there is the issue of what to do with the gentlemen. The Englishman? I have no use for him." He looked at his wives. "You ladies may take him for yourselves. Use him as you wish before you kill him."

"The longer he performs, the longer he lives," snickered Lan.

Vo continued, "The other, the Marine scum, is mine. Be careful. Remember, he is a vampire, like us, but"—there was victory in his voice—"we know how to destroy him." He turned his attention directly at Robin. "In the credenza, among my wartime souvenirs, is my officer's sword. I have honed it to a razor's edge. The Japanese, you know, consider beheading an honorable death. As for me, I call it expedient."

Tien said, "May we play with the Englishman now?"

The other two grinned, the younger-looking Lan moving her head up and down rapidly, like a child being asked if she wanted candy.

"I don't see why not. Take them both topside." The women untied the men's feet. "Oh, Tien, before you do, would you bring Rowena's father in from the other room?"

"Of course."

Rowena drew in a breath. "Bring him in?"

Tien left, and seconds later returned with a square wooden box measuring about two feet per side. It was cut from raw lumber, unfinished, the top fastened with a pair of cheap brass hinges. Something thumped inside when she handed it to Vo.

"Would you like to see your father?" he cooed. "When I offered him a choice between his life and your mother's . . . well. Let's just say he was noble to the end."

Rowena shrieked, swore, strained at her bonds. But she refused to morph, refused to bite through her bonds, refused to attack, despite the confused stares from Robin and Naomi and the pleading look from Matthew. "Don't!" she cried. "Not yet!"

Robin muttered through gritted teeth, "Vo, I promise I will kill you for this."

Ignoring Rowena's outburst and Robin's threat, Vo gestured toward his wives. The three Vietnamese vampires pushed the men to the door. Matthew looked back at Rowena one more time. He tilted his head to the side, his expression pleading.

Rowena glanced at her mother, lying in her fugue state, then back at Matthew as he was herded from the stateroom behind Robin. She inclined her head. "Now would be a good time," she said.

Chapter Thirty-Nine

Once in the saloon again, the women pushed the men onto the overstuffed chairs. Lan stared frankly at Matthew, her eyes zeroing in on his slacks, specifically on his crotch. She licked her lips. Phuong walked behind him and twirled a finger in his hair, then scratched a sharp fingernail down the side of his face, leaving a trickle of blood to mark its path. She bent down and licked his cheek clean. The cut healed almost immediately. Matthew said nothing and kept his eyes to the front.

Tien, meanwhile, slid open the doors of the credenza. Robin gaped at what he saw inside: helmets, coolie hats, American and Chinese rifles, handguns, grenades. Medals and awards, along with photographs of Vo with American victims, his lower face bloody and their throats torn out, another photo of Vo standing amid the corpses of his fellow Viet Cong. He'd probably killed his squad to keep his secret safe, and then he'd killed the photographer too.

Tien withdrew Vo's sword from the credenza and danced the tip beneath Robin's chin. "Yes, Mr. Bradford, as you have said, I am indeed an angel. The angel of death. I would love to do this myself, but the colonel has claimed you. Pity for me." She placed the sword atop the credenza as she returned her attention to Matthew.

The three women began undressing Matthew from feet to waist—his shoes and socks first, followed by his slacks and shorts. They made approving remarks when they exposed his crotch.

"Bigger than Vo's," said Lan. "Finest kind. We have fun with this one."

Matthew appeared unfazed, which made Robin frown. The Englishman's breathing was steady, and for a moment, Robin thought he saw the merest flicker of a smile.

"Ladies," the ex-pat said, "if you are determined to have your way with me, I could give you even more pleasure if you untied my hands."

Tien smiled. "That is not an option for you," she said.

"But I'm not really into bondage. Unlike, I suspect, your master."

Tien bridled at the word *master*. "We are not interested in what you are *into*. It is what *we* are into that matters." She pulled him off the chair and threw him to the carpet. He lay sprawled on his back.

Matthew turned his head to face a clearly perplexed Robin. "You know, mate, under ordinary circumstances, being *attended to* by three beautiful women would be a man's most glorious imaginary scenario, would it not?"

Robin only stared, unable to speak, marveling at Matthew's studied nonchalance. A part of him thought back to his first contact with then Captain Vo, in a village in Vietnam. Had he acceded to his men's request after the battle, to pile the VC bodies inside a hooch and set fire to it, none of this would be happening today. Vo would've been incinerated with the others, before having had a chance to reanimate. But instead, he'd told his men to gather up their own dead and wounded and return to a clearing where he would call for medevac.

If he'd said yes, Rowena's beloved parents, and his dear friends, would still be alive. And he would not be in danger of imminent decapitation. And Matthew—what in the hell was Matthew doing?

The women had stripped off their clothes, and despite himself, the artist in Robin couldn't help but admire their beauty—long dark hair, slim bodies, shapely legs—but for their Asian facial features, they reminded him of Daciana.

Daciana, who had sired him. Daciana, who blessedly had been killed by Rowena's friends. Friends whom he'd hoped to meet one day, if only to offer his profoundest thanks. For payback for the scourge Daciana had visited upon Naomi. For what her thrall Alphonse had done to her and her family. And for what they'd both done to Naomi's son Joseph.

Robin shook his head, snapping out of his reverie. He listened as the ladies discussed who would be the first with Matthew. Tien, as the senior wife, said the privilege was hers, but she decided she would be last, because the last would then be the first to feed. The other two hovered over him, as if daring him to try something. But Matthew seemed compliant, even eager to acquiesce. Tien knelt above him and pulled his bound arms over his head, pinning his wrists to the carpet.

Lan squatted on Matthew's ankles, squirming lasciviously as she ground her hips against him. She leaned forward and held onto his knees, forcing his legs down.

Phuong, the next-senior wife, stood spread-eagled over Matthew's hips and looked down. "Soft," she said in a tone that suggested disbelief. "Three naked women, and yet you are still soft." She stared into his eyes. "Phuong will make you hard," she promised as she squatted over him.

And Matthew, his voice mellow, said, "Phuong you, little lady."

Suddenly, Lan screamed as Matthew's knees pushed her up and back and claws, claws springing from inhuman feet, gouged deep into her abdomen. Coarse fur sprouted from his body. His palms became leathery, grabbed Tien's own wrists, and tossed her over his head into Phuong, still frozen mid-squat.

Horrified, they watched his face elongate, his snout turn dark, his teeth extend into wickedly curved canines. Drool spilled over black lips, and his jaws closed on and through the nylon line that once restrained his wrists.

Robin bounded from his chair and backed against the credenza as the three women retreated to the cockpit door. Tien opened it with fumbling fingers, and they spilled onto the aft deck, where an hour ago a buffet of appetizers had been spread for the enjoyment of their guests.

In seconds, they would become the main course.

As Matthew created carnage in the cockpit, Robin grabbed Vo's sword and braced it between his knees. He rubbed the nylon line against the razor edge. No sooner had he freed himself than Vo sprang into the saloon, eyes wide.

He stopped dead, ears assaulted by the screams beyond the door, by the bestial roar that silenced them one by one, by the blood pooling on the once pristine teak decking. Then he turned to see his enemy, the Marine dog, holding his ceremonial sword.

The screams and the snarls outside subsided.

271

For an instant the two men stared at each other.

And Robin, acting contrary to every principle he espoused, dropped the sword.

Vo charged him, and the two grappled like enraged lions—no rules, no quarter asked, none given. Robin threw Vo to the deck and wrapped his fingers around his throat, but Vo brought a knee up smartly into Robin's groin. Robin grunted and rolled over, and before he could recover Vo grabbed the sword and swung it in a savage arc.

Robin twisted his head to the side and felt the blade bite into his right shoulder, breaking his clavicle. The pain was excruciating, but he managed to swerve to avoid yet another blow. Vo took measure of his target, raised the sword for another slash—and tumbled to the carpet as Robin's legs scissored his ankles. The blow knocked the sword from his grip, and as he turned back to reach for it, Robin encircled his neck with his left arm, got to his feet, and stumbled back against the credenza.

Vo reached his arms up and back, trying to get a grip on Robin's head. Then he froze as he saw, standing in the doorway to the cockpit deck, a creature, half man, half wolf, covered in blood, naked but for a ragged shirt.

With his collarbone already healing, Robin reached his right hand into the credenza. His fingers, fumbling at first, managed to find a familiar object, and he pulled it out.

It was an American-made grenade.

Not the pineapple-looking grenade of World War II, where the shrapnel took the form of squared-off cutouts. This newer model was smooth, its shell designed to explode in millions of near microscopically thin pinwheels, spinning through the air and shredding anyone and anything within range.

"Can I help?" called Matthew from the doorway, returned to full human form.

"Come here, quick!"

His speed was uncanny. "What can I do?"

Vo screamed and opened his mouth. His viper's jaw dropped and his fangs fell into place. He tried to wriggle free, but Robin held him firm. Before Vo's viper teeth could strike, Robin shoved the grenade into his distended mouth.

"That's just what I wanted you to do, Vo." To Matthew he said, "Pull the pin! Then get out of here! Hurry!"

Vo tried to spit out the grenade, but he couldn't dislodge it, because Robin's left arm held his head fast, and his right hand pushed his teeth tight against the grenade. Matthew reached into Vo's mouth and pulled the pin, and the spoon sprung free.

"God bless you, mate," he said as he turned and made for the door, again with inhuman speed.

Robin pushed Vo's chin up far as it would go and sealed the grenade inside his mouth. He held his enemy's head tight against his own body.

In the movies, it was common to see a soldier pull the pin on a grenade and count to five or more before hurling it at the enemy—because everyone knew that it took ten seconds for the fuse to ignite the charge, and the soldier didn't want the enemy to have time to throw the grenade back.

But in reality, it doesn't work that way.

In reality, the soldier holds the grenade with the spoon pressed into his palm. He pulls the pin and immediately throws the grenade—not stiff-armed, the way the movies show it—but like a baseball, as hard and fast as he can. The spoon flies off in flight, arming the grenade, and from that point there's no telling when it will go off, whether in ten seconds, five seconds, or instantaneously. On the other hand, it might just be a dud. The fuses on a grenade are notoriously fickle.

Robin held tight as Vo struggled to free himself. He realized the explosion would probably shred his own head along with Vo's, but into his mind sprang the immortal words uttered by legendary Marine Dan Daly, as he spurred his men to action against the Germans: "Come on, you sons of bitches, do you want to live forever?"

Robin waited for the blast, his final thought that of Naomi.

Eight, nine, ten seconds . . . eleven, twelve, thirteen . . .

Nothing happened.

From the cockpit deck, Matthew poked his head inside the saloon and couldn't believe what he was seeing. "Get down, you suicidal bugger! You've a wife to think of!"

Robin heard something from within Vo's mouth, a muffled click—as something else clicked inside his own head.

He dropped to his knees, wrapped his arms around Vo's legs, and closed his eyes.

273

On the heels of the click came a muffled boom.

A boom, followed a millisecond later by the sound of metal shards ricocheting off bone; shards that sliced through Vo's face, through the back, sides, and top of his head; shards that spewed bloody effluent upward and outward, in an almost spherical bloom, like one of the red starburst fireworks Robin and Naomi had enjoyed, exploding above and behind the Washington Monument last Independence Day.

Robin let go of Vo's legs and fell prone to the deck as hot blood and spongy brain matter splattered onto his head and back. At the same time, what remained of Vo toppled forward, bumped against the credenza, and fell onto the carpet.

Robin could barely catch his breath. Some shrapnel had managed to find his shoulders and back; the fine steel needles hurt like hell. But already, his body was pushing them out onto the carpet, and his nearly cloven collarbone was fully healed. He looked up to see Matthew, once again standing in the middle of the saloon, staring at him, shaking his head.

It was Matthew who finally broke the silence. He glanced at the carnage in the cockpit and looked back at Robin.

"Ruined my bloody shirt, they did."

Chapter Forty

There was no time now for conversation. Both men ran below to find Naomi and Rowena, still sitting on the berth opposite Kim-Ly Mitchell. The wooden box stood on the nightstand, mercifully unopened. Kim-Ly was barely breathing, her gaze distant; the other two women sat immobile, still bound, watching her. They looked up when the men entered, and relief flooded their faces. Naomi saw Matthew's nakedness and averted her eyes.

Rowena looked at Matthew. "Thank you," she said, her voice soft.

"How are you doing?" asked Robin as the men untied the women's hands and feet.

"That depends," said Naomi, shaking her hands to get circulation back in her wrists. "What happened up there?"

"They're all dead."

Rowena said, "You guys all right?"

"Much better now, thank you, luv."

"Go topside," Rowena said. "All of you, please. I need to be alone with my mother."

"We'll go to the bridge station," suggested Matthew. "I want to weigh anchor and get going."

"Going where?" asked Naomi.

Rowena looked at her husband. "Are you thinking what I'm thinking?"

"I'm thinking that the Chesapeake Bay is about seventy miles from here, which this boat should be able to make in about two hours. The water's over a hundred feet deep out there."

"Then you are thinking what I'm thinking. Now go. Please. Before I have a complete breakdown in front of all of you."

Naomi was staggered at what she saw in the saloon and nearly fainted when she looked at the women's remains scattered about the aft deck. Robin urged her to divert her eyes, but she said that's like telling someone with a tooth-ache not to touch the tooth with her tongue.

Matthew had put his undershorts back on before climbing to the bridge station but left the rest of his clothes on the saloon's blood-spattered carpet. His shirt he wadded into a ball and left next to his slacks. "I'm going to ask one of you to find the washer and dryer aboard this tub and give our clothes, all our clothes, a good cleaning. Once under way, Robin, I'm going to ask Naomi to join Rowena here at the steering station while you and I strip the carpet and clean any and all traces of blood from the saloon."

"That's a tall order. What about the bodies themselves?" asked Robin.

"You mean the body parts," said Naomi, suppressing a shiver.

"We'll take care of those."

Matthew started the engines and raised the anchors using the yacht's electric winches. Once they were secure, he fed full throttle. The boat cut smartly through the water, and the shoreline seemed to fly by. He sat at the covered bridge station and seemed to relax for the first time since boarding the yacht.

Naomi and Robin, dressed in robes they'd found in the master stateroom's en-suite head, sat on a settee to the port side and looked at Matthew, their expressions blank, waiting. From below, they could hear the washing machine as it agitated their clothes clean.

"Right," as we English say to buy time when we're not quite sure what to say. "A little history while we wait for my wife to recover her composure and join us. That probably sounds insensitive; I apologize. Rowena has lost everyone in her family, everyone she's ever loved, and it's like I'm passing her grief off as inconsequential. Believe me, I want nothing more at this time than to be holding her in my arms and sharing in her sorrow. But when she says she needs to be alone, she means it."

Naomi reached over and touched his hand. "You look like you're about to cry yourself, Matthew. It's all right."

Robin remembered the words of Jessie Stover. "Tears can show strength as well as weakness."

"And Robin is living proof," Naomi said as she wrapped an arm around his shoulders and rested her head against him.

"Yes. Well. Stiff upper lip and all that. Let's continue. When Rowena and I met, she concealed the little tidbit about her being a metamorph from me, and over a period of time, during which we experienced both heartache and triumphs, I fell hopelessly in love with her."

Robin said, "I don't know if that's a good thing or a bad thing, her not telling you."

"Turns out it was an exceptionally good thing, as I carried with me trauma issues from childhood that would've sent me flying from her had I known. But as things worked out, we ran afoul of another of Daciana's depraved disciples, and he managed to kill me. Rather, I was near to certain death, when Rowena made the decision to share blood with me. Forced it down my throat, I'm told, yours truly being unconscious at the time. She said later that what it came down to was she'd already lost her first husband and their child; she couldn't bear to lose me too. And that's how I came to be a metamorph like her."

"She was aware of your childhood trauma issues, I assume," said Robin.

"She was. On the one hand, she knew that saving me would turn me into the type of creature I most feared— but she also knew that my living was more important than whatever form that living took. As I was unable to make that decision for myself, Rowena made it for me. Because she was as much in love with me as I was with her. So the question is, was she being selfish in saving my life? In other words, did she make her decision more for my sake, or for hers?"

"A philosophical conundrum."

"Correct, mate. But really, isn't everything we do selfish?"

Naomi frowned. "My head's spinning. You're saying Rowena's saving your life was selfish?"

"I know what it sounds like, I know. But think of it, luv. You want to make Robin here happy. Why? Because making him happy makes you happy. On the other hand, he was willing to sacrifice himself for you an hour or so ago. Robin knew that shoving a grenade into Vo's mouth and holding him close while it exploded would lead to his own death too. But he did it to save you, and the rest of us, and that made it worth it . . . for himself."

Robin said, "Fortunately, my limey friend here shouted some sense at me, and I ducked."

Naomi kissed Robin's cheek. "Thank you for that, Matthew. But thinking about what you said, you make us sound totally self-absorbed."

"No, luv, you see, it's just semantics. Not self-absorbed, but self-aware. Not selfish in the greedy sense at all."

She thought about it. "This is what you and Rowena talk about?"

"Oh, that and lots of other things."

"Like what?"

"Like why don't you go below and see if Rowena is ready to take over the helm for me?"

In the saloon, they found Rowena sitting on the settee, in tears. "Mom died," she said, her voice a whimper. "I told her I loved her, and it was like she smiled, or tried to, and then her eyes just rolled back and she stopped breathing." She looked at their faces. "Yes, I know what you're thinking, that with my blood I could have saved her. But I couldn't make myself do it. Without my father to be there with her, to share her life, I just . . . couldn't. She died still believing me to be her little girl, not knowing what I am, not knowing what I've become."

"Let us help you," said Naomi, and Rowena took her hand, stood, and nearly collapsed into her arms.

Then she braced herself and took a step back, holding onto Naomi as if she were afraid to let go, lest she crumple to the carpet.

"You wondered why I didn't morph when Vo had us tied up below. Now you know, it was for my mother's sake. As long as she was alive, I couldn't let her see me like that."

She released Naomi and took a breath. "We made a pact earlier, Matthew and I. We had our suspicions about what we were getting into here, but we agreed not to reveal ourselves unless it was absolutely necessary for survival. Matthew said he would take his cue from me."

Rowena steadied herself as the yacht crested a passing boat's wake.

"Look at us," she sobbed. "Monsters. We're evil and vicious. We prey upon the innocent. We have no morals; our only instinct is to kill. That's what all the books and movies say, right? And look at what we've done." Her gesture encompassed the gore-spattered saloon. "But it's not true, is it? Tell me. Make me believe it's not true at all."

"Not all monsters are evil, Rowena," said Naomi. "And remember, a lot of people are monsters without the fangs and . . . and the werewolf-type things. It's a matter of intent."

"Thanks for that, sweetie." Rowena continued, her voice becoming clinical. "I took the IVs out of Mom, and the catheter. I wrapped her in some clean bedding. We'll bury her at sea. Well, by *at sea* I mean the Chesapeake Bay. And we'll bury . . . the box with her, weighted down and fastened to her so they can remain together."

Chapter Forty-One: Naomi

Naomi sat to the side of the bridge station as Rowena, silent and apparently deep in thought, steered them past the mouth of the Potomac and into Chesapeake Bay. The men stood on the aft deck, ready to step onto the swim platform with their burdens.

Rowena turned the vessel north. The depth sounder showed progressively deeper water, and when it registered a hundred thirty feet, something caught her eye. She cut the engines to idle and pointed. "A blitz," she said, finding her voice again.

Naomi saw the surface of the bay erupt with leaping tiny fish as seagulls flying above dived upon them. "What's going on?"

"Probably a school of bluefish on the hunt. They get underneath the baitfish and drive them to the surface, where they have no place left to go. Then they come up from behind and eat them. Blues can be as vicious as piranhas, they tell me, when they've got the blood lust on them." She snapped her fingers. "Take the wheel for a second. I'll be right back."

With that, she disappeared down the aft stairway and returned moments later. "Thanks. We're going to mosey on close to the blues and dispose of our, uh, disposables there. At least as much as we can. The guys are slicing and dicing as we speak. What won't slice easily, Matthew can snap his way through."

Naomi grimaced. "Thanks for the warning. Remind me not to look."

Rowena forced a weak smile and took the wheel, adding just enough power to creep close to the roiling surface.

"Listen," she said. "A few years ago, we were docked at Solomons Island a few miles north of here, and some creep beat Matthew nearly to death. Long story, I can fill you in later. Anyway, while Matthew was recovering in the hospital, I lured the creep onto the boat and killed him. It wasn't pretty, but it was gratifying. The next day, while I was in the hospital with Matthew, our friends Claire and Dale took *Semper Fi* out to the Bay and disposed of the body. What was left of it." Her look grew distant as she remembered. "No mercy, and no regrets either. Monster to monster."

"No, avenging angel to instrument of evil." Naomi changed the subject. "I like that little star around your neck. Is there any significance to it?"

Rowena looked down at her necklace, the five-pointed medallion at the end of a thin golden chain. "It's a pentacle," she said. "Not to split hairs; yes, it's a star, but it has meaning beyond that. It was a gift from my friend Claire, after she turned me. It used to be hers. How she got it is another story for another time."

"I can't wait."

"Close enough!" interrupted Matthew's call from below, and Rowena idled the engines again. The women heard the sound of flesh slapping the water, followed by a symphony of splashes from below and raucous cries from the seagulls swooping down from above.

Naomi swallowed hard as she envisioned the scene. The only thing that kept her attention focused was the knowledge that the four people—make that four vampires—whose remains now fed the voracious bluefish and their airborne counterparts had themselves been just as vicious, just as bereft of morality as the predators their bodies now nourished.

"Circle of life," Rowena said, as if reading Naomi's thoughts.

When the feeding frenzy subsided and the call came from below to press on, Rowena fed power and steered farther north, toward the middle of the bay and the shipping channel. Then she placed the yacht on autopilot, slowed the speed to a crawl, and led Naomi down to the aft deck, where Matthew and Robin—dressed in newly-washed clothes, Matthew wearing a blue polo he'd found in Vo's stateroom—stood alongside an elongated bundle of bedding, encircled by anchor line and weighted down with spare parts they'd scavenged from the engine room. Lashed to the bundle was a wooden box, the lid now fastened shut with stainless steel screws.

The men carried their bundle down to the teak swim platform, followed by the women. They stood silent, as if waiting for Rowena to say something. But she couldn't; she looked down at the wrapped remains of what had been her parents and sobbed. Matthew put an arm around her, and she leaned into his shoulder.

Naomi looked at Robin, who cleared his throat.

"I first met the gunner, Marcus Mitchell, at a parent-teacher conference," he began, "back when Rowena was one of my high school students. He commissioned me to paint a portrait of Kim-Ly as a surprise birthday present. It wasn't long before we became friends, and the hardest thing I'd had to do in a long while was take my leave of them before my lack of growing older became noticeable. We promised to keep in touch, but for obvious reasons that would have been impossible, at least in person."

Naomi clasped his hand.

"Marcus Mitchell sacrificed himself protecting his beloved wife and daughter, and in so doing he demonstrated the last full measure of devotion. *No greater love hath a man,*" he quoted, "*than he lay down his life for another.*" Robin took a moment, his own voice beginning to grow unsteady. "A more nearly perfect couple I could not have imagined, and I believe their spirits live on, and will live on forever, in the person of their daughter. Now, as their souls are free to ascend to heaven's grace, we commend their earthly bodies to the deep."

Silence followed. Robin looked to Matthew and Rowena, whose heads were bowed, then to Naomi, whose eyes reflected the setting sunlight. Then Matthew and Robin arranged the parcel, narrow end first, on the edge of the swim platform.

"Godspeed, my dear friends," said Robin as he and Matthew tilted the bundle and it slid into the calm waters of the Chesapeake Bay.

They watched it descend until they could no longer see it. Then Rowena hugged Matthew in an embrace that would have broken the ribs of a normal man.

"So," she said after a bit, "where to next, Captain?"

Matthew piloted the swift yacht north to the mouth of the Patuxent River and radioed for dock space at the Solomons Island Marina. It was dark when they pulled in, but the dock lights were bright. He and Rowena managed the lines, and once the boat was secured they all walked together to the office.

They were greeted jubilantly by an attractive young woman whose nametag read CASSIE. She hugged Matthew and Rowena, then glanced at the vessel tied to the dock. "Well, well. Come up in the world, have we?" she said.

Matthew made introductions and told her that the boat belonged to a friend.

"Did you at least bring your guitar, for a moonlight sing-along? If not, Elvis, the price doubles."

"Sorry, luv, I guess we pay double."

Cassie directed her attention to Rowena. "How have you been? I mean, since the incident here back in '09? More than that, *where* have you been? I missed you guys."

Rowena shrugged her shoulders. "We cruised New England for a couple of years. Matthew's company left New Jersey for China, and he quit and moved to Boston with me."

"Well, it's good to have you back. How long will you be staying here in the Land of Pleasant Living?"

The four of them looked at each other.

They left the next day, Monday, with Matthew and Rowena promising to return later in the summer, aboard *Semper Fidelis*—and with Matthew's guitar. Matthew piloted the mega-yacht out of the harbor and fed full throttle as they sped south toward the Potomac. He kept the throttles engaged as they headed upriver toward Washington.

"Think you can handle this beast, luv, while Robin and I head below?" he asked Rowena.

"If I have trouble, I can send you a pan-pan. You guys going to finish cleaning up the saloon, I suppose?"

The two men exchanged a look. "Right, luv. Send that distress call if you need me."

"What was that look for?" Naomi wondered after their husbands had left.

"No idea," Rowena replied; but Naomi got the feeling she might have suspected.

"Beautiful morning," Naomi observed.

"I like mornings better aboard our boat. She's slow, she's stately, and oh so serene. You can really enjoy the scenery when it's not whizzing by you at thirty-plus miles an hour. Furthermore, our flying bridge is outside on top of the boat deck, not down a few steps like this one and enclosed like a cocoon."

"Still, you don't look like you're suffering." *Bad choice of words,* she thought, tightening her lips. *Rowena just lost her parents; of course, she's suffering.*

Rowena saw Naomi's expression. "I know what you're thinking. Don't worry about it. As for this boat, I wouldn't refuse it, if someone offered to take me on a round the world cruise in it; that someone being Matthew, of course. As for what you were thinking, don't worry about it. Yes, I'm hurting. But no worse than you were hurting when you lost your family. I have to tell myself Mom is better off now. I'm pretty good at coping, really."

"Thank you. I try to be tactful, but sometimes I just blurt things out without thinking."

"Girlfriend, you blurt all you want. But don't be alarmed if you hear me howling at the moon tonight."

They motored on, saying nothing, for a few moments, as they took in the sights on the wooded shorelines. Rowena finally broke the silence.

"Now, let's talk about your demons. Tell me about Alphonse. His name sounds familiar. What's his last name?"

"Puglio, why?"

Rowena looked at her. "Ah hah. He have a son, Alphonse Junior?" Naomi said yes, and Rowena gave her a sardonic smile. "My metamorph friend Claire and her werewolf boyfriend at the time came upon young Junior along the Appalachian Trail. He'd slaughtered a pair of campers, just for kicks, understand, and guess what? They morphed into wolf form and tore him apart. There was nothing left of him but fingers, toes, and teeth."

"Whoa. I knew he was dead, but—"

"Yeah. Then Daciana came along, killed Claire's boyfriend, and started a vendetta against her."

"Why?"

"Because her boyfriend refused to give Claire up for Daciana."

"Oh. Big mistake."

"Claire was working as a junior editor at Jones Publishing at the time, and that's what brought me into the picture."

"I see."

"So, Alphonse, Senior?"

Out of habit, keeping her voice low as if ashamed, Naomi said, "You know he raped me and got me pregnant, and as an unmarried woman in those days I was branded with a scarlet *A*. I was ostracized by the faculty and administration and fired. Over time, I developed that infamous victim mentality you mentioned. I moved away from Newark, but somehow he found me and even managed to get a job in the high school in Silver Spring so he could keep harassing me. But when Robin got your email saying Daciana was dead, I realized that there was no need for me to be afraid of him anymore. I realized Daciana was the specter that was haunting me, not Alphonse, but she was doing it through him. So back at work, I told him, in no uncertain terms, to, um, auto-fornicate."

"Auto-fornicate? You actually said that? Girl, you don't like dropping the F-bomb much, do you?" Rowena was laughing.

"Actually, *girl,*" said Naomi returning the laugh, "you've got to remember I was born in 1945, which makes me a lot older than you. And in my day, swearing was considered crude and unladylike."

"Understood. Claire calls cussing lazy language. She says the philosophy goes, if you can't dazzle them with brilliance, baffle them with bullshit."

As they neared National Harbor, Matthew took over the helm as Rowena prepared the lines. The bow and stern thrusters nudged them sideways, making for easy docking. They made a final inspection of the yacht, with Matthew and Robin taking rags and wiping down for the last time anything any of them might have touched. Matthew pronounced it ship shape, and Robin confirmed it was properly squared away. The four of them walked casually up the floating dock to the mainland, and once on dry land Robin surprised the women by hailing a cab for them.

"Matthew and I have an errand to run. We expect to be late, so don't hold dinner for us." He refused to tell them more.

As the cab pulled away, Robin checked his watch. "It'll be dinnertime soon, but I think we should wait until around closing time. How do you feel about Vietnamese food?"

When the men returned to Takoma Park it was well after midnight, and their clothes were filthy with soot and splashes of blood. They put their clothes in the hamper, showered, and slid into their beds without waking their wives.

Next morning, the women let their snoring husbands sleep in and drove to a local deli for breakfast. They sat near a wall-mounted television tuned to a local station. The sound was low, but Rowena's sensitive hearing was able to pick up every word being spoken, and when the news segment came on, she perked up visibly.

"What's up?" said Naomi.

"Shh. Just a minute." Then, "Look at the screen."

What Naomi saw was an image of the ruins of a restaurant gutted by fire, above a banner reading ALEXANDRIA. More images flashed, videos of firefighters fighting the inferno, blinking red and blue lights from police and emergency vehicles, the building finally crashing down upon itself before the picture returned live to an on-the-scene female reporter.

From behind the counter, a server turned up the volume with the remote.

"Vo's Vietnam was a popular ethnic eatery here in Alexandria," the reporter said, her tone breathless. "It's too early, I'm told, to pinpoint a cause of the fire, but authorities speculate that it might have been caused by spilled cooking oil. What makes this tragedy even more bizarre is the fact that investigators found in the basement a number of charred bodies, all female and all burned beyond recognition. It appeared that they lived there, because steel bedframes, warped by the intense heat, were found on site as well." She consulted her notes. "The owner, a Colonel Vo, had been known to import young women from Vietnam to staff the restaurant. Some believe that he housed them, illegally, in the restaurant's basement. I'm told that authorities haven't been able to locate the colonel himself."

She collared a middle-aged man wearing a jacket with ME stenciled across the chest. "Excuse me, sir," the reporter said, "but might it be possible to identify the women by their dental records?"

The medical examiner, a middle-aged man who appeared annoyed at the interruption, barked his answer before leaving the reporter standing alone and stunned: "Maybe . . . if their heads hadn't been chopped off."

The server hurriedly muted the volume as some diners pushed their plates away and others just stared at their food as they grew progressively paler. Rowena stared at Naomi, her expression grim. Softly, she said, "Looks like Dracula had more than three wives."

When the women arrived back at the house, the men were dressed and finishing off a huge breakfast. A large glass coffee carafe stood between them, nearly empty.

"We saw the news. How many?" Rowena asked.

Robin said, "Six. All young looking, all beauties. Colonel was a busy boy. They were ready to put up a fight, too. Until they noticed Vo's sword in my hand and saw my lupine friend here transform." He held his hand to the side of his mouth, as if not intending Matthew to hear. "Frankly, he scared me too."

"Their heads?" asked Naomi.

"You don't want to know, luv," said Matthew.

Robin agreed, and the subject was dropped.

"But we did bring home a souvenir," Matthew said. "Have you looked in the fridge this morning?"

The women said no.

Robin opened the refrigerator and withdrew a translucent plastic gallon-sized jug with a pour spout. It resembled a miniature gasoline carrier. It was filled to the top with a dark liquid.

"Is that what I think it is?" asked Rowena.

"Nectar of the gods, luv."

Robin added, "We didn't think they'd have any more use for it. Shall I break out the glasses?"

Chapter Forty-Two

The Cessna Caravan ("Dale's Skyhawk on steroids," remarked Rowena) landed with barely a squeak of its tires at Montgomery County Airpark in Gaithersburg, Maryland. It taxied to the terminal area and shut down its turboprop engine. The two couples watching from the pilots' lounge saw a distinguished looking elderly man disembark, then a woman, each holding a piece of carry-on luggage. The man waved briefly to the pilot, still inside the plane, and escorted the woman into the terminal building.

A motorized cart hooked the airplane's nose gear behind it and towed it to the tiedown area. Once it was parked, two pilots emerged and tied the plane to the tarmac. One was a tall, striking blonde, the other a slightly taller man with a definite military look and carriage. They did a walk-around before leaving and headed toward the pilots' lounge.

"Family reunion, kind of," said Rowena, her face reflecting pure joy.

The pilots entered the lounge, and the blonde strode to the desk to fill out paperwork as the man ambled toward the waiting group. Matthew held out his hand; but, with a grin and sideways glance at the Englishman, the man went instead for Rowena and lifted her off her feet. After a kiss, he turned toward Matthew and accepted his hand with a firm grip. "Sorry, young man, age before beauty," he quipped. "Although come to think of it, you're not that beautiful at all."

"Age may be irrelevant for people like us," responded Matthew, "but if you're going to be a stickler about it, maybe you'd better greet our senior citizens over here. Naomi was born in 1945, and Robin sometime around the late 1500s."

"Well, I'm impressed. Dale Keegan," the man said, shaking their hands. He looked the pair up and down. "Rowena told us about you on the phone. Not all, but enough for now. That's my wife Claire at the desk. She was pilot in command on this trip."

"Come a long way from her Skyhawk days," said Rowena. "No surprise, though, knowing her."

Claire Delaney Keegan finished the paperwork, approached the group, and gave Rowena and Matthew hugs that would've crushed a mortal's ribs. Rowena made the introductions and cautioned her not to squeeze her new friends too hard—"They're hemophages, not metamorphs. At least, not yet."

At Robin and Naomi's, the newcomers plopped their bags in the third bedroom, and after a quick shower they joined the others downstairs.

"Our passenger Mr. Cullington's in-laws live in Brinklow," Claire explained. "His wife's mother has multiple cancers, and they're afraid this is the end. The Caravan may look gawky, but it's actually faster from point to point than having to schedule a hop from home base in Bozeman to Denver or Chicago, from there to Dulles or Reagan, and finally renting a car and slogging through D.C. traffic. Their son met them at Gaithersburg and took them directly to Brinklow. It's an expensive charter, but to people like the Cullingtons it's chump change."

"Nice folks, though," added Dale. "Old money, no pretention."

"Is that magnificent machine your personal aeroplane?" asked Matthew.

"Ah, the proper pronunciation," chimed in Robin.

Rowena cast the others a wry glance. "He also says *aluminium* and *jewellery*. Can't break him."

"I wish it were my *aeroplane*," said Claire, "but it belongs to the company. I work for a firm that caters to campers, hunters, and fishermen. We take them to the bush and bring them back when their vacation's over."

"Certainly not in that plane?" said Naomi.

"No, usually in four- to six-place utility planes, Cessna 206s and 207s. We also have a few 185s for the deep bush. They're taildraggers," she explained, forgetting that like all non-pilots, Naomi couldn't have appreciated their advantage in off-airport landings. "The owner bought the Caravan for parties who want to fly from Bozeman to Kalispell so they can visit Glacier National Park. Recently, the Cav's become a popular alternative to the airlines for those who can afford it."

"Witness our latest mission," said Dale. "Claire usually flies it single pilot while I teach history in school. But school's out for the summer, so I tagged along. Seeing you two again is a plus. And meeting these two new ... um, nice people ... well, that's an added bonus."

The six shared their stories into the night and confirmed that they all shared one link—Daciana Moceanu.

Daciana: whom Dale and Claire had barely managed to kill years before; whose body they'd converted into fishing chum; and whose remains were now dispersed on the ocean floor, digested and excreted, at least once; in all likelihood, more than once.

After the next morning's breakfast, the subject of Alphonse Puglio returned to the discussion. Naomi said, "Thanks to Rowena here, he's no longer a threat. And his sons are dead too, one from a drug overdose and the other—"

"Attacked by wild animals on the Appalachian Trail in Massachusetts," finished Claire. "Which, on a positive note, got Dale here snooping around trying to find my trail."

"Another unintended but in this case happy consequence. But Daciana's gone," said Dale, "and the Puglio gene pool has been thoroughly drained. Good riddance to bad rubbish all around."

Claire's cell phone rang, and she excused herself to the living room. When she returned, she advised them that Mrs. Cullington's mother had passed peacefully during the night, with her family by her bedside in Brinklow. "She chose to die at home," Claire said. "The viewing's tomorrow night, one time only. Funeral and interment will be the next day." She looked at Dale. "We should be there."

"I agree."

"They're going to stay a week longer to straighten out the family's affairs. Mr. Cullington asked if we minded waiting around all that time. He said he'd pay for the plane's down time and our hotel expenses. I told him we were staying with friends. I hope that's all right with you."

"More than all right," said Robin and Naomi together.

"I've an idea," said Rowena. "When you fly back home, how about taking four more passengers with you? I'd love to show Robin and Naomi the Bozeman area. And it's close to Yellowstone and Jackson Hole. We could do some exploring together."

Claire raised an eyebrow. "Don't even think of hunting, Rowena. The wildlife there are protected."

"Hey, girlfriend, remember, the Yellowstone wolves can hunt to their hearts' content. Who's to notice there are four more wolves in the park?" She looked at Naomi and Robin. "Or even six?"

Epilogue: Rowena

Upon our arrival in Montana, Matthew and I called the marina in Boston where we berthed *Semper Fidelis* and told the harbormaster that we'd be postponing our cruise for a couple of weeks. Her food lockers were stocked only with non-perishables, so there was no need for him to unload anything that needed refrigeration. He asked how long we'd be gone, and I told him I wasn't sure. We were vacationing with friends and might be gone a month or more. In fact, if we set off as late as the fall, we could join the fleet of snowbirds, the legion of northerners who spend winters on their yachts in the sunny South. Some hire crews to take the boats down; others do the piloting themselves. We, of course, would happily number among the latter.

Waiting until September or so would allow us the summer to be with Claire and Dale and Naomi and Robin. Robin put a Closed for Vacation sign on his shop—he had no new commissions to fill—and Naomi, in a ballsy move none of us would've expected before her near-fatal rendezvous with Alphonse in Rock Creek Park—resigned from her position at Montgomery Blair High School. I asked her what she would do for income. She gave me a wink and said, "Have you seen our offshore account lately?"

It was mid-September before Matthew and I returned to Boston. We flew commercial from Bozeman to D.C. in September and stayed with Robin and Naomi for another few weeks. Robin's lease on the store was up, and he decided not to renew. Matthew asked what he would do now for work. He said he had plenty of time to think about that. "I've stashed some money away over the years. And thanks to you, now we're not only rich, we're filthy rich."

"Nice to have options, isn't it?" he said.

When Matthew and I got settled back in our Boston home, we looked at the recent NOAA reports and decided to postpone our trip until spring. We were in the middle of hurricane season, and the deep blue sea wouldn't be the place to be during a seventy-four-mile-per-hour-plus wind and the seas that accompany it.

Figuring the provisions we'd stocked (essentials like Doritos and potato chips—and pork rinds) would be stale before the spring sailing, we drove to the dock to unload them—and saw to our shock that our beloved forty-two-foot trawler was missing from its slip.

The harbormaster was gone, too.

We tore into the chandlery and learned from a teenager behind the counter that the harbormaster had taken the boat out a week ago to deliver emergency engine parts to a boater in distress on Block Island. Matthew challenged that, saying if the emergency were real, he'd have taken a boat with a cruising speed a lot greater than eight knots. In fact, didn't he have a high-speed boat of his own? The teenager worked only occasional evenings and most weekends. He had no seagoing experience, and therefore no seagoing expertise. He told us his employer's excuse for not using his own boat was that it was made for bay and sound cruising but wasn't seaworthy enough for ocean going. He thought a bit more and said he'd assumed, when he saw his boss and his companion board the boat with only their duffels, that the engine parts were already aboard.

What companion?

The teenager gave us a grin, totally not apropos, considering the situation. She was a looker, he said, probably somewhere in her twenties. Long legs, big—

That was enough; we didn't need to hear more. I reminded the boy that the harbormaster had a wife, and she was due to deliver their first child in just a few weeks.

He shrugged and said something like you think you know someone. He gave us the harbormaster's home address, and we rushed over to find the wife, Jean, in tears. She'd called the police and filed a missing persons report, but they'd told her what the boy in the chandlery had told us—that he was gone on a rescue mission of sorts to Block Island. They turned the investigation over to the Coast Guard.

Her husband wasn't answering his cell phone.

He also, in allowing his little head to do the thinking for his big head, probably wasn't following the NOAA reports. *Semper Fidelis*—or what was left of her—was but one of hundreds if not thousands of pleasure boats up and down the Atlantic coast destroyed in the wake of Superstorm Sandy. The Coast Guard found her documentation plate attached to a piece of debris and called Matthew with the news.

As for the acting captain and his long-legged female crew, the Coasties had no information. The lieutenant who called did say that the debris was found on the ocean side of the New Jersey barrier island, which would indicate that the boat was at sea when it was destroyed. Had it been on the bay side, the people might have found some safety ashore, but at sea they would not have stood a chance.

So long, *Semper*. Matthew went into depression for about a week, and I joined him in his funk for a couple of days. But then we realized there were some things that needed doing, and the first was to see that heavily pregnant Jean, a housewife who had married her husband right out of high school, would be taken care of. She assured us that she had family in the area, but Matthew still felt he owed her something; after all, he could've flouted a time-honored boating tradition and taken the boat's ignition key home instead of leaving it in the harbormaster's care. So, with the insurance money from the boat's loss and with my blessing—not that he needed it—Matthew set up a college trust for Jean's newborn son. A boy she named, you guessed it, Matthew. We may have lost a boat, but we've gained a pseudo-nephew. As we can't have children of our own, we're delighted with the arrangement. Jean has found deskwork at a local chain hotel, and her mother, who lives nearby, has become a doting nanny.

Which reminds me of Naomi's arrangement when she was a single mother. Fortunately, there's no vampire living next door to threaten Jean, her mom, or baby Matthew.

Naomi and Robin visited us for Thanksgiving week and got to meet Jean and baby Matthew. As did Claire and Dale, who had flown in to join us. Jean asked us to join her family for Thanksgiving dinner, but we politely declined, as we had a prior invitation.

It was to the home of Elliott Tavender, the schoolteacher husband of Bentley Williams, my boss at Jones Publishing. Bentley, along with the rest of the staff, was killed in
the building's explosion, an explosion targeted for me. She
had acquired the firm after the death of its owner Ray Jones
at the hands—and claws—of Daciana Moceanu. Bentley
had almost immediately become a dear friend.

Added to their deaths was the horrific loss of my parents as well. I would sometimes wake up screaming, cursing the fates that had visited violent death to those around
me—all because of me. Matthew would be there beside me,
calming me, soothing me, coaxing my uninvited change
back into fully human form.

At least I knew better than to curse God—it wasn't His
fault, and I knew better than to cop out and make Him my
scapegoat. All He did was give us free will; what we did with
it was up to us.

We were greeted at Elliott's door not only by Elliott, but
also by Emma and Benjamin, his elderly chef and housekeeper, who had once worked for Ray Jones and comprised
another part of our extended family. Hugs and kisses were
exchanged and introductions made, drinks were served,
and—forget turkey—we were treated to Benjamin's famous
standing rib roast; in fact, three standing rib roasts, and
we consumed them all. We've yet to tell Elliott the reason
for our appetites. I don't know if we ever will, but if his proposal comes to fruition, some day we might have to.

His proposal? He'll be ready to retire from the classroom in a couple of years, and he told us that he'd like to
consider resurrecting Jones Publishing, putting me at the
helm. With Claire as its managing editor, if he could convince her to relocate back East.

We stared at each other, bewildered. Then Claire looked
at Dale, who gave her a barely-perceptible nod, and she
said that with her being originally a Jersey girl, and Dale's
being a Jersey boy, they found that they both missed the
East Coast more than they'd thought. I caught the unspoken fact that the non-aging process would soon catch up
with them in Montana and they'd have to move anyway.

Naomi, who had been listening quietly, mentioned her
background in art and suggested, if there were room for

her, she might contribute toward layout and cover design. Elliott's smile said everything that needed to be said.

As for Dale, he could continue with his teaching career in Boston, and with his treasure trove of historical lore he'd be a credit to any school with the wisdom to hire him. And as for Robin, he could not only provide first-person historical information to Dale, but he could also set up a new studio and art gallery in the city.

If that didn't work out for him—hey, they're rich. Just ask his wife.

Oh yes, about that.

It seemed that as products of their past, Naomi and Robin hadn't kept up with the present as well as they might. When Naomi was a young woman, a blood test to check for venereal disease and rubella was mandatory before a marriage license could be issued. Nowadays, in the vast majority of states, including their current Maryland home, those blood tests are no longer required. On our Yellowstone vacation we brought them up to date on that, and they nearly whooped for joy. As soon as we returned to Maryland last September, and with Matthew and me as witnesses, they marched to the county courthouse and took out a license. They are now and forever Mr. and Mrs. Robert Bradford.

That meant an official honeymoon was in order; in fact, they'd never even taken an unofficial one. But Robin put it off, refusing to explain, but—looking like the proverbial feline that had swallowed the proverbial songbird—he said he'd tell us why in due time. I grilled Naomi, but her lips also were sealed. What was going on here? Inquiring minds—well, mine anyway—wanted to know.

Meanwhile, having seen Claire, Dale, Matthew, and me hunt as wolves in Yellowstone, Robin and Naomi had mixed feelings about our offer to make them metamorphs as well. The transformation would give them powerful strength, hawkeyed visual acuity, highly sensitized senses of smell, taste, and hearing. And, maybe best of all, great sex.

It was Naomi who balked more than Robin. She said based upon her history of being an underdog—pun unintended—she might find herself a lone omega among five alphas, which was understandably an undesirable place to be. I told her that considering what I'd seen in Rock Creek Park the night we took out Alphonse, I didn't think she needed to worry about caste. Matter of fact, one of the things that separates us from our lupine cousins is that we don't have a hierarchy.

But we do have great sex. Monogamously, of course.

That turned out to be the clincher. Sex was Naomi's friend these days, thanks to Robin's love, but even so the poor thing had no idea what she had been missing all these years. And the longer she waited, I told her, the more she would hate me for not insisting on the transformation. She told me they would both think about it. They'd been what they are much longer than the rest of us have been what we are—Matthew and I are actually the babies of the group, but Robin is . . . wow. I hope I look as good when I'm four hundred years old.

But then, of course I will!

So they thought about it, and long story short, on Thanksgiving Friday, 2012, we turned them into full-fledged metamorphs. The four of us oriented them to their new lives in the White Mountains of New Hampshire, not far from Criterion University, Claire's and my alma mater. And last March, after we all settled into our new lives setting up the Jones-Williams Publishing Company; after Claire and Dale bought a home near Matthew's and mine on the Charles River, two blocks away from Naomi and Robin's; the newly-weds, as it were, finally announced their honeymoon plans.

Robin told us the full story of Joe Paris, husband of Aimee and father of April Naomi. The war denied Joe the chance to give his wife the vacation he'd promised. But his friend, nicknamed Rembrandt, decided to honor Aimee and Joe's memory with their daughter, who was now officially Rembrandt's wife.

As I write, my sentimental friends are celebrating April in Paris.

Rowena Mitchell Parr Collins
Boston, Massachusetts
April 4, 2013

The Pentacle Pendant (Book 1)

When Claire Delaney's lover confesses he's a were-wolf, she laughs; when he asks permission to turn her, she laughs again; but when she regains consciousness, she isn't laughing anymore.

In fact, she's howling mad.

As Claire learns to adapt to her new life, as both a career woman and a self-appointed star chamber, she becomes conflicted by the dubious righteousness of her human kills. Her dilemma intensifies as she finds herself pursued on two fronts: by a covert agent who seeks to protect her; and by a mysterious seductress who seeks to eliminate her. In the cruelest way imaginable.

When their paths finally cross, there will be hell to pay.

Metamorph (Book 2)

What happens when Beauty *becomes* the Beast?

A vampire who has slaked his taste for terror through centuries of history's darkest eras puts a hold on his covert attacks on America in order to pursue a secret vendetta against a beautiful bi-racial woman who has scorned him.

But the woman has a secret of her own. She is a metamorph, a hybrid shape-shifter with the healing powers of the vampire, the heightened senses and strengths of the werewolf, and the needs that accompany both. Needs that conflict with her strong moral code; needs which compel her to conceal her extra-human identity from the mortal man she has grown to love.

Metamorph combines known history with speculative fiction, a strong female protagonist, and the pitting of a creature of unmitigated evil against a pair of unsuspecting lovers in a complex cat-and-mouse pursuit.

MORE TALES OF THE FANTASTIC AND SURREAL
By Stephen M. DeBock
Published by Gypsy Shadow
and available for your e-reader

The Bridge Between Worlds
A novel, also available in trade paperback edition

Alden Walker—sport pilot and skydiver—finds himself and his light airplane mysteriously transported into an alien world: a parallel Earth peopled by exotic-looking humans as well as a host of animals that have evolved into human-like form, with human-like powers of thought, but which have retained their appetites for flesh and blood. Especially human flesh and blood.

Accompanied by a beautiful indigenous woman with a score of her own to settle, Walker must set out upon a covert mission to retrieve a vital element from the creatures who have stolen it, employing his piloting and parachuting skills in combination with her superb swordsmanship.

On their quest, they will encounter a host of anthropomorphic predators, until they finally reach their goat: a mountains fortress occupied by a coldly calculating race of humanoid vampire bats. And upon the success or failure of their mission hangs the fate of both their worlds.

"Heroic characters, flesh-eating monsters, alternative universes, and even a love story worth rooting for . . . Mr. DeBock has a flair for writing characters that come to life, creating fantastic new worlds, and terrorizing the reader with horrifying creatures that keep you up at night."

—Ronni Arno Blaisdell, author of *Ruby Reinvented*

Can't Take My Eyes Off You
A novella

Society has made the death penalty obsolete; instead, convicted killers are condemned to serve humanity as living organ donors. Paparazzo Patsy Galiardo publicly contends that former friend turned backstabber Peter Serafin belongs in that select prison population. True, the coroner has ruled the suspicious death of Peter's affluent first wife a suicide. But when Peter later remarries, his bride this time a wealthy supermodel, Patsy vows to pursue his personal vendetta with even greater zeal.

Further, because the paparazzo has designs of his own on the newest Mrs. Serafin, Patsy has even more motivation to get Peter out of the picture—thus giving Peter more motivation to get Patsy out of the picture. Permanently.

The Testament of Charlie Fairweather

The voodoo queen cursed him as she lay dying, and now, years later—dogged by guilt and haunted by the memory of her murder—Charlie Fairweather is compelled to seek atonement by returning to the Southern swamp where he committed his foul deed.

What he doesn't know is that someone else has been looking for him; and that some*thing* else has been waiting for him.

—Rated among the top ten horror stories of the year in an online readers poll.

Catamount

Allen Foss, a college senior with a history of tormenting his teachers and pissing off his peers, has decided this time to charm his way into his beautiful professor's bed—and then publicly humiliate her.

What he doesn't know is that his 16-years-older professor—a Native American Indian who was abandoned by her tribe while still a baby—has an agenda, and a grisly secret, of her own.

Some "cougars" just refuse to be tamed.

"An intelligently written horror tale that combines Native American folklore with modern academia in a satisfying story where predator and prey are not readily apparent."

—George R. Appelt, Jr., author of *Shepherd's Fall, Life Bites,* and *Spooked*

Morgen

Two months ago, college junior Lori Stark was found dead of unknown causes along the Appalachian Trail. Today, the police bring a beautiful girl to the grieving parents' door. She appears around Lori's age; is amnesiac from an as yet unknown trauma; and her only link to her prior life consists of two words: Lori Stark.

—Rated among the top horror stories of the year in an online readers poll.

A Cross to Bare

Reporter Lucille Easton's nose tells her that the full moon murders plaguing the city are the work of a vampire, and thanks to the efforts of the newspaper's researcher, she learns that the undead do indeed exist.

Lucille deduces that the vampire is the town undertaker's new assistant; among other reasons, his job guarantees an endless supply of blood.

The reporter plans to seduce the vampire in his apartment, while hiding a crucifix in her blouse and a vial of holy water in her purse. She's already framing in her mind the story she'll write and the Pulitzer she'll win. Surely, a TV anchor's slot will follow—won't it?

Lucky Break

His fraternity brothers have warned Brian not to surf alone, but the beach is empty, the ocean is calm as a lake, and this overindulged son of privilege figures a couple hours' dozing on the board won't do any harm.

That is, until he wakes up enveloped in fog. Until he feels the sudden swirl of current beneath the board. Until he sees the triangular fin slicing through the water, coming straight for him.

And as his guts turn to water, Brian realizes that the last thing he'll probably ever see is a cavernous, jagged-toothed tunnel leading straight into hell.

The Heart and the Crown
For younger readers

Whenever the beautiful Princess Malory so much as bats her eyes, all the knights in the kingdom take notice, but none so much as Sir Nicholas. Thus, when Mallory sweetly asks him to kill a dragon for her, he is eager to be on his way.

Meanwhile, in the forest far from the castle lives a witch who also has reason to want the dragon killed, a dark purpose known only to her. Every day she travels to the castle on a secret mission, leaving her poor servant girl to clean and cook and keep her hovel in repair.

The dragon, the servant girl, the witch, and the knight are all destined to meet in a fearsome battle, where the knight discovers that things are not always as they appear—not even his adored Princess Mallory.

About the Author

Stephen M. DeBock is a Marine Corps veteran who served in the Presidential Honor Guard during the Eisenhower and Kennedy administrations. A private pilot and former liveaboard boater, his non-fiction has appeared in *American Heritage, AOPA Pilot Online,* and *Living Aboard* magazines. He wrote the text for a coffee-table book titled *The Art of H. Hargrove* and writes the artist's quarterly fan newsletter.

His novel, *The Pentacle Pendant,* in which a contemporary werewolf becomes a one-woman star chamber, is currently available in hard cover, eBook, and trade paperback. Two of his e-publications from Gypsy Shadow have been listed among the top horror stories of their respective years.

Stephen and his wife Joy live in Hershey, Pennsylvania.

FACEBOOK:
https://www.facebook.com/pages/Stephen-M-DeBock/295034173887998

CPSIA information can be obtained
at www.ICGtesting.com
Printed in the USA
BVOW03s1429150917

494969BV00001B/1/P